"What have you got?"

The police technician pointed to the floor. The room was dark in spite of the glow of one naked light bulb, and it took Gardner a few moments to adjust his eyes. At first, he observed nothing out of the ordinary. Then he saw a few dark brown spots on the floor and the back wall.

"We'll check them against Bradshaw's type. Someone washed up most of it. The victim's wound would have caused profuse bleeding. There should be a lot more blood than this."

"Assuming he was killed here," St. Croix said with a slight note of skepticism.

"Oh, he was," Fitzpatrick said. "I even think we've got the murder weapon." The lab man carefully displayed a long-bladed, all-purpose knife.

"Where was it?"

"On the floor, over in that corner." Fitzpatrick pointed to the darkest part of the room. Garner noticed how clean the blade was.

"Find any prints?"

"I seriously hope you mean that as a joke, Mike."

★

THE DROWNING POOL

JACQUELINE SEEWALD

W🌐RLDWIDE®

TORONTO • NEW YORK • LONDON
AMSTERDAM • PARIS • SYDNEY • HAMBURG
STOCKHOLM • ATHENS • TOKYO • MILAN
MADRID • WARSAW • BUDAPEST • AUCKLAND

For my mother, Anna, a loving, compassionate
human being as well as a natural storyteller, and for her
three special sisters: Sarah, Fanny and Molly

Recycling programs
for this product may
not exist in your area.

THE DROWNING POOL

A Worldwide Mystery/February 2012

First published by Five Star Publishing.

ISBN-13: 978-0-373-26787-3

Copyright © 2009 by Jacqueline Seewald

Printed in U.S.A.

Acknowledgments

A special thanks to Alice Duncan, who edited this novel, as well as The Inferno Collection, with her usual thoroughness. Alice, a veteran writer of mystery and romance herself, provided fresh eyes and perspective.

"Lord, Lord, methought, what pain it was to drown,
What dreadful noise of waters in my ears,
What sights of ugly deaths within my eyes!"
—William Shakespeare, *Richard III,* Act I, Scene iv

ONE

KIM REYNOLDS WAS haunted by ghosts, but only a select few knew about this since it wasn't something she discussed openly. To most people, Kim appeared to be a perfectly normal woman. Her life was about service to the community—in her case, service to the university where she worked as an academic reference librarian at the humanities library. Wanting to pass as ordinary, she repressed her psychic sensibilities as best she could. But Mike Gardner knew and understood, because he himself had a unique awareness.

At the moment, Kim was much more aware of the living than the dead as Mike held her in his arms and proceeded to kiss her thoroughly, his body quickening in a way that sent delicious sensations rippling in waves across her skin. All he had to do was touch her and she went up in flames.

Suddenly she became aware of a persistent beeping sound. Mike groaned and cursed softly as he moved away from her. The loss of his touch left her bereft, as if part of her had been surgically removed.

"Gardner." He practically spat the word into the cell phone, then listened impatiently. "I'm off-duty. Can't you put someone else on it?" He listened again.

Kim could tell he was withdrawing from her, moving into the orbit of his work. She rose from the couch that doubled as her bed in the small studio apartment and adjusted her clothing. When Mike finished the call, he looked over at her apologetically, his strong features solemn.

"Suspicious death," he said without preamble. "They need me now."

"Then I guess you'd better go," Kim said. She tried to ignore her sense of disappointment.

"Yeah, well, I have an idea. Why don't you come with me?"

She stared at him in amazement. "Isn't that against procedure?"

"I'm not supposed to be on duty tonight, but I suddenly am. Besides, there's something I've been meaning to talk to you about." He sounded very serious and thoughtful.

There was no way that she was going to refuse.

"You'll find this interesting," he told her. "The death occurred here in La Reine Gardens."

Kim looked at him in surprise. "Here?"

"No other."

They left the apartment, and Mike opened the door for her to enter his black Ford on the passenger side. Mike concentrated on his driving as they moved through the garden apartment development. It was an attractive complex, brick buildings set around large courtyards, lushly landscaped, the lawns elegantly manicured. How could anything evil ever happen in such a place? And yet, according to Mike, it had.

"What did you want to talk about?" she asked him.

"About us." He gave her a sideways look.

"I think things are going pretty well with us."

He grinned, his ruggedly handsome features lighting up. "I sure agree. In fact, I think maybe it's time we thought about making arrangements more permanent between us."

She instinctively moved closer to the car door. "Define permanent."

"Well, like maybe I should make an honest woman of you. What would you say to us getting married?"

She stared at him. "I had a feeling that's what you meant."

"Of course you did." His eyes twinkled.

She looked away from him, staring into the darkness. "I suppose you'd want me to move into your house, fit into your life." Kim felt her heart start to beat faster.

Mike kept his eyes on the road, but his expression was one of concern. "Would that really be so bad? I know you like your independence, but don't you think we could be happy together?"

"What about the girls?"

"Evie and Jean like you. I don't really see a problem there."

Kim bit down on her lower lip. "I couldn't be their mother."

Mike reached over and took her hand. "No one expects that. You could be their friend."

"I need to think about it."

"I'm not pushing," he said. But it was clear to her that he was hurt, disappointed by her reaction to his proposal.

Still, Kim knew that although her feelings for him were deep and strong, it wasn't going to be a simple decision for her. She wasn't ready to give up who and what she was to become Mrs. Michael Gardner. Maybe she never would be ready for that.

"Do you want to just move in with us for the time being? See how it goes?" he asked.

"No, I need to keep my own apartment," she said in a firm voice, sounding more certain than she actually felt.

Mike didn't respond, but his silence spoke volumes. He pulled up in front of the pool club and they both got out of the car. Kim wondered if their relationship was about to end. God, that would hurt! She really cared about him. And yet she was afraid to completely trust him—or any man, for that matter. Still, losing him might kill her. And knowing she'd only have herself to blame didn't help the least little bit.

AROUND THEM ON this humid night in early August, the world breathed in a hushed gasp, lit darkly by a cloud-obscured moon.

Detective Bert St. Croix was already on the crime scene when they arrived. To Gardner, she looked tired. He introduced her to Kim.

"Ms. Reynolds is going to consult with us on this case," he said.

Kim stared at him and raised her brows questioningly. He gave her an enigmatic smile.

"So what have we got so far?"

"Positive I.D. of the deceased as one Richard Bradshaw, a member of the swim club and tenant of La Reine Gardens. Found floating in the pool," St. Croix reported in a crisp manner.

He turned to Kim. "You know him?"

She shook her head. "No, but that's not surprising. A lot of people live in the apartment complex."

"Who found him?" Mike asked.

"Martha Rhoades," St. Croix responded, nodding to a tall, stern woman who looked mighty unhappy. "She manages the pool club."

"Good, I'll talk to her now."

"The lab people will be going over the place tomorrow morning."

Gardner stared at his watch. "It's already tomorrow morning. Sounds like you got things well-organized." He figured by the time they were back on duty the next day some concrete facts would be established.

Kim appeared to be listening intently to the exchange. He was pleased that she was taking a real interest. He felt the same fierce attraction he always did when he looked at her. At this moment, all he wanted to do was make love to her, to bury himself in her female essence.

With reluctance, he turned his attention to the pool manager, introducing himself. "Could you take us through what happened here tonight?"

"Again? I already told those other policemen, the ones in uniform."

"Humor me."

She sighed with annoyance. "All right. I was walking my dog, Caesar, and I decided to walk in the direction of the pool. During the summer, the pool club is under my control, and I take pride in its management. Although I believed the pool had been properly closed, it's part of my routine to double-check such procedures."

"What do you do the rest of the year?" he asked.

"I'm a physical education teacher at the township high school."

"So what did you see exactly?"

"Caesar and I walked up to the main gate around midnight."

"Do you always walk your dog that late?"

She frowned at him. "Caesar sometimes suffers from insomnia. Rather than let him bark and keep everyone awake, I take him for a walk. I don't mind on summer nights. It soothes both of us."

"So what tipped you that something was wrong?" Gardner said.

"I was satisfied that the gate was securely chained, but when I was about to turn and go, something out of the ordinary caught my eye. The brightness of the lights on the water illuminated the figure of a man floating face down in the pool."

"Okay, thanks. I'll want to talk with you again about this. Meantime, the pool club is shut to everyone except authorized personnel."

"I'll have to notify the owner you're closing the pool. Mr. Page won't like that. You can expect to hear from him. The man has a temper—not that I've ever seen it," Ms. Rhoades hastily added, "but I've heard other people say that about him." She compressed her lower lip as if worried she might have said the wrong thing. "I've always found Mr. Page to be a model employer. But this will upset him. And the tenants, they won't like it, either. Are you certain the club has to be closed?" Her expression was grim.

"For the time being, it can't be helped," Gardner said. He had no intention of debating the matter with her.

"Even the tennis courts? There's a separate entrance to them."

"Sorry. Until we have a chance to go over the place, everything stays locked." He maintained a quiet but assertive tone with her. Gardner sensed he had to be firm with Ms. Rhoades because she seemed the sort of person who confused kindness for weakness. "Who closed up for the night?"

"Sonny did. He locks up every evening. It's part of our regular routine."

Gardner pegged Ms. Rhoades as the type of individual who rarely broke with routine. "At what time did Sonny lock up?"

"Punctually at eight."

"You're sure?"

She glared at him.

"All right, and who opens the club?"

"I do, punctually at noon each day."

"How many people work here altogether?"

"There are four of us. Myself, two boys and a girl. We act as lifeguards and do most of the maintenance work, as well."

"And how reliable are the other three?"

"They were all students of mine at the high school. I hand picked each one of them." She gave him a look that made it clear no further comment was necessary.

"We'll be back. We'll have more questions for you," he said.

She sighed loudly. "I just cannot believe this. What a shame Mr. Bradshaw had to drown himself in our pool. So messy. And I suppose I'd better check the chlorine level. To-tally unsanitary." She turned her nose up in disdain.

Gardner smiled inwardly. The woman should have been a drama teacher. She'd clearly missed her calling. He glanced at Bert St. Croix but couldn't tell what she was thinking. The hard features were expressionless, the eyes obsidian.

Usually, Webster Township kept its police force working singly rather than in pairs because it was one way of saving on expenses. But Mike Gardner knew the captain didn't ex-actly trust St. Croix. She was a newcomer and the captain wanted him to keep a careful eye on her for a while. The bad part was that St. Croix seemed to understand that and resent it.

"Before you go, Ms. Rhoades, do you have Mr. Bradshaw's address?"

"No, but you can get that information from the rental office when it opens in the morning."

"Did Bradshaw have a wife?"

"Not a wife. He was living with someone. The women around here will gossip and one cannot help overhearing. This Bradshaw person apparently gave them quite a bit to gossip about. Besides the girl he was living with, there appar-ently were others. Someone said he was divorced, too, but I wouldn't know anything about that. He really didn't interest me at all—nor I him."

That seemed true enough; Ms. Rhoades was not the type to be noticed by a womanizer. Her physique was decidedly masculine: flat chest, small hips, broad shoulders, cropped, curly hair, and a certain tightness about the mouth implying repressed hostility. He concluded that she was not a promis-ing candidate for a *Playboy* centerfold.

"Would you happen to know the names of any of Bradshaw's friends?"

"I'm trying to think of them. Well, I suppose one really does stand out. The last few weeks he was with a woman named April Nevins. No one could help noticing them. They were awfully friendly for such a public place."

"How so?"

"Well, it was her fault more than his. She wears the skimpiest bikinis imaginable. And she didn't seem to mind at all when Mr. Bradshaw put his hands on her. One day, the woman he lives with showed up here while the two of them were cavorting in the pool. Seeing all that kissing and touching must have set her off. She made quite a fuss. Luckily, it was late in the day and there weren't many people around."

"Would it have made much difference?" Bert St. Croix asked, voice and eyes switchblade sharp.

"This is not a swinging singles establishment. We're family-oriented, and we have a large clientele of retired people who can afford gracious suburban living. Why, some people come all the way from New York City just for membership in our golf club. Everything here is first-rate."

"But there are young tenants, as well?" Gardner probed.

"Oh, yes, mostly young married couples with two salary checks coming in."

"And Bradshaw, was he friendly with any of these young couples?"

"Yes, the Wallings and the Scofields. I saw him with them all the time."

"Were either of those two couples around last evening?"

"You'll have to ask Sonny. I left at four."

"We'll do that. Thank you, Ms. Rhoades. Like I said, we may have a few more questions tomorrow."

She looked less than pleased as she stalked away.

"I think it's a crock," St. Croix said. "If this kid Sonny locked up after everyone else left, how did Bradshaw get in?"

"For that matter, why did he want to get in?" Gardner let out a yawn. "We'll find out more tomorrow. As for tonight, or what's left of it, I'm too tired to do anymore thinking."

"Right. You old geezers need your rest."

"Just refer to me as experienced," he responded dryly.

"Experience is overrated. Frankly, I don't know what I could learn from you."

"Maybe just one thing—you can't ever afford to think you know it all. I never stop learning, and I've had some very unusual teachers along the way."

St. Croix smiled at him tolerantly and left. He ground down on his back teeth. No, it wasn't going to be easy working with her.

"So what do you think?' Mike asked Kim on the drive back to her apartment.

"I don't think Mr. Bradshaw died in the pool. I don't think he drowned in it."

He glanced over at her. "What makes you say that?"

She shrugged. "Just intuition I guess. I looked at the pool and I didn't sense death in it. Does that sound weird?"

"Not to me."

She was pensive. "I suppose police detection is a lot like reference work."

"How so?"

She turned her head to one side, considering her words. "People bring you a problem and you need to find the solution. It's kind of like putting the parts of a puzzle together to get a complete picture."

"So you plan on helping me with this particular puzzle? You have vacation time this week, don't you?" he asked.

"I do indeed. The university is pretty much shut down. Most summer school classes are over. We're informally on hiatus. Ma wants me to visit her in Florida, but I thought I'd wait and fly down over the winter semester break. I'll have a week off then too."

"Maybe you could spend some of the week with the girls and me," he said.

She glanced over at him questioningly. "You still want to bother with me?"

He pulled up in front of her building and shut off the engine. "Ms. Reynolds, you underestimate my feelings for you. I have every intention of courting you."

She smiled at him. "Do you?"

"Yeah, I do. See, I'm a real old-fashioned kind of guy. And I don't give up easy when I want something. As it happens, I want you bad." With that, he pulled her into his arms and planted a sound, smacking kiss on her lips.

As she observed later, it was no ordinary kiss. He took her mouth like a conquering warrior, then he groaned and shuddered as she returned his passion. She felt dizzy with need for him. But then suddenly, he was pulling away. Her skin still tingled from his touch.

"Much as I regret it, I have to go. We'll take up where we left off very soon," he said. "The girls are alone. Evie may be fourteen and old enough to babysit for Jean, but it's getting late. I'm sure they're both asleep—it's just that I worry."

"Of course, I understand." And she did. Mike Gardner was a responsible parent. It was one of the things she found so attractive about him—that and the fact that he was a studly hunk.

Kim wondered if it made her superficial that she found him so physically attractive. Mike Gardner was a tall, dark-haired man with rock hard abs and a powerful build, broad-shouldered and lean-hipped. She couldn't imagine why Detective St. Croix had referred to him as old. Mike was only in his late thirties. Of course, to a woman like the detective, who was likely in her middle twenties, he might appear mature. But Kim suspected Detective St. Croix was baiting him, being deliberately antagonistic. Kim had to wonder about the detective's motives. But she had enough of her own problems to deal with.

She and Mike exchanged a final kiss and parted at her door. "I'll be in touch," he said. "Count on it."

"I certainly will," she said with a smile. It was nearly two o'clock in the morning, but for some reason, she didn't feel the slightest bit tired. Mike had a strange effect on her.

Kim wished her feelings for Mike weren't so confused and uncertain. Did he want more from her than she could ever give him?

TWO

BEFORE RETURNING TO La Reine Gardens the next day, Gardner began going over lab findings. The basic facts were deceivingly simple and could be concisely summarized. Richard Bradshaw, male Caucasian, somewhere in the neighborhood of thirty-five years of age, was found floating in the pool fully clothed. He had received a hard blow to the head. However, the victim's death was caused by a stab wound, a lethal puncture just above the sixth thoracic vertebra. The murder weapon was most likely a knife, judging from the nature of the wound. Estimated time of death, somewhere between six and nine o'clock of the previous evening.

"They haven't pinned down the exact time of death," St. Croix noted critically. "And there's nothing here as to where the guy was killed. You think the killer concealed the body somewhere, then came back after everyone was gone and dumped the vic?"

"Real possibility," Gardner agreed, "but I'm keeping an open mind. Right now, I've got no opinions."

The swim club looked different in the light of day, as though nothing sinister could possibly have occurred there. Cushiony chaises and rustic redwood tables shaded by yellow and white umbrellas beckoned for occupants. Finely cultivated flowers and shrubs grew from decorative brick encasements. The tennis courts glistened smartly in the smoldering August sun. The pool itself was seductively inviting; the water very clear, more aqua than the pictures he'd seen of the Mediterranean. Gardner, already sweating through his shirt in the tropical forest heat and humidity, wished he could heed the siren's call, just jump in and feel the cooling waters wash over him. He turned regretfully away.

Ms. Rhoades and her staff were waiting for them. There were still police technicians on the premises continuing with their clinical investigation. Otherwise the place was deserted. Ms. Rhoades began by introducing her helpers. There was an anorexically thin girl named Beth whom she introduced first, patting the girl's hand in a friendly gesture. Then there were two male lifeguards, both young, not yet out of their teens. The taller of the two was blond and muscular. He looked as if he belonged on the California surfer scene rather than a pool club in New Jersey. The other boy was dark and much slighter in build. His manner toward Ms. Rhoades was deferential, and although he didn't look much like a lifeguard, Gardner saw that he would be the kind of worker she would prefer.

"You're Sonny?" Gardner asked, not waiting for Ms. Rhoades to continue with what was an unnecessarily long-winded introduction of the taller lifeguard.

"I am," the light-haired youth said. He stepped forward and flashed a near-blinding smile.

The teeth were so perfect that Gardner wondered fleetingly if they were capped. "You close up yesterday?"

"I close every day."

"What time?"

"About eight in the evening."

"Anyone still here?"

"Nobody."

"Did you know Mr. Bradshaw?"

Sonny nodded his head but didn't speak.

"Was he here yesterday?"

"If he was, I didn't see him."

"What about you?" Gardner turned to the other lifeguards and glanced quickly at each in turn, but their response was also in the negative. He looked back at Sonny. "Did Bradshaw come here often?"

"Almost every evening," the youth said. "See, children aren't allowed after five, so all the mothers leave then. The place is practically deserted on weekday evenings. Just a few of the same people show. Some retired folks who don't like using the club when kids are around and younger people who get home from work late."

Gardner studied the boy. His manner of speech, the broad, open smile implied honesty and straightforwardness. Still, Gardner was wary; he'd been a cop too long not to know that appearances are often deceiving.

"Were any of Mr. Bradshaw's friends here yesterday after five?"

Sonny scratched his towhead thoughtfully. His eyes were small and dull in contrast to the dazzling porcelain smile. "Yeah, there was Miss Nevins, Mrs. Walling and Mrs. Scofield. They were all sitting together. Mr. Walling and Mr. Scofield, they came by later."

"Did they come together?"

"No. Mr. Scofield came first and practiced on the tennis court. Mr. Walling showed up later."

"Is it possible that Mr. Bradshaw might have come and you didn't see him?"

"Not likely. Of course, I was busy part of the time, picking up trash around the pool, putting away chaises, like that." He looked about furtively and seemed relieved to observe that Ms. Rhoades was occupied elsewhere for the moment, giving orders to the rest of her staff much the way Napoleon would have done with his field officers. "See, it's like this," Sonny said in a soft, confidential tone of voice, "some guys I know dropped by wanting to shoot a few hoops. So we went outside for a while." He indicated a small, concrete court outside the fence.

"Weren't you supposed to be watching the pool?" St. Croix asked pointedly.

Sonny's face turned red. "Well, yeah, sure, but there wasn't nobody in danger of drowning and these guys are friends. And I gotta keep in condition. Next year I start college on an athletic scholarship."

Gardner noted the youth's thick neck and bulging biceps. Football player, he decided.

"You lift weights?" St. Croix probed.

Sonny's wary look indicated that he did.

"How much you press?"

"Usually two-hundred and ten, about fifteen pounds more than I weigh, but I intend to bring that up—and I don't use steroids." There was definite pride in the voice.

"I guess the girls around here are impressed," Gardner said in an easy, friendly manner.

Sonny relaxed perceptibly. "The young ones maybe, but it's real hard to figure women."

Gardner was well-coordinated and appreciated athletic skills in others.

"How well did you know Bradshaw?"

"Hardly at all."

"And his friends? Ms. Nevins, for instance?"

"I just knew them all by sight 'cause they were regulars, but I don't know anything about them. I was pretty much invisible to those people. You know how it is."

"Mike!" Gardner turned around and saw Herb Fitzpatrick from the lab coming toward him. "We found something in the utility room."

Quickly, he and St. Croix followed.

"What have you got?"

The police technician pointed to the floor. The room was dark in spite of the glow of one naked lightbulb, and it took Gardner a few moments to adjust his eyes. At first, he observed nothing out of the ordinary. Then he saw a few dark brown spots on the floor and the back wall.

"We'll check them against Bradshaw's type. Someone washed up most of it. The victim's wound would have caused profuse bleeding. There should be a lot more blood than this."

"Assuming he was killed here," St. Croix said with a slight note of skepticism.

"Oh, he was," Fitzpatrick said. "I even think we've got the murder weapon." The lab man carefully displayed a long-bladed, all-purpose knife.

"Where was it?"

"On the floor, over in that corner." Fitzpatrick pointed to the darkest part of the room. Gardner noticed how clean the blade was.

"Find any prints?"

"I sincerely hope you mean that as a joke, Mike."

If there were anything else, Fitz would find it. Except for an occasional drinking binge when his wife was out of town visiting her family, Fitz was competent—and having met the termagant, Gardner could readily understand why Fitz felt the need to celebrate her infrequent departures.

"I think we ought to bring Ms. Rhoades and Sonny in here."

St. Croix remained silent but left immediately, only to return like a Mercurial messenger moments later with both parties in tow.

"How accessible is this storeroom?" Gardner asked Ms. Rhoades.

"Obviously, we keep it locked at all times. There are a lot of valuable pieces of equipment in here. Only staff have keys." As Gardner scrutinized Martha Rhoades more closely, he decided her unattractiveness went beyond mere physical appearance; it had more to do with her attitude, which struck him as patronizing and overbearing.

"And the same key opens both doors?"

"Of course."

Gardner looked around. One door led to the pool area, and the second led outside. If Bradshaw had been able to enter through this second door, no one in the pool area would have seen him.

"Do either of you know who owns this knife?"

"It's mine," Sonny said, his lips drawn thin.

"Where do you usually keep it?"

"Right here in the utility room."

"In plain view?"

"Well, sure, it has to be handy. I need a blade sometimes, 'cause of the maintenance work."

Gardner couldn't think of any more questions to ask for the moment so he let them go. Besides, the glare from Sonny's teeth was hard to take even in a dark room.

ON THE BRIEF DRIVE to Richard Bradshaw's apartment, Bert began to talk. "It must have been a man. A woman couldn't do it."

"Why not?"

Bert shot him a disapproving look. "You saw the size of that Bradshaw guy. Must have weighed at least two hundred pounds, and he was easily over six feet tall."

"Six feet two," Gardner corrected.

"And you think a woman could have carried or even dragged him to the pool from that utility room?"

"An especially strong woman." He thought fleetingly of Martha Rhoades and her physical characteristics. "I've seen some women body builders who were amazingly strong. And then, of course, a woman might have a male accomplice, or it could have been two women acting together."

"Wacko theories. Nine times out of ten it's the obvious choice that's right."

"So you think it was Sonny?"

"That's right, I do."

"What was his motive?"

"How the hell should I know right off? They say around headquarters that you got some special kind of insight into people. I think maybe you're overrated."

Gardner trusted his instincts; they told him Bert's hostility was directed at the world in general, not himself in particular. Whatever was troubling her, and something definitely was, she needed to talk it out—still, that couldn't be hurried or forced.

St. Croix rang the bell to the Bradshaw apartment and then waited with impatience.

"Who is it?" a woman's soft voice wafted through the door.

"Police," Bert called out in a throaty voice.

The door was opened by a willowy brunette whose age Gardner estimated to be around twenty-five. She was wearing a blue halter and matching shorts. Her tall, slender model's figure radiated elegance and style rather than sex appeal. Something about her made Gardner think of his daughter Evie, who had a similar natural grace and poise. He politely introduced Bert and himself, explaining that they wanted to talk to her about Richard Bradshaw. She agreed to speak to them only after he told her that Bradshaw was dead. She stood immobile, completely expressionless. The color drained from her face like wine escaping a shattered decanter.

"It's all over, then," she muttered, more to herself than them. Her eyes met his. "If you don't mind, I'd like you both to leave." She seemed preoccupied, but it was impossible to tell what she was thinking. There were no tears in her eyes; her expression was guarded, not at all what he would expect.

"As a matter of fact," he said gently, "there are a few things we need to discuss with you."

"Am I supposed to be able to help you in some way?"

"Just a few minutes of your time."

She led them into a large, expensively furnished living room. It had all the glamour of a fashion showroom and was just as impersonal. Pushing back a long chestnut mane of hair, she seated herself on a carved, Mediterranean chair. He and St. Croix located themselves on an avocado, crushed velvet sofa. The thick, matching wall-to-wall carpeting felt incredibly soft under his feet. Bradshaw had obviously been a man of expensive tastes and had the means to indulge them.

"You're listed at the rental office as Mrs. Bradshaw. Is that your legal name?"

"No, it's not. Rick and I weren't married." She met his gaze in a direct, bold manner, defying him to comment or snicker. "That was just so we wouldn't raise any eyebrows when we took the apartment."

"Your name, then?"

"Cheryl McNeill—*Ms.* Cheryl McNeill."

"The questions I have to ask, some of them will tend to be personal, Ms. McNeill. I hope you understand."

"No, not really. What I mean is, I don't understand why you're asking me any questions at all. I don't know anything about Rick's death. You seem to know a lot more than I do. I ought to be the one asking questions."

"Sure, go ahead." His tone was sympathetic. If the young woman knew nothing about Bradshaw's death, then this experience was at best difficult for her.

"Was he in an automobile accident?"

"No, why would you think that?"

"I don't know. He did enjoy driving fast and taking chances. Rick could be reckless, wild at times. He felt it made life more exciting. He didn't like anything that was too predictable. It was part of his charm and his charisma. He always stirred up excitement around him."

"In what other ways was he reckless?"

Her nostrils flared and her cheeks flushed. "With women, always with women."

"How do you mean?" He was more than a little surprised by her candor.

Cheryl McNeill stood up and paced the velvet carpeting.

"Rick was insatiable. No one woman could satisfy him for very long. He had to keep on proving his virility, always the need for new conquests."

Gardner noticed that she was no longer meeting his eyes, not even momentarily. He sensed that he was touching on a very raw nerve. At any moment, she would likely stop being cooperative altogether if he didn't in some way make this easier for her.

"Would it be all right if Mr. Bradshaw's belongings were examined? Nothing will be disturbed."

She nodded her head. He gave Bert a meaningful look and she rose and walked toward the bedrooms.

"What was your arrangement with Bradshaw?" With St. Croix gone, an aura of intimacy was established, and Cheryl seemed less tense.

"Our arrangement? That's a quaint way to put it. We lived together, as so many couples do."

"Just that?"

"Well, not exactly. Rick didn't want me to work. He paid me the equivalent of my old salary."

"To stay here?"

"To behave like a wife in every way. He liked nice things surrounding him. And weird as this might sound, he loved my cooking. I'm something of a gourmet chef."

"Would you have preferred it if he offered to marry you?"

She sat down again, this time as if she were suddenly very weary. "Not at first, but we've been together almost a year. I won't lie about it. I wasn't thrilled with the arrangement. I don't think of myself as a kept woman. That sort of thing went out with zoot suits. I dislike chauvinism in any form. When it all started, Rick said he wanted it this way because he'd been burned once before. He was afraid of remarrying.

He figured we could live together like we were married but there wouldn't be any demands or formal commitment. If I wanted to date someone else, even bring him here to the apartment, then I could. The same was true for him. Rick rented this apartment with that in mind. Two bedrooms, two complete bathrooms."

"And has it worked out?"

"For him—definitely."

"But not for you?"

She bit down on her lower lip again. "I haven't wanted to date anyone else."

"Did he bring anyone here?"

She nodded, the long mane of brown hair falling forward like a melting mound of rich, Swiss chocolate. "During the time I went home to visit my family in San Diego, he had another woman here. I could smell her cheap perfume on the pillow."

"How did it make you feel?"

She viewed him with a pensive stare. "You want me to say that I was jealous? Well, I was. But I didn't even ask him about it. I didn't have the right." Her eyes met his again, level and direct. "I think the situation was changing though."

He raised his brow and waited for her to continue. She took a deep breath and exhaled slowly, her tension all too evident.

"Last month he neglected me completely. Didn't show up for days at a time. When he was here, he barely spoke to me. I knew he had to be sleeping with someone else. Rick always had sex with me at least once a day until then. Occasionally, someone phoned, but when I answered, the person hung up."

"Never a voice?"

"Not ever."

"Did you plan a confrontation with Bradshaw?"

"I thought I'd wait it out, but I couldn't."

"Something happened at the pool?"

Her face began to redden. She stood up and began pacing again. He thought her a private sort of person and this must be proving difficult for her; yet she seemed to want to talk to him.

"You know about that incident? That nosy-body lifeguard at the pool told you, didn't she? No need to tell me. Rick used to make fun of the way she would eavesdrop and then throw disapproving glances at him as if she considered herself so morally superior."

Gardner changed the subject. "Did you go to the pool looking for Bradshaw that day?"

"Yes. He'd dropped by the apartment after work to pick up a bathing suit and towel as he often did. Then he left."

"You didn't suggest going with him?"

"No, I rarely go to the pool. Rick preferred going alone anyway. I made my mind up to follow him there on impulse. I was bored and lonely. I thought it might help our relationship if I joined him for a swim."

"What happened at the pool?"

"I think you already know. Besides, I'm answering too many questions." Her tone was becoming noticeably wary; her luminous brown eyes burned with what must have been painful memories.

"Forgive me, Ms. McNeill, but someone murdered your friend yesterday. We do need information. These are not idle questions."

"You think I had something to do with it?" Her eyes widened.

"We believe he was killed at the pool club. That's why we want to trace his movements when he was there. Again, what happened that prior day?"

"All right," she responded in a reluctant voice. "When I got to the pool, he was there but not alone. He and some virtually naked woman were splashing around and laughing together in the center of the pool. He was disgustingly familiar with her. I would never have let him treat me that way in public."

That struck Gardner as being true. Cheryl McNeill was young and attractive, but there was something of a ladylike reserve about her.

"I was angry, but still under control. When Rick saw me, he got out of the pool. Then he started mumbling some words to the effect that I was following him around and spying on his activities. He could be terribly insensitive and cruel at times, a total bastard. I suppose that's when I started shouting. I didn't mean to. I was just so furious. I told him that I was going back to California permanently. I never have liked the East Coast and I hate living in New Jersey. God, the pollution makes L.A. seem like the Garden of Eden! Anyway, I guess I might have called him a few choice names. I started to leave but he came after me and began apologizing. He said he wanted to take me out to dinner that night, someplace intimate and private where we could talk things out. I refused to discuss it with him and left immediately."

"Did you forgive him?"

"Eventually. He came back to the apartment soon after I did. He told me the woman I'd seen him with was just a slut who meant nothing to him. When I strongly suggested he was lying, he claimed he really loved me. Then he said he'd prove it was true. He was going to marry me. He said he wouldn't let me go back to California alone. He was very passionate and I really believed him. Rick insisted that he just needed a few days to tidy up his affairs. He said he was through with other women. I promised to be patient and didn't ask any questions. I honestly believe he meant to make a clean start."

If she were lying, she was very good at it because she convinced him. "You came with Mr. Bradshaw from California. Did you know his wife out there?"

"No. I met him while the divorce was becoming final."

"What caused their break-up?"

Cheryl lowered her eyes; long, silky lashes hid their expression. "He said she was frigid. He didn't know until after they were married because he respected her demand to keep herself pure until their wedding night. It turned out that she was an ice queen. I guess the experience was what made him so bitter and cynical about women. Rick felt she'd made a fool out of him. That was one reason he decided never to re-marry without a trial period."

"And you believed what he told you?"

"I wanted to. Rick was such a fantastic salesman. By profession, he was a sales executive, a very successful one. That's why they brought him out here: to improve the organization of the corporation in the East. He'd smile at you and you'd believe whatever he said."

"Did you hate him?"

The question didn't seem to throw her. "You can't love someone without hating him a little sometimes. But I really did believe Rick when he said he loved me and was going to marry me."

"Do you happen to know the name of the woman you saw him with in the pool?"

"April Nevins—at least that's who Joan Walling said she was."

"You know the Wallings?"

"Yes. Rick was Martin Walling's boss. In addition to working for the same company, they seemed to have a lot in common."

"For instance?"

"Like Rick, Martin was divorced. He and Joan have only been married around six months."

"How did Bradshaw and Walling get along?"

"Just as you'd expect, very well. Of course, they were both salesman, so it's hard to separate appearance from reality. But I always thought that Martin admired Rick very much."

"Are you and Mrs. Walling friends?"

"Not really, but they've had us over and we've reciprocated."

"Do you remember how Mrs. Walling happened to mention Miss Nevins?"

"She was at the pool the day I blew up. Joan witnessed the whole scene. I guess she called to dig around for information. Anyway, she dropped by the next evening."

"By herself?"

"Yes. She and Martin don't seem to spend much time together."

"Unusual for newlyweds, isn't it?"

"Not if you know Joan and Martin. He belongs to a lot of organizations and things, claims it's important for business. Mostly men's groups. And Joan's quite independent. Mostly keeps to herself. In fact, before that evening, I never realized she was the nosy type. They're very different people, she and Martin, but then they do say opposites attract, don't they?"

"Actually, I've always thought that like people have a greater tendency to come together," he responded. "But that may just be the cynical eye of a policeman."

Bert returned and he rose to his feet.

"Thank you for your cooperation, Ms. McNeill. We may have to call on you again."

She let out a deep sigh. "I understand."

Outside the apartment, Gardner turned to St. Croix. "Did you find anything?"

"Except for a lot of expensive clothes that we couldn't afford on a cop's salary, no, not one damn thing."

"And her story? I know you were listening. What did you think of it?"

"You're the one who's supposed to have all the answers so why ask me?" She began walking away from him. He moved quickly to catch up with her.

"A man keels over at a concert performance. The conductor calls for a doctor who finds the man has died of a massive coronary. From the balcony, a little, old lady shouts out: 'Give him some chicken soup!' The exasperated doctor says: 'Madam, the man is dead.' The old lady calls back, 'so what can it hurt?'"

Bert shook her head. "Is that supposed to be funny? What does it have to do with our case?"

"People think differently. Sometimes, the way they think isn't logical. Take Ms. McNeill for instance. She doesn't appear to be taking her boyfriend's death hard. Yet she claims she loved him. It almost seems as if she knew about what happened before we told her."

"You got nothing there," Bert said, "just conjecture."

Gardner felt St. Croix's quick anger, the way he'd have felt a box cutter blade. "Don't suppose you'd care to talk about what's really bothering you?"

Bert narrowed her hard, electric eyes. "I don't follow you."

"Look, we can't work this way. I'm not trying to force the issue. It's just that when cops aren't working as a team, it can be dangerous."

"Maybe I just don't trust small-town cops."

"If you really feel that way then why did you come out here to work? Why didn't you stay in New York City? I know you had a good record there."

"Let it alone," Bert said.

"You hate it out here?"

"You really don't quit, do you?" Her eyes blazed.

"What? You haven't found happiness here in beautiful suburbia?"

"I made a mistake."

Gardner didn't know what to say. The shuttered eyes, the clenched jaw, the bitter tone of voice testified to St. Croix's inaccessibility. Her secrets were her own and she would be a hard person to know.

"It's all changing and especially here. Plenty of middle-class people of all races are moving into the suburbs. This area is becoming more multicultural all the time."

"I didn't like the way the captain came on to me with that bogus rap jive about how much I was going to learn from you. I'm not a novice. I don't need training. I mean, this is a hick town police force in a place where the local industry is sweet shops. I resent the attitude of superiority. I could show all of you a thing or two. There isn't much I haven't seen or had to deal with." She squared her shoulders and set her angular jaw, a handsome woman with skin the color of mocha cream and an aura of determined pride.

Gardner didn't doubt Bert could handle just about anything. Merely the physical size and power of the woman would intimidate most lawbreakers. Yet Gardner had the feeling she was like a time bomb, just ticking away and waiting for detonation. He had a choice: either figure a way to defuse St. Croix or else stand back and avoid the explosion. The latter would be the sensible, safe course of action, but Gardner knew better than most that all of life was uncertain and entailed risk.

"Are you hurling a challenge at me?" He kept his tone quiet, non-threatening.

"No, just stating facts."

"Generous of you."

There wasn't much point in telling Bert that he hadn't always lived or worked in the suburbs, that he started his career patrolling the streets of Newark—mean streets that looked a whole lot worse than pictures of Berlin after it was leveled in 1945. He recalled a statement of past Mayor Ken Gibson that if you wanted to know where other cities were going, all you had to do was look where Newark had already been. But no, there wasn't any point in trying to explain.

THREE

KIM SLEPT LATE, which was unusual for her. She dreamt about her friend Lorette Campbell, whom she hadn't thought about for several months. It was a strange dream. In it, they were back on campus taking an English class together as they once had done.

Halfway through the lecture, Lorette turned to her. "It's such a shame we can't do this anymore. I hate being dead."

Kim woke up with a start. She found herself sweating and at the same time chilled. Such a creepy dream. Lorette was dead, murdered. Probably it was visiting the pool club last night that had precipitated the nightmare.

She felt a sudden longing, a need to talk to her mother. She reached for her cell phone and scrolled down to her mother's number. The answering machine picked up. It seemed Ma wasn't available at the moment. Kim left a brief message and clicked off. She didn't much like talking to machines. Too impersonal for her tastes.

She had the whole day ahead of her and wasn't certain quite what to do with it. She wanted to be with Mike but knew he was working. Besides, after their discussion last evening, it might be better if she gave him some space, no matter what he might say to the contrary. Too bad about the murder at the pool; she wouldn't have minded lounging there herself today. Under normal circumstances, she couldn't think of a better place to relax.

Kim looked at herself in the mirror and decided a haircut might be in order. Her hair was getting long, the dark mahogany falling in thick waves. She usually wore it pulled back in an austere chignon at work, and during hot weather like this, in a ponytail around the apartment.

The phone rang; she assumed it was Ma calling back but it turned out to be Mike.

"So what are you doing on your first day of vacation?"

"Not much of anything so far. I might sit in the courtyard and read a novel for a while. Soak up some sun."

"How about spending the evening with me? I'd like to take you and the girls out to dinner."

She smiled. That was thoughtful of him to want to include her. "I'd like that a lot."

"Great. I'll pick you up as soon as I get off work. The girls will be home from day camp by then. We can all chow down and share our day."

"You don't think it might be awkward between us?" she asked in a tentative manner.

"Who says we have to agree on everything. I'm not that insecure. Besides, I intend to be very persuasive."

"You really think you can change my mind?"

"I know I can. I've got plans."

Funny how just hearing his deep, masculine voice thrilled her straight down to her toes.

So he planned on courting her. Well, she could certainly do with a bit of that!

"WHERE TO?" BERT ASKED.

"How about April Nevins' apartment?"

But they did not go directly there. It was lunchtime and they were both hungry. They drove out to Route 9, and Gardner fittingly stopped at the La Reine Diner just a mile from the garden apartment development complex. Too bad he couldn't be with Kim for lunch. Well, he was looking forward to the evening.

The air-conditioning provided a welcome relief from the

sweltering heat outside. Bert chose the rear booth and slid
into the gunfighter's seat, back to the wall. Gardner, sitting
opposite her, smiled at her degree of caution.

St. Croix wasn't stupid or reckless; Gardner found that reassuring. A heavily perfumed waitress brought them some
menus then swiped their table with a few strokes of a dirty
cloth.

Gardner caught sight of himself on the mirrored ceiling.
He saw his own thoughtful, calm gray eyes reflected back
at him. There was nothing exceptional about the light gray
summer suit that matched his eyes, or the sprinkle of gray at
the temples of his dark brown hair, which made him look deceptively more like an accountant than a cop. Only the hard
lines and sharp angles of his face gave him a certain air of
granite strength.

After they ordered, Gardner sat back and relaxed in the
coolness. The waitress returned quickly with two frosted
glasses of iced coffee. About then, Mike heard a commotion
in the front of the diner and twisted around to see what was
causing the disturbance. There were three boys arguing with
a man he recognized as the manager. Then he saw the gun,
black and shiny. Bert was fast on her feet. For such a big
woman, she could move with surprising speed and agility.
She zeroed in on the scene, impressive Smith & Wesson
327TRR8 revolver drawn.

"I'm a police officer. What's the trouble here?"

The manager, visibly shaken, glanced at the badge Bert
flashed.

"I told these punks never to come back here again. Every
time they show up, they buy a lousy Coke, then hang around
and bother the customers and my waitresses. Now they come
here with a gun!"

The boys exchanged looks, the weapon holder giving the
other two a cocky smile.

"Drop the pistol, kid." St. Croix spoke with easy authority.

The boy ignored her and continued to point his weapon at the manager, arrogantly surveying Bert as his two friends moved slightly away.

"What if I don't like giving it up, bitch?" St. Croix moved toward him. "Hey, keep away, you get me pissed, something bad could happen to you!"

Bert brought the side of her left palm down on the boy's extended arm, the movement hard and fast. Then she followed up with one sharp kick to the knee. The arrogant expression disappeared from the boy's face, replaced by one of agony as he fell to the floor and began moaning. Bert picked up the boy's gun and holstered her own.

"Damn, it's not even real."

"It's just a toy, officer. We were going to play a little joke on the prick manager is all," one of the other two boys said nervously to Bert, his pockmarked face reminiscent of craters on the moon's surface.

"Assholes, you got no sense at all. I want the three of you out of here right now. I'll keep your little toy. Don't ever try anything like this again, and never come back here." Her voice softly insinuated all kinds of harm.

"My knee! I can't walk!"

"You're lucky it wasn't your groin."

The two boys helped their companion to his feet. He was still breathing hard and moving unsteadily but managed to leave fast enough.

"Thanks a lot, officer," the manager said, a grateful smile spreading across his thin lips. "Anything you want is on the house. It's the least I can do."

St. Croix frowned. "I pay my own way," she responded. "If those kids show up again, call us right off."

Back at the booth, she shoved the toy pistol across the table to Gardner, who examined it with interest.

"Damn thing looks like a real Luger," she said with contempt.

"Sure does," Gardner agreed, turning it over in his hand. His opinion was confirmed: St. Croix was very comfortable in situations that demanded immediate and violent action.

"You never told me, is Bert a nickname?"

"Short for Roberta. My mother favored that name. Had an Aunt Roberta once upon a time."

BERT GLANCED AT her watch when they reached the apartment of the Nevins woman. It was just six o'clock. The apartment was located on the ground floor and she could see into the front window, but it was dark inside. She heard voices. The lights went on as soon as she rang the bell the second time. Still, no one came to the door. Impatiently, she rang the doorbell again. Finally, a woman's voice with a shrill edge called out to them.

"Go away, whoever you are. I'm busy."

"Police, Miss Nevins, we want to ask you some questions concerning the death of Richard Bradshaw." Gardner's statement was clear and concise. He was well-spoken; she would grant him that. He was different from most of the cops she knew in many ways, more of a gentleman, better-mannered.

"Come back some other time." The voice sounded irritated.

Bert spoke up. "If we have to come back, you'll be answering questions at police headquarters." That got results; the door opened a crack.

"Look, I can't see anybody right now," the woman said. "I'm not feeling good. Come back later."

"We need to see you, and it has to be now," Bert insisted.

"Get a warrant, then." She started to shut the door, but Bert gave it a quick heave with her shoulder and walked inside. Gardner quickly followed.

"Hey, what the hell are you doing?" Nevins shouted.

"We aren't here to give you a hard time," Gardner said in

a conciliatory, soothing manner. "We just want the answers to a few questions."

Bert could tell from the way Gardner glanced at her that he was not exactly thrilled with her methods. She shrugged; getting results was what mattered. She began looking around the apartment, which was in the nature of a studio or efficiency. The room they were in served as both bedroom and living room. A convertible sofa was pulled out, and had obviously been occupied at the time of their arrival.

The room was messy, clothes scattered, newspapers and magazines thrown around, accumulations of dust on the furniture. Smells of stale tobacco and burnt coffee permeated the atmosphere, offending her nostrils. Slovenly bitch, this April Nevins.

Her eyes shifted to the woman. She wore a gossamer thin, close-fitting vermilion negligee and nothing underneath. The full swell and hardened nipples of her breasts were clearly defined by the negligee that came open as she moved, revealing firm, well-tanned thighs. She glanced over at Gardner and was amused by the fact that he appeared uncomfortable.

"Look, I can't help you. I hardly knew the guy."

"We got a different impression," Bert said, keeping her tone flat.

"From who?"

April Nevins was shorter than Cheryl McNeill and definitely more voluptuous. Her well-rounded body was that of a woman, not a girl. Bert judged her to be at least thirty—although carefully made up, she could have passed for younger. Tousled, light brown hair was sun-streaked with blond, as if she spent a lot of time outdoors. Looking away from her, Bert caught sight of some articles of interest lying on the floor. The first was a condom, the second a pair of men's briefs. She called Gardner's attention to both.

"Now how do you suppose jockey shorts ended up lying on your floor? They don't look much like something you'd wear."

Most women would have blushed in embarrassment, but not April Nevins. "Sonny, I think you better come out here."

The bathroom door opened and Sonny, with nothing but a bath towel wrapped around his torso, walked into the room. His face was very red. Bert tossed him the underwear and then the other clothes she found nearby.

"Get dressed. Then we'll talk," Gardner said.

The boy took the clothing back to the bathroom without uttering a single word.

"Okay, what did you want to ask me?" April's voice was too loud and shrill. It grated.

Bert didn't speak, waiting for Gardner to take the lead. This was really his show; she was just along for the ride, at least for the time being.

"Let's sit down," Gardner said. Again the soothing voice. He was trying to get the woman to relax. Good strategy, she decided, but not likely to work under the circumstances.

The woman seated herself on the edge of the convertible couch while Gardner moved a coffee cup off the nearest chair. Then April Nevins picked up a half-used pack of cigarettes from an end table and lit one.

"How long did you know Bradshaw?"

"Only a couple of months."

"Were you intimate with him during that period of time?"

The Nevins woman took several vigorous puffs on her cigarette, then rubbed it out with ferocity into an already overflowing ashtray. "We only slept together a few times, that's all. I dropped him the day after his live-in maid caused a scene at the pool club."

"Wasn't it the other way around?" Gardner asked.

"You think he dropped me? That wouldn't make sense. I had good reason for dumping him, not the reverse."

"What reason?" Bert interjected.

Nevins whirled, gold-edged hair swirling around her face. "It's damn personal!"

"We're not voyeurs, Miss Nevins," Gardner said. "But it is necessary for us to know. Otherwise, we might end up arresting the wrong person."

Her hands were shaking as she lit up another cigarette. Bert would have liked to rip it out of her hand and crush it, but she kept her cool.

"If you must know, for all his big talk and smooth manners, Rick Bradshaw was pretty lousy in the sack. He'd come here, drink off enough of my good Scotch to get loaded and then grope around in bed. He'd satisfy himself and then pass out. I tolerated it a few times and then got fed up. Oh, he took me to some fancy places, but that wasn't enough. I can always find men who'll take me out, and I can always get men who want to screw me. But I don't sell my services. I expect to get as much enjoyment out of having sex as the man does. Otherwise, I don't want anything to do with him. Do I make myself clear?" She tossed her tawny mane. "Rick Bradshaw had a very selfish attitude. He was strictly a taker, a user."

Sonny came back into the room and April Nevins abruptly stopped talking. Gardner turned and faced him.

"You pretended you barely knew Miss Nevins, why?"

"I thought you'd get the wrong kind of idea about me."

"Or the right one," Bert said.

"Did you think we'd suspect you of killing Bradshaw out of jealousy?" Gardner was scrutinizing the kid with care.

Sonny wasn't meeting their gaze. Bert reminded herself it was Sonny's knife that had been used to kill Bradshaw.

"Look, I already told you I broke with Rick. Sonny had no reason for being jealous." April Nevins ran her hand through the gold-crested hair.

Bert wondered how truthful she was. April wasn't easy to read.

"All right, you can go," Gardner said to the lifeguard. "But we'll want to talk to you again."

Bert did not miss the meaningful look the youth shot at April Nevins. As to what it meant, she had no idea. These weren't her kind of people. She watched the lifeguard leave with an abrupt, almost clumsy stride.

"How involved are you with the boy?" Gardner asked with a directness that surprised Bert.

April Nevins looked away from them. "Sonny knows I like my freedom, and he's too young to get seriously involved with anyone. But sexually, we're very compatible. Look, I know what you're thinking. How come a woman of thirty-two is sleeping with a boy of nineteen? Well, it's simple. He's got a beautiful body and he knows how to use it to gratify a woman's needs as well as his own. That's more than I can say for lots of older men." Her face was screwed into an intense, militant expression. "Frankly, it isn't any of your damn business! We're not hurting anybody, and what we do is private."

Bert thought April Nevins was talking straight. But then again, who could tell? Lying to cops was as typically American as slurping beer at a ball game.

Gardner gave April time to calm down, and then he continued with his questions. "When did you and Sonny first become intimate?"

"I met him at the beginning of the summer when the pool opened Memorial Day. We hit it off right away. I was thinking of taking some swimming lessons at the time. That's how it got started."

"And eventually you dropped him for Bradshaw?" Gardner suggested.

"Just for a few weeks. But I didn't actually drop him. I just couldn't conveniently see both of them at once. Rick seemed more interesting at first. Sonny wasn't jealous. If you want to know the truth, Rick was the jealous one, although he had no right to be."

"Why was that?"

She took a few more puffs of her cigarette and flicked the ashes at the tray. "Rick was immature for his age. He had very shallow feelings. Using other people to feed his ego seemed to be a pattern with him. While he was seeing a woman, she had to be completely under his spell. He couldn't stand to have it any other way."

"And Sonny was different?"

"Sonny's okay. Dumb but decent. He wouldn't deliberately hurt anyone."

"And Rick would?"

She shrugged uneasily. "Rick liked hurting people. He was sadistic." She turned and faced Gardner. "Look, Sonny couldn't have done anything to Rick. It wasn't his way. Besides, Sonny and I have nothing more than a physical relationship. No emotional commitment."

It occurred to Bert that the woman was making it sound too simple. She had the feeling April was just trying to protect the kid.

"Miss Nevins, did Bradshaw ever discuss his views on marriage with you?"

"Yeah, sure, once when he was drunk. Not that he was talking about marrying me. No man's ever seriously considered marrying me." She paused reflectively. "I don't mean that the way it sounds. I'm not feeling sorry for myself. I did a long time ago, but that's over. A woman's better off on her own and independent anyway."

The woman struck an empathetic feeling in Bert. They had nothing in common, but Bert could sense when another human being had been deeply hurt.

"What exactly did Bradshaw say about marriage?" Gardner was good at keeping people from digressing and getting back to the heart of the matter, she granted him that.

"Rick said he'd never get married again. He couldn't be faithful to any woman for very long."

"Did he happen to discuss his relationship to Ms. McNeill with you?"

"Only once. He said she was trying to get him to marry her and he was about ready to dump her."

"When did he say that?"

"The day after she made that scene at the pool. I remember because it was right after that I told him I didn't want him coming around here anymore."

"A week ago?"

She thought for a moment. "Less I think. I don't know. I'm not the kind of person who keeps track of time. I'm generally late wherever I go. I don't even wear a watch." She stared off into space, her expression pensive. "I did feel sorry for her, though."

"Why?"

"I've gotten to the point where I can recognize men who use women selfishly. Rick was one. A definite womanizer."

"Did you hate him?"

"Hell, no, and I didn't kill him, either! He was just a creep, and I didn't want anything more to do with him." She looked from Gardner to Bert. "Listen, could you leave now? I got to go to work. I need to get dressed."

"Certainly. Just one last thing. Do you know if Bradshaw was seeing any other woman?"

"Knowing Rick, I wouldn't doubt it. But he didn't tell me anything, so I can't give you any information."

It was twilight. The air had grown cooler and less humid by the time they left April Nevins' place. Of course, her apartment faced woodlands that bordered the development on two sides.

"We're getting conflicting stories from Bradshaw's two lady friends. Which one do you think is lying?" Bert was curious to hear Gardner's analysis of the questioning.

"It could be that they're both telling the truth as they know it. Maybe it was Bradshaw who did the lying, told each woman something different. What's your take on this? Got some woman's intuition to offer?"

"More likely he told the Nevins woman the truth," she said.

"Could be."

Bert was aware Gardner's nickname around headquarters was *the psychologist*. It was used in a respectful manner from what she could see; it suited Gardner. The man had a talent for interrogation. He asked questions in a nonjudgmental way that got people to open up to him. But it was more than that. There was a sympathetic quality that encouraged the sharing of confidences. Most of the good cops she'd known used intimidation tactics during questioning. Personally, she wasn't above scaring the crap out of people when a confession was called for or information needed to be solicited. Gardner's approach was different, and she had to wonder at it. Still, he did have a way with people.

"A case like this is like a giant jigsaw puzzle. Each suspect furnishes a different piece of that puzzle. Then we've got to examine them critically to see how they fit together. Naturally, the complete picture is going to look very different from the individual pieces."

"The whole is equal to more than the sum of the parts?" she said.

"Exactly. No single point of view will be free from distortion. Even a person who believes he's telling the whole truth is bound to be partially inaccurate."

"Sounds good in theory," she said.

"But?"

Their eyes met.

"I'm a practical person, and I live in the real world. You're spouting theory at me. You talk the talk, but can you walk the walk?"

"What if I said I can walk the talk?" His eyes twinkled.

She wondered if he took anything very seriously. "I'll have to wait and see."

"You just do that," he said with an easy smile. "So now it's time for my lamb chop story."

"I'm not following you."

"You will. There's this little old lady who goes to the store to buy lamb chops."

"Let me guess: would this be the same little old lady who went to the concert?"

"How did you guess? Anyway, she asks the butcher how much the lamb chops cost and he tells her. She complains that the store down the block is selling them two bucks cheaper per pound. So the butcher says, 'Lady, why don't you buy your meat there?' She tells him the other store is out of lamb chops. So he says: 'if we were out of lamb chops, we could sell them just as cheap, maybe even cheaper.'"

Bert rolled her eyes. "I suppose there's some point to the story?"

"Did I make you smile for a minute? Did I relieve your type A angst momentarily?"

"I repeat, does the story have a point in the context of the crime we're investigating?"

"Maybe, then again maybe not."

She let out a deep sigh. "You think Rick the prick was out of lamb chops?"

He gave her a noncommittal shrug. "Let's say from what we've learned about our victim, he wasn't the kind to offer what he advertised. You know how angry some shoppers get when an advertised product doesn't exist."

"Angry enough to kill?"

"You never know about people," he said with another shrug.

FOUR

KIM WAS READY when Mike came by that evening. He looked so handsome, his dark hair falling in waves over his forehead, his lean, muscular build emphasized by a close-fitting blue knit shirt and jeans that hugged his hard body in all the right places.

"You look great yourself," he said with a smile.

She found herself blushing. He'd read her mind.

His two daughters were in the backseat of the car.

"Hi, Ms. Reynolds," Jean said with a sunny smile. "I'm glad you're coming with us."

"Please call me Kim," she said. "And I was happy to be invited."

Kim noticed that Evie didn't acknowledge her. The older girl transmitted a general air of disdain. Well, what could Kim expect? Evie was a teenager, probably eager to demonstrate her independence and growing maturity. Jean, by contrast, was a fair-haired ten-year-old with a friendly, outgoing personality. Evie was guarded and reserved, careful and cautious. Kim understood all about that. As a teenager, she too had been old beyond her years. It wasn't surprising that Evie might have trust issues and be wary around women. Kim knew that Mike's wife had left him and the girls several years ago. Evelyn Gardner had not just divorced her husband; she'd divorced herself from the entire family. Still, Kim conceded, it was easier to warm to Jean.

"Well, ladies, what's it going to be? Italian, Chinese, Mexican or plain old American?"

"I like them all," Jean said.

"And it shows," Evie remarked, looking pointedly at her little sister's chubby figure.

"Yeah? Not everyone needs to look anorexic like you," Jean countered.

"Enough of that," Mike said, his tone firm. "Kim, why don't you decide?"

"I'm really not fussy about food," she said, feeling uncomfortable with three sets of gray eyes focused on her. "Where do you usually like to eat?"

Mike drove to a restaurant that served buffet style, had a casual, relaxed atmosphere and was suited to families. Kim thought it was a perfect choice.

"So how is your murder investigation going?" Kim asked as she munched on salad greens.

"Yeah, Dad, what's going on?" Jean's enthusiasm was emphasized by her punctuating the air with a French fry speared on a fork.

"Sorry, but it isn't suitable dinner conversation."

The girls groaned in unison.

"He doesn't like telling us about his work," Jean confided.

"You treat us like babies," Evie agreed.

Mike cleared his throat. "So Kim, what did you do today?"

She understood that he wanted to change the subject and responded accordingly. "My day was pretty dull I'm afraid."

AFTER DINNER, Mike let the girls rent a film. And with her tacit approval, Mike took Kim back to his place with them.

"I like your house," she said, looking around. "It has a homey, lived-in look."

"A polite way of saying it's not very neat," he said with a wry smile.

"It's great," she assured him, and she meant it.

The girls started watching the film rental while she and Mike went out to the kitchen.

"Tell me more about your house," she said.

"Not much to tell. Fifteen years ago, I bought two acres of land and slowly set about clearing them. With the help of my brother, who's in the contracting business, I had a proper foundation laid plus plumbing and electrical work put in. Then I set about building a house. It took quite a while, but I enjoyed the manual labor, found that it relaxed me.

"Five years ago, I was wounded in a shoot-out following a liquor store robbery. The recuperation period was one of the things I always remember with special pleasure. In the mornings, there was the sonority of the birds. I watched a robin building her nest and then hatching her eggs in the crab apple tree outside the bedroom window. And there was the sense of peace and stability I felt watching the kids play in the backyard as the sun set through the woods." He stopped as if embarrassed. "Hey, you don't want to hear that kind of stuff."

"I really do," she said. "I like knowing things about you."

"I feel the same way about you," he said, stroking her cheek and then kissing her lips.

Weird how the barest brush of his lips made her shiver with longing.

LATER, WHILE MIKE checked his calls and the girls watched the movie, Kim looked around the downstairs area of the house by herself. No, she hadn't imagined the good karma in this place. Mike's rock-hard steadiness was ingrained here. How could any woman want to leave a home and family like this one? She had to wonder what kind of person Evelyn Gardner was.

Kim returned to the living room. Evie came toward her. "Your bag was ringing. I pulled out your cell phone and answered it for you. Hope that was okay."

"Yes, thank you. I always forget about it."

Evie handed over the phone and Kim checked the caller I.D. "Hi, Ma. How are you?"

"Just fine, dear."

"How's Florida?"

"Hot and humid."

"Same here."

"You phoned earlier."

"I just wanted to say hello."

"You usually phone on the weekends."

"I'm off this week."

"You should have told me. I would love to have you come down for a visit. You know that."

"I'll come down this winter if that's all right."

"Any time you like."

"I'll phone you again soon."

"Good." So much was always left unsaid between herself and her mother. She regretted that. It was always that way between them.

When Kim finished the call, she looked up to find Evie studying her, a question in her eyes.

Of the two girls, Evie reminded her more of Mike in manner and appearance.

"Thanks for getting that for me," she said to the girl, "I wouldn't have wanted to miss my mother's call."

"She asked for Karen Reyner. I wasn't sure she wanted you. If that lady's your mom, how come she doesn't know your name?" Evie stared at her with a puzzled expression.

"It's complicated," Kim said.

Evie rolled her eyes. "That's what adults always say when they don't want to answer questions."

"I don't mean to treat you like a child." Kim sat down heavily on the couch. "At a certain point in my life, I decided to reinvent myself. I wasn't very happy and I wanted to be a different person. So I legally changed my name. It was a symbolic act. My mother and I disagreed about it. She's never accepted it."

Evie was thoughtful, solemn, her gray eyes owl-like. "I was named for my mother. Eve is the short version of Evelyn. She was a rotten mother. I'd really like to change my name, too." There was a mist in the girl's eyes and an edge of bitterness in her voice.

Instinctively, Kim reached out. Evie sat down beside her, letting Kim place an arm around her. "I don't pretend to know why your mother left or how she could, but I will tell you this much. It had everything to do with her and nothing to do with you."

"Yeah, whatever." Tears welled over Evie's eyes. She rubbed at them with a fisted hand.

Mike found them sitting together when he entered the room. "Lousy movie?" he asked.

"Sort of," Evie agreed. "Jeanie likes it, though. The humor's childish, on her level."

Mike looked at his watch. "Time for you and your sister to start getting ready for bed."

"Dad, I'm older than Jeanie. I should get to stay up later. Besides, it's summer vacation."

"Don't you have camp tomorrow morning? Jean may just be a camper, but you're a junior counselor. That means responsibility. You need to be sharp, at your best, well-rested."

"Okay, okay, I get it," Evie said, exasperation dripping from her mouth like acid. "You don't fool me. You just want some alone time with Kim."

He gently swatted her bottom. "That too, smart girl."

After he'd hugged both girls, gotten them to go upstairs and settled down for the night, Mike seated himself on the couch beside Kim.

"You have a very good relationship with them," Kim observed.

"Glad you think so. It can get a little hairy at times."

"At least they know you love them." She thought of Carl Reyner and shuddered inwardly.

"Evie was right. I do want to be alone with you." He took her hand and kissed the palm.

"To woo me?"

"How does that work for you?" He gave her his sexy smile, then put his arm around her.

"So what happened today with your homicide case?"

He looked at her from the corner of his eyes. "You're not going to make this courting stuff easy for me, are you?"

"I'm many things, but definitely not easy."

"Tell me about it. Okay, I'll give you a nutshell summary of my day."

She listened attentively as he described the questioning of Cheryl McNeill, April Nevins and Sonny Blake.

"So what do you think? Any flashes of intuition as to who might have killed Bradshaw?"

Kim was pensive. "I don't have those kinds of powers. Sometimes I see things other people don't, just like you do. Mostly, I just put things together. Ms. McNeill sounds like she might have a motive. A woman scorned. Yet she claimed he intended to marry her and had apologized for his infidelities. This April Nevins…she sounds like a troubled individual. But if she dropped your victim as she claimed, then she really wouldn't have any motive, either. Sonny Blake. Obviously he was physically able to move a body on his own and he would have had the opportunity, but what possible motive would he have? This is frankly perplexing."

"Maybe I can manage to arrange for you to meet the people who were directly involved with the vic. Are you willing?"

Kim worried her lower lip. "Won't Detective St. Croix object? She might resent my interference."

"We'll see. In the meantime, I don't want to waste the time we have together talking shop. I plan to champion my cause."

"Which is?"

There was a wicked gleam in his eye. "I intend to persuade you how much you want to be the significant lady in my life."

"Do I?"

He rubbed his thumb erotically across her palm. "I'm convinced you do." He kissed each finger of her right hand, playfully nipped her thumb, then licked it.

She laughed. "Are you going to try to seduce me?"

"Good thinking."

He kissed her on the lips, and the earth went out of orbit. Being close to him was the definition of spontaneous combustion. Mike slipped his hand around the back of her neck, angled her head, his mouth returning to hers. His tongue outlined her lips, then provocatively urged her mouth open. Their tongues touched, dueled and joined. His mouth was hard and soft at the same time. She heard the pounding of his heart as he pressed himself against her. She buried her hands in the waves of his hair. As the kiss became deeper and more passionate, desire burned in her body. She ached for him.

He pulled back. "Let's continue this upstairs," he urged in a husky voice. "Stay over tonight." He kissed her again as if to seal the deal and counter any possible argument on her part.

"With the girls upstairs, I don't think I'd feel comfortable. I'd feel depraved."

"Well, I'm feeling deprived." He leaned over and kissed the nape of her neck.

"I have to think about it."

"You're too uptight. Let me give you a massage," Mike said.

"I've never had one," she admitted.

He gave her a heavy-lidded smile. "I'm not the only one

who's been deprived. And a little depravity wouldn't hurt you, either. Let's go upstairs. I've got magic hands."

"I'll just bet." She put her arms around him and held tight for dear life. Mike Gardner did have quite a way about him; she had to concede that. His raw, masculine essence was hard to resist. When they were together like this, she stopped thinking, lost in passionate feeling.

And then her cell phone started to ring. She tried her best to ignore it.

"Damn all phones to perdition."

"I'll just shut it off."

"And have you worry about who was calling? No, Kim, you answer it. Then shut it off for the night."

She clicked the phone on as the third ring vibrated.

"Hello, Kim. How are you?"

"Don?"

"The one and only. I was reading Byron and immediately thought of you. 'She walks in beauty like the night/Of cloudless climes and starry skies/And all that's best of dark and bright/ Meet in her aspect and her eyes.' See what I mean?" Don's melodic baritone was seductive. He certainly did justice to the poet, and then some.

"I'm flattered," she said. Uneasily, she noted Mike's eyes narrowing.

Don Bernard's suave, cultured voice insinuated itself into her ear. "I dropped by the library today to do some research for an article I'm writing. When I asked for my favorite reference librarian, I was told you were on vacation. I hope I'm not phoning too late, but I was wondering if you'd care to go to the theatre with me this weekend, or any evening this week, for that matter, while you're free."

"I'll have to get back to you."

"Of course. Bad time?" Don's voice was knowing.

She glanced at Mike, who definitely looked none too happy. "You could say that."

As she disconnected, Mike was studying her. "Professor Bernard, I presume?"

She sometimes forgot how perceptive Mike was. She nodded her head with an almost imperceptible motion. Mike was frowning deeply. He looked formidable, too much the tough cop for her taste. Gone was the tender, teasing lover. His eyes were dark gray thunder clouds ready to burst with a dangerous electrical charge.

"Think maybe I ought to have a talk with Bernard."

Kim rarely lost her cool, but this was too much. "Leave Don alone."

"What I ought to do is shoot him—nothing lethal, just give him a warning not to poach."

"Mike, don't even joke about that."

"Who said I was joking?"

She stiffened. "That's it. Take me home or I'll call a cab."

"Fine, let's go to my car. I just can't believe you'd consider encouraging that guy anymore." He grabbed his car keys in an angry motion.

"Don is a friend. A person can never have too many friends. And I've known him longer than I've known you."

"But not as well—or have you forgotten?"

No, she hadn't forgotten anything. "You don't have any cause to be jealous."

"Is that right?"

"I hate you acting this way."

He wasn't even looking at her now. "I had an unfaithful wife. I don't ever want to deal with something like that again."

"If and when I marry a man, I won't cheat on him."

THEY DIDN'T DO MUCH talking on the drive back to her apartment. How had things gone so wrong between them? She hadn't wanted bad feelings to exist, hated confrontations of any sort. Yet she must face the fact that they were two very different people and just might want very different things. She admitted, at this moment, she was pretty much confused about what she did want out of life—and possibly who.

FIVE

BERT WAS DREAMING about Alva; there was a smile in her friend's brown velvet eyes. Then suddenly, Alva was gone. A feeling of panic took over. Where was she! Where was Alva? Why had Alva disappeared? Bert looked everywhere but couldn't find her friend. She was seized by the conviction that something terrible had happened.

The dream ended where it always ended. Bert woke up that morning gulping air, and for a moment or two wasn't certain where she was. Her breath came in short jags, the sense of grief and pain washing over her anew. Her three-year friendship with Alva had been the best thing that ever happened to her. Now her life was empty and lonely again; she was out of place and out of time.

She envisioned Alva, wishing her friend was here, her usual smile on her face. Bert never understood how she managed it, particularly since so many of Alva's patients were terminal. But she had a relaxed outlook on life, an optimism that was infectious.

Life was so ironic. It made no sense at all. If anything, she should have been the one to die first, not Alva. She was in a dangerous line of work. Alva should have survived. A good woman like Alva was really needed in this screwed up world. Bert saw Alva clearly in her freshly laundered white uniform, a smell of spring lilacs perpetually about her. It should never have happened. She still couldn't believe it; a living nightmare. Bert clenched her fists, raging at the injustice of life, desolate in the awareness of her own inability to change things. At least police work gave her a sense of purpose.

SHE AND GARDNER MET the Wallings that evening and proceeded to examine two more of the puzzle parts. It was strange how Gardner's analogy seemed to stick in her mind. Bert didn't want to like or respect the guy, but she had to concede, however grudgingly, there was something about the older cop that another professional couldn't help but admire.

Martin Walling greeted them warmly, if not over-enthusiastically, with a sweaty handshake. He was fat and short—several inches shorter than his wife. His ruddy complexion implied that he might make an agreeable drinking companion, and it seemed like there was more hair in his mustache then on his head.

"We want to help the cops all we can," Walling said. "Rick was a good friend of ours. The damn bastard that murdered him ought to be strung up by the balls." He quickly turned to his wife. "Sorry, honey. I know I shouldn't talk that way in front of you, but I feel very strongly about this."

His wife's expression seemed either indifferent or just detached.

"How long did you know Mr. Bradshaw?" Gardner asked.

"Ever since he came east."

"And Mrs. Walling?" Gardner turned to the lady, but it was her husband who answered.

"Joan's known him for maybe five months. Right, honey?"

Mrs. Walling glanced from Bert to Gardner with suspicious eyes. "I suppose," she replied. Her bored, indifferent expression made Bert wonder.

"Say, would you folks like a drink or something?"

"No, thanks, Mr. Walling," Gardner said. "Could we just sit down and talk for a few minutes?"

"Sure thing, I'll just turn up the air-conditioning. I'm sweltering. Since both Joan and I go to work every day, no one's around, so Joan says it's more sensible to keep the cooler off until we get home. Keeps the electricity bills down."

"You're a practical woman, Mrs. Walling," Gardner said with an easy smile that showed a dimple in his right cheek.

"Very practical," Walling responded, and turned down the thermostat.

Bert was struck by the vulgarity of the room's decor. She was no interior decorator, but the garish reds and purples dominating the color scheme were a little bit much, even by her uncritical standards.

Walling observed her looking around. "Place is something, isn't it? Bet you couldn't help noticing my favorite painting, right? Do you like it?" Walling pointed to an oil painting of a half-naked Spanish dancer on a background of black velvet set in a heavily gilded baroque frame. "Those gypsy gals really know how to turn a man on. Every time I look at it, I get horny." Walling winked at Gardner, who did not bother to respond. "Yeah, that picture really set me back a bundle. Hell, it's an original. I spent a fortune decorating this room, and you know what? Joan hates it! She says it's loud and tasteless. What do you folks think?"

Joan Walling went up a notch in Bert's opinion.

"Did Mrs. Walling have input in making the selections?" Gardner inquired.

"After my first wife and I split, I moved out and rented this apartment. When Joan and I got married, she was still living at home with her folks. Imagine that? So naturally she moved into my place. I can't afford to redecorate just now, but any time Joan wants to do it herself from her salary, she can go right ahead."

Mrs. Walling shot a sharp look of annoyance toward her husband, which didn't seem to disturb him in the slightest. Clearly his skin was thicker than a rhino; maybe his brain, as well. He just kept right on talking. "I can't get Joan to part with a cent of her earnings. She won't even buy decent clothes for herself. She earns more than I do, but all she does is squirrel her money away. Myself, I believe in women's rights. A woman shouldn't depend on a man to support her. I admire a liberated woman. I think it would be just fine if a woman wanted to support me."

"Be quiet, Martin! You're making an ass out of yourself. The police didn't come here to discuss our personal lives." She turned to Gardner. "You'll have to excuse Martin. He tends to ramble on aimlessly. He also exaggerates everything. That's the way salesmen are. They love to talk and tell stories. He suffers from diarrhea of the mouth and constipation of the brain." She glared at her husband, but he chose to ignore her.

"All that complaining about me being in debt," he continued. "I guess I figured I'd needle you a little in return. Anybody who's been soaked for child support the way I have deserves some sympathy. My ex-wife was a rotten bitch. She really took me to the cleaners. We only had one kid and he's seven. She can work while he's in school, but will she? Hell, no! Rather drive the nails into my hide."

There was an uneasy silence and Gardner looked uncomfortable. Bert wasn't too thrilled herself. Walling made her feel like puking.

"Mrs. Walling, what kind of work are you engaged in?" Gardner turned his steady gray eyes in her direction.

"I'm a systems analyst."

Bert studied the woman. She was unexceptional in height and build, maybe five-five with a medium frame. The plainness of her face was underscored by a sharp chin. Her lips were thin and her nostrils seemed pinched. There was no sparkle to her hazel eyes. If she wasn't homely, then she was close to it. The fact that she was reticent to speak made Bert think she had an introverted personality. Then again, she seemed to be weighing every response as if making certain she wasn't giving anything away, in direct contrast to her husband, who was too blunt with his comments. Bert found herself neither liking nor trusting either of them. Then again, in police work, it was best to be short on trust. She'd learned long ago that lying and distortion come as easily to people as eating and drinking.

"You have a responsible job," Gardner said.

"Joan's a very responsible person," Martin interjected, digging into his wife again with mockery in his voice.

"One of us has to be responsible, dear," she returned, dripping acid.

Bert shot a significant look in Gardner's direction. The Wallings were clearly past the honeymoon stage.

"It would help us if you could get back to discussing Richard Bradshaw."

"Sure, Lieutenant, what do you want to know?"

"You worked with Bradshaw. Tell us about that."

"Martin worked *for* him, not with him," Mrs. Walling said.

Walling threw his wife a killing look. "We worked for the same outfit. In fact, it was me who suggested these apartments to him. See, we hit it off right away. Our relationship was always as much social as it was business."

"Why was that?"

"Well, he was just a great guy to work with, really nice and easygoing. Nobody had a sharper mind."

"In what capacity did the two of you work together? Did he supervise you closely?"

"He was my boss in theory, but he wasn't standing over me. I'm a district sales manager. I'm on the road a lot, working with different salesmen, checking over accounts. Rick was put in charge of the entire east coast operation, all the managers. That meant that he was out on the road a lot, too. But he had an office in New York at company headquarters."

"What kind of company are we talking about?"

"Pharmaceutical. You know, drugs."

Bert raised her brows with interest but said nothing. Big money, deep pockets.

"Could we have the name of your company and the address of the main office?"

"Sure. I'll get you guys a business card." Walling checked a desk drawer and came back with a white card that had *Marcom* elaborately embossed on it.

"Who was Bradshaw's boss?"

"Fella named Briscoe. He's the regional sales manager."

"I thought that was Bradshaw's job."

Walling seemed momentarily flustered. Bert picked up on it and noticed that Gardner had, as well.

"Did I say he was? Sorry, I must have given you the wrong impression. Briscoe can explain things better. That is, if you can ever get through to him. He's always either out of the office or busy in a conference. You know how executives are."

Actually, she didn't know, and was certain she never would.

"Did Mr. Bradshaw have any business or personal enemies that you know about?"

"Rick? Impossible! He was one terrific guy. Charm and class all the way. Everybody liked him, even Joan. Right, honey?"

"He was more interesting than your other friends," she agreed in a detached tone of voice.

"Interesting doesn't hope to cover it. Christ, did he ever know how to score with the ladies. What a stud!" Walling's smile was an envious leer.

"I have some questions about a few of those ladies."

"Shoot, Lieutenant, I'll enjoy answering. Say, would you like a cigar?"

Gardner responded negatively. It would figure that someone like Walling would smoke cigars; Bert always associated cigars with fat, bald men, wannabes with no taste or common sense. Walling fit the stereotype perfectly.

"Well, I think I'll have one."

Mrs. Walling let out an agonized groan. "Thinking about it is as far as you get," she said, showing some real spirit for the first time. "That hideous smell never leaves once you've smoked one of those things."

"Joan doesn't approve of drinking or smoking. Regular Puritan. Sometimes I wish I were a bachelor again. Hell, I got screwed twice. Big dummy, that's me. Guess I shouldn't have been in such a hurry to remarry. You got me on the rebound, honey."

Mrs. Walling stood up, her face red to the hairline. "Well, I certainly didn't get any kind of bargain, Martin."

That was for certain.

"You were over thirty and lucky to get me." Walling seemed much more composed than his wife.

She walked away with quick strides through the dining area and opened a sliding glass door that led out to a terrace. She betrayed her anger by slamming the door in a forceful manner.

"Do you and your wife quarrel often, Mr. Walling?"

"Now and then, like everybody. You know how it is. We're still newlyweds." He grinned through nicotine-stained teeth that gave him an almost sinister look. "We need time to adjust to each other. Joan's got a heart like one of her computers. She doesn't lose her temper much, mostly just ices over when she's angry. She doesn't understand that most of us aren't as pure and free from vice as she is."

"No vices?" Gardner probed.

"Well, she fucks pretty good. I mean, you know how important that is. And she wasn't no virgin when I met her either, in spite of living with her folks."

Bert found it hard resisting the temptation to stuff Walling's cigar down his throat.

"I was playing the field. She invited herself up to my apartment, bold as brass. When a woman like her acts that way right off, I get uneasy. So I told her that I didn't want to get serious with anyone for a while. But she decided to stay for the weekend. Joan can be very aggressive when she wants something. She set out to change my mind and she did a real job." Martin flashed his leering smile, displaying pinkish white gums against crooked, yellowing teeth.

"Did you know Richard Bradshaw's women friends? Would any of them have reason to kill him?" Gardner's tone was neutral, nonjudgmental. How did he manage it?

"Rick was such a popular fella. He really turned the broads on. Handsome son-of-a-bitch. But he played it cool. He wasn't dumb like me. Rick didn't rush into a second marriage."

Bert found it increasingly difficult not to betray her visceral reaction to Walling. She couldn't tell about Gardner because he was good at keeping his cool, but she had an idea that Gardner felt the same way. She also realized that Walling wasn't aware of their reaction to him; he was too obtuse an asshole.

"Did any of Bradshaw's former women friends dislike him?"

"Probably, but that doesn't mean they'd kill him. I figure it was likely some mugger or drug addict."

Gardner ignored the comment. "Do you know Cheryl McNeill?"

"Sure, Rick brought her over a couple of times and we went out with them once. Stuck-up bitch. She puts on airs. Wants everyone to think she's a real lady. Never even laughed at any of my jokes, like they were too vulgar for her refined tastes. Shit, even Joan laughs at my jokes sometimes. Just to give you an idea of the kind of deadhead she is, Rick and her had some kind of fight at the pool club. He was supposed to come here that evening—I don't know which broad he planned to bring. Anyway, he calls up and says he can't make it. I could hear her yapping in the background: 'don't ask them to go out with us. I can't stand that big blob of protoplasm.' She didn't care whether I heard her or not."

"Did they patch things up?"

Walling shrugged. "I don't know. Joan might. I didn't get to talk with him after that. Like I said, I'm on the road a lot. I was away for a few days around that time."

"Do you know April Nevins?"

"Who doesn't?" The leering smile returned to Walling's lips.

"What's your impression of her?"

"A real nice piece of ass. Rick brought her over once. We had some drinks together. She was real lively, not a dull broad like Cheryl. She and Rick really put away the booze. And she laughed at my jokes. I don't think I took my eyes off her the entire time. She was wearing this skimpy black dress with nothing underneath. What a bod!" Walling let out an appreciative sigh.

"Did you ever see her socially? That is, not in Bradshaw's company?"

"Only at the pool. Don't get me wrong. I'm human, but when my first wife and I weren't hitting it off so good, I started visiting pros. A guy has to get it somewhere, right? Except that only caused me more trouble. I picked up a nasty case. It sobered me fast. I mean, it could have been something more serious, even deadly, if you catch my drift. I got real careful after that. The way I see it, April is an easy lay, just begging for it. I'm keeping away from the kind that sees too much action. Rick even told me he was using rubbers whenever he slept with her."

Bert could tell by the expression on Gardner's face that he'd taken all he could stand of Martin Walling for the present. Personally, she was grateful she hadn't eaten dinner yet.

"Thank you, Mr. Walling. I would like to speak with your wife now."

"Go right ahead. You sure I can't get you a drink? Some nice cold beer maybe?"

"We're still on duty," Gardner replied.

"Well, I'll just pour myself one. All this talk made me damn thirsty."

Bert was already on her feet, quickly following Gardner out to the terrace. The beauty of the view immediately struck her. The terrace faced out on a huge, landscaped courtyard.

"Very nice here," she commented to Mrs. Walling who, was resting her well-tanned legs on a stool.

"I find it relaxing to sit out by myself when I come home from work." She spoke in a low monotone and avoided looking at either of them.

"Do you mind answering a few questions for us?" Gardner asked.

She yawned softly, almost deliberately. "No, but I doubt I know anything that could help your investigation."

"Let us make that decision. Your husband mentioned the fact that you know April Nevins."

"I know her but we're not close friends." Her manner remained distant.

"And Cheryl McNeill?"

"She's also an acquaintance."

"You do, however, know some of the more intimate details concerning their relationship to Mr. Bradshaw?"

"Neither one ever tried to conceal anything." Joan Walling gave the impression that the conversation bored her, but Bert decided that might be a careful pose. She sensed wariness beneath the disinterested facade.

"Do you know if Ms. McNeill made up with Bradshaw after the incident at the pool?"

"Yes, as far as I know."

"And he promised to marry her?"

"That's what she told me."

"Did you speak to Bradshaw at any time after that? If so, did he confirm the story?"

"I didn't see him, so I really don't know."

"What about Miss Nevins? Did Bradshaw break off with her after the pool incident?"

"They had a fight. I'm not exactly certain who did the breaking off. Probably it was a mutual thing. But I know it didn't end on a friendly note. April was bitter."

"Did she say why?"

"I told you everything I know."

Her coldness didn't deter Gardner; he kept after her. "Was Bradshaw seeing any other women besides those two?"

"None that I'm aware of, but then I don't qualify as an expert on the life and times of Richard Bradshaw."

"Do you think Bradshaw might have confided that kind of information to your husband?"

"Hardly. Martin is a blabbermouth. Rick was only open with people when it suited his purpose. I'll admit we were both curious, but Rick kept his personal affairs pretty much to himself. Unlike my husband, he was discreet. I consider that sensible, don't you?"

"Mrs. Walling, your husband mentioned being in debt. To your knowledge, did he ever borrow money from Mr. Bradshaw?"

She sat up straight in her chair, posture stiffening visibly.

"No, he didn't owe Rick anything. I'm the one he always pesters for money. I think there's something I ought to explain about my husband, since he does tend to give people distorted impressions. When we first married, I paid some of the outstanding bills. For example, I took care of the phone bill and had the line reopened. Also, the utilities were in arrears. Martin's salary is quite satisfactory. He doesn't have to be in debt. He's just totally irresponsible with money. He claims I'm stingy, but the truth is, he's extravagant."

"Extravagant in what respect?"

She was reluctant to answer, but Gardner wouldn't let up. God, the guy was a regular pit bull!

"For instance, does he like to visit Atlantic City or the track?"

Mrs. Walling eyed Gardner sharply. "He doesn't have a gambling problem, if that's what you're implying. Sure, he might play a little too much when he's down there, but that's typical of most people."

Loses money he can't afford to lose, Bert thought to herself. Walling's financial situation opened all kinds of speculation. Money was always a strong motive for murder, maybe even more compelling than passion. Joan Walling looked nervous now, as if realizing that she'd told them too much.

"Could you go? I'm very tired. I really don't have anything more to tell you about Rick."

As they proceeded back through the apartment, Martin Walling grabbed Gardner's arm with his fat, sweaty hand.

"I don't want you getting a bad impression of me and Joan or thinking that we don't get along. What I mean is, we have these little spats from time to time. I'll take her out to dinner and she'll forgive me. I know I shouldn't dig her about being cheap, but it's been eating at me. You understand how it is, don't you? Anyway, I hope you find out who murdered Rick. He was one hell of a guy. And if I can be of any further help to you, just let me know." He shook Gardner's hand in a final effusive gesture.

The beefy paw did not extend to Bert, as if maybe Walling thought the darkness of her hand was caused by dirt that might just rub off on him. Prejudice took many forms, subtle and otherwise. Bert knew most of them well, but then wasn't she just as prejudiced against the Wallings of this world? She wasn't about to beat up on herself over it though. Walling deserved it. But she knew this was a form of rationalization. Prejudice didn't need to be logical and rarely was.

SIX

BACK AT HEADQUARTERS, Gardner began discussing the case with Bert St. Croix, fully aware she had barely spoken at all during his questioning of the Wallings.

"What do you think of Martin Walling?"

"Not much. He's a slob, but I notice he never got around to lighting up that cigar."

He smiled at Bert's observation. "True. A small penance to pay for the fact that he humiliated his wife in front of us."

Bert nodded in agreement. "He's got a very low opinion of women in general. You notice he didn't talk to me, only to you. Then again, being a woman of color gave me a second strike."

Gardner decided it was safer to change the subject. "Did you think they were telling the truth?"

"Hard to say. In spite of the fact that ol' Martin's got a bad case of diarrhea of the mouth, just like his wife said, I wouldn't trust him to speak the truth any more than a snake oil salesman."

"And his wife?"

"She was playing it close. Can't say that I really care much, either." Bert's eyes were dark and unfathomable.

"What worm's eating on you?"

She didn't answer him right away. Gardner understood instinctively that they'd arrived at a moment where St. Croix had to decide whether or not to trust him, and clearly, it wasn't an easy decision for her to make.

"The whole case stinks. I hate it. All we do is talk. No action, no doing anything real. It's like being buried alive."

"Not exactly like New York, is it?"

"I'm used to being where there's excitement, things happening. That's my lifestyle. I'm out of my element here, and I feel damned useless. In New York, I felt like something was being accomplished, even if most of what I did proved futile in the long run. Even when I was scared and gone beyond my limits, the adrenalin rush made me feel real. At least, I was alive. I don't find any challenge for me here. I don't belong." She ran her hand over braided hair as dark as a raven's wing. "How could I expect you to understand? In all your life, have you ever had to shoot another man?"

"I served in the military. I've also been a policeman in the inner city, and yes, I've been forced to take several lives. Does that make me less of a wimp and more of a good cop in your eyes?"

She looked away, obviously embarrassed. "I didn't mean to insult you. Maybe some of the things I've seen and done have brutalized me, but I know I can't take this sitting still very well. Don't get me wrong. I know there are all kinds of ways to be a cop. I just wasn't cut out to be a clerk and sit around typing out petty reports."

"They also serve who only stand and wait."

"Sounds familiar."

"Milton—now there was a fellow who could see without eyesight."

"I didn't know you were a literary scholar, too," she said in an amused tone of voice.

He shrugged, feeling embarrassed. "It's Kim's influence. She's got me into reading some classics."

Bert gave him a knowing smile.

"Look, we don't always work on homicide cases around here. Usually, if there is one, it's assigned to me. But like you said, this is just a small-town police force. We handle everything. We also cover a lot of physical area, since there's no teeming mass of people. A lot of the terrain is still farmland and forest, looking no different than it did fifty or a hundred years ago. So we don't have the kind of violence and excitement that comes from policing an area of concentrated population. But things do happen around here, and your kind of police person is needed. Why don't you give it a fair chance and try not to get too restless or impatient. Not yet anyway. This can work out for you. You couldn't have been very happy in New York or you wouldn't have left in the first place."

A look of pain passed over her face. "It's the memories that were killing me." She didn't seem willing to elaborate and Gardner had no desire to push. He respected the right to privacy. Whatever made Bert St. Croix so angry and restless was her own business as long as it didn't interfere with her judgment on the job.

"We're going to make a breakthrough on this case soon. I can feel it. Things aren't as placid as they seem. It's like that pool we found Bradshaw floating in. On the surface it's clean, peaceful. But just get close enough, look down into the depths, and you can see the murky residue of slime undulating. We're getting deeper into it all the time, and the truth is just waiting to be located."

"E.S.P.?"

Gardner smiled. "Call it cop's instinct. Want to make a call?"

"What call's that?"

"To Bradshaw's boss at Marcom Pharmaceuticals."

"Sure, if you trust me to do the talking."

"Why wouldn't I?"

She took the card Gardner handed her. "You might as well listen in."

Gardner nodded his head in agreement. He thought he felt the tension lessening between them. He wondered if he could keep things moving in that direction. Bert was beginning to open up to him, and that was a good sign. As she dialed the

New York phone number, Gardner picked up on the extension. At the other end of the connection, a young woman's voice answered wearily. Bert asked for Briscoe.

"The offices are closed for the day," the receptionist said. Gardner glanced at his watch. He'd forgotten that it was well past six. Still, some executives did work late. Bert must have been thinking similarly because she identified herself and told the woman to ring through. On the fourth ring, a man picked up the phone and it turned out to be Briscoe.

"You're lucky," he said. "I don't usually stay here this late but we had an important conference."

"Concerning Mr. Bradshaw?"

There was a hesitation on the other end of the line. "Yes, as a matter of fact, it was. He won't be easy to replace."

"We're conducting an investigation into Mr. Bradshaw's death and we'd appreciate your cooperation."

"I was just leaving," Briscoe responded in a tired voice. "I don't think we ought to discuss this matter over the phone. Why don't you make an appointment with my secretary and come by the office one day this week."

Gardner made a note of the man's reluctance to talk. But Bert wasn't buying it; she kept after Briscoe.

"The questions are pretty standard. They'll only take a few minutes. I'd rather not waste the time traveling back and forth to the city unless it's absolutely necessary. Tell you what, if you aren't sure of my identity, just phone back to Webster Township Police Headquarters and ask for Detective Bert St. Croix."

There was a deep sigh at the other end of the line. "No, I guess it's all right. What do you want to know anyway?"

"Why did Bradshaw come east?"

"We needed him here. He was good at his job. Certain districts haven't been functioning properly. Profits are down. We thought Bradshaw could shore things up for us, make some useful recommendations, that sort of thing."

"And did he?"

"Yes, he did."

"Was he finished with the assignment at the time of his death?"

There was a long pause. "Not entirely."

"What about Martin Walling's district? Were his profits down?"

"Things weren't going well for Martin lately, even though he has a solid area. But Bradshaw hadn't made any suggestions concerning him yet. Of course, I've known Martin for years and I'm well aware of his problem."

"Which is?"

"His divorce, naturally. It drained his energy and concentration for quite a time. We're hoping that the situation will improve now that he's remarried. Bradshaw informed us that Martin's new wife is very ambitious for his advancement. She ought to prove a good influence."

"Walling have any other problems?"

Another reluctant pause. "There was something else. We've had thefts from our warehouses in Martin's district. Some valuable drug shipments were stolen. As a result, delivery dates were set back and a few clients cancelled their orders with us in favor of other companies. It's a highly competitive business."

"Were the thieves ever caught?"

"No. The police told us that the robberies were well executed. Professional jobs, they said."

Bert threw a meaningful glance at Gardner, indicating that she thought Walling was looking more in the nature of a likely suspect all the time.

"Did Bradshaw have any enemies you were aware of?"

"None. He was well liked. The fact is, we're really sorry about losing him around here. He was one of our best. Clever mind, charming personality, a salesman's salesman. He knew the business from every aspect. Was there anything else?"

"No, that's it, Mr. Briscoe, but we may have to contact you again."

"Feel free—just don't call me this late in the day next time."

The line went dead and Bert hung up.

"What do you think?"

Gardner met her gaze. "You were very good. Handled him just right. As for Walling, I agree with what you're thinking. He may very well have fingered those jobs. It's obvious he needed money."

"Yeah," she agreed. "His first wife was making demands and his second disappointed him."

"Joan Walling's not exactly a benevolent benefactor. Still, I don't know how easy it would be to connect Martin with the thefts." Gardner didn't want to get sidetracked.

"We could get the reports and think about it."

"It doesn't mean that he murdered Bradshaw, but there might be a connection," he acknowledged.

"I wonder if we'll find any link between Walling and Sonny. You don't mind if I look into that?"

Gardner nodded his head in approval. He wanted her to get involved in the case, to care about solving Bradshaw's murder. Maybe working in Webster Township wasn't the greatest thing in the world for Bert, but Gardner had the feeling that returning to New York would be worse. Whatever the source of Bert's unhappiness, she needed distance from it. He was about to suggest making a visit to the Scofields, the other couple that had been friendly with Bradshaw, when a call for detectives came through.

The call took them to County Highway 683. They drove quickly along the single lane road as it snaked a serpentine path through well-forested land. A patrol car was there waiting for them. Although two blankets were securely wrapped around her, and the night was warm, a young girl stood shivering on the dirt shoulder of the road, an uneasy, fresh-faced uniform patrolman beside her. Her dark hair hung limp and matted, plastered with blood against her face. Bert helped the girl sit down in the backseat of the blue and white cruiser. She was trembling so badly that her movements were completely uncoordinated. Carefully, Gardner took down her statement, writing the key facts he intended to deposit on another detective's desk for further investigation.

The girl spoke in a disjointed manner, but he was accustomed to that and listened patiently. She was a local resident who'd decided to hitchhike to the shopping mall. Two young men picked her up. Her description of them was vague and confused, but Gardner decided not to prod her; she was still in a state of shock. All she could remember about the car they drove was that the color was a metallic silver. She had no idea of the make, model or license plate number of the vehicle.

"They drove off the main road and into the woods. Then they took turns raping me." She began to sob uncontrollably. "I begged them to stop but they wouldn't listen. They were animals!" Bert held the girl and comforted her until she could resume her story.

The young men had left the girl naked, beaten and humiliated in that isolated spot. Eventually, bruised and bleeding, she managed to make her way back to the main highway. There a cruising township police car had spotted her and stopped to lend assistance. Gardner finished taking down the girl's statement by the time the ambulance arrived.

"They'll take good care of you at the hospital," he said, trying to sound reassuring.

"Do I have to go there?" She seemed very frightened, her eyes enormous in a small, heart-shaped face.

"You'll have to be examined," Bert said gently.

"No. I'm scared."

"How about if I call your parents so they meet you there?" Gardner said.

She shook her head. "My dad, he's going to kill me! He'll say it's all my own fault for hitchhiking."

"I'll talk to him," Gardner promised. "They really need to know so they can help you."

As the ambulance moved away, lights and siren piercing through the growing twilight, Gardner was thinking of his own two young daughters and how he'd feel if something like this happened to one of them.

He'd call the girl's parents and make certain that someone sympathetic took charge of the investigation. From his point of view, helping people was the most important function of his job. About ninety per cent of his time on duty was devoted to assisting people with one type of problem or other, only about ten percent to making actual arrests.

"Imagine, crime exists even in beautiful suburbia," Bert said with a note of sarcasm in her voice.

"Anywhere there are people," Gardner replied, his features taut and grim. He didn't miss the sadness in Bert's eyes.

KIM SAT ON A LARGE tree trunk that had somehow managed to drift on to the beach. The sea lapped up against her toes. In the distance she could make out Staten Island and Brooklyn. Sailboats, motorboats and jet skis meandered their way about the water. She loved it out here, loved the bay and the beach. Out on the jetties, people were patiently fishing. She was alone but not lonely. This was such a peaceful place. Not far from here the house she'd grown up in stood, rented by her mother to strangers. Just as well. There weren't many happy memories there. She didn't think she wanted to ever go back there again.

Thinking about the past, she pulled her cell phone from her shorts pocket and scrolled down to her mother's number. The phone rang several times before Ma picked up.

"I couldn't really talk when you called me back," she told her mother. "I was with Mike over at his house."

"That's the policeman, isn't it?"

"Yes."

"He's the one you care about, isn't he?"

She hesitated, but why keep things from Ma? There had been too many secrets between them while she was growing up, and it had been so destructive. "Mike proposed to me. He wants us to get married."

Ma's reaction was immediate. "That's wonderful!"

"Maybe."

"I don't understand, dear. I thought you told me you love this man."

"I did. Maybe I still do. I don't know. I'm confused, Ma." She picked up a small scallop shell and turned it over. "The thing is, I was nearly killed last fall. Mike was there for me. I think I might have reacted too strongly to the situation. Not that I don't have feelings for Mike, but I'm just not certain. He's about ten years older than I am. He's been married before. He has two daughters who live with him. I don't know if I'd fit in with his life. And besides, you don't need to be married to have great sex with someone. Sorry, Ma, I hope I didn't scandalize you with that comment."

"Dear, it takes a lot to shock me. But you'll be thirty on your next birthday. Isn't it time you started to think about marriage, maybe having children of your own?"

She watched someone unleash a German shepherd, allowing the animal to prance into the ocean. How joyful that dog must feel being released and free! It would be great if she could be released from her personal prison. But Kim knew only she herself could do that; only she held the key.

"I'm not certain exactly what I want, Ma."

"Or who? What about that professor friend of yours?"

"Don Bernard phoned me. He wants to take me out."

"That's the professor you said was sophisticated and charming? Is he the sort of man you want?"

"You're asking me questions I just can't answer."

"Well, think carefully about what you're doing. I think marriage would be good for you. And Mike sounds like a good, steady man."

"I imagine you thought that about Carl at one time." Why had she said that to her mother, knowing it had to be painful? She was angry with herself.

"Honey, Carl was a good man. It was the army that ruined him. You know he was permanently disabled. It made him bitter, made him do things, things he wouldn't have normally done."

"Ma, Carl murdered other people. When are you going to stop making excuses for him?"

"I don't want to talk about it! Let's discuss other things, please."

So the conversation got casual again. Ma talked about Florida, how nice it was, and how she would probably sell the house in New Jersey.

"But, Karen, if you decide to get married, let me know. I want to be at your wedding."

"Sure, Ma, and I'll phone again soon."

She disconnected and put the phone away. Talking to Ma really hadn't helped. She buried her toes into the sand and turned her face to the sun.

Maybe she thought too much. It made life complicated. When she was in Mike's arms, all she knew was that he wanted her, and she wanted him just as much.

SEVEN

MIKE GARDNER OPENED his desk drawer and took out the brown paper bag that contained his dinner. Evie had neatly packed two turkey sandwiches, but he found them soggy with excess mustard. He had a sneaky suspicion it was Evie's punishment for him not eating dinner with the family, even though she knew perfectly well that he had to rotate shifts. Again he reached into the bag, discovered a large, ripe Jersey peach, and bit into that first. That made him think of Kim Reynolds. She was a true Jersey peach, juicy and sweet, but with just an underlying edge.

What was going to happen with them? He'd thought he knew where the relationship was headed, that they were in a really good place; he wasn't so certain of that anymore. Kim was special. They shared a connection very few people ever had. He'd lost Evelyn. He didn't want the same thing to happen with Kim. He shouldn't have been so jealous, so possessive of her. He knew how she felt about her independence. He could be sensible and in control on the job, but when it came to Kim, emotions got in the way.

The office was unusually quiet at this hour. He was alone in the drab room shared by the plainclothes detectives. The frosted glass door that led to Captain Nash's office swung open and the captain barreled toward him.

"Mike, is St. Croix around?"

"No, she went out for something to eat."

"Just as well. I was looking for a chance to talk to you alone. Think you could eat in my office?"

"As well as anywhere else." Gardner picked up one of the offending sandwiches and took it with him.

Nash was a big, burly man possessed of homely features. His nose, broken at some indefinite time in the past, had never properly mended and gave him the intimidating appearance of a former boxer. Gardner seated himself across from the captain.

"What's your take on the Bradshaw case?"

"We're questioning people," he said carefully. "We have several suspects."

"Translation, you got nada."

"We've got some solid leads."

"I'd like to see you wrap this one as soon as possible with no screw-ups."

"I always try to be thorough. What's the problem?" He took a bite out of his sandwich, the oozing mustard stinging the corner of his mouth.

"You know how local politics are," the captain said with an uneasy shrug.

"Someone putting on the pressure?"

Nash cleared his throat. "I got a call from Pete Ginley this morning. Maybe you know him?"

"Know of him. On the town council, right?"

"Yeah, and he also heads the planning commission. He's a pal of George Page."

Gardner felt like a character in a comic strip, a lightbulb glowing incandescently over his head. "Let me guess. Page, who happens to be the builder and owner of La Reine Gardens, is worried about unfavorable publicity."

"You got it. Ginley says that his friend Page is concerned because it's not just a local story anymore. An article appeared in *The Star-Ledger,* which means people are reading about the drowned man all over the state. I think what's really bothering Page is the fact that he's eager to double the size of his complex. He also put in a bid to build a big shopping center. The planning commission is very sensitive to public opinion and pressure. If the newspapers start giving this story a big play with articles on crime in suburbia and how unsafe it is to walk out alone at night in this township, well, you see what could happen." Nash waited for him to say something. When he didn't, the captain continued. "A lot of people would benefit if Page put a large shopping center into this community. I'm not talking another dinky strip mall. And the apartment complex is quality stuff. That can only improve the town and life for the homeowners. A lot of us wouldn't like to see the council deny Page approval on his plans. Let's face it, we've had enough shoddy, substandard housing tracts thrown up around here. We've got to encourage people like Page. You ought to know that the chief's involved in this, too."

"Not another friend of Page."

Sarcasm was wasted on the captain; he never reacted to it.

"You got it. And he wouldn't be the only unhappy camper if Page doesn't build further in Webster. Take Mayor Ryan, for example."

Should he start taking notes? Gardner felt like he was a student back in high school, but he listened politely without interruption.

"The Mayor is also a friend of George Page, as it happens."

"I guess a person can never have too many friends," Gardner said with a hint of irony, thinking of what Kim had said the other evening.

"And I don't have to tell you about the feud that the mayor and the chief are having. Now to some folks, it all seems like petty crap, but to those of us who understand the situation, we see that it's a serious matter, a question of power and control with significant implications."

A question of who gets the most pay-offs. Gardner couldn't help being cynical. He'd lived in the town enough years to suspect graft and corruption, not that he could really prove anything. They were too smooth for that. Hard evidence was difficult to come by. Then again, the entire state had been controlled by corrupt politicians for as long as he could remember.

"So the mayor and the chief have put aside their personal differences to help Page?" Gardner surmised.

Nash eyed him askance. "You implying something?"

"Not a thing. I just find human behavior fascinating."

"Helping Page is the only thing the chief and the mayor agree on these days." Nash cleared his throat and continued. "I've decided to keep you working evenings for a while. Since Bradshaw was whacked in the evening, and most of the people involved are available then, it seems the smart thing to do. Hope you don't object."

"Would it matter? I'm sure my kids will be thrilled. You want to explain it to them?"

Nash quickly sought to change the subject. "How's St. Croix working out? You breaking her in?"

"More like the other way around," Gardner said with a wry smile.

"I knew she wouldn't be easy to work with. A real pistol. That's why we gave her to you."

"Should I send a dozen roses as a thank-you?"

"Don't be a wiseass. The chief says she's a first-rate cop. They wouldn't have hired her otherwise."

"Unless the chief was under pressure from the mayor and the department had been criticized publicly because of its discriminatory policies."

Nash put up his hand as if to dismiss the matter. "Everybody knows Mayor Ryan is after the chief's scalp."

"So now the department has its own female Jackie Robinson."

"Well, something like that," Nash conceded. "Anyway,

just get this murder solved as fast as possible so the big shots don't come after our asses."

At that moment, a red-faced man bustled into the office, looked around quickly, eyes lighting on Nash.

"Speak of the devil," Nash muttered.

"And he'll hear you," Gardner said.

"Okay, where's Chief Morgan?" the red-faced man demanded.

"Not here right now, Mr. Mayor," Nash responded.

"Damn it! Where is he?"

Gardner had never seen the mayor so angry; he was usually very affable and in control.

"Really, sir, I have no idea," Nash said.

"Well, you can give him a message for me. Just say that this business of having his policemen harassing me won't work. I don't appreciate you guys following me around day and night, and I especially don't like coming out and finding twenty-two tickets on the windshield of my car! It's overkill. Gestapo tactics. And I'll see to it that everyone knows about it, too. The story is going to the newspapers. Make sure you tell him that. I know him for the crook he is, and I'm bringing the old fart up on charges of corruption and insubordination." With that, Mayor Ryan stormed out of the office, furiously slamming the door behind him.

"Jesus Christ!" Nash let out, "I can't believe it!"

Gardner made no response. He tried to avoid involving himself in petty local politics as much as possible. The chief considered himself above the law, and so far he'd gotten away with it. Mayors came and went but the chief stayed in power. As long as the chief did his job honestly, Gardner kept out of the political forum.

Back at his own desk, Gardner got down to business. He phoned Herb Fitzpatrick and, after quickly disposing of the amenities, dug into the Bradshaw case.

"What new info have you got for me?"

"The knife we found is definitely the murder weapon. It matches up. No question that Bradshaw was killed in the utility room, either. It was his blood, just as we suspected."

"That should make it easier. Oh, one other thing. Did you find any keys?"

"The victim's house keys? Yeah, they were still in his pants pocket, along with his wallet containing a hundred bucks or so and a bunch of credit cards. Your perp's not a thief anyway."

"Never thought so. Find any keys that would open the utility room?"

"Strictly negative."

"What else was on the body?"

"Just the usual stuff—a half empty pack of cigarettes and an expensive lighter with the vic's initials."

"Okay, thanks."

When Bert returned, they went over the information together.

Gardner thought she seemed more involved—or was it just wishful thinking?

"I still think the killer had to be a man," she said.

"How can you be sure?"

"It's obvious. Look, Bradshaw must have had an appointment to meet somebody there. He came straight from work. That utility room isn't exactly a romantic hideaway. Did you get a whiff of the place? It reeks. Not the kind of place a guy uses for a bang."

"Don't be too sure of that. I've seen stranger. If he meant a meeting to be kept secret, as in the case of a married woman, it might be the perfect spot."

She threw him a look of annoyance. "Clearly, he wanted his meeting kept private, but that only implies something confidential was being discussed. When we fished him out of the swimming pool, Bradshaw was fully clothed. We never even located a bathing suit that could have belonged to him.

Sounds like business dealings to me. Maybe he confronted somebody—Martin Walling, for instance. Bradshaw could have told Walling he had evidence showing complicity in certain warehouse robberies."

"A decided possibility, but where did Walling get the keys to the utility room?"

"From Sonny. Walling could have put the kid on the payroll. I think Walling hired him as an accomplice." Bert's dark eyes shone with intensity and total concentration. "Figure whoever put Bradshaw in the pool had to be strong. Sonny had the keys, and we know for a fact that he lied to us about how well he knew April Nevins. He could have helped Walling for more reasons than money. He had to feel jealous of Bradshaw muscling in on his territory. I say we break the kid down."

Gardner didn't deny that Bert might have the solution to the homicide, but something bothered him, even if he wasn't certain what it was.

"Yes, we should have another talk with both Walling and the boy. But first, I'd like to finish questioning the rest of Bradshaw's friends. Besides, it's standard procedure to interrogate all possible suspects and witnesses before we go after anyone in particular."

Bert acquiesced grudgingly. "I guess you want to meet the Scofields."

"Looks like a good evening for making new friends. I keep losing the old ones."

Bert frowned at his tone of levity. She didn't talk again until they reached the Scofields' apartment. Mr. Scofield answered the door and led them up a flight of carpeted stairs into his living room. Gardner's first impression of the Scofields was that they were a handsome couple. Louise Scofield had auburn hair stylishly coiffed, and large green eyes dominated her pretty face. Yet she gave the impression of being frail and vulnerable, partly due perhaps to the unusual pale-

ness of her milky skin. Although small-boned and of delicate build, her figure was as perfect as her face. On the other
hand, Bill Scofield, equally attractive, seemed a different
sort of person. He had a self-reliant, macho look about him,
a determined hardness, as if he considered himself more than
ready to cope with the world for his wife as well as himself.

"Thank you for seeing us this evening. We understand
that you were friends of Richard Bradshaw."

"Friends?" Scofield said. "Hardly. He and I played tennis
together and sometimes chess. He was good at both games
and offered a challenge. But we were never friends. Bradshaw wasn't just competitive. There was a vicious aggres-
siveness about the man. He always had to prove he was better
than anyone else."

"Mrs. Scofield, how would you characterize the deceased?"

She didn't answer immediately, sinking down on a chair
instead. In a shimmering silk dress, she looked delectably
cool. Gardner noted that the living room was furnished in
a deceptively simple, modern style. Some original abstracts
and landscapes hung on the living room walls, and he observed that the artist had signed with the initials L.S.

"They're waiting for an answer, Lou," Scofield said. There
was the slightest hint of a southern accent to his voice, giving
it a softness that was in direct contrast to the harshness of his
expression.

"We knew Rick through Joan and Martin Walling. Joan
and I became friendly in the beginning of the summer, but I
never knew Rick well at all. Bill knew him much better."

"Did I?" Her husband's response was acrid.

Gardner studied Scofield. He was a tall man, over six feet.
Scofield had sand-colored hair and sapphire eyes that suggested the coldness of a mountain lake.

"Mr. Scofield, you mentioned Bradshaw was competitive.

Aside from tennis or chess, how did he communicate or demonstrate that to you?"

Scofield ducked his direct gaze. "Lots of small ways. He'd pull cute little tricks in front of the ladies to impress them and at the same time put me down. It was mostly subtle and not easy to explain."

"If you could give even one example, it might help us understand the kind of man Bradshaw was and give us a lead. Very often, the way to solving a murder of this kind is to find out as much about the victim as possible."

"I don't see how that would help you, but all right. Bradshaw knew I had a fear of swimming underwater. One evening we were over at the pool with the Wallings and April Nevins. Bradshaw started needling me about my phobia, betting me I couldn't swim half the length of the pool underwater. He claimed he could swim the whole distance at one shot, that he had the breathing technique down pat. For a heavy smoker, he did have surprisingly good wind. I told him if he wanted to show-off, that was his own business, not mine, but he wouldn't let up. He even got Martin on his side—of course, that was no surprise. Walling was his stooge. When I flatly refused, he started making snide remarks about men who pretend they've got guts but are really cowards."

"No one took him seriously," his wife said gently.

"Didn't they?" Scofield turned back to Gardner. "He made me look like a jerk in my wife's eyes. Had a good laugh at my expense. Then he sat down with the women and basked in their admiration."

"Not mine," came his wife's quiet response.

"That's so much bull and you know it!" he fumed. "You ate up his attention like bonbons."

Louise Scofield's great green eyes took on an apprehensive look. Gardner wondered what lay behind her fear. A more natural reaction to her husband's apparent jealousy would have been anger rather than fright.

"Lose your temper often?" Bert asked Scofield with a directness that was almost as unnerving as it was hostile.

"I think of it as righteous indignation. You got some criticism of that?"

"It all depends on what you got to feel righteous about."

Scofield's eyes took on a metallic luster. His wife, by comparison, looked paler and more frightened than ever. Gardner decided to try and ease the tension in the room.

"Mrs. Scofield, you don't appear to be much of a sun worshipper."

"No, I go to the pool late in the day, use sunblock and sit in a shaded area. I'm one of those very fair people who always seem to burn rather than tan."

"She gets sick if she's out in the sun," Scofield said.

"You're not in ill health I hope," Gardner commented.

"Oh, no," she interjected hastily. "I just haven't been feeling very well lately. Sort of a general malaise. Run-down I guess."

"She's taken the last few days off from work. Bradshaw's death really seems to be hitting her hard."

Louise was livid. "Stop it, Bill!"

Out of the corner of his eyes, Gardner saw Bert clenching her fist.

"Mr. Scofield, you obviously didn't work with Bradshaw, did you?"

"No, I'm happy to say that I did not. I'm in advertising."

"And Mrs. Scofield?"

"Lou's a commercial artist. In fact, that was how we met. She started working for the same agency I did."

"And you still work together?"

"No, she's stayed with the Baincroft Richardson ad agency in Manhattan. I've changed agencies since then. I got a better paying job elsewhere."

Mrs. Scofield stood up slowly and took a few steps toward the kitchenette.

"Where are you going? Can't you see they still have questions?"

"I—I thought I'd see if the steaks were thawed for dinner."

"Well, sit down! If Bradshaw were here instead of being talked about, you'd probably be riveted to your chair."

Mrs. Scofield resumed her former place, head down, obviously intimidated. Bert moved toward Scofield; her face wore the same hard expression Gardner had observed in the diner when the snickering teenager had insulted her.

"I don't like the way you talk to your woman. Don't dis her. Show some courtesy. That's what a real man would do."

Gardner did not miss the grateful look Mrs. Scofield shot in Bert's direction. Then she quickly cast her eyes downward again. Scofield looked surprised and taken aback by Bert's remark, and the hostility implied by her tone of voice.

"Just a few more questions," Gardner interceded smoothly. "Did Bradshaw give you cause to be jealous, or did he observe a weakness and simply play on it?"

Scofield seemed just as surprised by the straightforward nature of Gardner's question as he had by Bert's hostility. He took a moment to collect himself before answering. "Bradshaw was always after Lou, trying to flirt with her, paying her compliments, sitting as near to her as he could possibly get."

"Doesn't sound worth getting excited over," Bert said.

"Who are you to judge? You didn't see the guy in action. He only let up a tad when I explained my personal philosophy to him. He actually blanched then. His face turned as white as the belly of a dead catfish."

"What philosophy would that be?" Gardner asked.

"My attitude toward adultery." Scofield flashed a quick, inscrutable glance at his wife.

"You might explain it to us."

"It's very simple. I believe if a man catches his wife in bed with another guy, the husband has every right, a duty, in fact, to kill both of them."

There was a moment of absolute silence in the room.

"You don't consider that harsh?" Gardner asked.

"It's justice. You think it sounds extreme? I say it's fair."

"Most men would be satisfied with a divorce."

"I'm not most men! I was brought up to believe people should be made to pay for their transgressions."

Gardner glanced over at Mrs. Scofield. Her coloring resembled nothing so closely as a peeled summer squash. She rose abruptly to her feet, only to begin swaying unsteadily as if she were about to faint. Bert went to her, took hold of her arms and gently seated the young woman again. Mrs. Scofield gave Bert a small, grateful smile, but her eyes looked terribly sad.

"Are you all right?" Bert asked with genuine concern.

Lou's hand rose to her forehead. "I was just a little dizzy for a moment. Everything suddenly went dark. As I said, I haven't been feeling too well lately. I guess it must be a touch of the flu." She folded her hands primly in her lap.

"I am sorry, Mrs. Scofield," Gardner apologized. "We don't have any more questions for you. So if you'd like to lie down, please feel free."

"Thank you," she said. Slowly, she got to her feet again and then left the room.

They all watched her go, then Gardner turned back and faced Scofield, eyes meeting with direct contact.

"Did you murder Richard Bradshaw?" He kept his tone of voice quiet but intense.

"What? Of course not! I could have, should have, but I didn't." Scofield met his gaze unflinchingly.

"Are you certain that your wife was having an affair with him?" He looked at Scofield directly.

"That's none of your goddamned business," Scofield fired

back, his face turning the color of a blood sun. The man was coming toward him, his fists raised, a savage expression on his face.

"Take it easy," Bert warned.

"We're through with our questions," Gardner said. The last thing he needed was for them to get into a physical confrontation in this situation. Scofield backed off, and Gardner signaled Bert that it was time to leave.

Once on the outside, Bert took long, rapid strides toward their parked car. "I would enjoy taking that bastard apart."

He decided that although Scofield was a big man, Bert was probably capable of doing a job on him.

Bert climbed into the passenger side of the unmarked, dark blue Chevy he was driving tonight. "Scofield makes a real good suspect. And don't tell me you can't see him having a motive."

"Possibly, but according to his self-espoused philosophy, if he caught his wife cheating, he would kill her as well as the man. She is still alive."

"Just barely. He's punishing her with a living death, or haven't you noticed?" Bert vigorously slammed the car door.

"I definitely noticed. But is he the kind who would plunge a knife into a man's back? Whatever he is, Scofield doesn't strike me as being a sneak."

"I still say anyone who comes right out and tells us he's got a theory like that is practically confessing to murder."

Gardner had doubts. "Would he actually be that foolish if he'd killed Bradshaw?" Gardner started the engine.

"Why not? Plenty of psychos do exactly that. He could be a typical nutcase. And who ever said killers were smart?"

"We'll have to handle him differently."

Bert glanced at him, a deep frown creasing her forehead. "You think I came on too strong with him? I don't think you were strong enough. I didn't care one bit for the way he treated his wife."

"Neither did I. The scenario reminds me a lot of *Othello*."

"Shakespeare?"

"Exactly. Let's say Scofield is our Othello, an abnormally jealous husband. How did those doubts enter his mind? It had to be more than mere innuendo on Bradshaw's part. And if he'd actually caught his wife with Bradshaw, then both would be dead. No, something is missing here. Where's our Iago? Somewhere Iago lurks, feeding our Othello's suspicions. We have to find out who this individual is. Something tells me it's an important missing part in our puzzle." As he told Bert, since he'd been seeing Kim, he started reading some of the classics, hoping they'd have more in common. Shakespeare did understand human nature. Shakespeare might have been a good cop himself.

"We ought to take Scofield down to headquarters for further questioning. That'll shake him up. I could apply some pressure."

"What kind of pressure? You don't need an assault charge brought against you."

Bert frowned at him. "I didn't say anything about getting physical. Although, people like Scofield, all they understand is force. Personal fear, that's what they respond to. I learned a long time ago, with certain kinds of people, there's no appealing to their conscience or better instincts because they don't have any. With the Scofields of this world, fear and intimidation most often turn the trick."

Gardner took Bert's cynicism in stride. "That could be true. But we're still going to have to use restraint. You can't tell us from the bad guys if we start manhandling suspects."

"Thank you for that enlightening lesson."

"Don't mention it."

"Know what? I think from what we've learned about Bradshaw, he was a miserable jerk who couldn't keep his pants zipped. Whoever did him should probably get a reward, not a prison sentence. Why go after him? Why care? There are too many crimes that shouldn't go unpunished. Why waste our valuable time on this one?"

Gardner was thoughtful. "Maybe because we've sworn to uphold the law. Murder is murder, even if we don't personally like the vic. Doing our job right, that's what matters. We don't have the right to serve as judge and executioner."

Bert's face wore a troubled, pained expression. Gardner asked himself again: what was eating at St. Croix? He still had no answers.

EIGHT

GARDNER HATED to admit it, but the Bradshaw case was beginning to bother him. What should have been a simple, straightforward investigation was becoming complicated by the unpleasant nature of the victim, the fact that Bradshaw had caused disturbances in the lives of a number of people. Obviously, someone had hoped the upsets would end with Bradshaw's death, but in reality, it was just the beginning. He knew that Bert was right about one thing. The situation between Scofield and his wife was unhealthy. He suspected, just as Bert did, that Scofield had the potential to erupt into violence and abuse his wife at any time. Certainly, their visit had intensified the tension in that situation. He told himself he shouldn't feel any sense of responsibility but felt it just the same.

He had difficulty sleeping that night, something rare for him. As soon as he came on duty the next afternoon, he made a phone call. Bert, already at her desk, observed and listened silently.

Mrs. Scofield answered the phone as he hoped she would, and he quickly identified himself. Her voice was subdued, almost without energy.

"I wonder, would you be home later this afternoon? I'd like to drop by and talk with you again for a little while."

"Bill won't be here."

"I figured that. You won't have to mention this call or the visit to him unless you choose."

"All right." He thought there was a note of relief in her voice.

Bert rose from her desk and came toward him as he hung up. "We seeing Mrs. Scofield again?"

"I am, you're not."

She lifted her chin. "I'd like to be there."

"Not a good idea."

"Why not?" Bert wasn't going to make it easy.

"I'll say it straight out. I saw the way you looked at the woman and her husband. You're not objective about them." Her face hardened, her dark eyes screwing into bullets. She smashed her fist down on Gardner's beat-up hardwood desk with so much force that the antique groaned as if it would break in half. "What's wrong with feeling sympathy for an abused woman and wanting to help her? Sisters have to care about each other."

"Look, we don't know what's really happening between Scofield and his wife. I know what it looks like, but we can't be certain. Before we get any further involved, don't you think we ought to have some more facts?"

"But you don't trust me to handle it, do you?" She pointed an accusing finger in his direction.

"No, that's not what I think. It just seems like you're getting emotionally involved with the Scofields. I want to talk with the woman in a cool, calm way."

"I've seen vicious types like Scofield before. He looks civilized enough, but he's not. If she doesn't leave him, Scofield will stop being content with mental torture and start beating her up. I haven't ruled out Scofield as a suspect in the Bradshaw murder, have you?"

"No," Gardner admitted.

"Then let me come along."

"Mrs. Scofield won't talk freely in front of you, because she won't want to say anything that might make her look bad in your eyes, which means she'll be reluctant to answer the kind of personal questions I intend to ask."

"Can a detached guy like you help that woman? Will you even try?"

"That's not my primary responsibility in this case," he reminded St. Croix, "but, yes, in my own way, I always try to help people. I consider that the most important part of police work."

"I got Scofield pegged as a sadist."

"If that's so, then she could be a masochist."

Bert's nostrils flared.

"I know you don't like hearing that, but you've got to realize there are a lot of possibilities. Still, I promise if there's anything you or I can do for her, it'll be done." He dumped paperwork on Bert's desk and left her to sort through it. He could feel her negative vibes even as he turned his back to her.

He walked across the parking lot, got into his car, and phoned Kim from his cell.

"Busy?"

"Not especially." She sounded glad to hear his voice, definitely a positive sign.

"Want to help me out?"

"Sure. What do you have in mind?"

"Tell you all about it when I pick you up."

"Okay, I'll get ready."

It was a few minutes past five o'clock when he rang the doorbell of the Scofield apartment. Louise opened the door, looking as if she'd slept very little the night before; iridescent, lavender shadows had formed under her eyes.

"Come in, Lieutenant."

"I brought a friend. I hope you don't mind. She's a police consultant."

Louise accepted that. Kim looked very professional in her

librarian's skirt and blouse, her auburn highlighted brown hair, much darker than Louise's, neatly pulled back in a chignon.

They sat down in the cool, air-conditioned living room opposite each other, he and Kim on a gold-brocaded couch, Louise on a straight-backed chair. He noticed the paintings on the wall again.

"You do beautiful work," he said.

She smiled and seemed less tense. "Thank you. Most people don't notice."

"Your husband remarked that you're a commercial artist. You must be very good at it."

At the mention of her husband, her countenance darkened visibly, the fern-green eyes losing their luster.

"What agency do you work for again?"

"Baincroft and Richardson. Why?" Her expression was wary.

"Just curious. Your husband also mentioned that you worked together in the past."

"There's a good light today. I thought to do a little painting."

He was aware she was trying to change the subject. Bert was right. Mrs. Scofield did seem in need of protection.

"How long have you and your husband been married?"

"Two years."

"Have they been happy years?"

"Basically, yes." She didn't look at him.

"But he's always had a bad temper?"

"Not the way you saw him yesterday. He used to be very considerate of me. It's all because of this terrible idea he's gotten into his head."

"That you had an affair with Bradshaw?"

She shot a look at Kim, whose expression remained composed and nonjudgmental; then Mrs. Scofield nodded her head miserably.

"And did you have an affair with Mr. Bradshaw?" His incision was deft and delicate.

"No," she answered, her luminous eyes grave but steady, "I never had relations with the man."

"Sorry, but I had to ask. Have you ever attempted to discuss the situation with your husband outright?"

"Yes, on several occasions. Each time he'd get furious and refuse to listen to me. He shut me out and threatened to do something horrible if I didn't keep quiet. It's like he's already made up his mind and refuses to let me either confirm or deny anything. But the insinuations continue. He's playing some kind of sick game with me. He hasn't even slept in the same bed with me for weeks. If I so much as touch him, even accidentally, he pushes me away. There's just no reaching him."

"Is there any basis for your husband's suspicions? Please try to think. Is it all just in his imagination?"

Louise Scofield looked to Kim as if reaching for support. "I never had anything to do with Rick. I swear it! But I'm never going to be able to prove it to Bill's satisfaction. I love Bill, or I'd have walked out on him. Of course, I don't know what he would have done then. He hasn't been behaving rationally at all lately. He's out of control." Her eyes grew dark and anguished, filling with tears. Her long, artistic fingers trembled.

"We might be able to help you convince your husband."

"Is that possible?" Her voice was pitched high, like a taut violin string. "How?"

"Just hold on a little longer," he said in the tone of voice usually reserved for his daughters.

"Bill is a good person. Of the two of us, he's always been the strong one. I leaned on him, depended on him for emotional support. He understood my weakness but he never faulted me for it." Vulnerability and pain were etched in her eyes.

"Could be you're stronger than you realize and your husband weaker than you know," Kim observed.

Louise stared at Kim in disbelief. "No, he was my savior, my personal deliverer. You see, my father died when I was ten. Then it was just Mother and me. My parents were older when they married. I was the only child they were able to have. I suppose Mother fussed over me too much. She didn't mean to smother me, but that's how it was. I was the center of her universe, her obsession and life's work. I wanted to please her and I needed her love. When Bill came along, I wouldn't allow myself to become seriously involved with him at first. But he pursued me outrageously. Mother didn't like him. I suppose they were too much alike, both strong, domineering personalities. She didn't want me to see him.

"But two and a half years ago, Mother died suddenly of a massive stroke. The shock of losing her, of being completely alone in the world—it was just too much for me. I couldn't handle it. I had no friends. Mother had always been my best friend. I felt so isolated. I didn't think I could manage to keep on living without her. My depression was such that I could barely concentrate on my work. I was close to a total breakdown. That was when Bill stepped back into the picture. He made me feel loved and cared for. I came to depend on him the way I had on Mother. His moods could be unpredictable of course, but I could accept that. After all, he kept telling me how much he loved me. That was what really mattered. Three months after Mother's death, Bill and I were married. Until recently, he's been a rock of stability for me. Now he's like a stranger. I want my husband back, Lieutenant. I want things to be the way they were before."

Kim took Lou's trembling hands in her own. "Nothing ever remains the same. Maybe your relationship will grow and get better or maybe it will disintegrate, but you must start having confidence in yourself. You are very talented. You can be independent, your own person."

Louise nodded and put her hand to her abdomen.

"Are you still feeling ill? Nauseous, dizzy?" Mike asked solicitously.

A startled expression crossed her face. "How did you know?"

"That you might be pregnant? I have two kids. I must have lived every symptom with my wife. After a while, we weren't quite sure which one of us was having a baby. You haven't told your husband yet?"

"No, the way he's been acting, I've been too scared."

"Are you certain he hasn't already guessed?"

"I've been very careful. The evening I went to the doctor for my examination, I told him that I was going shopping with a friend. Bill never has been eager for children, and now, with his jealousy so acute, I'm afraid if I told him, he might think..." her voice trailed off.

"That it was Bradshaw's child?" Gardner said.

Her expression told him that he assumed correctly. "You can't keep it a secret from him forever. And the longer you wait, the more likely he'll consider that reason enough to believe the baby isn't his."

"You think I should tell him then as soon as possible?" She seemed desperately eager for advice.

"Not necessarily." It wasn't his place to counsel her.

"I've been thinking about getting an abortion, but I don't feel comfortable with the idea."

"I'm not the right one to advise you. You really ought to get professional help for you and your husband. A marriage counselor, a psychologist, or even a clergyman."

She listened intently, and he realized she was making a strong effort to appear calm.

"Do you think your husband might have killed Bradshaw?"

Her beautiful features registered pain. "A few weeks ago, I would have said it was impossible. Now, I just don't know."

Anyone could kill, he thought. It was just a matter of being placed in the right circumstances. That's what made a homicide like this one so difficult to solve.

"We'll be investigating and if we come up with something that can help you, we'll see that you know about it." He kept his tone of voice reassuring.

"Thank you. I know you both want to help me. I appreciate that."

He patted her hand paternally, aware that her fingers were as cold as ice cubes.

"When we leave, why don't you warm some milk? Ever seen a cow that needed to visit a psychiatrist? Maybe lie down and take a nap. Getting plenty of sleep makes most problems easier to cope with." Gardner was satisfied when he saw Louise Scofield smile as they left her.

Kim turned to him and brushed his cheek gently with her fingertips before getting back in the car.

"Did I do something you liked for a change?"

She smiled up at him. "You do lots of things I like. You were very good with her. In fact, you're very good at your job. You really didn't need me along."

"Yes, I did. More than you know." He got into the driver's seat. "So what about dinner?"

"Sorry, I've made other plans." She closed down.

Kim didn't need to tell him. He knew the professor was on the menu for tonight. His hands balled into fists, but he refrained from further comment.

"I'll drive you home," he said with stiff formality.

They didn't talk much on the short drive. But he knew he didn't want to leave it this way. "Kim, I'm off tomorrow. What about coming over to the house at lunchtime for a barbecue?"

She hesitated, looking searchingly into his eyes. "Are you sure that's what you want?"

"Absolutely certain. I was wrong to act jealous. I'm not another Othello or a Bill Scofield."

She smiled at him. "No, you're not. And I shouldn't have doubted you." She kissed his cheek and started to get out of the car.

Gardner pulled her back, took her into his arms and kissed her thoroughly. He loved the fresh smell of her, the sensual female essence. His hand glided over her breasts. Kim let out a soft moan. He felt a raw rush of desire. With deep reluctance, he released her.

"That's so you don't forget me."

Kim shook her head, meeting his gaze. "Not possible," she said.

HE HAD AN EARLY DINNER with the girls and then decided to check back at headquarters. It was a humid August evening with the temperature hovering around eighty-three degrees and the moisture in the air reaching saturation. He tugged at his shirt collar uncomfortably and removed his jacket and tie as a concession to the weather. Winter or summer, he wore the same short-sleeved white shirts, never varying his professional wardrobe. Tonight he wished he could drive back to the municipal complex in the buff. Wouldn't that have brought interesting comments as he walked into the office? Maybe he would've had to arrest himself. His irreverent musings made him smile.

Bert was waiting in the squad room when he returned. "Anything new?" she asked.

"Nothing that helps our investigation. How would you feel about phoning the Baincroft Richardson ad agency in Manhattan? Leave a message. We might find out why Scofield left his job there. Being the possessive husband he is, I would've thought he'd want to continue working as close to his wife as possible."

"Great minds think alike, or so they say. I already checked

on it and found out something interesting. Scofield didn't quit his job. He was axed. Seems he got into a violent quarrel with a coworker, a guy who he claimed was trying to hit on his wife. Scofield punched the dude right in the face there in the office. His boss asked him to resign." Her eyes were thoughtful, two candles reflecting darkly in a mirror. "This Scofield fits a classic pattern."

"Think so?"

"Sure. You still consider Scofield a suspect, don't you?"

"I haven't crossed him off our list."

That seemed to satisfy her. "He has a definite motive."

"Mainly, there are three motives for murder: love, hate and greed." He counted them off on his fingers as he spoke.

"What about insanity?"

"Not a motive, but certainly a cause," Gardner observed. "You think Scofield might be insane?"

"He's not too tightly wrapped. A few slices short of a loaf. But I'd definitely classify his motive as love. Oh, incidentally, I asked that our inquiry be kept in the strictest confidence."

"I agree. It's best Mrs. Scofield doesn't find out. She's got enough on her mind without worrying about that. And it's also better if Scofield doesn't know we're checking on him. We can get more from a suspect if he's off-guard."

In their mutual concern for Mrs. Scofield's welfare and suspicion of Mr. Scofield as a murder suspect, he and Bert seemed to have struck some sense of solidarity and mutual accord.

Gardner was just finishing his reports for the night when the telephone rang at ten o'clock, jarring him out of his thoughts. He quickly lifted the receiver and identified himself.

"I need your help!" It was a woman's voice, shrill, nervous.

"Miss Nevins?"

"Yeah, it's me."

"What's the problem?"

"Sonny's here where I work. He's stinking drunk and causing trouble. He came in that way," she quickly added, probably afraid Gardner might think she'd been serving liquor to a minor in a public place. "He keeps saying crazy things. I'm afraid if someone doesn't get him out of here soon, I'll lose my job."

"Where are you?"

"It's the Galaxy Lounge on Route 9. Know it?"

"Right. We'll be there in just a few minutes."

Bert was eager to be on the move. Gardner was pensive as they drove along the highway. The Galaxy Lounge was a relatively new establishment in the area but already had something of a reputation for a pick-up joint. The locals or *townies* never went there—too new and fancy for their tastes. The townies liked their watering holes old and disreputable-looking. Their favorite place was Slater's, a tumbledown tavern with a huge sign that read Female Dancers in bold red letters. Every cop in town had been called on at least once to break up a fight at Slater's. The Galaxy was entirely different. It was strictly a hang-out for the emigrant New Yorkers who inhabited the luxury condos, garden apartments and housing development complexes, and as such, boasted a classy veneer.

The original residents of the area resented the presence of the city people, resented the term *bedroom community,* which had been tagged on to their township in recent years. They themselves refused to buy any of the new dwellings or rent the new apartments. Those who sold their farmland were looked down upon with scorn and referred to as "traitors" by the others. The locals were proud of the old sections of Webster where white frame, clapboard houses of another era stood on parcels of land that were still farmed. Many of the locals could trace their origins back before the Revolution.

Gardner was not unsympathetic to these people, although

he was certainly not one of them. He understood their point of view. His own home was between the largest of the housing developments and the old section, actually set off from both. His simple, modern dwelling was a real source of pride. Gardening or mowing in the large yard gave him a feeling of tranquility, no matter how hard a day he'd spent on the job.

He looked over at Bert and wondered how many of life's small satisfactions had been denied to her. "We're off-duty tomorrow. Why don't you come over to my house? The girls and I usually barbecue outdoors in the summer on weekends. It's pretty informal, but there's always plenty of food and we'd enjoy your company. Come around lunchtime."

"Aren't you a little sick of my face?"

"Not yet."

She refused at first, but Gardner was insistent. By the time they pulled into the parking lot of the Galaxy, the invitation had been tentatively accepted.

The inside of the cocktail lounge was very dark, walls black and tablecloths blood red. Tapered red candles were at each table, but only the bar itself was crowded. Soft music was being piped in from somewhere. The only unusual thing was the ceiling: some aspiring Michelangelo had painted the universe there. It was hardly the Sistine Chapel, but Gardner had to admit the artwork made the place stand out from most run-of-the-mill gin joints.

A number of single men and women were socializing at the bar. Gardner hadn't forgotten the murder he'd investigated here last year. A woman had been picked up here, never to be seen again. They'd found her raped and mutilated body in a drainage ditch, but the murderer was never caught. The victim left behind a small daughter and a grief-stricken mother. He'd always felt badly about being unable to solve that homicide. In his mind, it remained open and would until he finally did solve it, no matter how long that might take.

April Nevins had apparently been watching for them. She

came toward them almost as soon as they entered and quickly signaled the sequined hostess not to bother trying to seat them. April's blonde highlighted hair was pulled back from her face and neatly parted down the middle. Yet her costume was anything but prim. A black velvet micro skirt barely brushed the tops of her thighs. Her white satin blouse, cut very low, loosely covered her well-endowed breasts and emphasized her bronzed cleavage.

"He's in the back. I didn't serve him anything. Like I told you, he was totally polluted before he got here." She walked ahead of them with a brisk step; her voice trailed back in a breathy whisper. Gardner realized it was the first time he'd heard her make an attempt to speak softly.

"Why did he get drunk?" Bert asked.

"We had a quarrel this evening before I left for work. I wish you'd let them reopen the pool so he wouldn't come around so much. You're causing me trouble."

"What did you quarrel about?" Gardner asked, ignoring her comment.

"Rick's death."

"What aspect of it?"

"What difference does that make?" Her voice was shrill again. "Just get him out of here." She walked away as soon as they were in view of Sonny. The boy was holding his head between his hands. His pale blue eyes were glazed over. It was obvious he was not used to drinking.

"Come on, we'll take you home," Gardner said.

"I'm not going nowhere. Go away!"

"Get on your feet," Gardner said in a quiet but firm voice. He took the boy by the arm, but Sonny thrust him off with a strong heave. Bert pulled the youth out of his chair, pressing his arms together. Sonny broke free and tried to take a swing at her. Bert was quick. Before Gardner could even step in, she'd handled the situation. Ducking the punch that came at her, she moved into Sonny with a stiff karate blow to the gut. The kid groaned and sat down heavily on the floor.

"Get up," Bert demanded in a tight voice. "We'll help you walk. Any more trouble and we'll have to cuff and arrest you." She positioned Sonny between Gardner and herself. The boy, no longer protesting, leaned on Gardner for support.

April Nevins watched at a discreet distance, but as they marched the boy out, he caught sight of her. "It's all your fault," Sonny yelled back at her as they guided him toward the door. She turned on her stiletto heels and clicked away.

Once they were outside, Sonny quieted down. They seated him in the back of the car, and Bert positioned herself beside Sonny.

"Where do you live, kid?" she asked. Bert had to ask a second time before Sonny answered in broken, near incoherent syllables.

Gardner knew the street and took a sharp turn on to Jake Blackwell Road to head toward the old section of town. He didn't need to use the GPS.

"Why did you get drunk?" Gardner asked, keeping his eyes on the road to look for street signs.

"'Cause of her. I tol' her I want them back. She says she don't know what I'm talkin' about." Sonny's voice trailed off.

"What did you ask her to return?"

Sonny didn't seem to hear him. "Called her a liar. She got mad, real mad. Said I was good for only one thing. She said never to come back. After all I done for her."

"What was it you did for her?" Gardner got no response.

Bert smacked both of Sonny's cheeks. "What was it, kid?" Her voice was harsh and demanding.

"I got him in the water. For her. Pull over, I'm sick. Gotta barf. Come on, pull over for Christ's sake!"

Gardner drove off the road and pulled the car over on the shoulder. Sonny staggered out and pushed his way through brambles and briars into the woods.

"Think he killed Bradshaw for the Nevins woman?" Bert asked.

"Maybe, but a confession now isn't worth much. He's too drunk. Even if we read him his Miranda, it wouldn't stand up."

"Advise him anyway," Bert urged.

"I suppose we ought to get him to talk regardless, hear whatever he's got to offer. If it sounds like the real thing, we can pick him up for further questioning tomorrow morning."

They waited a few extra minutes. It started to drizzle and Bert walked impatiently up and down the side of the road. "That's it. He's had long enough." Just as Gardner went to get him, Sonny reappeared.

"Gotta go home. Lie down. So sick."

He staggered toward them and they got him back into the car. Sonny smelled foul, so foul that Gardner's own stomach became queasy. He quickly opened the car windows in spite of the fact that the drizzle was fast becoming a downpour. He did not immediately switch on the ignition.

"Before we take you home, I want you to tell us everything you did for April."

"Don't remember." Sonny's speech was slurred, but he still had a certain amount of control. "Please, home."

"Come on, kid. What did you do for her?" Bert insisted. "Tell us and we'll take you home."

"There was blood." The boy didn't say anything else and Bert shook him.

"Who killed Bradshaw? Did April Nevins? Did you do it for her?"

"So sick. Gotta go home …" Sonny passed out.

"We'll get him in tomorrow. Guess he's more involved in the murder than we thought."

"Than *you* thought," Bert said.

"He's a material witness, at any rate. He obviously saw the body in the utility room after Bradshaw was dead."

"I say he's an accomplice. It was Sonny who moved the body to the pool. Seems he did it for April Nevins. Maybe you were right after all, and a woman did murder Bradshaw."

"It's a real possibility," Gardner agreed. "But we will need to interrogate Miss Nevins again."

"Looks like one of us is going to work tomorrow. There's no sense both of us coming in on our day off. I'll pick up Sonny tomorrow morning and bring him down to headquarters."

"That doesn't seem fair," Gardner said.

"What's the matter? Don't you trust me, a woman of color, to handle this alone? You figure only a white male cop can do it right?"

"Cut the crap!" Gardner swung the car back into traffic and drove steadily down the dimly lit highway doing his best not to lose his temper.

"All right, then why should we both be cheated? I don't have any family. Nobody cares if I work or don't. Besides, having a day off means a lot less to me than it does to you. And if I need you, I can always reach you at home."

"All right, on one condition."

"Which is?" She eyed him askance.

"You make it to my house later for the barbecue."

Then Bert did something that really surprised him—she smiled, completely transforming the belligerent expression on her face to one of amity. Had he ever seen her smile before? He didn't think so.

Gardner stopped the car in front of the address Sonny had given them. Then he got out and came around the other side to give Bert a hand with the unconscious youth.

"Damned kid's heavier than an elephant and smells worse than moldy cheese. Be glad to dump him," she said.

Slowly, they struggled up the stairs to a poorly lit front porch. Gardner noticed in passing that the old Victorian style house badly needed a fresh coat of paint. He rang the doorbell and they waited. A middle-aged woman with puffy bags under her eyes answered the door. She saw Sonny and gasped.

"What's wrong with my boy?"

They brought him into the house and deposited the boy on a well-worn sofa.

"Just too much to drink," Gardner reassured her. "He'll be fine in the morning except for a headache."

Sonny's mother wrung her hands anxiously. Gardner studied her. Sonny had inherited his blond hair from his mother, although hers was paler, substantially invaded by white so that the original color had faded. She was tall, had washed-out blue eyes and was thin to the point of emaciation. Her checked cotton housedress hung listlessly from her frame. Everything about her suggested yesterday.

"Was he with that horrible city woman again? I know he's been keeping fast company. A whore has corrupted him with her evil ways, forced a young, innocent boy like that to drink and fornicate." The woman's face became unnaturally flushed. "That harlot will burn in the fires of hell. Don't think she won't! And just who are you?"

"Police officers, ma'am," Gardner responded courteously. He showed her his shield.

"Did Sonny get into some kind of trouble tonight? If he did, it was her fault."

Gardner ducked the question. "Detective St. Croix will be back here to talk with your son tomorrow morning. Please see that Sonny remains here and waits for her."

"I don't understand," she said in an alarmed voice.

"Nothing to be upset about," Gardner said. "But there are some questions Sonny has to answer related to the Bradshaw homicide at the pool club. You heard about it?"

She patted down her short, thin hair. He recognized it as a nervous gesture.

"Sonny told me about the murder, and there was also an

account in the newspaper. Well, I suppose I should thank you for bringing my son home." But the woman didn't appear grateful; if anything, she looked frightened.

As they left, Gardner had a premonition that Bert would not have an easy time tomorrow, and it worried him. Yet he realized there really wasn't anything he could do about it.

NINE

Mike Gardner yawned and relaxed after having spent the morning marketing with the girls and doing a few needed home repairs. The sun warmed his back and he felt like a lizard resting on a rock. His nose told him it was time to inspect the barbecue. Reluctantly, he lifted himself off the chaise and walked the few steps from the grass to the well-shaded patio. The charcoal was finally turning white, and there was no longer any flame. This was the kind of even heat he considered perfect for cooking. Although the coals looked deceptively ashlike, in reality, the hibachi was experiencing its greatest intensity of heat at this time. Everyone raved at the perfection of his barbecuing skill, but he knew himself to be no great chef; it was all a matter of patience and subtlety. With care, he arranged steaks and burgers on the grill, setting hot dogs aside for later use.

"Hey, Dad!"

Gardner looked up as his younger daughter, Jean, splashed him. She was with her two cousins, Mark, nine, and Jerry, twelve; the three got along well together. They were still young enough to enjoy the above-ground pool he put up some years ago, which was in reality little more than an oversize bathtub. He found himself thinking idly of the beautiful pool at La Reine Gardens with its magnificent Olympic size. He let out a deep sigh. Swimming was a sport he enjoyed but had little time to indulge in.

"Dad, give me a hand with these." Evie, as usual, was carrying too many things at once. She tried so hard to act like a grown-up that it made his heart hurt.

He relieved her of some items and helped set down buns, potato salad, pickles, relish, ketchup and mustard on the long, redwood picnic table.

"I put up corn and I'm fixing vegetable salad. You want beer as well as soda?"

"Bert might want it. I'm not certain of her tastes."

"You're sure she's coming?"

"No, but she hasn't phoned, so I guess she'll be by."

"What's she like?" Evie tilted her head.

Gardner shrugged. "Different from anyone else I've ever worked with, but she's a pro. Why should I say anything? You can make up your own mind—you always do anyway."

Evie eyed him narrowly, putting her hands on her slim hips. "Is anything wrong with her? She's not chasing after you, is she? I bet Kim wouldn't like that."

He laughed and gave his daughter a reassuring hug. "Nope. Bert's only got to the point of tolerating me. Try to be friendly and avoid snarling. Bert's the sensitive type, although she doesn't look or act it."

Evie raised her chin. "I am always polite. Don't I put up with those snotty little kids?" She inclined her head toward the pool.

"They are respectively your sister and your cousins," he pointed out.

"They're still annoying."

Actually, he loved having all the kids around. He enjoyed the boys; they played rough as he and his own brother once had, but they were good-natured and fun to be with. He never objected to his brother and sister-in-law leaving the boys with him when they wanted some alone time.

Jean climbed out of the pool and shook herself like a dog.

"Hey, watch that!" Evie said.

"Dad, do you think I'm getting fat? Mark says I'm a blimp." There were tears in Jean's eyes.

"No, honey, you're pleasingly plump. I think you look just right. Very attractive in fact." He put his arm around her waist, gave her a squeeze and kissed her cheek.

"Still, a diet is in order. I'm not looking forward to some future time when people refer to my sister as 'ravishingly rotund.' You've got to start cutting down on calories."

Mike could tell that Evie's remark made Jean feel worse.

"You're beautiful just as you are," he assured his younger daughter. "But if you want to lose weight for health reasons, that's fine with me."

"As the Duchess of Windsor said: you can never be too rich or too thin," Evie remarked.

Gardner cocked an eyebrow. "Girls, your old man's a cop. You're never going to be too rich unless you earn the big bucks yourself or marry money, and trust me, there really is such a thing as being too thin."

"Dad, speaking of money. I plan to go shopping with my girlfriends later. I need new jeans for my date tonight."

"The twenty pairs she has in her closet aren't good enough," Jean said.

"I think I'm missing something here," Gardner said. "What date? You're too young to be dating."

"No, I'm not. Anyway, it's just another camp counselor. He asked me out because we're friends."

Gardner walked over to check on the meat.

"Well, I expect to meet this boy you plan on dating."

"Dad, must you be so old-fashioned?"

"Something bothering you about him?" he countered. "Are you ashamed to have him meet your old man?"

"God, you're actually interrogating me!" Evie placed her arms across her chest, her expression fierce. "You're treating me like I was one of your criminals."

Evie might be outraged, but he had no intention of backing down on this. "I ought to meet all of your dates regard-less, but this one in particular since he's your first."

"I've gone out in groups with guys and girls before. This is no big deal." The flush on her face told him different.

"We'll have to see about that. The way you're behaving, I don't like him already."

She rolled her eyes. "You're overprotective."

"In my line of work, I see what can happen to young girls."

"Your work gives you a dark view of life."

"No, just realistic." He and Evie faced each other like two gladiators.

"I know him, Dad," Jean interjected. "I don't think you'll like him."

"Why not?" Gardner asked.

"To begin with, he wears sloppy, torn jeans and his hair needs to be cut."

"That's in style," Evie said, turning toward her sister.

"I prefer the clean-cut look," Gardner said.

"And he wears sunglasses he never takes off," Jean con-tinued.

Evie's eyes narrowed. "So what?"

"A guy who won't look you in the eye is up to no good."

Evie shrugged. "He just might have a good reason for keeping them on."

"Sure, like being a drug addict?"

"Like wanting to look cool." Evie's face had turned scar-let. "Jean, you're letting your imagination run away with you. Why assume the worst? You're just jealous, aren't you? You want to ruin my date for me."

Jean stuck her tongue out at Evie.

Evie turned from Jean back to her father. "Don't listen to her. She's just a little kid who watches way too much TV. Dad, how can you criticize a boy you've never met? Why do you discount my opinions as if they aren't worth taking seriously?"

"I do value your opinion," he said. "Okay, I promise not to pass judgment too hastily. Satisfied?"

Evie nodded her head, still frowning.

"But someone has to watch out for you kids."

"You're out all day and night arresting criminals, making like super cop. You hardly have time for us."

Every once in a while, Evie expressed her frustration and dissatisfaction with his job. Evelyn used to accuse him of being married to police work rather than her. In some ways, Evie reminded him of her mother. It wasn't a simple matter to reassure her. He hated it when she got into one of her dark moods.

He heard the doorbell ring at the front of the house and walked around to greet his guest. Kim stood there looking beautiful in denim shorts and a hot pink shirt in a silky material.

"Why are you staring at me that way?" she asked self-consciously.

"I was just noticing how great you look."

"You like the outfit?"

He folded her into his arms. "I love it."

"This morning I realized I had no casual clothes, nothing appropriate for an outdoor barbecue. So I went to the mall and did some shopping. Terrific bargains on sportswear this time of the year."

"You ought to wear casual clothes more often. I'm used to seeing you as a professional. Let me tell you something, Madam Librarian. You are truly a gorgeous gal, one sexy woman."

She blushed deeply. "I'm glad you find me attractive."

"Oh, it goes beyond that." He held her close and whispered in her ear. "All I can think about right now is stripping you naked and having wild sex with you right here on the lawn."

"And scandalize your neighbors?"

"Place is like a morgue. It's needs a little excitement."

She shook her head at him. "You say the most outrageous things."

"Isn't that why you love me?"

"I'm not going to answer that. Where are the girls?"

"Everyone's out back. I'll introduce you to my two rowdy nephews." He took her arm and led her around to the yard.

"Hey, guys," he called out to his nephews, "we're about ready to eat. Hustle on out of there!"

His declaration was greeted by good-natured splashing in his direction. A fracas began over the towels, of which only one dry one remained. Mark, being smaller, lost the battle and was forced to run into the house for one. A few minutes later, he returned with an odd expression on his face.

"Uncle Mike," he said, large brown eyes opened wide, "there's this big black lady, must be seven feet tall, kind of messy looking, and she asked for you."

Everyone turned to look at him. "Oh, that's Bert St. Croix," he said, flipping a hamburger. "Mark, go bring Detective St. Croix around back before she sweats to death on our front lawn."

The first thing that Gardner noticed was Bert's face. It was battered, just the way Mark had observed. He made no comment, instead introducing Bert to his family. Everyone looked at her for a moment with a kind of awe; the woman definitely had presence.

"Please sit down," Evie said, moving toward Bert. "You must be hot. Have something cold to drink, 'cause everything's ready." She put a place setting in front of their guest.

Gardner smiled at his daughter, pleased by the courteous way she had behaved.

"I'm not hungry," Bert said dejectedly.

"What happened?"

Bert looked around at the gathered family and Kim.

"You can talk in front of them. I'll vouch for their integrity. They've all taken the oath of silence."

"If you say so. The fact is, I blew it, just like you thought I would."

"Would you like me to take a lie detector test to prove that I didn't think you'd blow it?"

"Come on, don't hand me that bull!" Bert was clearly in a foul mood.

"Did you pick up Sonny?"

"No!"

He was going to have to pull the information out of her, like a tooth extraction, but he had to know what happened.

"You might as well tell me. Get it over with."

He watched Bert clench her fist in a militant manner and saw that the knuckles were bruised and raw. "I got to the house around 11:30 a.m., figuring the kid would be straight by then. The mother—her name, incidentally, is Nora Blake—came to the door and refused to let me in. Well, to make a long story short, I got in anyway. She proceeded to yell hysterically. That must have been some kind of signal, because three big blond dudes materialized, and they all looked like Sonny except they were older and two of them were actually bigger. They came on pretty strong, but I wasn't going to back down. So then they eased up a little, claimed the kid was still asleep and I couldn't talk to him until after they'd held a family conference. The oldest acted as spokesman, claimed they were thinking of hiring a lawyer for the kid. It seems the mother told them about last night. Anyway, they're convinced the police want to stick Sonny for the Bradshaw murder. I told them we only wanted to question him, but they told me in no uncertain terms I couldn't see him until later. I wasn't having it. Then the mother started to cry and they told me to clear out. It got a little physical."

"You should have called me."

Bert shook her head.

"At the very least, you could have called for backup."

"It happened too fast."

"You want to haul them in for assault?"

"No point. I gave as good as I got. They weren't being malicious, just trying to protect family."

"Suppose I go back with you after we've eaten? They'll have talked to Sonny. Whether they've decided on a lawyer or not, we still get to question him."

"Sounds good. I think the kid's got the answers we're looking for."

"I agree," Gardner said, passing Bert a plate with a steak and a burger on it. "Sonny's got a child's mind in a man's body. We'll have to probe that mind, and it won't be easy. Children are known to be perverse, even the dull ones." Gardner passed Kim the bowl of potato salad.

"The kid appears to be our key to solving the murder. He's the one real link to our perp, who I hope won't realize that until after we've had a chance to extract some info."

Bert grabbed some buns for the meat. "You're thinking April Nevins, aren't you?"

"I don't know. As far as I'm concerned, the field's still wide open."

Evie heaped some of everything on Bert's plate.

"You could let our guest take what she wants," Gardner told his daughter with some amusement.

"We can't let a guest in our house starve. Stop talking so much, Dad, and eat or you won't have strength to track down criminals."

Mike never argued with Evie when she acted that way; she reminded him too much of her mother. Apparently Bert was not about to argue, either; she dutifully ate most of the food on her plate and then downed a cold beer.

"Wonderful meal," Bert said, "especially the salads."

"I fixed the salads," Evie said, beaming. "You have to take

home some fresh vegetables from the garden. We grow them organically."

"The girls are great at that," Gardner said with a warm smile in his daughters' direction.

"Dad helps us with it," Evie said, lowering her eyes.

"Working the earth gives me a feeling of satisfaction. Let me get you some coffee and dessert. Kim brought us a terrific chocolate cake."

"Don't say that until you've tasted it," Kim said.

Jean and the boys were loud in their appreciation and praise. Kim smiled at them. He liked watching her face light up that way.

"Chocolate's always a winner with these kids. Good choice." Gardner squeezed Kim's hand.

"I've got to be going." Bert was already on her feet.

"Oh, no! Dessert's the best part of the meal." Before anyone could stop her, Evie was hurrying back into the house.

"I'll give her a hand," Kim said, following Evie.

"You've got a fine daughter there," Bert said, sitting down again.

"And a determined one," Gardner said with a smile. "Just sit back and enjoy it. Evie won't be happy until she sees you forced to loosen your belt a notch." He noticed although Bert was tall, she was trim, nearly gaunt.

Coffee, fresh fruit, cake and chocolate chip ice cream materialized as did an ice pack for Bert's bruises.

"Thanks, Evie. You're a terrific hostess," Gardner told his older daughter. She smiled, pleased with the compliment.

The phone rang and Evie went back into the house to answer it. Kim cut the cake and gave everyone plates. When Evie reappeared, she was frowning. He could tell from her expression that the call came from headquarters.

"They say it's important," she said in a subdued voice.

He and Bert went into the house immediately. He sent

Bert to the kitchen phone while he ran upstairs and listened on the bedroom extension.

"We're here. What is it?"

"This is Nash. We don't have all the facts yet, but I thought you'd want to know. About twenty minutes ago, Louise Scofield was admitted to County Regional through the emergency entrance. We got a call from a neighbor lady who heard a loud quarrel going on in the Scofield apartment. You know how thin the walls are in those new flats. By the time the patrol car arrived, there was already an ambulance."

"Know what went down?"

"From the report, I'd say Mrs. Scofield was beaten up."

"What happened?" Bert demanded.

"Her husband claims she accidentally fell down a flight of stairs."

"What does she say?"

"Nothing, she was unconscious when they brought her in."

Bert muttered some curses under her breath.

"Are you holding Scofield?" Gardner asked.

"Nope. Granted it looks suspicious, but we have to wait until the wife comes around to hear her story."

"Scofield at the hospital?"

"He was when the patrol car left."

"We'll be at the hospital as soon as possible." Gardner hung up the receiver and rejoined Bert in the kitchen.

Her eyes narrowed to an angry squint. "You bring in Sonny. I'll take care of Scofield."

"We can handle both of them together."

"And waste valuable time?" Her full lower lip set.

"You're not fooling me, you know."

"I don't know what you mean."

"Wasn't one fight enough for today? I know you want to go after Scofield so you can beat him up."

"Someone ought to beat the crap out of that bastard!"

"That won't accomplish anything."

"Won't it?" The initial explosion was over, but she was far from controlled. "I've handled cases like this before. Husbands, boyfriends, stalkers. The women get restraining orders, but it never stops these creeps. Scofield will understand to leave his wife alone only if someone throws the wrath of God into him."

"So you're just going down there to knock the guy around before you find out what actually happened?" They faced each other like gunfighters at high noon.

"All right, I see your point. I'll talk to the asshole first."

"Aren't you kidding yourself? Can you manage that kind of restraint?"

"I can handle it," Bert asserted. "I'm not a rookie. If we're going to work together, you've got to start trusting me."

She did have a way of making things personal. Gardner knew he ought to refuse outright, but he just couldn't bring himself to do it. Things hadn't gone right with Sonny, and her ego didn't need another putdown. Still, what if his vote of confidence turned out to be at Scofield's expense? Besides, violent manhandling of suspects would not be tolerated by the department. But in the end, he decided she was right: he had to trust her. There was no way they would be able to continue to work together otherwise.

"Bring Scofield in," he yielded. "Just remember, we don't know what really happened between his wife and him. If you touch him without provocation, you could lose your job. Maybe that's what you want, but I hope not. I'm putting my faith in you, just like you asked."

Bert viewed him with a fixed, sullen stare. "Anything else?"

Gardner shook his head. "See you back at headquarters later."

As she left, Gardner wondered if he would have been as sensitive to his partner's feelings if Bert weren't black and a woman. Probably not, he conceded. Kim came into the kitchen and looked at him questioningly.

"I have to go out for a while."

"So I gathered. I'll give the girls a hand cleaning up."

"Could you stay? I hate to ask it, but my nephews need supervision. And Evie's going out this afternoon."

"No problem. I don't have any special plans."

"I really appreciate it." He hugged her and kissed her lips, trying hard to keep it casual.

"Really, Dad, they don't let you alone even on your day off." Evie stood there, hands on hips, giving him a Medusa-like stare as he adjusted his shoulder holster.

He walked to the front hall closet and grabbed a tie and jacket. They weren't exactly a match, but who cared anyway?

"Dad, don't worry if you can't get home in time to meet my date tonight."

"Oh, I'll be home all right."

Evie gave him a dubious look.

"I mean it."

"Yeah, whatever."

"I'll be back as early as I can. I won't forget."

Evie's mouth puckered as if she'd been sucking on a sour lemon. Then she walked away.

"It'll be okay with her," Kim said. She squeezed his hand reassuringly.

"You're just saying that to make me feel less guilty about leaving."

Kim shook her head. "No. Honor bright. You're a good dad. Evie will figure that out. She's a smart girl." Kim hugged Gardner.

He gave Kim one last regretful look and took off. He drove his own car to Sonny Blake's house, listening to police calls on the way. He called himself all kinds of a fool for letting Bert go after Scofield alone; it was just asking for trouble. She should be coming back to Sonny's house with him. The business with Scofield could have been allowed to cool for a while. He should have handled it better.

Sonny's house looked even more dilapidated in the daytime. The sight depressed him as he rang the doorbell. As before, Sonny's mother came to the door, but this time, she opened it no farther than a crack.

"Oh, you again." Annoyance at his presence was undisguised by her manner of speech.

"May I come in?"

"Did that big black woman come back with you?" She looked at him through the faintly down-turned corners of her washed-out blue eyes.

"At the moment, Detective St. Croix is on another assignment."

"All right, I guess you can come in." She grudgingly opened the front door. "She was real pushy. My son decided to call your office and complain about her."

"Because she's African-American?"

"No, she was rude, too. She talks nasty, real tough."

"Don't expect a police detective to act sweet as strawberry jam while investigating a homicide."

She began wringing her hands as she had done on the previous evening. "There's no excuse for bad manners."

"Please tell Sonny I've come to talk with him."

"He ain't here no more."

Gardner felt as if he'd been dealt a severe body blow. "I thought we agreed last night that you would keep him here until we had a chance to talk."

"He's grown now—nearly grown, anyhow. I can't keep him where he don't want to be."

"You realize his lack of cooperation makes him look guilty."

"Guilty of what? Not murder!" Her pale eyes widened.

"Complicity, at any rate." He managed to keep his voice cool and steady.

"Sonny would never do anything wrong, except things that wicked whore might have forced on him."

"And what would that be?"

"Well, how should I know!"

"You had a family conference. Did you decide whether or not Sonny should have a lawyer?"

"He didn't want one. Told us all to keep out of it, said he was going to tell everything he knew. But first he had to find something, something that would prove he wasn't guilty of murder." She paused to rub her sweating palms against the flowered housedress she wore.

"Go on. What else did he say?"

"I already told you every word."

"Not quite. Where did he say he was going?"

"He don't tell me everything. Just said he was going out."

Gardner knew enough to ask first, because without a warrant he was violating the law, but Bert's attitudes seemed to be rubbing off on him. Gardner quickly walked upstairs and glanced around. There were three small bedrooms and a bath. None of the rooms were occupied. Old wallpaper was peeling in a room that had Webster High banners and football clippings hanging. The bed was unmade, so he was reasonably certain that Sonny had slept there.

Mrs. Blake followed him. "What are you doing?"

"Just looking around." He glanced at the high school awards and letters for athletics. There were no clues as to where the boy might have gone. "You're certain he didn't say where he was going?"

"I already told you he didn't."

Gardner walked back downstairs and glanced through the rest of the house with Mrs. Blake following. "Your other sons didn't press him for an explanation?"

"He wouldn't give any."

"Did Sonny ever mention Richard Bradshaw to you?"

"Once maybe. I think he said that the harlot was dropping

him for a slick, city fella, a fancy dresser with lots of money to spend. I told him it was for the best, but Sonny, he got real huffy and never confided in me again."

Gardner was about to leave when the phone rang. Its loud reverberation pierced the air with menace.

"Excuse me," she said, and walked swiftly back toward the front parlor.

Gardner watched her reach for the telephone that rested on a small, white table near the foyer. He glanced around the room, taking it all in. The wallpaper in the living room was an old-fashioned rose pattern, and like that upstairs, it had begun to fade and peel. Apparently nothing had changed or improved in the domicile in many years. He could hear the woman's anxious voice with clarity.

"Where are you now? There's a policeman waiting to see you. Yes, same one as last night. Please come home." For a few brief moments, she listened intently. Gardner was already beside her. "I don't care about that. I'm worried." There was another pause as she listened. "Keep away from that whore. I'm frightened for you."

Gardner took the phone, which she surrendered reluctantly. "Sonny, this is Lieutenant Gardner. Why didn't you stay at home?"

"There's something I have to find." The boy sounded near panic.

"Let me help you. I'm terrific at finding things. It's my life's work. Where are you now? I'll pick you up and we'll look together."

There was a hesitation he didn't like at all. "I gotta go alone."

"No, you don't. Pick a place and I'll meet you." Gardner did his best not to sound impatient.

"Okay. April's apartment in a half hour."

"Are you there now?"

"I was before, but she wasn't there, and I couldn't figure how to get in."

"Is that where your 'something' is located? Did you leave it there?"

"No more questions. Not now."

"All right, but definitely later. Half an hour. I'll be there. Don't forget. I'll help you."

"I got something to do first. Then I'll go back there."

The line went dead.

"He says he's okay. Do you think he really is?" She was wringing her hands again.

"I don't know, but I intend to find out." Gardner walked to the front door.

Once he was outside and back in his car, he sat for a moment, thinking out what his course of action should be. No point waiting. He started his dependable Ford and drove directly to La Reine Gardens. Although it was only a fifteen-minute drive, the time passed very slowly. He wanted to drive by April Nevins' apartment at least once, just to see if anyone was around. No, the area looked deserted. He parked in the vicinity, a block up the street, where he had a good view of the apartment but was unlikely to be noticed.

Half an hour came and went. Still no sign of Sonny Blake. He began to grow irritated. Police work always meant lots of waiting around for things to happen, but he hated surveillance and always would. He walked up to the apartment, rang the doorbell; when no one answered, he tried looking through the front window. The apartment appeared to be dark and unoccupied. He wondered where April Nevins was. There was no sign of either her or the boy. He went back to the car and waited another twenty minutes. The fact that Sonny had not shown up was a bad sign.

Gardner came out of his reflections, realizing there was a call for him.

"Urgent you report to headquarters," the dispatcher said in a nasal voice.

"I'm on something important."

"Captain Nash wants you on the double."

Gardner decided on one more tour of the block before he would consider leaving the development. He drove slowly, keeping a look-out for the tall, towheaded youth, but the area was still deserted. When he circled for the second time, there was no sign of anyone in or near Nevins' apartment. He swung his car around into the main street of the development, then entered the steady stream of highway traffic past Burger King, driving faster than he ordinarily would. He was obeying the captain's order less than enthusiastically, convinced that leaving La Reine Gardens now was a serious error. Sometimes he had a clear intuition about things, and this was one of those times. He was certain something had gone very wrong, dead certain. He sensed evil hovering in the thick summer air.

TEN

WHEN BERT ST. CROIX arrived at County Regional, she immediately checked on Louise Scofield. At first, no one would tell her very much. All she could find out was that Mrs. Scofield was in stable condition. No, the doctor who treated her was not available; Bert would have to return another time. It was also too soon for visitors. She thought the blue-haired nurse was an old crone with a serious attitude problem but refrained from telling her so. Gardner would have been impressed by her self-control.

Assured that Mrs. Scofield really was all right, Bert turned her attention to Mr. Scofield. But she struck out there, as well, because Scofield had already gone home. All the way over to the Scofield apartment, Bert kept thinking about Louise. Gardner was right when he said the element of objectivity was lacking. Louise Scofield reminded her of Alva. It had nothing to do with looks, because Alva's appearance was nothing like this white woman. No, it was something that went deeper. There was a soulfulness, a sensitivity about Louise Scofield that reminded her of Alva. In her mind's eye, she could picture Alva even now; skin like coffee lightened by cream, brown eyes soft as velvet, a smile that lit the cold chamber of Bert's heart.

Alva. Giving, loving, gentle and kind but with an inner strength. Alva, dressed in her starched nurse's uniform. Then Bert remembered how she'd last seen Alva with the crimson stain of her blood coloring that fine white uniform. She felt the anger rise in her all over again. People like Alva needed to be protected. But she hadn't been able to protect her friend. If the justice system could just be changed. Everyone worrying about the perp; no one giving a damn about the vic. Christ, it was so damn frustrating!

Of course, Louise Scofield wasn't Alva; she didn't have Alva's strength of character, but there was a gentleness about her. She didn't deserve a husband who terrorized or beat her. Someone had to protect her. It was time to handle things her way, time to make Scofield understand how he should be treating his wife. Women had to care about each other, had to watch out for their sisters.

Bert knocked several times before Scofield answered the door. He stood before her hollow-eyed, a glass of Southern Comfort in one hand.

"Come to arrest me?" Scofield had a stupid grin on his face and his breath reeked like a distillery.

"I'd like you to come down to headquarters and answer a few questions about what happened today." She kept her tone as unemotional as possible, but it wasn't easy.

"I'm not going anywhere with you."

She pushed him off-balance then pinned Scofield's arm behind his back. "You're coming with me."

Scofield dropped his drink on the rug. "The hell I am! Woman or not, I'll kick you out if you don't go away and leave me alone!"

The words were slurred and Bert understood that she was dealing with a drunk, but still, it was very hard not to lose it.

"You're coming with me," she repeated.

Scofield tried to shove her toward the door. She was prepared, moving out of his reach. Frustrated, Scofield charged at her. She brought up her fist and punched Scofield right in his face. The blow landed with a hard sound. Bert realized that her knuckles had been further bruised, but somehow it seemed worth it. She thought that would be the end of it, but Scofield wasn't satisfied. When he realized his nose was bleeding, enraged, he half-charged, half-staggered toward her. Bert felt forced to land another punishing blow, karate style to the rib cage. There was a nasty thud as Scofield landed on his knees gasping for breath.

"That's it," Bert said, regaining her composure. "It's over, man. We'll talk at headquarters."

As she cuffed Scofield and led him to the car, she thought this had been something of a victory. She hadn't really hurt Scofield the way she could have. Guys like him disgusted her. What right did the bastard have to mistreat his woman? She wanted to protect them all, every one of them, all the good, beautiful, sensitive, caring people. She viewed the drunk in front of her with contempt, and grimly asked herself again: how was she going to live the rest of her life without a friend like Alva?

AT HEADQUARTERS, Gardner knocked once and walked directly into Nash's office. He wasn't planning to waste any time. Finding Sonny was too important. The Captain was pacing the tiny room like a caged lion that hadn't been fed recently. The way Nash looked at him, Gardner had the feeling that he was the delivery of raw meat. Sitting in front of the worn, wooden desk was Bert, eyes fixed uneasily on the floor.

"Something wrong, Captain?" he asked warily.

"You could say that." His eyes flashed electricity. "Your partner. I want restraints on her. Did you tell her to pick up Scofield by herself?"

"I did." He would have to be the calm eye in the center of a hurricane.

"Damn it, how could you be so stupid? You were supposed to be with her, work as a team until further notice. This Amazon thinks she's still in the ghettoes of New York dealing with homeless derelicts." Nash glowered at Bert, looking as fierce and intimidating as a bull charging at a matador's red cape.

Gardner braced himself. "What went wrong?"

"Want the whole list? I damn well would like you to hear it." Nash continued to pace the room. "First, I took a call from one Eric Blake, who was furious because he claimed St. Croix harassed his mother. Said the poor woman was near mental collapse because St. Croix was hounding her. Said St. Croix pushed her way into their family home and when asked to leave, got into a physical altercation with him and his brothers. You, of course, weren't with her then either, were you?"

"Those guys assaulted me, not the other way around. I came to pick up Sonny Blake for questioning. We have reason to believe he was an accomplice in the Bradshaw homicide. His brothers were obstructing justice. Believe me, I got the worst of it, outnumbered the way I was, and I did not draw my weapon. If anything, I used restraint."

Gardner was pleased at the way Bert stood up for herself. The Captain seemed to calm down a little.

"Okay, that's all right. That means the department is protected there. By the way, I did stick up for you when I spoke to Blake. I always do that for my people, but what I say privately is something else. That was why I called you in, Mike, before I even knew about Scofield. Now let's talk about that incident."

"What about it?" Bert said, her forehead wrinkling as she took a defensive stance.

Nash smashed his fist down on the desk. "Jesus Christ, just take a look at the guy!"

"He swung on me first. Ask him yourself."

"Doesn't make a damn bit of difference. He was intoxicated, stinking drunk. You used undue force. The guy looks like he was flattened by a steamroller. I expect my detectives to use their brains before their fists."

"I didn't beat on him for kicks. You weren't there, Captain, so how can you judge?"

"My football coach used to say that assholes and excuses have one thing in common: they both stink."

Gardner could see that Bert was close to losing her temper. "In case you forgot, neither Bert nor I is technically on duty today. We're giving up our free time voluntarily to solve this homicide as quickly as possible. If Detective St. Croix is guilty of anything, it's being conscientious."

Nothing pleased the captain more than cops working extra hours, but Gardner wasn't through applying balm yet.

"I trust Bert. If she says it took force to subdue Scofield and get him down here for questioning, I believe it. Scofield has a violent temper. I can testify to that."

"All right, I accept what you say. But I better not get any more reasons to suspect you of abusing and manhandling suspects. Got that?"

Bert stared back moodily but didn't respond, and Nash appeared placated. Gardner took that as a cue to move toward the door.

"Wait a minute! Where are you going?"

"I've got to look for Sonny Blake."

"That can wait. I want you to question Scofield first. He's waiting for you."

"Bert can do that."

"No, she can't. Not by herself anyway. I thought it was settled. You and St. Croix work together."

"Then send someone over to wait by April Nevins' apartment. Sonny was supposed to show up there. He's got important information."

"All right, I'll see to it. Satisfied?"

"I suppose I'll have to be. One thing. I want a good man."

"All our people are good. Drew Mitchell is here. I'll send him."

"All right, but if Blake isn't around, I want Mitch to sit in his car and wait."

Very rapidly, Gardner followed Nash out to find Drew

Mitchell. From the precise description he furnished, even an untrained observer would have little difficulty identifying Sonny.

"Got it." Mitch practically yawned in his face. So why did he still feel so uneasy?

Bert joined him in the small interrogation room where Scofield sat impatiently, smoking a cigarette. The suspect seemed relieved to see him with Bert. He stood up as they entered, but Gardner motioned him to sit down again. Gardner surveyed Scofield and observed that the man did look battered. His lower lip was puffy, almost ink-blue in color, and there was dried blood around his nose.

"Grind it out," Bert said. "No smoking allowed here. You know that. Poison yourself if you like when you're alone, but the rest of us don't want to breathe that crap."

Scofield did as he was told. The fight seemed to be totally out of him. He took a few gulps from a foam cup of the rotgut squad-room coffee someone had provided for him. His hand trembled slightly.

"Did you resist Detective St. Croix when she tried to bring you in for questioning?"

"I guess I tried to hit her. It's all kind of a blur. When I got home from the hospital, I was in a bad way, really upset. I had a few drinks. Then she showed up." Scofield pointed an arched, accusing finger in Bert's direction. "Acted haughty and hard-nosed, insinuating I deliberately tried to hurt Lou. Provoked me."

"Don't ask the Lieutenant to waste any sympathy on you, not when your wife's lying unconscious in the hospital and you put her there." Bert glared at Scofield with such violent intensity that Scofield drew back involuntarily.

"I never meant to hit her. It was an accident. I've smashed my fist into the wall dozens of times when I was angry just so I wouldn't touch her. You have to believe me. I'd never hurt her on purpose. I don't hit women."

"Is that so?" Bert gave him a meaningful look.

Coffee sloshed onto the hardwood table.

"What about that adultery business? You were going to murder your wife and anyone you caught her with? Wasn't that what you told us?" Bert accused.

"All right, I felt she deserved to be punished."

Bert stood over him. "So you tried to kill her?"

"No, only to frighten her. She deserved that."

"Easy," Gardner said.

"Keep her out of my face, Lieutenant."

"You didn't even care enough to hang around the hospital to find out if she was all right?"

"Why did you go home?" Gardner asked evenly.

"They told me she had a concussion, but I couldn't see her until the morning. They wouldn't allow me in. The doctor kept urging me to leave. They were looking at me funny. If the doctor said that her condition was serious, I would have stayed regardless. But there wasn't much point in me just hanging around cluttering up the place. I couldn't do her any good, so I left."

"You said you meant to punish your wife, Mr. Scofield. Did you intend to punish Bradshaw, as well?" Gardner studied the man carefully.

"He's dead. I can't do anything to him."

Gardner leaned toward Scofield and spoke quietly. "Did you kill Bradshaw? You can tell us, Bill. We want to know all about it. We can make it easier for you." Gardner's voice was friendly, personal.

"He deserved to die, but I didn't do it. I swear it."

"All right. That will be it for now. We'll have someone drive you home. But we'll want to see you again tomorrow, after we've had an opportunity to talk to your wife. You'll be at the hospital in the morning?"

"Of course, I will."

Gardner carefully kept himself between Bert and Scofield

until they were outside the interrogation room and Scofield was claimed by a patrolman.

"I'm going to phone the hospital and check on Mrs. Scofield's condition," Gardner said.

He waited patiently and finally got through to the resident on duty. When he replaced the receiver in its cradle and turned to Bert, she looked at him with keen anticipation. "Mrs. Scofield's going to be okay. She's got a mild concussion and a broken arm. She regained consciousness a little while ago. The fall left her bruised and shaken, but there's nothing really serious. I left instructions that Scofield not be allowed near his wife unless we're there with him. We'll have her story first. I don't want him getting a chance at her."

Bert nodded approval, looking satisfied. There was one piece of information that Gardner decided not to share with Bert: Louise Scofield had lost her baby.

Gardner turned to Bert. "Let's get going. I want to head over to Nevins' apartment."

Outside of headquarters, the sky had become dark. Storm clouds swelled above them. He admired the flowers that had been planted in the center of the square. The buildings of the municipal complex flanked the square as if to offer protection to its frail beauty. There really wasn't much natural beauty in Webster Township, but at least they didn't have the remaining factories and refineries spewing pollution like North Jersey did. Of course, illegal dumpers had managed to do quite a job on some of the wooded areas, turning them into chemical cesspools. It would take years more of cleaning to redevelop some of the toxic dump sites.

A few minutes after they got on the highway, rain began to beat down on the roof of the car with a steady drumbeat. April Nevins' apartment still showed no signs of occupancy. Gardner rang the bell, knocked on the front door with no response, only silence. Drew Mitchell was staked out half a block from the apartment. It was raining too heavily to talk outside. Gardner and Bert slipped into the unmarked vehicle, Gardner in front with Mitchell, Bert in the rear.

"Anything?" Gardner asked.

Drew shook his head. He was a big, burly cop who looked uncomfortable jammed behind the wheel of the compact vehicle. "No one's come or gone from the apartment since I've been around." He spoke in a monotone as if the assignment were one he found particularly boring.

"You're certain?"

"Absolutely. I've been parked here by these woods for half an hour easy."

Gardner studied the wooded acreage that paralleled the apartments. "See anyone answering the boy's description in or near the woods?"

"Nobody. I've been watching. Believe me, he didn't show, and in this rain, I don't think he will."

Gardner felt let down. He knew the other detective well enough to be satisfied with his competency. Still, he had misgivings. There was definitely something wrong. Somehow he'd missed Sonny; maybe the boy had come when he went back to headquarters. But why hadn't he waited? Gardner's sense of foreboding chilled him more thoroughly than his rain-soaked jacket.

"I want you to stay here anyway, just in case he turns up later. I'll see that you're relieved soon."

"What now?" Bert asked as they walked back to their own car.

"Stake-out Sonny's home, as well. Put a bulletin out on him. We want the boy picked up as soon as possible."

Gardner started the car and the engine hesitated slightly, as if to complain. *I don't like being out in this miserable weather any better than you do,* Gardner thought, as if to send a telepathic message. The steady, hypnotic sound of the windshield wipers pushing back the rain was like a heartbeat struggling for survival. It caused him again to ponder what might have happened to Sonny Blake.

"I'm beginning to think we're giving Sonny too much credit. Truth is, there's just as good a chance that Scofield murdered Bradshaw in a jealous rage."

Gardner wasn't convinced and told Bert so.

"It could be Sonny found Bradshaw's body and somehow got the dumb notion into his head that his girlfriend killed the guy. Scofield is something else altogether. For instance, why didn't he complain to Nash about me hitting him? He could have made a big fuss."

"You're going to say he didn't because he knew that he deserved it. You think he was feeling guilty."

"Sure, what else?" Bert gave him a hard look.

"Probably right, but his guilt was caused by his wife's condition, not Bradshaw's death."

"And doesn't one relate to the other?"

"Without proof, I'm not convinced. Granted, Scofield is a viable suspect, but we'll have to interrogate him a lot more to get beyond mere speculation. Also, it's pretty humiliating for most men to get into a physical altercation with a female, let alone get beaten. I think he was too embarrassed to complain."

"Serves him right," she said with grim satisfaction.

Gardner concentrated on the road as the downpour intensified; it was coming down as a perfect sheet of water and, even with the windshield wipers and defroster going full blast, visibility was poor. He felt as if they were in a tropical rain forest.

"Mike."

Gardner shot a glance at Bert; it was the first time he could remember her calling him by his first name.

"I guess I owe you for getting me off the hook with Nash. I appreciate the way you stood up for me."

"Skip it. You don't have to eat eggshells around me. Like

Nash said, we're a team. I accept half the responsibility in everything that goes down." He looked over at Bert again and noticed a momentary smile flicker.

"Hope I didn't cost you Sonny. You think he showed before Mitchell got there?"

"Maybe, or he might not have come after all." Gardner didn't think that was the case, but there wasn't any point in making Bert feel rotten. Besides, anything could have happened to Sonny. Somewhere, a murderer was freely roaming. There was no telling who could be the next victim. Disheartened, Gardner decided the opportunity for an easy solution to the Bradshaw case had vanished along with the golden-haired lifeguard.

GARDNER ARRIVED BACK at his home at seven in the evening. Kim was waiting for him.

"Evie's date is coming at eight, or so she informed me. You have time for something to eat. Would you like coffee and a sandwich?"

"Just coffee," he said, "if you'll join me."

The caffeine restored his drained energy. Kim placed a bowl of tapioca pudding in front of him; never having cared for the stuff, he pushed it away. He could tell she was surveying him.

"You ought to change your clothes. You look soaked."

"I am," he replied with a wry smile.

"Where are the boys?"

Kim sat down at the kitchen table with him. "Your brother came by and picked them up about an hour ago. He's very nice. Looks a lot like you."

"I hope the babysitting wasn't too much of a chore for you," he said. He felt the need to apologize.

"I didn't mind. I like children."

"That's good to know." Their eyes met, but then she looked quickly away.

"The rain really cooled things down," she said, pouring him another cup of coffee. "How about some chocolate cake? I spent all last night baking it."

He laughed, enjoying her attempt at levity. "Sure you did."

"Okay, Mr. Policeman, you force me to confess. I bought it at the bakery. What gave me away?"

"Cop's intuition. That and the bakery box with the pink string tied around, which didn't hurt, either."

"Evie says that you work too hard and the department doesn't deserve you."

He didn't bother to respond, just drank his coffee slowly. This was old ground, and he didn't much care to tread over it again. Evie had picked up that idea from her mother. In his mind, he replayed the last time Evelyn had harangued him about his work. She'd wanted him to quit the force.

"The people who live in this town are so apathetic. Nobody appreciates a good, honest policeman. You get so little for your trouble—not recognition, not appreciation, not wealth or power. If you were in industry or business, at least they'd pay you properly for your sacrifices and all the extra time you put in. Look at your old friend Tony. How many years did he give to the force? Twenty-five? Thirty? What did he have to show for it? And who besides you cared when he left?"

"True about life in general," he'd told her. "No one's missed for very long. Nobody's indispensable. We can all be replaced. It's a sad fact of life, but then again, maybe that's just the way it should be. Makes mortality a little less painful."

"But what's the point of it?"

"The point is that I like what I do. As far as money, let's face it, we're conditioned to a certain life style. We've never had much money so we know how to manage without it. But if there's ever anything you want that you don't have, go out and buy it with my blessings. Whatever I've got is equally

yours. Besides, there's no reason we have to ever think poor or feel small. That's all a matter of mind. There's plenty of wealthy people who feel poor. As long as we've got enough and no one in this house ever goes hungry, I'm satisfied."

"My husband the philosopher. I've been thinking I might like to get a job, go back to work. Everyone works these days. I'm a dinosaur. I'm the only woman I know who still stays at home. It's not like I have small children anymore."

He'd leaned over and kissed her forehead. "If that's what you really want, but don't do it for the money. We don't need the money. That's not so important. Just do it if you think it'll make you happy and less restless."

He'd meant that and hoped she understood how he felt. Evelyn had been awfully moody, and he thought it had something to do with the fact that she was bored at home. She donated time to the P.T.A. and the local hospital, but that wasn't enough. With the children getting older and becoming independent, she probably needed something more challenging. He just didn't want her taking on more than she could handle. Too many women thought that if they didn't work outside the home, they weren't worth anything. He thought that was wrong, but he also knew that his beliefs went against popular opinion. Still, she needed to feel good about herself; if a job would do that, then he supported it. Too bad things hadn't worked out better. Over and done with. He wouldn't dwell on it.

He let out a deep sigh and turned back to Kim. His relationship with Evelyn was in the past. Hopefully, Kim would be his future. "Where are the girls?"

"Evie's getting ready for her date. Jean's upstairs with her."

"I'll see if we can't talk before she goes out."

"It's obvious she loves and respects you." Kim's dark brown eyes were warm as toast.

"Not true. Evie blames me for her mother leaving us."

"I don't believe that."

He knew Kim was being kind. "Believe me, it's true." He took Kim's hand and held it.

"They love you, but they tend to take you for granted because you're always there for them. You do what needs to be done. I see that and I admire it."

"I think you're pretty special, too." He gave her hand a gentle squeeze.

Her cheeks flushed with pleasure, and she pressed her mouth against his in a brief but giving kiss. He smiled, mussing her hair.

"You think Evie's mad that I had to go in to work today?"

"She said all you ever think about is police work. But I really don't think she meant it."

Contrary to Evie's opinion, he observed an ironclad rule: off-duty he did not worry about work. It was just he sometimes considered himself on-duty when he might well be off. But he refused to take himself too seriously. That was his technique for keeping things in perspective. Maintaining a proper degree of objectivity was crucial. Stepping outside himself and being the impartial observer of life, the spectator sitting on the sidelines, he was able to analyze events, to develop insights. He refused to brood over the Bradshaw case. This evening he had family responsibilities, and that was what mattered most. He felt he had his priorities straight.

He went upstairs and changed into comfortable, casual clothing, then knocked at his daughter's bedroom door.

"Who is it?" His older daughter's voice reminded him of a flute.

"Your father, last I heard. Can I come in?"

"Sure, Dad."

He opened the door and looked at her. Even without any make-up, Evie was very pretty. She was innocent-looking and would always appear younger than her years, possibly due to the small pug nose with freckles scattered over it. Her eyes, like his, were gray. They sparkled with smoky warmth. Jean sat cross-legged on the bed while Evie studied herself in the mirror over her dresser.

"How was your shopping expedition?"

"Very successful. I found just the right pair of jeans."

"Jean says you already have twenty pairs."

Evie shook her head. "She tends to exaggerate. Don't you?" She nailed her sister with an accusing look.

Jean lowered her head. "Think I'll go watch T.V. for a while." She left quickly, aware Evie was annoyed with her.

Gardner sat down on the chair by her desk and watched as Evie combed out her medium-length, shiny hair. Her face glowed with youthful enthusiasm and vitality. He could still remember when he felt like his daughter, full of the sense of possibility.

"So how old is this boy?"

"He's going into his senior year."

"I suppose that means he'll be driving?"

Evie nodded her head and gave him an anxious look. "He's a really safe driver."

"And you would know that because?"

Evie bit down on her lower lip. "Everyone at camp says so. He's the most responsible counselor."

"The kid's what, seventeen? How long has he had his license?"

"Don't give me the third degree, Dad."

"Does he know you're only fourteen? Does he know you're going into your freshman year of high school?"

Evie stood up, trembling. "Dad, please don't ruin this for me. Go back to work again. That's where you want to be anyway, isn't it?" Evie started to cry, and Gardner took her into his arms and held her.

"I'm sorry, honey. I just want to keep you safe. You're my little girl and I worry about you."

Evie shook her head. "I'm growing up. Please don't smother me."

He nodded. "All right. By the way, you were terrific today. Very mature. A big help with our company."

"Thanks for noticing," she said, mollified. "Mom never thought I was very mature."

Gardner frowned. "Your mother did have a way of telling people what she thought. Her opinions were often negative. Doesn't mean what she said was true. She won't ever be asked to give a course in public relations. If she could have seen you today, she'd talk differently."

Evie lowered her eyes. "If you say so."

"Tell me one thing. Do you like the boy as much as the idea of going out on a date, or is it difficult to distinguish between the two at this point?"

"Daddy!" She gave him a hurt look that made him regret his comment. "Gary really is nice."

At that moment, Kim called him downstairs. From the tone of her voice, he knew Evie's date had arrived.

"Honey, I'll chat with him for a few minutes while you finish getting ready."

"Okay, but no more third-degree tactics," she warned.

He gave her a quick hug and left the room. Downstairs in the living room, a nervous young man sat on the sofa.

"So you're Evie's date," Gardner said.

"Yes, sir, and you're her father?" The question was rhetorical.

Gardner's mind moved ahead, framing a few questions. He seated himself opposite the teenager.

"I've heard a lot about you from Evie. She says you're a great police detective."

"My daughter tends to be prejudiced."

Kim smiled and gave him a meaningful look as she left the room.

The youth looked far from relaxed. Gardner took a

moment to look him over. Evie's young man was a sloppy dresser. Jean was right. His jeans were faded and ripped over one knee, shirt open carelessly at the neck. At least the kid wasn't wearing an earring; that always put him off. No tattoos or visible piercings. Gardner went through a mental checklist. The shaggy head would have benefited from a haircut and the youth did wear dark glasses. That bothered him.

"I don't think I caught your name."

"It's Gary Sargent. I like your daughter very much." Gary Sargent's face turned red.

"Nothing wrong with that," Gardner assured him. "We're pretty fond of her, too."

The boy smiled for the first time.

"Where are you planning to go tonight?"

"I was thinking about taking Evie to a movie. Do you think she'd like that?"

"I'm certain of it. You will try to bring her home early?"

"Sure," he mumbled.

Gardner carefully studied the sunglasses the young man wore.

"Are those prescription lenses?"

"These? Yeah, they are."

"May I see them?"

Gary removed the glasses and handed them to Gardner. The gold rims were expensive and stylish.

"I'm kind of myopic—nearsighted, that is."

"So I see," Gardner responded, looking through the tinted glass. He observed the boy's eyes. The pupils were not dilated and the irises were a clear, bright blue. He was convinced that Gary Sargent was not on drugs. He returned the eyeglasses. "Attractive frames, but isn't tinted glass a little tiring on the eyes in the evening?"

"Sure, but my regular glasses are so wimpy-looking. I'd feel like a dork wearing them."

"You might consider contact lenses. Evie wears them."

"She does?"

"When they begin to bother her eyes, she wears her glasses. She's slightly nearsighted herself. If you were to wear your regular glasses, I'm certain she'd think nothing of it." Gardner hoped he wasn't delivering his message in too heavy-handed a manner, but Gary didn't seem offended.

His daughter made her entrance looking very attractive, and her escort was quick to tell her so. Gardner called Kim back into the living room and they exchanged good-byes. After the young couple had gone, Kim turned to him.

"So what do you think?"

Gardner shrugged. "He's okay I guess."

"Does that mean you approve of him?"

"I'll tell you all about it. But first, where's Jean?"

"She's watching television upstairs. I think Evie said something to her about staying out of the way."

"Let's give her something else to do."

"Like what?"

"A walk in the mall maybe. It's a perfect evening to go out for some ice cream."

"It's probably going to rain again," she hedged.

"Doubt it."

"The truth is, I'm trying to lose weight. Ice cream will only tempt me."

"Frozen yogurt then. And we'll start a diet together tomorrow."

"You don't need one."

"Neither do you. You look terrific. Come on, Kim, it's Saturday night. Let me take you out for a little while. A walk on the wild side. I feel like having a sundae."

He ran his hand down her arm, saw the goose bumps form there. She turned her face up to his.

He knew she was expecting him to kiss her. He decided not to disappoint her. Their lips touched, brushed, and then the kiss deepened. When they came apart, she was just as breathless as he was.

"Stay over tonight. Don't go home. We need to be together."

"I'm not sure," she said.

He saw the doubt in her eyes. "I'm not giving up on you, on us. We belong together. I know given your past, it's hard for you to trust men, and particularly cops. But I'll always be there for you. I've made some mistakes in my life. I don't intend to repeat them."

He kissed her again, this time hot and hungry.

ELEVEN

ON SUNDAY MORNING, Mike Gardner woke up a little before eight o'clock, glanced at the clock radio, and then closed his eyes again, rolling over on his side. Patterns of color and light danced beneath his eyelids as he reached over and felt for Kim. His hand lightly brushed her thigh. She moaned and moved slightly toward him. The touch of the soft curves of her body made him want her again. They'd made love last night, but he wanted her still. His groin pushed up against her buttocks, pressing into her.

"Are you asleep?" he asked.

"No, I'm awake now. I'll go put the coffee on and start breakfast." She mumbled her words in a tired manner.

"You're a guest here."

"I'd like to fix breakfast for you."

"I'm not hungry—for food." He nibbled her earlobe then kissed the curve of her neck.

She pulled away from him. "You're really attracted to me?"

"More so than ever. You're a beautiful woman."

"Funny, my mirror doesn't tell me that."

"Let me be your mirror."

They didn't do much talking after that, instead making love in a passionate manner that reflected their affection and shared intimacy. Hands, lips and skin touched. His hands moved downward over her hips, over the roundness of her derriere. She explored his body, as well. His mouth went dry with lust as her tongue trailed down his chest and stomach.

And then her clever hands took over. She came astride him and took hold of his erection. She spread her hands on his chest and closed her eyes, lowering her body on to his with erotic slowness. She was moist and open and exciting. She clenched her inner muscles around him. The pleasure was almost too much to endure. He realized that this was the first time she'd taken the initiative in their lovemaking.

"Ride me hard," he demanded.

She opened herself to him completely, trusting him. Her body met each thrust as he joined with her, completing her, filling her. When he came at last, she was right there with him. He felt the explosions that rocked her body. They shattered together.

"God, how I love you," he gasped, as she collapsed against his nude body.

She caressed his cheek and kissed his brow. "I love you, too," she said.

"Do you?" He wasn't certain he'd heard her correctly. It had been a while since she'd told him that.

"I must be totally crazy, but I do." She playfully traced the dimple in his cheek with her forefinger.

AFTER KIM HAD SHOWERED, dressed and had gone downstairs, Gardner took his turn in the bathroom. As he dressed, he could smell the fragrant scent of fresh coffee brewing in the kitchen. He heard someone knocking lightly on the bedroom door.

"Dad." It was Jean. "Kim sent me up to tell you that breakfast is almost ready. She seems really happy. She's singing."

Gardner smiled to himself. This was turning out to be a special morning. When he got down to the kitchen, he found Jean helping Kim with the preparation of what looked like a terrific meal. There were scrambled eggs, cantaloupe, toast, blueberry waffles made with fresh berries, and hot oatmeal.

After that breakfast, he was ready to face whatever the day might bring.

"You're a wonderful cook," he commented as he rose from the table. "I didn't know that."

"Actually, I don't cook much. It doesn't pay for just one person. But Jean was a big help. You could say I felt inspired this morning."

They exchanged a meaningful smile and he squeezed her hand.

"I wish you would stay with us all the time," Jean said to Kim. "It would be so cool."

Kim turned to him, hands on hips. "Mike, did you tell her to say that?"

"Me? No way. I guess great minds think alike." He kissed his daughter's forehead. "Right, Jeanie?"

"Sure, Dad."

Kim followed him upstairs and watched as he got into his gray suit. "I thought I'd head home this morning."

"Can you come with me? I have to visit a frightened young woman who's in the hospital."

"Anyone I know?"

"Louise Scofield."

She paled visibly. "What happened?"

"Tell you all about it on the way."

"First, I need to stop at my apartment and change. I'm not dressed properly for a hospital visit."

"Anything you say." He gave her a quick kiss. "Before we go, I'll check on Evie."

He knocked on his older daughter's bedroom door. She'd slept through breakfast in spite of the clatter they'd made. Now she called out for him to come in. She was still in bed with the sheet pulled up to her neck, her young, oval face flushed with morning radiance.

"How was your date with Gary last night?"

She yawned and smiled. "Just great. I really like him."

"Why don't you tell your sister about your date while you have something to eat? The waffles are still warm." He gave her forehead a quick peck and hurried downstairs.

Kim watched as he went through the daily ritual of unlocking his holstered revolver from the desk drawer in the living room. He checked his .38 caliber Smith and Wesson Chief's Special in a precise manner. He checked his Smith & Wesson 327 TRR8 revolver in a precise manner. He preferred it to the Glock automatic, the latest issue. "You be careful," she said, eyeing the weapon.

"Me? I was born careful."

"Sure you were." She shook her head in a dubious manner.

"Did I ever tell you that my mother named me Michael Careful Gardner at birth, just to make certain?"

She groaned, which made him smile and want to hug her.

"Sometimes you're a very strange man."

"But sexy?"

"Definitely that."

COUNTY REGIONAL was a twenty-minute drive from Kim's apartment. Mike parked his car and checked his watch as they walked briskly through the main entrance. It was clearly later than he'd anticipated arriving.

"Sorry for slowing you down," she said.

He gave her a slightly lopsided smile and squeezed her hand. "Hey, don't apologize. I don't regret a moment spent with you. Besides, you're doing me the favor here. I prefer having you with me today, and so no regrets. I just want to make certain we speak with Louise Scofield before her husband does."

At the information desk, Mike got Mrs. Scofield's room number and two visitor passes. It was only two flights up, and Kim agreed to walk instead of waiting for the elevator that, Mike explained, he knew from past experience was slow.

There was something oppressive about the sterile, institutional corridors and the omnipresent smell of antiseptic. She never would feel comfortable in a hospital. There were many ghosts here, crying out in pain. She found herself shivering. Mike put his arm around her. He radiated strength. Even under these circumstances, his mere touch sent a chemical reaction surging through her.

They found the correct room without difficulty. Mike didn't seem the least bit surprised to find both Bert St. Croix and Mr. Scofield waiting outside like two pillars of granite contemplating eternity.

"She says I can't see my wife until after you've talked to her." Scofield's voice was angry and he pointed an accusing finger at Bert.

"Under the circumstances," Mike said, "that seems best. Don't worry, you'll see her. I just want to talk to her first. You'll have to be patient. It's a great virtue, so they say. I haven't fully mastered it yet, either. You can practice on Detective St. Croix. She'll remain here with you."

Bert looked far from pleased but said nothing and gave a stoic nod of her head. Walking into the hospital room beside Mike, Kim quickly glanced around. The room was a private one, which made it a lot easier to talk. Mike positioned himself next to the bed. Kim sat down on a chair beside the bed. Mrs. Scofield, who had been staring out the window, now turned and faced them. Against the white pillows her faced looked smaller and paler than ever. Kim observed that her arm had been set in a cast.

"How are you feeling?" Mike asked, his expression sympathetic.

"Physically? I've had better days. My head hurts badly. But at least I'm not afraid anymore. I don't have to live in dread because the worst has already happened. It's over and done with."

Kim wasn't certain that she understood Mrs. Scofield's

reasoning. She studied the younger woman thoughtfully. Louise Scofield did seem much calmer.

"Did your husband do this to you intentionally?" Mike asked. He could be awfully blunt. Kim supposed that came with the job he did.

"Intentionally?" Louise parroted, her russet hair spread out on the pillow like a fan.

"Do you want to press charges against him?"

"No, he doesn't deserve that."

"It would help if you told me what happened yesterday."

"There isn't a great deal to tell. We were quarreling as usual. He kept at me with his barbs and innuendoes. He just would not stop. When I began to cry and begged him to leave me alone, he became angrier. Finally, I lost control and began shouting at him, told him I was pregnant and couldn't stand any more of his abuse. I told him I was going to leave him. He became like a madman. I've never seen him quite that way. He kept saying I was just like his mother. There wasn't any reasoning with him."

"You think he lost it because he believed the baby wasn't his?" Mike had a direct way of asking hard questions that was not offensive. It seemed as if he'd perfected it as an art. Kim supposed it had something to do with his innate intuition.

Mrs. Scofield's green eyes were reflective. "I don't even know if that was it. Odd, because I was so afraid for him to know. It was when I said I was leaving him that Bill went wild. I thought he'd be glad for an easy out of our marriage after the way he'd been behaving. He's been acting as if he hated me. When I said I was leaving him, his rage bordered on insanity. He started coming toward me, looking as if he were going to kill me, and I was terrified. I remember backing away from him, moving toward the steps that lead down to our front door. I told him again that I was leaving and that he shouldn't think of trying to stop me. I said I would return for my things some other time. His features became distorted and his fist lunged forward. I thought, dear lord, he's going to strike me! Involuntarily, I flinched, jerking backward. I lost my balance and fell backwards down the stairs."

"He would have struck you if you hadn't fallen?" Mike's expression was intense, concentrated.

Louise Scofield gave a bitter cry from somewhere deep in her throat—or maybe it was her soul. "Probably not. As I lost my footing, his fist went crashing into the wall. He looked as shocked as I was when I fell backward that way. I can still see the expression on his face. It was the last thing I remember before I woke up here."

"You hit your head."

"So they tell me. As I told you, I have a terrible headache. But the worst part is losing the baby. I really feel awful about that. Yet I suppose it's probably better this way. What kind of father would Bill be? What kind of childhood could my baby have?" Tears welled in her eyes.

Kim reached over and placed a comforting hand on Louise Scofield's arm. "I'm sure there will be other babies under better circumstances in the future," she reassured.

Louise lowered her tearstained eyes.

"Mrs. Scofield, in cases of this kind, it's not uncommon for a wife to cover up for her husband, even when he doesn't merit it. Sometimes the motive is fear of reprisal. Other times, it's caused by a misguided sense of loyalty. Some women foolishly believe that being beaten by a man shows he loves them."

Kim wondered if Mike intended to charge Louise's husband.

"No, it isn't anything like that." Louise's denial was vehement.

"You're not protecting him, are you? That would be a serious mistake. Because if you do decide to stay with him, and what he did was deliberate, there's every possibility, every likelihood, this will happen again. I don't want to scare you, but it could be even worse next time. Wife-beaters tend to follow a pattern. They apologize, beg forgiveness, say it will never happen again, then repeat the same ugly behavior."

"You sound experienced."

"Unfortunately, I am."

Her long lashes fluttered like butterflies in a strong wind. "It's just as I told you, Lieutenant, it really was an accident. I was afraid and I lost my balance." The sparkle was completely gone from her eyes.

"All right. I have no choice but to accept your statement. Are you up to seeing your husband?"

"Yes, I think so."

The tears remained in Louise's eyes. Kim took Louise's cold, delicate hand in her own and silently offered comfort. Louise turned a grateful look to her. She closed her eyes as Mike went outside to get Mr. Scofield. It was obvious that Mike had no intention of leaving the two of them alone together until he'd had a chance to talk to Scofield in his wife's presence. Kim fully agreed; the first concern had to be for the woman's safety and well-being.

Bert St. Croix did not demand inclusion, but waited while Mike followed Scofield back into the hospital room. Bill Scofield's sandy hair was unkempt and he hadn't bothered to shave. His clothes were rumpled, as if he'd slept in them. Was this to demonstrate atonement for his behavior of the previous evening?

"Mr. Scofield, your wife has confirmed that her condition was caused by an accident. There won't be any assault charges filed against you at this time." Mike's steady gray eyes connected with Mr. Scofield's slightly unfocused light blue orbs.

Scofield signaled that he understood with a weary nod of his head.

"You look tired," Louise said to her husband.

"I didn't sleep last night." Scofield turned to Mike. "Lieutenant, can I please talk to my wife alone?"

"I'm too exhausted for another emotional scene."

"I wasn't planning on one. I just want to tell you that I love you. Everything I've done was because I love you." Mr. Scofield dejectedly shoved his hands into his pants pockets.

Louise turned her face toward the wall.

"God, I didn't mean to hurt you. If I can't win you back, I don't want to live anymore, I want to be dead!"

Kim exchanged an alarmed look with Mike, who placed a hand on Scofield's shoulder. "You sound irrational right now. You're close to the edge, too close."

"I just don't want to live without Lou. I didn't mean to hurt her. I'll make it up to her, if she'll let me." He clutched at his wife's delicate hand and grasped it to his lips.

Kim could see panic seizing the young man when his wife appeared unmoved by his passionate anguish.

"Lou, please say you won't leave me."

She turned and looked at him, eyes dark and stormy. "You can ask me that after yesterday? I think our marriage was a mistake from the start. If I get a divorce, I would be doing us both a real favor."

Her words appeared to strike him to the heart. "That's stupid! We love each other."

"But what kind of love is it? You and I got married for all the wrong reasons. You loved me for my weakness, because I needed to depend on you. I loved you for your kindness and supposed strength. We've been like two parasites feeding off each other. It's not love. It's sickness. God help me, I've been nothing more than a coward, running from responsibility and decision-making. But the price has been too high. Some people turn their dreams into reality. I turned reality into a dream. I dreamt you were some kind of hero, come to rescue me from all of life's sorrow. But you can't help me, can you? It's time for me to help myself. Time to grow up.

In memory of the baby that will never be born, and for my own self-respect, I know I have to walk away from you."

"That's why I never confronted you outright about Bradshaw. I knew you'd leave me for him. My mother left my father and me when I was six years old. She never came home, never even wrote us a Christmas card. I was afraid it would be like that all over again."

She stared at him in surprise. "You told me your mother died."

"As far as I was concerned, she was dead. I never loved another person until I met you." He pressed her hand again, but she turned away. "When this thing started with Bradshaw, I became obsessed with the fear of losing you just the way I lost my mother. I never saw the man my mother went away with, but it was different with Bradshaw. I knew him and I hated him. As for you, I'm never going to let you go."

Kim was disturbed by what Scofield was saying. It seemed very possible that Bill Scofield had murdered Bradshaw and was on the verge of admitting it. She hoped Mike would proceed cautiously. She wasn't certain that Scofield was entirely rational.

"Your wife understands that you didn't intentionally hurt her. But the Bradshaw homicide is a different matter. Did you kill him?" Mike probed Scofield with intensity.

"I didn't kill the bastard, although I would have liked to do it."

"Then again, you aren't demonstrating a very high level of emotional stability, are you?"

"I have reasons for what I've done, good reasons."

"Really? What are they?"

"I don't care to discuss them with you."

"Would you prefer Detective St. Croix?"

"Don't threaten me. Look, I just want to be alone with my wife."

But Mike clearly had no intention of letting up on Scofield. "You're a prime suspect in a homicide investigation. I can have you brought back to headquarters for formal questioning."

"What do you want from me?" Scofield ran his hand through the shock of sandy hair as if he were in agonizing pain.

"Cooperation. I want to know every bit of information you're holding back. First, why were you so certain that your wife was having an affair with Bradshaw?"

"Little things mostly, like the way she wants and needs me less all the time."

"That's awfully general, in fact, downright vague. Give me some specifics."

"All right. One day after we'd been playing tennis for a while, Bradshaw and I took a break. We had this conversation I was never able to put out of my mind. He told me about a special date set up for that evening. I told him that I wasn't particularly interested. He kind of laughed at me, asked if I thought I was superior because I was a married man. Then he said I'd be very interested in knowing who the woman was, in fact, I'd be very surprised because the lady in question was also married. He laughed right in my face. Next thing I knew, he was asking me about Lou. 'You've got a real beauty there,' he said. 'Be careful someone doesn't steal her away from you.' Another time, we happened to get on the same bus for work and he sat down beside me. I tried to read my newspaper, but he just kept on talking during the entire trip into the city. Know what he talked about? Lou. Said how she was the most beautiful woman he'd ever seen and how lucky I was to have her. He even got kind of poetic, for a creep like him. He claimed Lou's hair reminded him of flaming autumn leaves. That wasn't the way he usually talked about women, believe me."

"It sounds as if he were baiting you, Scofield. Is that what you based your suspicions on?"

"In part." Scofield appeared reluctant to talk further.

"There has to be more," Mike prodded.

"Lou became very secretive. It wasn't like her. We'd always shared everything. She used to be open with me."

Louise turned to Mike. "When I found out I was pregnant, I was too afraid to tell him."

"Because of his jealousy over Bradshaw?"

Louise surprised Kim by shaking her head. "No, more than that. Bill always said he didn't want to have children, that it wasn't right to bring them into this miserable world. I was scared he'd be angry with me for being careless about taking my birth control pills. Then as his jealousy grew stronger, it became more difficult to tell him."

"You should have told me. It would have saved us so much misunderstanding."

"Would it really?" She faced her husband squarely.

"Just don't leave me, honey. I'll do anything."

"I won't promise that."

"Give me another chance," Scofield begged.

"If I do, what's to prevent you from acting this way again? Some man might look at me and you'd fly into a rage. If he so much as glanced at me a second time, you'd be convinced we were sleeping together. I won't live in fear anymore."

"I'll do anything you say. I promise I will."

"Mr. Scofield, would you be willing to see a psychiatrist?" Mike kept his tone calm and paternal. Kim admired his restraint.

"I'm not a lunatic." Scofield's face burned scarlet.

"No one's saying you are, but your mind is troubled. Talking things out with a qualified person could help you."

"I tell you, there's nothing wrong with me!"

Louise turned and faced him. "What about the way you behaved that evening we went out with Joan and Martin?"

"What evening? I don't know what you're talking about."

"About two months ago when you tried to punch a total

stranger whose only mistake was to look at me. Don't you remember? We were at the Galaxy Lounge."

"Just looking at you? He was flirting with you, or trying to. And you obviously didn't hear the remark he made as he passed our table. No man would allow his wife to be talked about that way."

"The truth is, you lose your temper too easily."

"Damn it, you're unfair. I only try to protect what's mine."

"I belong to myself, Bill. I'm not a possession. You don't own me."

"Lou, I'll do whatever you want, even see a shrink if you'll stay with me. For God's sake, I'd do anything for you." Scofield's voice betrayed fear and vulnerability. He seemed overwhelmed by passion.

Kim was surprised to observe that Lou's fine features were, in comparison, unrelenting and controlled. "I'll try to forgive you. That's the best I can do for now. Please don't ask any more of me. Emotionally, I'm numb."

"Why don't we let her rest?" Mike suggested, leading Scofield toward the door. "You can discuss getting counseling another time."

The man was suffering; that was obvious, and he appeared emotionally exhausted. Louise no longer seemed quite as helpless and vulnerable. Kim was aware that a subtle reversal of roles had somehow occurred. Was there another side to Mrs. Scofied she hadn't realized existed?

A sudden disconcerting thought struck Kim. No one had ever considered Louise Scofield as a possible suspect in the Bradshaw homicide. They had responded to her emotionally rather than rationally. A shrewd murderess might well feign such a pose. It was conceivable that a distraught Louise Scofield could have murdered Bradshaw when he threatened to expose their affair to her husband. With Bradshaw dead, she would be able to convince her husband the relationship never existed. Bradshaw, after all, would be in no position to confirm or deny anything. Scofield would end up apologizing to his wife, just as he had done.

Bradshaw's death at the hands of Louise Scofield was, of course, not likely, and at best, a distant possibility, a decidedly unpleasant one. No, of the two, Mr. Scofield was the more likely to be guilty of murder. Yet, she couldn't shake the fact that Bradshaw had been bragging to Scofield about having an affair with a married woman. The implication had clearly been that Louise Scofield was that woman. Kim decided to keep this conjecture to herself for the present. Sharing it with Mike didn't seem sensible until there was more than theory to rely on. And there was no tangible evidence against Mrs. Scofield.

"Mr. and Mrs. Scofield, we have no more questions for either of you at the present time, but please keep yourselves available."

Mike walked Scofield out into the hospital corridor. Kim was thinking that something was missing. The Scofields had not told Mike everything. They knew more. She sensed it, felt it in nearly a tangible way, as one held a grapefruit.

Bert St. Croix looked from Mr. Scofield to Mike. "How is she?"

"Mrs. Scofield will be fine. She's already stronger."

She saw Bert breathe a sigh of relief, then look back at Scofield and glower. "I'll walk you out to the parking lot," she said.

Scofield eyed Bert's imposing figure. "Lieutenant, keep her away from me."

"Just a few words," Bert said, and took Scofield by the arm, steering him down the corridor.

"What do you think she's going to do?" Kim asked Mike. Bert's anger had come at Scofield in waves.

"Come on." Mike took her by the hand as they hurried after Bert and Scofield "I'm hoping Bert won't do anything stupid." They caught up to the detective in the parking lot as Scofield was driving away.

"I hope you had the common sense to keep your hands off him this time."

Bert gave Mike a satisfied smile. "I'm loaded with common sense."

"Einstein once said common sense is not so common. Who am I to argue with genius?"

"Obviously, you don't have a high trust level. The fact is, I only gave him a little warning."

"Which was?"

"Let's just say he'll think twice before laying a hand on his wife again."

Looking at Bert St. Croix's grim expression, Kim fully believed it. Kim instinctively liked the black policewoman. The demeanor might be fierce, but Kim sensed genuine compassion and generosity of spirit present in Bert. Kim also recognized something else. Like herself, Bert had suffered. They were kindred spirits.

TWELVE

Monday afternoon, Gardner was already at his desk when Bert came on duty. Bert watched him taking notes on what appeared to her to be official written reports.

"More paperwork?" she asked in disgust.

"Not exactly. These are the police reports on those Marcom warehouse robberies."

"Anything interesting?"

"I'd say so. Apparently, Walling's company had him covering quite a big chunk of territory. Altogether, there were three robberies and three different police departments involved. Believe it or not, no one's ever bothered to collate info."

"Hard to believe."

"I guess it never seemed worth their time."

"Cases still open?"

"Do birds fly."

"So you're going over the reports. Find anything?" Funny how Gardner's enthusiasm kind of rubbed off on her. There was something about the guy that made her feel as if Gardner were okay. Still, it wouldn't be smart to trust him too far.

Too much was in a state of flux in her life. True, she'd taken this job, but it was just to get away from everything that tortured her. She didn't want to commit to anyone or anything right now. It would have been okay to talk to someone about Alva. But how could anyone else understand? Gardner might not be judgmental, but if she told the guy what had gone down—no, she couldn't. No way! He'd think she was some kind of nutcase. Probably, he already did. She might be able to talk to his girl friend though. She liked Kim Reynolds. There was something about the woman, like she'd suffered through her own personal torments and had compassion for others.

Gardner was examining the reports carefully. "Each job was slick, professional, very clean. They knew just when no one would be around. Nobody saw them and nobody got hurt."

"Real neat. Jobs had to be pulled by the same people. Any other pharma companies hit with the same M.O.?"

"I had it run through the system—believe it or not we hicks do know something about computers. Only Marcom has had this dubious experience."

"So the jobs had an inside man."

"Has to be. Highly marketable drugs in large quantities were in the warehouses at the time of each robbery. These thieves are very good, too clever, in fact."

"So I guess it's time we have another talk with Walling."

Gardner put his head between his hands thoughtfully. It seemed to her that this cop looked more like a high school math teacher or maybe an accountant, dressed as he was in a conservative gray suit, white shirt and dark tie. But if a person were sharp and looked closer, they'd notice the chiseled features and the hard body of a strong man who commanded respect. Bert was learning not to underestimate him.

"I'd like to see if we can dig up more on Walling's connection with the robberies before we tip him that we're on to him. If we don't have anything but our suspicions, he can laugh in our faces. I'd rather hit him hard, catch him by surprise, and that means getting concrete evidence."

"You think his wife knows?"

"Wouldn't surprise me, but she keeps a tight lid on, too shrewd to give us anything on Walling, no matter how she might feel about him."

Bert had to agree. "So we're going out to the warehouses."

"One of them anyway. It's about an hour's drive from here. We're not likely to uncover anything the North Ridge Police haven't already found. On the other hand, they didn't know about Martin Walling. Could be our questions will be a little different from theirs."

"Anything on Sonny today?"

A shadow crossed Gardner's face. That was a sore point for both of them. "He hasn't turned up. No one's found a trace of him. Seems he hasn't contacted anybody, not April Nevins if we can believe her, not his mother or brothers."

She saw the look of dejection on Gardner's face deepen. "Hey, the kid'll probably turn up in the next couple of hours." She could only hope her optimism was warranted.

"I checked with Martha Rhoades at the pool club. Sonny was supposed to be in on Friday but he never showed, not then, not since."

"So you think something's definitely wrong."

"Let's just say there's a creepy sensation running down my spine. I usually trust my instincts. They're seldom wrong."

"It sure looks like Sonny was the murderer's accomplice. He did admit to putting Bradshaw's body in the pool. Could be he was in a state of panic and figured to get as far away from here as possible."

"Maybe. Anyhow, we've got a stake-out round the clock on April Nevins' place and the mother's house. Of course, if he phoned, we won't know. There's no wiretap. I couldn't justify it."

She knew what he meant; wiretaps were only for serial killings, major drug busts, high profile criminal cases. Bradshaw's homicide was strictly small change in the scheme of things, just like this nothing little town itself.

"I'd like to know what Sonny thought April Nevins has that belongs to him," Gardner said.

"If we had him here right now, he'd only lie to us anyway."

The drive to North Ridge was relaxing; the sun was already going down, red and round on the horizon, drawing toward it the long shadows of late afternoon. The winding country road took them through cultivated farmlands. North Ridge was a suburb composed mostly of farms and expensive residential tracts. Unlike Webster Township, there were no garden apartments out here; not even elegant ones were permitted. It was zoned for houses on no less than two acres of land.

As they drove, Bert observed the differences between the old, stately Victorian homes and the showy, new development houses. She didn't even consider which she'd personally prefer because she could never afford, either. It was a far cry from the teeming city, all this open well-tended land, all these expensive homes. She had a sense of being in alien territory.

The warehouse was not near any houses. It was off the main road and isolated from the town as if anything smacking of commercialism should be hidden since it was a source of shame. As they drove near, Bert noticed large trucks in the process of being loaded. They parked their car and quickly found the manager's office.

"I've already been questioned about the robbery," the irritated manager told them after the introductions were completed.

"We're aware of that, but we were hoping there was some information you could give us that the North Ridge Police don't already know."

"Like what?" The manager was wiry, but with a whining quality to his voice that Bert found annoying.

"How is it that the thieves managed to come and go when no one was around?"

"Luck, I guess. Our security man had just stepped out for a sandwich. By the time he came back, they'd disappeared.

Needless to say, our man brings all his food with him nowadays. Another slip and he's out on his ass."

"Mighty slick trick, getting in and out before he got back."

"Kind of like magic," Bert agreed.

The manager narrowed his eyes.

"Is your security guard around?"

"Not until later."

"Then I'd like his home address," Gardner said.

The manager went over to a large file cabinet. "You ought to know he's been questioned already, just like I was."

"Don't worry about it." Gardner waited as the manager wrote out the information for him. "One last thing, do you happen to know Martin Walling?"

"District sales? Sure, he's here now and then to check on shipping orders, see how things are going."

"Has he been here since the robbery?"

The manager chewed thoughtfully on the tip of his pen. "Guess not. Don't remember him coming lately."

"When was the last time he was here?"

"How should I know?"

"It's important," Gardner persisted. "A month before the robbery? A week? Maybe you could check your records or something."

Gardner wasn't willing to let go. His tone was smooth and courteous, but he was like a pit bull clamping his jaw down on prey. You really couldn't judge by appearance, Bert supposed. Gardner was outwardly laid back, easygoing, but caught up in a case, he was focused and intense.

"Okay, maybe it was two weeks, maybe even three," the manager finally allowed.

"Maybe right before the robbery?"

"It could have been a week," the manager conceded.

Gardner politely thanked him and they left. Locating the security guard's place turned out to be difficult since he lived in an old bungalow, little more than a shack off a bumpy road no wider than a driveway. It was also a good half-hour farther south.

Roy Gunther was a hermit. He lived alone under primitive conditions. Bert heard dogs growling inside as she knocked at the door. When it was opened, an old man came out, followed by three mongrels. She judged Gunther to be close to seventy. His grizzled white hair and bent posture made him look even older. Gunther scowled at them as Gardner made introductions. The old guy looked ready to growl just like his dogs.

"Well, what do you want with me?" The voice was gruff as she'd expected.

"We understand you were on duty the night the Marcom warehouse was robbed."

"What if I was?"

She sensed fear in the man. She could smell it. What was he scared of?

"Do you go out to eat at the same time every night?"

"I used to."

The sharp, bared teeth of the dogs were in contrast to Gunther's gummy mouth. She didn't much like the man or his animals, all of whom seemed decrepit and degenerate; funny how dogs just naturally took on the qualities of their owners.

"Did you eat at the same place every night?"

"What's it to you?" The wrinkles on the old man's face were like a mosaic pattern.

"This is important, understand?" Bert gave him a menacing look and noted with some small satisfaction that the old man seemed to wise up.

"I always go to the same place to eat."

"Were other people aware of it?"

"No one ever said I couldn't go out for a little while, not until after that robbery."

"But technically, you're not supposed to leave the premises," Gardner supplied.

"There's a clock at both ends of the warehouse. Each hour, I'm supposed to make my rounds and punch in my card at the opposite end. Dinnertime, I'd walk out to the diner just after punching in at one side. Diner's open all night. I never got much anyway, just a bowl of soup and maybe some crackers. Can't eat much 'cause of my bad choppers. When I got back, I'd punch in at the other end. Nobody ever knew the difference—until that night. Then I caught it good from the boss. Nearly got canned."

"Who knew your schedule?"

"Nobody. I never shoot off my mouth. Hardly talk to people."

"Except maybe Martin Walling?"

"Never heard of him." Gunther stared at them blankly.

"Wasn't he around to check on things? A short, heavy man, small bald spot on top of his head, sporting a mustache. He's the district rep for sales."

"Rosy and round-faced like an apple?"

Bert decided Walling had more of a porcine puss; in fact, if an apple were stuffed in his mouth, he would have been ready for a spit.

"I guess I seen him around a few times," Gunther conceded.

"What exactly did he ask you?"

"Nothing much. We just talked a little. But he give me ten bucks, I sure remember that."

"What was it for?"

"Eating money. Says to me I do a real fine job and he appreciated it. Heck of a nice fella. Real friendly. Looked like the kind who knew how to enjoy a good meal himself. Except for his sweaty hands, he was fine."

"Did he happen to discuss your habit of going out to the diner for supper?"

"I don't tell people."

"But you told Walling because he gave you the money."

"Maybe. Can't remember." Gunther rubbed the gray stubble on his face in a nervous manner. "Am I gonna be in trouble all over again? I can't afford to lose my job. After the robbery, the boss started talking about how a younger man might be better for security. It ain't easy for a man my age to find work." Gunther looked at them pathetically.

"We don't want to get you fired. We're not pushing the robbery investigation any further than knowing how it fits in with a homicide."

The old man showed his relief by exhaling noisily.

"Did you ever meet a man named Richard Bradshaw?"

"Can't say as the name is familiar."

"Another salesman. Tall, good-looking, well-dressed. He may have asked you a few questions about Walling, the way we've been doing."

The dogs panted, moving toward Gardner and Bert, their sharp teeth and lapping, pink tongues fully exposed. The dogs made her nervous, but much to her relief, the old man restrained them.

"Yeah, there was a fella like that. Said he was from the main office and out to check things over. He asked about Mr. Walling some, but that wasn't all he talked about."

"Did he happen to ask if Walling had discussed your schedule?"

"Maybe. I'm getting old. I don't always remember so good. You sure I won't get in any trouble over this?"

"You're a witness. That's all."

They left the old man and his mean-looking mutts standing outside the tumbledown bungalow. She did the driving on the way back, taking the road faster than Gardner had coming.

"I believe we can connect Walling to the other two robberies, as well," Gardner said.

"You think Bradshaw confronted Walling with his suspicions and was murdered for his trouble?"

"A real possibility. I don't think Walling is very eager to end up in prison, do you? There's no doubt that Bradshaw discovered the truth. He was many things, but obviously not stupid."

"Funny, Walling was the only one who had anything good to say about Bradshaw. Could be Bradshaw wasn't planning to rat on him—or maybe he never did get to confront Walling." She was trying hard to ferret out fact from supposition.

"Or that was just a smokescreen meant to throw us off. If we thought Walling liked Bradshaw, then we were less likely to investigate him. Don't forget, Marcom brought Bradshaw here to find out what was going wrong with the east coast operation of the company. He wasn't just another salesman."

"I still think Walling's attitude toward Bradshaw was genuine," she said.

"Maybe, but never trust appearances. I remember my great aunt Mindy, who enjoyed going to funerals. I don't think the old gal owned a dress that wasn't black. She generally cried louder than any member of the bereaved family, even if she hardly knew the deceased. You'd swear it was she who sustained the greatest loss."

"Okay, I get the message. Where to next?"

"Let's have a change of pace and visit a good-looking lady," Gardner said with a smile.

BUT IT WASN'T GARDNER who ended up at the front door of April Nevins' apartment. Gardner was stopped by the cop on surveillance duty. Impatient to get the interview over with, Bert offered to talk to the woman herself. Gardner agreed. At least he was beginning to trust her.

April Nevins answered the door to her apartment after Bert rang the bell three times. She was wearing a black silk kimono with a red Chinese dragon on the back and nothing else.

"You again." She did not bother to conceal her agitation. "If you're here because of Sonny, I don't have anything more to say." She preceded Bert into the living room. As before, the bed was unmade. She noticed Bert looking at it. "I just woke up. Want some coffee? It's fresh. I made a whole pot. It's good and strong."

Bert agreed to the coffee and looked for someplace to sit down. Glancing around the apartment, she found that it was just as chaotic as before. Clothes, shoes, old newspapers and glossy magazines were scattered around. There was dust on the furniture and dirty dishes piled up in the kitchen sink. The place reeked of cigarette smoke. She wondered in disgust how anyone could live that way and had an overwhelming urge to open the windows wide.

April Nevins handed her a white ceramic mug of black coffee, then began sipping some of the brew from a matching cup.

"I need this to wake up. I haven't been getting much sleep lately."

"Guilty conscience?"

April put down her coffee cup, folded her hands across her full breasts and threw Bert an annoyed look but took her time responding. "What do you want with me now?"

"You know that Sonny disappeared?"

"I don't know anything about it."

"Didn't he arrange to see you on Saturday?"

April turned her handbag upside down, letting the contents drop randomly. Scooping up a pack of cigarettes, she started looking around the apartment for matches. "I wasn't home."

"Where were you?"

April's hands were none too steady. "Say, do you have a lighter or matches on you? I seem to be out of them."

When Bert responded negatively, April resumed her hunt, much to Bert's irritation.

"Let's get on with it," Bert said.

"After I have my first cigarette, I'll be ready."

"You don't need those coffin nails."

Apparently, April wasn't listening because she'd located a lighter under a magazine and was pulling a cigarette from the pack. What happened next, Bert really didn't intend to happen. Since she'd lost Alva, she found her temper much shorter than it should be, and this woman in particular provoked her. Bert put the coffee cup down, found herself grabbing April's hand, seizing the pack, and crushing it.

April's eyes opened wide and her face turned red as a blood sun. "You rotten bitch! That was mine, my last pack. You had no right." She started crying in frustration.

"All right, I'm sorry. I'll buy you another pack to replace that one. But you're only killing yourself with that garbage. Christ sake, girl, you smell like a human ashtray."

"Why should you care about me? What's the difference to you if I do smoke myself to death?"

"It's personal," Bert said, trying to look away from her.

"Tell me and you can forget about buying me that pack."

Bert let out a deep sigh. "My mother died of emphysema. She had a heavy habit and smoked herself into an early grave. I promised on her deathbed that I'd never smoke again, and I hate it when I see other people puffing their brains out. I especially hate to see what it does to their families."

"I don't have any family, and I need caffeine and nicotine to get me going each day. I've got a lousy job and a lousy life. It helps get me through. You understand?"

"There are other ways to pull yourself together."

"Like what?" Her eyes flashed an angry challenge.

"I'm not the best one to tell you. I haven't done so great with my life, either."

"You couldn't be as messed up as me." April Nevins

started crying again, her hair falling forward over her eyes. Bert held her, patting April's back as if she were a child that needed comforting. Finally, April pulled back, rubbing the tears from her face.

"Are you married?" she asked.

The question surprised Bert. "No, why?"

"I just wondered."

"Most men find me intimidating because of my size—which is just as well."

"You're not bad looking. If you dressed better and wore make-up, you could have guys."

"Don't want them. Don't need them. Don't trust them. That's enough about me. As for you, Ms. Nevins, it's time you got your act together. Don't be so needy."

"Easy for you to say. I'm not independent like you. I need a man in my life. I'm afraid."

"We're all afraid, but we women need to know how to rely on ourselves first and foremost."

Bert heard someone clear his throat and turned to see Gardner standing in the doorway. She could tell he'd over-heard some of the conversation, likely he disapproved of the personal turn it had taken.

"Has Miss Nevins told you where she was on Saturday?" Gardner asked.

"Not yet."

April hugged the silk kimono against her body. "After that little incident on Friday night, I was pretty upset. I didn't want to hang around here. I was afraid Sonny might come around later. One of the other waitresses invited me to stay over at her place when I told her about my problem during our break. So I slept over there. I didn't come back to the apartment at all. Lisa and me spent the entire day together and then went to work that evening."

"And your friend Lisa will confirm this if we ask her?"

April ran her hand through her tawny mane of hair. "Why do I need an alibi?"

Gardner sidestepped the question and posed one of his own. "Did Sonny phone or contact you at any time since you saw him at the lounge?"

"No, I haven't heard from him at all."

"Don't you find that a little odd?"

"Why should I? Considering the fight we had?" She was defensively belligerent again and looked with longing at the crushed pack of cigarettes.

Bert found herself wishing Gardner would ease up on the woman.

"I never quite understood what the argument was about, Miss Nevins. Maybe you can explain it to Detective St. Croix and me."

"How would I know what was going through Sonny's screwed-up little brain?" Her voice approached shrillness.

"But he did make some accusations. What were they?" Gardner wasn't going to let up on her.

"He told you, didn't he? You don't have to play games with me. I know what he said. But I didn't kill Rick. I don't care what Sonny said. It's not true." She turned to Bert, her eyes pleading for support and understanding.

Bert didn't say a word, but it wasn't easy.

"The question is, what reason did Sonny have for thinking that way?" Gardner kept his tone cool, but there was fear in April Nevins' eyes.

"He claimed that he left something here and I took it. He said I hid it somewhere. I didn't know what the hell he was talking about."

"He wanted to search your apartment Friday evening, didn't he?"

"Yeah, but I had to go to work and I didn't want him hanging around when I wasn't here. Honestly, nothing he said made any sense to me. I never took anything that belonged to him. Why would I? What did he ever have that was worth anything, other than his hot bod? Sure, sometimes he left stuff here, but never for long. Anyway, I didn't know he was going to get drunk and make a scene where I work. I think he'd had a few before he even came here. Jerk. He didn't even know how to hold his liquor." She shivered.

"Did he give you any idea at all about what he thought was missing?"

She went to the kitchenette, poured herself a fresh cup of coffee and then began sipping it. "He was too excited to make any sense."

"Miss Nevins, is your apartment usually like this?"

Her face colored. "Messy, you mean? I guess so. I'm kind of disorganized. My sister says I'm a hopeless slob. You disapprove, don't you? So did that snobby bitch."

"Who would that be?" Gardner asked.

"Oh, Cheryl McNeill. She stopped by for a few minutes once and made some nasty comments about how I keep the place. That's one reason I referred to her as Rick's live-in maid."

"When did Ms. McNeill call on you?"

April moved around the room restlessly. "It was the day after the scene at the pool."

"Why did she come?"

"She came to find out if Rick really had broken off with me."

"Why come to you?"

Her full lips twisted into a bitter smile. "Because Rick was a liar and she knew it. I felt sorry for her. She wasn't so bad. I told her that he dropped me, even though it was the other way around."

"And she was satisfied?"

"With that part of it anyway."

"Was something else bothering her?"

"She asked if I phoned Rick the night before. I told her I

didn't. But you could see that she was convinced he was still seeing another woman. Personally, I don't think he had any intention of marrying her."

"Was this just intuition on your part, or are you basing it on something concrete?"

April ran her fingers through her hair. "I really don't like talking about this. It was something Rick told me when he was blasted. A few months ago, Cheryl became pregnant. She expected Rick to marry her then, but instead he arranged for her to have an abortion. She went through with it like he wanted. It seems to me if he ever had any intention of marrying her, that would have been the time."

"Never know when it comes to people," Gardner said, his expression pensive.

She began to fidget. "I haven't caused her any trouble? Right?"

"I wouldn't worry," Gardner said.

Bert couldn't help wondering whether April had offered the information to draw some of the suspicion away from herself. Regardless, Cheryl McNeill might have had more of a motive for murder than they'd realized. Bert made a mental note to check out the abortion story. A verification could prove significant. Cheryl might have hidden her resentment and waited to get even with Bradshaw. Bert knew from personal experience that unexpressed anger could fester like an open sore.

"When you told Ms. McNeill you weren't the other woman in Bradshaw's life, what exactly did she say?" Gardner moved his questions smoothly back to key information.

"I think she would have liked it if I told her I was still seeing Rick. Then she would have had it out with me right then and there, but she believed me when I told her our brief fling was definitely over."

"Did you speculate with her as to the identity of this other woman?"

April looked away from them. "I didn't know anything, and I'm not a gossip."

"Did you think the other woman might have been Louise Scofield?"

Bert flashed a reproachful look in Gardner's direction.

"She's a real nice person," April said, mirroring Bert's own thoughts. "I'd hate to think she was mixed up with a creep like Rick."

"But you do think she might have become involved with him?"

She nibbled nervously at her lower lip. "Anyone could see that Rick was crazy about her."

"Does anyone include Bill Scofield?"

She nodded her head miserably. "Especially Bill. He was very jealous of the way Rick acted toward her. Rick would rush over to sit and talk with Louise the minute she arrived at the pool. He'd give her compliments, which wasn't like him at all. Bill was furious, but he didn't know how to handle it because Rick was so smooth. He kept making Bill look dumb in front of Lou."

"Did this go on from the beginning of the summer?"

"I'm not sure. I think so."

"Could Bradshaw have been interested in starting trouble between Mr. and Mrs. Scofield? Possibly he found it amusing."

"I suppose. Rick considered Lou a challenge, maybe because Bill was always very devoted to Lou, watching over her."

"Abnormally devoted?"

"More than most husbands I've seen let's say. I thought it was very romantic. But Joan said that she personally couldn't stand the idea of a man hovering over her like that. Joan's very independent. She does as she pleases. The truth is, Bill would probably keep Lou locked in a chastity belt if they hadn't gone out of fashion after the Middle Ages."

"Have Louise or Joan ever visited your apartment?"

"Sure, they both have. I'm in walking distance from the pool club and sometimes I invite people in after we've been over there for a while, especially on my days off."

"Were they here in the week preceding Bradshaw's death?"

"I guess so." She bit her ragged fingernails as if trying to remember. "Yeah, Joan was suggesting that we all go away together for the Labor Day weekend but we never made any serious plans."

"I see. Did Martin Walling or Bill Scofield ever drop by?"

"No, Bill was never here, though he did phone when Lou was by, checking up on her I suppose. Martin was here once."

"What reason did he have for coming by?"

April glanced at Bert then lowered her eyes. "Martin Walling has two interests in life: food and sex, in that order. He's a perfect pig."

"And what was your reaction to his proposition?"

"I told him to go to hell. I don't sleep with married men, and Joan's a friend. Besides, that fat slob makes my flesh crawl. I don't need to get into bed with every man I meet. Believe me, I'm not on an ego trip, and I'm not a nympho."

"Walling hit hard on you?"

"Let me put it this way, if he had Rick's good looks and easy charm, Martin Walling would try to hit on every woman he met."

"Wasn't that what Bradshaw did?"

"I wouldn't know." Her face became icy as a glacier. Gardner picked up on that and changed the line of his questioning. "About Ms. McNeill's state of mind when she visited you, did she say anything specifically that would indicate she didn't really expect Bradshaw to marry her?"

April hesitated. "I guess not. I mean, we both agreed that Rick couldn't be trusted. That was all. She's not an open person the way I am."

Gardner thanked April for her cooperation and started toward the door. April placed her hand on Bert's arm as if to detain her. "You don't think I killed Rick, do you?" Her eyes were open wide, imploring an encouraging response.

Bert felt put upon. She didn't want to think April could have killed Bradshaw, but she sensed if provoked enough, April was certainly capable.

"How am I supposed to answer that?"

"Straight out."

"Okay, no bullshit, then. At this point, I don't know who killed Bradshaw or why. We're just talking to people, trying to fill in on his background." Bert turned to Gardner. "Am I speaking for both of us, Lieutenant?"

Gardner nodded his head. April looked much more at ease as she showed them out. She grasped Bert's hand momentarily as if she didn't want to let her go.

"Hey, it'll be okay," she told April. "All anyone has to do is tell the truth and they got nothing to worry about."

As they left the apartment and began walking down the street to the car, Bert had the feeling that April's eyes were following her from the front window. She didn't want to believe that April murdered Bradshaw. It had to be someone else. For a moment, she resented Gardner's emotional detachment and thought there was a suggestion of smug superiority in it.

"What was that business about Louise Scofield?" she lashed out. "You're not putting her on the list of suspects?"

"I know you're sympathetic to both Louise and April, but we can't let personal feelings get in the way of professional judgment."

"Thanks, Mr. Psychologist. Happens where people are concerned, I have gut instincts just the way you do and they're not often wrong."

Gardner obviously wasn't interested in a confrontation. "The pool club isn't far from here," he said. "Why don't we take a walk? Maybe it's time we had another little chat with Miss Rhoades."

"What makes you think she's at the pool?"

"A dedicated person like her? Where else would she be?"

GARDNER TURNED OUT to be right. They found Martha Rhoades sitting in her office, her German shepherd obediently by her side.

"I was going to phone you, Lieutenant. You saved me the bother. When are we allowed to open again? The members are quite unhappy. Mr. Page, the owner of the club, even came down here personally to ask questions. Naturally, I couldn't tell him a thing. I suggested that he contact you. Mr. Bradshaw really did make quite a nuisance of himself." She enunciated the final statement with what struck Bert as a surprising degree of antagonism. Did Martha have some strong, personal reason for her intense hostility toward the man?

"How would the day after tomorrow suit you as a reopening date?"

"I have your word on that?"

"You have—unless someone else is found murdered in the pool during the interim."

She offered an indulgent smile. "That's hardly likely."

"We have a few more questions to ask you."

"Certainly. I'll be glad to help."

"How many keys are there to the utility room?"

"Just four. Each of us has one."

"Only four?"

"Precisely what I said." Her voice was stern and patronizing, treating Gardner as if he were one of her less intellectually gifted students.

"Suppose one of your employees lost a set of keys? What procedure would be followed?"

"They would report it to me, naturally, and I would loan them the spare set."

"Then, in reality, there are five sets of keys."

This time, she gave Gardner a supercilious smile. "Didn't I say that?"

"No, you didn't. Did Sonny happen to borrow the spare set of keys?"

She gave him a deep, puzzled frown. "Why should he?"

Gardner ignored the severity of her voice. "He never mentioned losing his pool keys?"

She sighed in a manner that indicated she was losing patience. Her lips were as tight as her short-cropped curls.

"Really, Lieutenant, I don't wish to be rude, but your questions are ridiculous, petty and redundant."

Gardner seemed to have cultivated a shell as hard as a mollusk, which protected him from the abusive remarks people often inflicted on policemen. He ignored the woman's petulance.

"Sometimes getting facts and evidence together in a case like this involves attention to details. Just bear with me, okay? Did either of the other two lifeguards, or you, for that matter, mislay those keys?"

"No, certainly not."

"Then may I please see the spare set of keys?"

"Of course, I keep them right here." She opened her top desk drawer and began searching around. When she didn't find the keys, she methodically went through the other drawers. "I can't seem to find them," she finally admitted.

"Do you generally keep your desk open or locked?"

"During the day it's open, but I lock it when I leave. When members bring guests, the money they're charged is kept in the drawer, so I'm very careful."

"Is anything else missing?" Gardner kept at her in a dogged manner.

"No, just the keys."

"Did Sonny ever borrow your keys?"

She gave the matter some thought. "Yes, he did. One day, he forgot his own and said he needed mine to lock up in the evening, but he returned them promptly the very next morning."

"Did you ever see the spare set after that?"

"I had no reason to check."

"If you saw that particular set of keys, could you tell them apart from the other ones?"

"From all but my own. You see, I placed my keys and the spare set on identical rings. The others were responsible for supplying their own. Naturally, each one was different."

Gardner thanked Miss Rhoades for her help, which seemed to please her.

"I do my best to fulfill the obligations of a responsible citizen," she responded in a pompous manner Bert found irritating.

They departed as the sun was setting through the trees, dancing on the aqua waters of the pool. Bert couldn't help thinking it was the perfect time for taking a swim. She let out a deep sigh.

"You think Sonny was looking for his pool keys at April Nevins' apartment?"

"Seems more than likely." Gardner said as they walked back to the car.

"And that's why Sonny figured April killed Bradshaw. He remembered leaving the keys there. He must have thought she took them, made a date with Bradshaw, let herself into the utility room, and killed him there."

"No point writing a scenario until we know a little more. But with those keys lying around, anyone who dropped by April's apartment could have seen them and taken them. You looked around her place. What did you notice?"

"It's a pigsty."

"Things could lie around there for days or weeks and go

unnoticed. April might never have seen an unfamiliar set of keys."

Bert's mind was working at a fevered pace. "But someone else who recognized the keys could have taken them."

"I have a feeling whoever killed Bradshaw made the mistake of keeping those keys."

"What makes you think that?" Bert wasn't convinced. She wondered if Gardner wasn't making too big a thing over Sonny's lost keys.

"Let's say I'm the murderer. The smart thing would be to wipe all fingerprints off the keys and leave them in the utility room or just outside of it after the murder. I'm smart enough to wipe the prints off the murder weapon but I forget all about the keys. Maybe I absently drop them into a pocket or purse."

Bert had to admit that Gardner made sense, but she still didn't think it meant much. "The murderer could have remembered about the keys later and ditched them somewhere."

"More than likely, but there's always a chance that the keys will incriminate the killer."

"You want to search April's apartment since we know what we're looking for?"

Gardner's eyes were nearly charcoal in the fading light. "I have a hunch we wouldn't find anything. Plus, it might tip off our murderer."

"If it's not April after all." Saying the words made her feel rotten; Bert didn't want April to be the one. She tried to consider some of the other suspects in the Bradshaw case. "You think what April said about Cheryl McNeill is true?"

"I wouldn't doubt it." An alert intelligence showed on Gardner's face. The elongated forehead wrinkled.

"But the McNeill girl can't be our murderer."

"Why not?" Gardner could be annoying.

"Why wouldn't she have killed him right there in the apartment?"

"If it were a premeditated murder, she wouldn't want to kill him there, would she? We'd have arrested her on the spot. Case closed."

"You think it was preplanned?"

"I have no idea," Gardner conceded.

"I want to make a good collar just as much as you, but all this shadowboxing is getting to me."

THEY WERE BACK AT headquarters when word came that Sonny Blake had been located. From the expression on Gardner's face, Bert knew to expect the worst.

THIRTEEN

KIM WAS HAVING a busy morning. It felt strange being back at work after a week of doing so little. In a way, it was a relief to be working again. She wouldn't have to think about her life and where it was headed. Her feelings for Mike Gardner ran deep. Kim meant it when she told him that she loved him. But she still wasn't convinced that their relationship could or should be a permanent one. They were such different people.

Rita Mosler would be on duty at the reference desk with her most of the day. Rita was an old-timer and somewhat jaded by the job. People rarely went to Rita for help when they could ask Kim or one of the young grad students. Rita was just too sharp-tongued. Her caustic manner frightened students almost as much as her bony, arthritic fingers resembling bent twigs. Her customary expression was that of someone who'd recently swallowed a lemon whole.

As luck would have it, Rita received a phone call from the Mad Movie Fan, as she referred to him. "Take it for me," Rita said. "I can't stand talking to that moron again. The man's impossible."

Kim got on the line. The old man's familiar shaky voice greeted her. As expected, he asked her to look up information for him, and she did so as he held on. This time, he wanted the cast list, director and producer of *The Godfather*.

"No big thing," Kim said to Rita after she'd finished with the call. "I Googled it in half a minute tops."

"He's a pest. Calls every day with some silly question. We

have more important things to do here. This is a university library."

Kim shrugged.

"Oh, it's nothing to you, Miss Magnanimous. After all, you just came back from vacation."

"Rita, aren't you due to take some vacation time this month?" Kim hoped that was the case.

Rita harrumphed. "I'm much too necessary around here to take time off."

"It really is slow right now. Why not take a cruise?" Kim suggested as she went about organizing the materials in the ready reference shelf under the main information desk.

"A cruise? Why I'd get sea sick."

"They have medication to prevent that."

Rita harrumphed again, this time louder. "People get all kinds of stomach ailments on board ships. Much too dangerous."

"All right, what about going to the shore for a few days? Nothing like being near the ocean."

"I'm too old to sit in the hot sun and fry like an egg."

Kim was grateful when someone came to the desk.

"So glad you're back," Don Bernard said, giving her one of his most ingratiating smiles.

"So am I, I think."

He cast a sideways look at Rita and laughed. God, the man had a great laugh, deep and full of resonance. "You're not sure? How can I convince you? I know, lunch today with me. There's an elegant little bistro that just opened in walking distance." Don focused on his watch. "And coincidentally, it's just about lunchtime."

Kim glanced at her coworker's sour face. "I have to make certain it's all right with Rita if I take first lunch."

Don turned the full force of his debonair charm on the dour woman. "Miss Mosler, you wouldn't refuse me a chance to speak with another colleague, would you? I have some

Shakespearean research I need to discuss with Ms. Reynolds. I know how truly understanding you are. I would consider it a favor."

Rita blushed. "Well, of course, Professor Bernard."

And that was that. Kim doubted many women could resist him. Don had a way with women, even ones like Rita Mosler. Women just naturally found Don attractive. Every time they were together, some female or other would try to flirt with him, students or even other professors. He had a charismatic aura and a clever way with words.

The restaurant Don chose was lovely, with large pots of colorful flowers arranged around the cobblestones that graced the outside and vivid seascapes decorating the interior. He selected a table near the windows so they could look out on the busy street.

They talked about the concert they'd attended together at the state theatre.

"I'm so glad you enjoyed it," Don said, taking her hand across the table. "The truth is, I would like to spend a lot more time with you. I know you enjoy cultural events just as I do." When she didn't immediately answer, he continued. "I'll be doing a symposium on Renaissance poetry this fall. Perhaps you'll come?"

"Of course, I will."

His smile widened. "Good, that means at least I can count on one person attending."

She realized the statement was disingenuous. "Don, you know very well all those female college students pant after you. You can fill an auditorium by snapping your fingers. You're so persuasive you could convince a vegan to eat steak."

He laughed. "I don't know any such thing." Then he playfully kissed her fingertips.

When she withdrew her hand, he merely smiled.

"There is written her fair neck round about:

'Noli me tangere,' (Don't touch me), for Caesar's I am;
And wild for to hold, though I seem tame."

Kim thought for a moment. She recognized the poem. "Sir
Thomas Wyatt I believe. 'Caesar' is a reference to King
Henry VIII while the doe is Anne Boleyn."

Don nodded his head in approval. "I was certain you
would know it."

"I disagree with your analogy. I don't belong to anyone
but myself," Kim asserted.

Don arched an aristocratic brow. "Not to that police detective?"

"I do care about him," she said carefully.

"I want you to care about me," Don told her.

"You are a very good friend. I value our friendship."

"I know how to be patient," he told her, caressing her
cheek, his voice mellifluous. *"'When I all weary had the
chase forsook,/ The gentle deer returned the selfsame way,/
Thinking to quench her thirst at the next brook./ There she,
beholding me with milder look,/ Sought not to fly, but fear-
less still did bide./Till I in hand her yet half trembling took./
And with her own good will her firmly tied./Strange thing,
me seemed, to see a beast so wild/So goodly won, with her
own will beguiled.'"*

No one recited poetry the way Don Bernard did. He had
a Shakespearean actor's voice, smoothly cultured and seductive. "That's how I see it with us, my dear. I have no doubt.
Patience will win out in the end." He squeezed her hand.

"You really know Tudor poetry."

"It might surprise you just what I do know." There was a
sensual suggestion to his statement.

Kim removed her hand from his and took a sip of cold
water. The restaurant suddenly seemed overly warm.

"So how did you spend your vacation?" He obviously
sensed she wanted to change the topic.

She shook her head. "I didn't do very much. Mike briefly

involved me in one of his homicide investigations. It was fascinating."

Don's eyes widened in alarm. "He shouldn't have done that. The kind of work he does is far too dangerous."

"He was just asking questions. No weapons were drawn."

Don's fine, handsome features continued to show concern. "Kim, I know how obsessed you became last fall trying to discover who killed Lorette Campbell, but that was an aberration. And it nearly cost you your own life. You're not the sort of woman who should be involved in such matters. Perhaps you'll consider it jealousy on the part of a rival for your affections, but I don't think Lieutenant Gardner is someone you should continue seeing."

"Let's not talk about that anymore," she said in a firm voice. Kim tried to sound confident, but her feelings were ambivalent.

THEY WERE DRIVING BACK to April Nevins' street and not the least bit happy about it.

"Ever feel we're getting into a rut with this case? If I were truly psychic, I'd probably be discussing *déjà vu,*" Gardner said lightly, trying to cheer his partner's gloomy mood, although he felt every bit as despondent as Bert.

"If you were psychic, *we'd* have found Sonny before anything bad happened to him."

Unfortunately, he had to agree with Bert about that. After parking the car, they made their way through the brambles and fir trees. The two patrolmen who caught the call stood in a slight clearing that appeared to overlook a jagged ravine.

"We located your man, Lieutenant. Male, Caucasian, six feet one, two hundred pounds, blond hair, blue eyes, late teens."

"And you knew right away it was Sonny Blake?" Bert asked.

The older patrolman shrugged. "The wallet was on him

with I.D. and a paycheck. Whoever nailed him wasn't a robber."

"Where is he?" Gardner asked. One of the patrolmen pointed downward to the bottom of the ravine.

"Some woman called it in. Her sons were playing over here and saw the body."

Bert took the lead and Gardner followed her down. It was Sonny all right; there wasn't any doubt. He felt a deep sense of regret, of wasted potential, as he looked at the twisted life-less thing before him. Bert knelt down to examine Sonny's remains.

"Neck's broken. Quite a fall he took."

"I don't see the kind of bruises that would indicate he was in a fight."

"No, nothing like that. But he's been down here a couple of days. No doubt about that." It was clear that Bert had seen her share of homicides.

It was a lot harder walking up, but he managed it, nego-tiating the brambles with caution. He began looking around for indications that a struggle had taken place here; there weren't any.

"Looks like an accident to me," the younger patrolman said, voicing his opinion with the certainty of unquestion-ing self-assurance.

"Yeah, usually when they're pushed, there's signs of a fight," agreed the second uniform.

"Unless the victim doesn't suspect the other person. It's not too difficult to push someone off a cliff if it's unexpected, even when it's a male that size. A woman could manage it as long as there was the element of surprise. She wouldn't even need great strength." Gardner realized that he was thinking out loud.

Bert exchanged a long look with him. "It could be any of them." She seemed lost in some sort of disturbing pattern of thought, electric eyes moving restlessly back and forth. "Weird, isn't it?"

"What's that?"

"Louise Scofield accidentally falls down a flight of stairs. Sonny Blake accidentally drops off a cliff."

"So what are you saying? Scofield is our murderer?"

Bert shrugged. "I don't believe in coincidence."

"You think Scofield wasn't satisfied with killing Bradshaw. He suspected his wife was involved with Sonny, so he killed him, as well?"

"Don't poke fun at my ideas." She was clearly beyond annoyed. Gardner forgot sometimes how sensitive she was. "You tell me what does make sense? Even if it was April who killed Bradshaw the way Sonny must have thought, he'd already told us about her. She had no reason to kill him."

"There could have been more to it. He might have had a lot more to tell us."

"About April?"

"Or someone else. Who knows?"

"I don't think that dumb kid knew who murdered Bradshaw any more than we do," Bert said.

"We'll never know for sure now," Gardner said. "But don't forget, the kid was on duty the evening of Bradshaw's death. He might have seen or heard something that didn't strike him as important but would give the murderer away."

"We can forget about finding out any of that now," Bert said glumly.

"There could be a way—if we were able to recreate the events of that evening. Maybe we could put it all together." Gardner was thoughtful.

"I don't think it would work," Bert said skeptically.

"Ever read about group encounter sessions?"

"A little. What's that got to do with this case?"

"I have a feeling our suspects would very much like to get

us off their backs. They might be in a mood to cooperate. Ever see one of those sessions in action?"

"Never."

"Too bad, neither have I. But I think we can handle it. As I understand it, the group turns on its individual members during the course of discussion. Each person is forced to face the truth about him or herself. The group can be very supportive but it also can be merciless. It's a truth hunt with nowhere to hide."

Bert still looked dubious. "Sounds more like a witch hunt. I don't like it. I think you're taking your nickname around headquarters too literally. No one should play the part of a psychologist unless he's qualified."

"In my own way, I am qualified. Besides, I'm not out to destroy these people. I only want to find Bradshaw's killer. Our suspects haven't faced each other. If anyone is lying, and we have to assume someone is, it's bound to show up through direct confrontation. There doesn't even have to be anything specific. It could be just a facial expression or vocal inflection that tips us."

"It's not standard police procedure," Bert objected. "We could lose control of the situation. Anything could happen. It's like throwing them into a pressure cooker. Turn up the heat and there's bound to be an explosion."

"Since when are you behaving like a regulation issue police detective? And who was the Machiavellian who told me it's results that count?"

She conceded the point moodily. "Who's going to tell Mrs. Blake that Sonny's dead?" Bert asked.

Gardner could see it was something his partner would rather not do. He also knew that talking to Mrs. Blake was not going to be easy. He anticipated a miserable scene with hysterical tears and anguished accusations. At least he could spare Bert that. "I'll do it myself later this evening. But first, we've got to get back to headquarters and issue personal in-

vitations for our little splash party tomorrow evening. A trib-
ute to Richard Bradshaw, you might say, kind of like a wake,
only without the kind words and Irish whiskey."

"Bradshaw seems to have touched all of them in some
way," Bert observed.

"More like contaminated them."

Several people had gathered to watch with the usual
curiosity and sick fascination that mortal beings have for
scenes of accidents and deaths. The crowd grew in size
as police pictures were taken of Sonny Blake's body, and
crime technicians searched the brush for evidence. An ambulance came for Sonny, and the two patrolmen climbed
down the ravine to help the paramedics bring up the body.
An assistant county medical examiner peered through thick,
black-framed eyeglasses as he gave the ambulance workers
authoritative directions for removal of the body after a cur-
sory examination.

The waste of human life disturbed Gardner deeply. As
a policeman, he knew something that the average citizen
was spared—the agony suffered by the victims of crime and
their families. It was an ugly, unpleasant knowledge he did
not dwell upon. But he knew his job involved an obligation
to the victims. They came in all sexes, ages, races and reli-
gions. Crime, like sickness and death, was egalitarian.

He guessed the do-gooders were right when they de-
clared that criminals were also victims, but was that supposed to wipe out personal responsibility? He never accepted
the notion that criminals were mere victims of bad environ-
ment. One killer had even blamed a murder he'd commit-
ted on "lousy luck." Gardner wouldn't buy that. People were
always looking for cop-outs: do what you want then give excuses when you get caught. Blame everyone and everything.
Killers never took personal responsibility for their own actions. He might not have liked Bradshaw as a person, but his

own duty was clear: Bradshaw's killer must be found. And now there was Sonny's death, as well, clearly connected. He owed the boy something.

BACK AT HEADQUARTERS, Gardner phoned the hospital first to find out if Mrs. Scofield had been released and learned that she would be allowed to leave the hospital on the following morning.

"Wish we didn't have to bother her," Bert said.

"She's part of it," Gardner responded.

Bert shook her head in a gesture of denial. "I don't think she killed Bradshaw, and she couldn't have murdered Sonny."

THEY DIVIDED UP the calls between them. Everyone was at home except for April Nevins, and Bert located her at the Galaxy Lounge. As they finished, Captain Nash came toward Gardner.

"You and St. Croix in my office now. Someone wants to talk to you." The Captain looked tense and irritable, making Gardner suspect that they were on his shit list again.

"Mr. Page, this is Lieutenant Gardner. He's in charge of the Bradshaw case."

Gardner considered Page thoughtfully. The land developer had the look of a shrewd businessman. He was middle-aged, average-looking, with olive skin, brown eyes and black hair, oily enough to skid on. He wore a blue summer suit that looked conservative but expensive. Gardner judged his height to be about five foot seven, maybe even shorter since he was obviously wearing lifts in his shoes. Page looked in good physical condition, not the kind of man who was content to sit still behind a desk for very long, but no one would have guessed from his appearance alone that he was the richest and most influential person living in Webster Township.

"Mr. Page would like to know, Mike, how we're coming along with the investigation on the Bradshaw case. He's here to get a firsthand report. I'll just let you talk." Nash hastily left them alone, shutting his office door behind him.

Gardner realized that he'd been put on the defensive, but he wasn't about to respond too quickly. He intended to turn the situation around if he could. Sure enough, when Gardner made no effort to speak and sat simply staring at Page, the builder became uneasy and started squirming in his chair.

"What's going on with this Bradshaw investigation?" he demanded finally, his voice like gravel.

"Nothing much to tell at the moment. We will be allowing the club to reopen day after tomorrow." He assumed that's what the builder was most concerned about. He had no intention of telling Page anything relevant to the case.

"About time the place reopened," Page grumbled in a raspy voice. "This damned murder happened on my property. It makes me look bad. I got a right to be informed of what you're doing to solve the crime."

"The homicide is getting our full and careful attention." Gardner's tone was placating. "We just don't have anything to report right at this moment."

"Does that mean the murder will go unsolved?"

Was it possible? Gardner thought he detected a certain degree of guarded hopefulness in Page's question; it puzzled him. He studied Page speculatively. "I don't want you to get the wrong idea. We have some very strong leads. It's just that we can't talk about them as yet. You can appreciate that, I'm sure."

Page fidgeted noticeably. "Listen," the builder said in a voice that was suddenly almost a whisper. "I know what you guys make a year. This case is important to me. I'll give you a nice healthy early Christmas bonus if you report back to me person ally on what you find out. Just give me a rundown on everything you uncover."

"As it happens, I don't spend a lot on Christmas," Gardner said, "so I won't be needing your money."

"Hey, everybody cuts himself a piece of the pie when it's offered. You wouldn't be doing anything wrong."

"I'm on a diet. I'm definitely off pie."

"Wise ass, huh? Well, you'll be sorry. I'll have a word with your superiors."

"Then I'd be forced to go public with the fact that you tried to bribe a public servant."

"Make it ten large apiece. How's that for an offer?"

Gardner exchanged a meaningful look with Bert then shook his head adamantly.

"I get it—you thieves want me to up the offer!"

"Up yours," Bert responded with an appropriate gesture. "Put your offer where the sun don't shine."

Page rose to his feet, his face drained of color.

"Just take it easy," Gardner said. "Detective St. Croix may lack subtlety, but she is correct in implying that your offer does not interest us."

Bert stood over the man, looming ominously. "You weren't getting the message."

"We'll be gathering together all the people who were involved with Mr. Bradshaw. It's scheduled for tomorrow evening at the swim club. Maybe you would like to join us? Then you could get your information firsthand. And it won't cost you a dime."

Page curtly refused and abruptly left the office. Gardner glanced at his partner. He could tell by the questioning expression on Bert's face that she was having similar suspicions regarding Page. The builder's concern seemed to go far beyond business. There was nothing to directly connect Page to the case. Still, Gardner was left with nagging doubts, wondering if he could have maneuvered Page into coming to the pool club the next evening had he been a little more clever.

"What he's so afraid of?" Bert mirrored his own thoughts.

"Does make a person wonder," Gardner agreed.

FOURTEEN

KIM HAD JUST arrived home when her telephone rang in the apartment.

"How was your first day back?" Mike asked. She'd know that deep baritone voice anywhere. It always served to send a rush of excitement through her.

"It was fine."

"You see Bernard?"

"How did you know?"

"Cop instinct," he told her. "I still think I ought to shoot him."

"And I still think that isn't funny."

"So you told him you're my sex slave and he needs to hit the road?"

"I did no such thing. He took me out to lunch to welcome me back."

She heard him mutter something under his breath. She probably should have been annoyed. But instead, she was smiling to herself. It was kind of amazing having two sexy, attractive men interested in her. Definitely a novelty worth savoring.

"I have an invitation to extend to you. It's really a favor. I want you to join me at the swim club tomorrow evening about seven p.m. It involves the murder investigation. Can you do it?"

She hesitated, remembering Don Bernard's admonishment. "I don't think I would be very helpful to you."

"I respect your insights. I think you might pick up on things other people would miss."

She was puzzled and asked for an explanation. After he'd finished talking and explaining, she was thoughtful.

"Kim, are you still there?"

"Yes, I'm just wondering what you'll be able to find out."

"Do you know any of those people?"

She frowned thoughtfully. "I might have seen them around. I don't go to the swim club often, but I did join this summer. I have to be honest with you. I still don't think I can be of any use in this situation."

"Why don't you let me decide that? You have a unique sensibility, a kind of sixth sense. And La Reine Gardens is your home turf."

"You just want to show off how good you are at your job," she teased.

"You got me there. I'm out to impress you by any means possible, fair or foul. It's all part of my diabolical plan to win you." Even the inflection of his voice was sexy.

She made up her mind. "If you really want me there, then I'll come."

"Thanks, I appreciate it."

She caressed the phone. "One thing, Mike, you don't need to impress me. I'm already impressed." She preferred he didn't know just how much.

GARDNER ARRIVED WITH Bert St. Croix at the swim club around six-thirty in the evening. They were not the first ones there: the Wallings and Scofields sat near casements of flowers where long shadows protected them from the fading sunlight. The moon would soon be rising, a crescent that would give little illumination to the coming night. *Lights, camera, action,* Gardner thought.

Puffing vigorously on a long cigar, Martin Walling sat slightly apart from the two women. Bill Scofield, dressed in tennis whites, looked ready to pose for a magazine commercial. The only thing missing was the little alligator on his shirt. When Scofield saw them, he went over and sat protectively close to his wife. Gardner found some irony in that.

The Scofields gave the impression of the perfect all-American couple. Louise was elegantly dressed in a sleeveless blouse of green silk with white linen slacks. The blouse emphasized her huge eyes and brought attention to her striking beauty. Only the cast on her left arm and some bruises were reminders of her recent ordeal.

Joan Walling looked even plainer sitting beside Louise Scofield, and yet there was a quickness and intelligence in her face that Gardner could not ignore. They all appeared nervous and unhappy, which didn't much surprise him. Bill Scofield stood up as he and Bert approached the two couples.

"I don't understand why you wanted us to come here, Lieutenant."

Gardner gave no real answer except to say it would all be explained in due time. Then he looked around for Martha Rhoades. He found her in the office and stuck his head in. "When everyone gets here, I'd like you to join us."

"Me?" she asked in alarm.

"Yes. I think you can help."

"Of course, if I'm needed," she replied dutifully.

Cheryl McNeill came a few minutes later. She was just as attractive as he remembered. Her long, silky brown hair was swept up elaborately in a braided crown on top of her head, and she wore form-fitting shorts that showed her willowy figure to advantage. He wondered if she had modeled at one time, because she carried herself extremely well. He could picture her on the catwalk.

"I'm not late, am I?" Cheryl asked. Her clear brown eyes scanned the group with interest.

"Right on time. Why don't you join the others?"

She glanced at them disdainfully. "If it's all right with you, I'd rather walk around until you need me."

"Certainly." He watched her walk away, head high, back straight, regal bearing.

"They're all here except April Nevins," Bert said. "Maybe she forgot and went to work instead."

"I doubt it. She said she'd get tonight off, didn't she?"

"Yeah, she did. They all look so straight. It's hard to believe one of them could be a murderer."

"Might be none of them." He couldn't help wishing George Page were here tonight. He had a feeling about the man, a hunch, that Page was somehow involved.

"I hope you know what you're doing."

"Thanks for the vote of confidence," Gardner said with a touch of amusement.

April Nevins made her entrance at seven. Martha Rhoades appeared outraged while the others gawked, except for Joan Walling who merely looked on indifferently. Dressed in a black wet-look string bikini, April's well-endowed body was a sight to behold. Gardner signaled Cheryl McNeill; the group assembled together, clustered around the Scofields. Gardner couldn't help thinking that Bradshaw would have appreciated this get-together in his honor.

He was just about to phone Kim on her cell phone to make sure she hadn't forgotten, when she appeared.

"Were you thinking about me?" She gave him a warm smile that practically melted his bones. Her demure appearance might not excite many other men's lust in contrast to April Nevins, but he knew better than anyone how really beautiful and hot she was. Kim Reynolds was a master of disguise. Lucky for him he had x-ray vision.

"Why don't we seat ourselves in a circle?" Gardner suggested in a deceptively pleasant manner.

The chairs were rearranged easily since they were lightweight plastic. Kim sat to his right, while Bert seated herself to his left. Everyone focused on Gardner. "Thank you all for helping us with our investigation."

Gardner was suddenly aware that Bert's attention was drawn behind him. He stood up and turned around. Mrs. Blake was standing there.

"I came like you asked."

"Thank you, did you bring it?"

"The ones that belong to the pool? Yes, I got them right here." She fumbled around in her purse, finally removing a metal ring with some keys on it.

Gardner took them from her. "Ms. Rhoades, whose keys are these?" He held them up.

"It's the spare set. As I told you, my keys are on an identical ring."

"Could you be so kind as to get yours?"

"Now?" Her narrow lips tightened.

"Yes, we'll wait."

In the tense silence that ensued, Gardner observed the unmarked car he'd requested as a backup positioned on the street outside the club. Drew Mitchell and another detective, whom he knew to be Chief Morgan's nephew, were looking very bored, slouched down in a black sedan.

Miss Rhoades returned, holding out a set of keys.

"You are right. These do appear to be identical." Gardner turned to the others. "Just so we all understand what this is about, I'd like to point out to you that whoever murdered Mr. Bradshaw apparently had Sonny's set of keys and probably still does." He looked sharply from one person to the other, but saw no unusual reactions. He turned to Mrs. Blake. "Thank you for coming. I realize how difficult this is for you."

Her watery blue eyes blinked in confusion. "That's all? I don't understand. You said by bringing those keys I'd be helping you find out what happened to my boy. Aren't you going to arrest somebody?" Mrs. Blake seemed to be working herself up.

He didn't respond. The truth was, he'd half-expected her

to make some sort of a scene; she was the sort of person who responded to stress and adversity with outbursts of angst and tears.

"One of them killed my boy!" She pointed an accusing finger at the group in general. "Sonny was meant to be a farmer just like generations before him. When the developers first came, they got folks like us who wasn't making a decent living off the land to sell their farms for next to nothing. Then they built lots of them houses and apartments. More city people came out here. Their children cluttered our schools so they had to build more schools and then they raised our taxes. Our way of life was destroyed. City people. Scum, I hate you all! You corrupted my boy with your sinful ways."

Everyone looked away, avoiding her malevolent gaze, but Mrs. Blake was determined to continue her diatribe. "It's her fault most of all. Tramp, whore, slut! I hope they hang you. Your life for his, like it says in the Bible." Mrs. Blake had turned her attention to April Nevins. The older woman was trembling. "Look at the way she dresses, exposing her flesh like that! It's indecent and sinful! How can you seduce young boys, harlot? Where's your conscience?" She raised her hand as if to strike April across the face.

Bert quickly sprang to restrain her. "Time to go home now."

"Let me be! She's responsible for Sonny's death. Sonny told me about her. Aren't you going to arrest her?"

April was livid. "You lunatic, I never killed anyone. Your son had some marbles missing, just like you. And he had plenty of experience with women before he ever met me. Your kid was far from innocent."

"Liar!" Mrs. Blake screamed out hysterically. Then tears began to flow down her faded cheeks. She sobbed convulsively and clung to Gardner for support.

"Keep her away from me, Lieutenant. I swear, I'm not responsible for what happens if you don't." April rushed off in the direction of the ladies' restroom.

"Detective, would you escort Mrs. Blake out?" He turned back to Sonny's mother. "We'll have you driven home."

"No, my daughter-in-law is waiting in her car for me."

Kim got to her feet. "I'll walk you to your car." Mrs. Blake seemed to respond better to Kim, to her innate kindness. In any case, she allowed Kim to take her arm, then rested heavily on her as they walked toward the gate.

"Poor woman," Gardner overheard Louise Scofield mumble softly to no one in particular. Cheryl McNeill stood up and resumed her restless pacing. Martin Walling continued to puff ferociously on his cigar. Only his wife seemed calm, composed, almost totally detached. Gardner walked over to the water fountain and took a long, cool drink. He was at some distance from the others, but could hear the hushed undercurrent of conversation. He wondered if anything of significance was being said.

Bert joined him. She brought her mouth down and drank deeply from the fountain. "Water's icy cold. I suppose you had some reason for setting that up?" Her facial muscles were taut. "In your own way, you're tougher than I am."

"No one felt much grief over Bradshaw's death. I don't think any one of them really cares whether or not his murderer is ever caught. But in Sonny's case, there should be some sorrow or guilt. A possible killer was brought face to face with Mrs. Blake's suffering which occurred as a direct result of the boy's murder. I'm hoping that it will have some psychological effect, no matter how minimal."

"Psych out the killer? I wonder."

"I'm not convinced either death was premeditated."

"Sonny's death might have been accidental," Bert agreed.

"Right. The motive must have been fear, panic. My thinking is that if we can upset the murderer enough, he or she will give something away."

"Right now, it seems we're long on motive and short on evidence."

April Nevins reappeared. Gardner could see that her eyes were slightly red and puffy. Nevertheless, she walked erect, head raised high, tossing her mane of tawny hair defiantly.

"Ms. Nevins, you provide magnificent scenery, but it might prove a distraction for the male element. Do you have something you could wear over your bathing suit?"

She removed a lacy black shift from her bag and put it on without comment. Gardner was very much aware that Louise, Cheryl and April were all beautiful women, each in her own way. If his ex-wife were here, without a doubt, she'd have made some cutting comment to the effect that she understood why he was so wrapped up in his work.

It occurred to him the common denominator in Bradshaw's attraction to each of these women was not actually their beauty, striking as it was. Most men desired a particular type of woman. Over and over, they selected women from the same mold. Some men liked their women dominant, others submissive. Most men were drawn to physical attractiveness, some to intellect, charm or wealth. The list of possibilities was innumerable. Bradshaw obviously admired beauty in his women. But more importantly, he looked for variety. Gardner saw Bradshaw as a man who was edgy and easily bored. Therefore, he always looked for the unusual—possibly even the bizarre? He would also crave admiration from women as well, since the man obviously had a major ego. Gardner was convinced that understanding Bradshaw's relationships with women was somehow essential to solving the case.

"Lieutenant, I really don't think my wife should be subjected to this."

Bill Scofield broke Gardner's train of thought, bringing him back to the situation at hand. Gardner was aware that Scofield's short fuse might present a problem; he resolved to handle him cautiously.

"You and your wife *are* involved in this."

Scofield's sapphire eyes hardened to glittering brilliance. "You know damn well Lou was just released from the hospital this morning. Hearing a bunch of insults and dirty accusations tossed back and forth won't do her any good, and it won't help you find out who killed Bradshaw. Frankly, I don't give a damn."

Gardner reflected that Scofield would have made a respectable Rhett Butler.

Louise reached out and put her pale, slender hand gently on her husband's muscled, tan bicep. "Bill, it's all right. I can take it. You don't have to worry about me."

"You're too fragile for this. I want to take you home."

"We have to stay," she replied calmly. Then she turned to Gardner. "I haven't murdered anyone. I'm not afraid to be here."

"It seems your wife has made her own decision."

"This is stupid," Scofield said angrily.

"You haven't any special reason for opposing it, do you? Is there a possibility that you've been holding back information or covering up to protect someone?"

"Of course not!"

Gardner watched him intently as did Bert.

"We're only here to talk." Gardner used a reassuring tone of voice.

"Could you please put out that foul-smelling cigar?" Cheryl said to Martin Walling, who was sitting to her right.

"Free country, isn't it?"

"If you don't put that thing out, I'm going to throw up all over you."

He gave her a dirty look, was about to say something, but thought better of it and finally tossed his cigar to the ground and stomped it out. As he stepped on it, Martha Rhoades let out a small but very audible gasp.

"Smoking is not allowed here," she said addressing the

group in general. Her chilling gaze rested on Walling. She bent down and picked the offending item off the ground ever so carefully as if it were a poisonous snake, then placed it in a trash container with emphasis. "Evil creature," she muttered audibly.

Kim quietly rejoined the group, exchanging a troubled look with Gardner. Sometimes he could read exactly what she was thinking, but at the moment, there was too much happening for him to directly focus on her.

Gardner could feel the tension stirring in the summer air. "There are a few questions I didn't get to ask you at the hospital, some points that need clarifying," he said addressing Scofield again.

"Like what?" Scofield asked irritably.

Gardner continued in a calm, polite voice that nevertheless conveyed authority. "You were vague about what started your belief that Bradshaw was having an affair with your wife. It's very important, vital, in fact, that you tell us everything."

Scofield's hand tightened on the arm of the chair so that his knuckles whitened. "In front of everyone?"

"Especially in front of them."

"I can't."

"Tell us the truth." Gardner gave Scofield a hard look.

Scofield lowered his eyes and acquiesced grudgingly. "There was an evening when Lou said she was going shopping with her friend. I didn't want her to go so I made a fuss over it. But she wouldn't back down, acted like her life depended on it. That just wasn't like her. She always yielded when I insisted."

"There must have been more to it."

"I neglected to mention it occurred on the same day Bradshaw told me that he was seeing a married woman, someone I knew quite well. He also mentioned he would be seeing her that evening."

"That was the evening I went to the doctor to find out if I

was pregnant," Lou said, her voice oddly detached and distanced.

"For Christ's sake, why didn't you just tell me?" Scofield turned an anguished look on his wife. "We never used to keep secrets from each other."

She sighed deeply as a sudden breeze mussed her auburn tresses. "I wasn't sure what your reaction would be. How many times did you tell me you thought it was wrong to bring children into our terrible world? I thought I'd better be sure I was pregnant before I told you anything. I was afraid of making you angry at me."

"What else was there?" Gardner pressed.

"That's all there was to it. Okay?"

He knew that Scofield was holding back, hiding something, and wondered if it were particularly damaging. "It's not okay. You're not being straight with us."

The final rays of sunlight glinted off Scofield's sandy hair. He stood straight and tall looking like a vengeful Nordic god. "It has no bearing on the case, Lieutenant."

"You're not the one to decide that, Mr. Scofield. You're too deeply involved."

Scofield looked away. "I gave my word, and I take that very seriously. In spite of what you might think, I am a moral man. I live by a strict ethical code of values, although they may be different from those of some people."

"I respect your feelings, Mr. Scofield, but holding back information of any kind makes you and your wife both suspect. You don't want that, do you? We must have all of the truth." Gardner had no intention of backing off. This was too important.

Louise took his hand and pressed it. "Please, tell them what they want to know."

Scofield looked at Joan Walling. "I'm sorry," he muttered, then he turned back, his cerulean eyes fixed on Gardner.

"After Lou left the apartment that night, I got a call from Joan. She asked to speak to Lou. Naturally, I became upset."

When Scofield paused, Gardner prodded him on. "Why would the call upset you? Doesn't your wife normally receive phone calls from Mrs. Walling?"

"Yes, but Lou told me that she and Joan would be out together shopping." His reluctance was evident.

"I see. Mrs. Walling was the girlfriend your wife claimed to be spending the evening with." Gardner pressed on. "Mrs. Scofield, wasn't it rather careless of you not to clear the story with Mrs. Walling?"

"I did. Joan promised to cover for me. I don't understand." Louise Scofield's expression was one of bewilderment.

"I forgot," Joan responded quietly. She avoided Louise's gaze.

"How could you? I even reminded you that afternoon. You knew I was going to the doctor. If Bill ever asked you about the evening, you were supposed to verify my story."

"When I phoned, I didn't realize you'd already left."

"I don't believe you. I told you the time of my appointment." Louise's face flushed with anger.

"She blew it. Just write it off, okay?" Scofield sounded embarrassed.

"Mrs. Walling, why didn't you tell Mr. Scofield where his wife really was at that point?"

"He didn't ask." Her voice was barely more than a whisper. "Anyway, Lou didn't want him to know."

"Bill, why didn't you come out and ask me that night, instead of thinking all those horrible things?"

Scofield shifted uneasily in his chair. "Joan was mortified. She knew you'd be angry with her if you found out what she'd done. So she begged me not to tell you. I gave her my word. Joan does value your friendship. Sometimes, Lou, you're not the most forgiving person."

"I've had a very good teacher in that regard." Her eyes

were bright with unshed tears. "You're being awfully chivalrous toward Joan, but then you always are to women who play up to your male ego. I can't remember a waitress who smiled at you that didn't get overtipped in return."

"What has that got to do with anything?"

"Joan was trying to cause trouble between us. I see that now. She was jealous of our relationship and you fell right into her trap."

"Who confided to her in the first place? She was your friend."

"She was never my friend. I just didn't know it."

Bert moved toward them but addressed her comments to Gardner. "I checked out Mrs. Scofield's story with her doctor. She was in his office nearly two hours on the evening in question."

Louise smiled at Bert with an expression on her face indicating that she considered Bert an ally; she sensed Bert's sympathy and instinctively trusted her.

Out of the corner of his eye, Gardner could see Martin Walling beginning to stir restlessly, like a bear coming out of hibernation. He turned his heavy body uncomfortably in his chair, perspiration standing out on the round bald spot near the top of his head.

"Look here, Lieutenant," Walling began, "I don't see any reason why Joan and I should have to hang around here. You seem to be dredging up a lot of dirt and destroying some good friendships in the process. And that's all you've managed to accomplish. If you have any specific questions to ask us, my wife and I are more than willing to cooperate, but I resent what you're doing here."

Gardner accepted Walling's criticism calmly. "You're right, Mr. Walling. But I do have some definite questions for you. So count on staying for a while."

"There isn't a thing I can add to what I've already told you.

I've been completely open with you, not like some people."
He tossed an accusing look in Scofield's direction.

"Not completely open, Mr. Walling. But then, a man in
your position can't be expected to do that, can he?"

The insinuation brought more beads of perspiration to
Walling's forehead. "What do you mean by that?"

"I was thinking about those warehouse robberies. You did
know we'd find out, didn't you? The way each job was pulled
indicates there was an inside man involved. That man had
to be you, Mr. Walling." Gardner paused giving Walling a
chance to absorb what he'd said.

"What the hell are you saying? You must have a few
screws missing!" Walling's fat face turned the color of flaming cherries jubilee.

"What if I were to tell you that a certain security guard
remembers talking to you about his eating habits just a week
or so before the robbery at the North Ridge warehouse?"

"We can trace you to the other two jobs, as well," Bert
said, a note of menace in her voice.

"Coincidence. Nothing more. I talk to lots of people.
That's part of my job." Walling wriggled in his chair like a
trout on the hook.

"Yet you managed to find out the schedule of each security guard."

"I know my rights. I don't have to discuss this with you
until I see a lawyer."

"Of course not. We're not arresting you, and we're not
asking for a confession of guilt. Oh, just one other thing, we
know that Mr. Bradshaw had been doing some checking on
you himself. He found out what we did. I suppose he must
have mentioned it to you?"

Walling managed a look of surprise that seemed genuine.
"No, he didn't." Walling's hand trembled as he reached into
his pocket and brought forth another cigar.

Cheryl McNeill immediately became agitated, but Martin

ignored her. From the look he gave her it was obvious that he held her in contempt.

"Do I have to hang around while this huge blob of protoplasm puffs pollution into my face?" Cheryl rose to her feet, hugging her slender arms around her willowy body.

"Don't even try to light it," Bert said, pointing a finger at Walling as if she were aiming a revolver. The short, fat man looked up at the intimidating figure and quickly put the cigar away.

"I got no luck with women," Walling muttered. No one looked sympathetic.

"Please let me go," Cheryl said. "I have nothing further to say."

"I have to insist that you remain," Gardner responded.

"But why? I wasn't here that evening."

"Can you offer some proof of that?"

"No one saw me. Ask any of them."

"We can't ask Sonny, can we?"

"I was at the apartment all evening."

"Any phone calls that you made or received during that time? Did you visit any of the neighbors or talk to one of them outside? Did anyone drop by?"

"No, I was completely alone for the entire evening. I sat and watched television. I waited with dinner until eight. When Rick didn't show up, I ate lightly and went to bed early. I never left the apartment." The look on her face defied him to prove otherwise.

"That may very well be true, but we have only your word for it. There's no way for us to verify your alibi."

She frowned worriedly, deep furrows invading her smooth forehead.

Gardner pursued his advantage. "Is it true that Mr. Bradshaw arranged for you to have an abortion several months ago?"

"What?" She was completely taken aback.

"Please answer."

"No one knew about that. How did you find out? Wait a minute." Cheryl turned to April Nevins. "That old woman had you pegged right—you are a bitch!"

"Say what you like, but you had a better motive for murdering Rick than any of us," April countered.

"Rick was going to marry me. Why should I kill him?" Cheryl raised her head haughtily.

"Come off it! That's a load of crap. He wouldn't marry you or any other woman. He was a user, a taker, and you knew it!" The two women confronted each other angrily.

"The last time I spoke to him, Rick told me we were going back to California, that his job here was about done. All he had left was to turn in his reports and recommendations. He said he was going to remove himself from the scene."

"Did he use those exact words?" Gardner asked. "The term *remove,* for instance, did he actually say that?"

Cheryl was thoughtful for a moment. "Yes, that was what he said. I remember it clearly."

"He wasn't talking about me," April responded hotly.

"I would like to go over what actually happened on the evening Mr. Bradshaw died. I'd appreciate it if we could be as specific as possible. Try to remember everything. If anyone recalls something different or can add to what's being said, don't hesitate to interrupt. It could make a difference."

The sun was setting, disappearing down through the pine trees, a huge, fiery ball that assured yet another hot tomorrow. Suddenly it was gone, and only the crescent moon was visible. With the coming of twilight, the people around him were momentarily mute. In the austere silence, the dark, rippling pool exerted an eerie, hypnotic fascination. But it was essentially a body of stagnant water—not like the ocean he loved or the small brook that rippled through the woodlands behind his own backyard. He could almost believe that beneath the tranquil surface of the pool lurked some hideous, amorphous monster poised and ready to strike. A sudden chill descended into his bones. He determined to shake off the fantasy, forcing his mind to return to the realities of the Bradshaw investigation. But the feeling of menace lurked, refusing to go away. Was someone else about to die? Kim tossed him a worried look. Somehow, he realized, she sensed what he was thinking. The connection, the bond between them, was stronger than ever.

FIFTEEN

"Mrs. Scofield, let's start with you. What time did you arrive at the pool?"

"Let me see, I went to work that day but left a little early. I arrived here about six o'clock."

"Where did you sit?"

"Right about where I am now. I prefer the shade and sit in approximately the same spot each day."

"Was anyone with you?"

"Joan arrived around the same time. We sat together. That was the usual."

"How long did you sit together?"

"The whole time we were here."

"Which was until when?"

She pressed her lips together in concentration. "Until around seven-thirty I think."

"And you both left the same time?"

She answered in the affirmative. It was not the answer he expected.

"Mr. Scofield, what about you? When did you get here?"

"Close to six-thirty."

"You didn't come with your wife then."

"No, I was later leaving the city. I also dropped by the apartment and changed."

"What were your actions on arriving here?"

"I talked to Lou and Joan for a few minutes. Then I went to the tennis courts to practice my serve."

"When did you leave the courts?"

Scofield set his jaw as he paused to reflect. Gardner observed the hard, angular lines in Scofield's face and sensed a tenacity of near ruthless dimension; a handsome man but capable of violence.

"I stayed on the court past seven, took a quick swim, then went in for a shower. I remember glancing at the clock over the snack bar as I came out of the water, and it was about seven-fifteen."

"Ms. McNeill, you've told us you weren't here that evening."

"That's right." Her voice held a distinct chill.

He'd half expected that she would change her story. "Of course, you don't have any proof as to where you were, but we'll let that pass for now."

He turned to April Nevins who struck a provocative pose. "When did you arrive here?"

"I guess it was around six-thirty or so. Bill was on the tennis court."

"And you did what?"

"Went over to talk with Lou and Joan, but I got bored after a short time."

"Any special reason for the boredom?"

"Lou wasn't feeling so good. She was tired. Joan's not much of a talker in general and that night, she seemed particularly remote, positively autistic. Anyway, I got restless. I'm the kind of woman who needs stimulating activity. It's my nature. Since I had my tennis racket with me and Bill was alone on the court, I figured being with him would be more fun. Besides, he always said if I asked, he'd give me a few lessons. I thought it was a good time. I mean, Lou wasn't in any mood to play. Anyone could see that. So I went on the court and asked Bill to give me some pointers. He was real nice about it."

"When did you finish playing?"

"I don't know. I stopped when Bill did and took a swim

with him. It's really nice when the pool is empty like that. You feel like you own the place. Makes you feel rich."

"And after the swim?"

"I went into the changing room. I brought my work clothes with me because I had to go straight to the job. I was there by eight o'clock."

"What was Sonny doing during that time period?"

"I hardly noticed him."

Gardner raised his eyebrows; that didn't ring true. "Wasn't he around?"

"I remember he was playing basketball with a couple of boys outside the fence around the time I was talking to Lou and Joan."

"Anyone else around?"

She chewed on a fingernail. "The place was kind of deserted, like it always is at that hour."

"Ms. Rhoades, where were you?"

"What?" She gave a startled movement, as if someone had woken her from a deep sleep. "I already told you, Lieutenant," she responded irritably. "I was at home. Mother and I were together all evening watching television."

"And your mother will confirm that?"

"There might be some difficulty. Mother is partially paralyzed and has difficulty with her speech. That's why I'm home every evening. Someone has to be with her to take care of her needs. I must say I resent you questioning me about this." Her tone was scornful and condescending. "Naturally, I did not approve of Mr. Bradshaw's conduct, but I would hardly murder him for that."

"We have to check out all possibilities. I'm certain someone as thorough as yourself understands that." He could see his last statement appeased her injured pride. "Mr. Walling, when did you arrive?"

"Around seven. I can't give you the exact time though."

"And what did you do with yourself?"

Walling was perspiring profusely, although with the setting of the sun, a cool breeze had come up. "I went over to the tennis courts and watched Bill give April a tennis lesson."

"Is that true?" Gardner turned his gaze from April Nevins to Scofield. They both confirmed Martin Walling's story.

"Martin was watching," Scofield said.

"The pervert kept his eyes on my ass every time I bent over to pick up a ball." April turned on Martin Walling accusingly. "Don't think I didn't notice."

"All right, Mr. Walling, let's go on from there."

Walling dabbed at his beefy face with a rumpled handkerchief. "Not much to tell. I was too tired for a swim. When Bill and April left the court, I sat down with the girls. We talked for a bit and then everyone left."

"Martin has that effect on people," Cheryl remarked.

Walling threw a nasty grimace in her direction.

"I drove my wife over to the diner where we had dinner."

Scofield corroborated Walling's story. Gardner wasn't at all satisfied; something important was missing—what had he overlooked? He looked at Bert, who shrugged, then over at Kim, who shook her head.

"What was Sonny doing when you entered, Mr. Walling?"

"Doing?" Walling blinked his eyes as if the question struck him as being in some way peculiar.

"Was he still playing ball with his friends?"

"No, he was here."

"Did you speak to him?"

"Only briefly."

"What did you say?"

"Nothing much. I asked him if he'd seen my wife."

Gardner raised his brows. "Didn't you see her? She was supposedly sitting right in plain view. Why would you have to ask where she was?"

Walling opened and closed his pudgy fist reflexively. "At the time Lou was alone."

Gardner felt his heart begin to beat more rapidly. "Mrs. Scofield, didn't you tell us that you and Mrs. Walling were seated together the entire time?"

She seemed surprised. "Well, yes, I thought we were." Her eyes displayed confusion. "I don't seem to remember when Martin arrived at the pool. I only recall him joining us later on."

"That's because you were sleeping when I first came."

"I was asleep? I felt exhausted, but I didn't realize I dozed off."

Gardner wanted to probe the inconsistency further, sensing that something might be gained.

"Mrs. Walling, where were you at the time your husband arrived?"

"I went to the bathroom for a few minutes when Lou fell asleep."

"Did Sonny later come over to tell you that your husband was looking for you?"

"No, he did not," she replied dryly. She rubbed one well-tanned arm with the opposite hand as if she suddenly felt cold. Her small, wide-set eyes narrowed.

"How did Sonny answer when you asked him about your wife's whereabouts, Mr. Walling?"

"Just that she was around somewhere. He wasn't very specific."

"I see. Mrs. Walling, suppose we return to your motives for phoning Mr. Scofield while his wife was away."

"I thought I made that clear. It was a mistake, nothing more, nothing less." She tossed a white shawl around her bare, tan shoulders, shivering in her sundress, but her control appeared unbroken.

"Was your husband aware of the phone call?"

"No, he was away on business at the time."

"That's true," Louise Scofield interjected. "I thought the fact that Martin wasn't going to be home that night would make it easier for Joan to claim she was with me. I considered Joan the sort of person who would keep a secret, but definitely Martin couldn't."

Gardner turned back to Mrs. Walling. Their eyes met for a moment and then hers slid away. Gardner realized although she appeared calm outwardly, there was turbulence within: Joan Walling was not so much composed as withdrawn.

"I would like to know why you really made that call."

She sighed and folded her arms. Her feet were pressed against the ground like a soldier on the Western Front digging into the trenches for the anticipated siege ahead. "I've already given you my answer. I have nothing more to say."

"You were absent from sight at the time Richard Bradshaw was murdered. Your behavior and actions are suspicious."

"Neither Cheryl nor Martin can prove exactly where they were, either. Why single me out? I don't have a motive for killing Rick."

"Let's explore that a little. You deliberately caused friction between Mr. and Mrs. Scofield, your so-called friends. Was that in reality the action of a jealous woman?"

"Nothing of the sort. I dislike having to say this, but you're forcing it on me. I thought just as Bill did, that Lou was seeing Rick. I didn't believe her story about going to the doctor. I thought there would be a better chance for their marriage if Bill were wise to what was happening. Of course, I couldn't tell him outright. So I made the phone call to alert him."

"Very considerate of you."

"I thought so."

Louise Scofield's normally milky cheeks were crimson. Gardner sat back and waited for her reaction; he knew she couldn't afford to let such a damaging comment pass.

"Joan, you're lying! You knew I suspected I was pregnant. I told you so."

"Of course, but that doesn't prove Bill was the father."

Louise rose unsteadily to her feet, trembling. "What are you saying?"

"I thought it was very clear. Rick never hid his feelings for you, even if you were clever enough to hide yours. Not that I blame you. Bill does have an insanely jealous nature."

"Mrs. Walling, did Mrs. Scofield ever actually tell you in so many words that she was having an affair with Bradshaw?"

"Must I really answer that question?"

"It's extremely important."

"Very well then, the answer is—yes." Joan Walling fixed her eyes on the ground.

"She's lying! Why are you lying?" Lou looked ready to topple over.

Kim reached Louise before Bert did and helped her sit back down. Kim was trying to soothe the trembling woman.

"Lou confided certain details to me. I'd rather not go into the specifics in front of everyone, but I am willing to make a statement privately."

"That would indicate Mrs. Scofield had a motive for killing Mr. Bradshaw, to keep him quiet about the affair, but she obviously did not have the opportunity to commit the crime." He waited to see how the two women would react.

Joan Walling took a deep breath and then exhaled slowly. "I suppose I'll have to admit everything now. Lou left me for about twenty minutes when the others weren't around. She looked at her watch and then left without any explanation."

"Liar!" Louise Scofield cried out. She rose unsteadily to her feet and then she began to sway.

Kim stayed beside Louise and got her to sit down again. Gardner observed that Kim's expression was sympathetic and her manner gentle. Bill Scofield appeared to be in shock. There was a horrified expression on his face, as if everything he ever feared had been proven true. Scofield seemed to be paralyzed by suspicion and doubt.

"What time did Mrs. Scofield leave you?" Gardner asked.

"Very soon after I returned from the bathroom," Joan Walling replied.

"I thought you told me Mrs. Scofield was asleep then."

"She woke up and looked at her watch."

"Go on," he urged.

"Well, she got up, said she had something important to do and left by the front gate."

"No further explanation?"

"None."

"You didn't see where she went?"

"No, I picked up a book and started reading it."

"And you're sure that she was gone twenty minutes?"

"About that. I didn't time it. The book was engrossing."

"Could she have used the outside entrance to the utility room, left the same way, then returned to the club by the main gate?"

"Quite possible," Mrs. Walling agreed in a noncommittal tone of voice.

"Joan, what are you saying? You know I never left, not even for a moment. What are you trying to do to me?"

Gardner felt badly about putting Louise Scofield through this, but felt it was necessary.

"She's right, Mrs. Walling, what you're saying is both serious and damaging. You do realize that, don't you?" Gardner's tone underscored the gravity of the situation.

"Believe me, if there were any other way, I never would have told you this. I'm sorry I had to do it."

Louise Scofield turned to her husband. "You don't believe her, do you? Tell me that you don't!" Her eyes had a childlike appeal to them.

There was a terrible silence and then Scofield jutted his angular jaw. "At the hospital, I prayed that you'd be all right. I promised myself that I would never doubt you again. I made up my mind that I was going to change. I suppose I'm being put to the test. No matter what, I trust you, and I'll stand by you." He took his wife's hand in his own and held it tight.

Louise Scofield's eyes filled with tears; then she turned back to Gardner. "Joan is lying about me."

Gardner focused his steady gaze on her. "Why would she do that?"

Louise sank back in her chair. "Jealousy, maybe. I don't know." Her voice admitted defeat. But in her despair she held fast to her husband.

Gardner was pleased to see the couple reunited, even under such dire circumstances. It seemed that Scofield had character after all.

"Maybe I can help you out," Gardner said and turned back to Joan Walling. "We did talk about jealousy in regard to your accusation, and certainly there had to be an element of malice."

"That's ridiculous."

"Weren't you interested in Mr. Bradshaw yourself?"

"Not at all."

"Weren't you jealous of your friend's pregnancy?"

"Lieutenant, what are you trying to do to my wife?" Martin Walling sputtered.

"Just trying to get at the truth. It can sometimes be unpleasant."

"My wife isn't interested in other men."

"I hope that's true, Mr. Walling."

Gardner retained a sharp awareness of each person sitting with him in the circle. When Walling made his declaration, an expression of disbelief had appeared on April Nevins' face. Gardner was aware that the Wallings were not happily married; he wondered what gave April Nevins a similar conviction.

"Miss Nevins, what makes you think Mrs. Walling isn't satisfied with her husband?"

The others turned and stared at April. She looked upset and began biting her fingernails again.

"Look, nobody's completely satisfied, not ever. I know lots of married people. Most of them are miserable, either they're thinking of getting a divorce or they want to switch bed partners. That doesn't prove that Joan..." Her voice faltered.

Gardner found enough in her statement to initiate a further line of questioning. "You mentioned once that Mrs. Walling suggested you all take a holiday together. Did she also suggest switching partners during the holiday?"

"Yes, but just for the sake of variety."

"Was Mrs. Scofield agreeable to that?"

April appeared less than eager to take sides or betray confidences. He felt like a dentist trying to extract wisdom teeth without Novocain.

"Lou wasn't in favor of it. Neither was I. Like I told Joan, if anyone got knocked up, we ought to know which man was responsible. But Joan said we had nothing to worry about where Martin was concerned because..." She stopped talking and her face became flushed.

Walling rose like a massive bull ready to charge, glaring angrily at his wife. "You had to tell them, didn't you? You know I didn't want anyone else to know. You go around telling your friends behind my back so they can laugh at me!"

"You're impotent, Mr. Walling?"

The question hung in the air like a guillotine ready to fall.

"I'm sterile. You'll have to pardon me if I'm a little sensitive on the subject."

"The effects of venereal disease?"

"I got the cure a little late," he acknowledged gruffly.

"Then there's no possibility for you and Mrs. Walling to have children together."

"I'm not exactly a stud," Walling acknowledged bitterly.

"Mrs. Walling, do you still claim that you had no reason to be jealous of Mrs. Scofield's pregnancy?"

"Absolutely. I don't have the slightest interest in having children. I'd just as soon be cursed by bubonic plague. Besides, I knew about Martin's condition before we were married."

"I never lied to her," Walling concurred.

"It's too bad that Sonny Blake can't be here. He probably could have confirmed or denied what you ladies have told us. In fact, that's a very good reason for Sonny to have been murdered."

He saw Bill Scofield tighten his grip on his wife's hand. When no comments or reaction were forthcoming, Gardner continued to speak. "However, it wouldn't make much sense for Mrs. Scofield to kill Sonny when she knew there was still another witness around who could incriminate her. I'm, of course, referring to you Mrs. Walling."

"I suppose Lou thought that I would cover up for her no matter what."

"Or could it be the other way around? Didn't you expect to have her create an alibi for you? We do know you were not with Mrs. Scofield when your husband arrived during the critical

period of time." He observed her sitting impassively. "Let's go back to the idea of a mystery woman in Mr. Bradshaw's life. We know he was seeing someone secretly. Mr. Scofield has informed us Bradshaw's unaccustomed discretion was due to the lady's marital status. But Bradshaw was never discreet about his feelings for Mrs. Scofield. In fact, he flaunted them in her husband's face. And she wasn't the only married woman in Bradshaw's circle of friends. Isn't that so, Mrs. Walling?" His gaze fixed on her.

She squirmed in her chair. "You can't prove a thing. It's all conjecture."

"Wasn't it you who Bradshaw was actually seeing on the evening of Mrs. Scofield's medical appointment?"

"Empty words, Lieutenant."

"What if I were to tell you that here in my jacket pocket, I have a John Doe warrant. With it, I am entitled to fill in your name and have your apartment searched immediately. I have two detectives standing by. On a signal from me, they're prepared to institute a search for Sonny's pool keys. They will be quite thorough."

"You won't find them in my apartment."

Somehow, the way she said it made Gardner believe her. Could he be wrong? He saw her hand reaching down into the big canvas bag she carried.

"People are creatures of habit. Do you always have that bag with you when you come here? I want to see the contents." He held his hand out.

"You won't need to do that," she said.

He assumed that she was going to hand over the keys. Instead she removed a small, snob-nose revolver, a .22 Saturday Night Special by the look of it, and aimed it at Gardner's chest.

"No!" Kim shouted, jumping to her feet.

Gardner signaled to her to stay back.

"I hope you're satisfied," Joan Walling said with open hostility.

He'd finally succeeded in shaking her loose, but there was no sense of exultation. Joan seemed ready to explode. He glanced over at Bert, who was eyeing Joan warily. It helped to know that his partner was no stranger to violent people or desperate situations.

Martin Walling with his lack of judgment, attempted to approach his wife. "Joan, this is crazy. Put that thing away. You don't even know how it works."

"I know enough. Keep away from me, Martin. I despise you! If you come any closer, I'll shoot you." Her eyes were wild, and there was a savage intensity to her voice. Gardner didn't doubt for a moment that she was capable of murder.

"Some way for you to talk. You cheated on me, didn't you? Screwed around with my so-called friend, and then you have the nerve to behave like this. Jesus, I thought you had some class!"

"Shut up, Martin! You don't have a clue what class is. I wish I'd never married you. This mess is all your fault."

"I traded one rotten bitch for another."

Joan Walling moved away from her husband. Her arm caught around April Nevins' throat as she positioned the barrel of her gun against the shorter woman's right temple. Gardner heard April gasp.

"I'm leaving here, and April is walking out in front of me." Her voice was unnaturally quiet and calm now that she felt herself to be in control of the situation. Her hand held the gun with a surprisingly steady grip. "Signal the other policemen. Let them know they better not try to follow us or stop me. Otherwise I'll kill her!"

April's eyes widened in terror, her face ashen.

"Joan, this isn't rational." Gardner kept his voice friendly and paternal. "You're a very logical person. Where can you possibly go? You've been caught. Surrender yourself and make the best of it. Hand over the revolver to me. Let's talk about this. The situation may not be as bad as you seem to think." He held out his hand in a coaxing manner. "I'll help you find a good criminal lawyer." He spoke gently to her in the soothing tone he used with his daughters when they were hurt physically or emotionally.

For a brief moment, she seemed to be responding, but then the wild, hunted look returned to her eyes and she tightened her grip on April, who flinched noticeably.

"Just stay away, Lieutenant. I don't have far to travel, so let me alone, or else I swear I'll have to kill you, too." A determined expression crossed her thin lips. "I mean it!"

They made no move toward her. Joan Walling kept the gun against April Nevins' head and backed her way out of the swim club. As soon as the two women got into Joan's car, Gardner and Bert ran to their own vehicle. The two waiting detectives came rushing toward them.

"What's going on?" Drew Mitchell asked.

"Just follow us and don't approach the women until I tell you it's all right."

They kept a discreet distance. April was at the wheel of Joan Walling's car. She drove with speed and awkwardness, screeching around corners and weaving through the development. Bert called headquarters as Gardner drove.

"Move in on her," Bert said.

"She's scared enough. We've got to wait for the right moment."

"Is that before or after she kills April?"

"It's a mistake to crowd her. I know what I'm doing. I've got the car in sight."

"I was afraid something like this might happen. Your splash party wasn't such a terrific idea."

At that moment, he saw April lose control of the car and smack into a tree. He thought they could move in, but Joan was still in control. She waved the gun threateningly as April tried unsuccessfully to extricate the automobile. Gardner pulled over and watched. When Joan half dragged a dazed April out of the car, he and Bert moved toward them. With any luck, this was the opening they had waited for.

Joan was still using April Nevins as a human shield. She edged away as she saw them walking toward her.

"I told you not to come after me. Why are you here? I'll kill her if you don't go away!"

April was too frightened to speak. With the panicked state Joan Walling appeared to be in, Gardner decided that April's silence would work to their advantage.

"You know you don't really want to kill anyone. You're just not thinking. It's normal to be afraid, but you must not let it control you. We're going to help you. That's what we're here for."

"You won't help me. You're lying."

"I wouldn't lie to you."

"Why should you want to help me?"

"That's my job. You have friends who care about you. They want you to put away the gun, to give it to me."

"I have no friends, only people like her who expect me to sit and listen while they babble on about their trivial problems. No one ever listens to me. No one cares."

"Talk to me. I'll listen. Tell me why you killed Bradshaw." He kept his eyes fixed on hers.

"I didn't mean to kill him but he made me so angry."

"What did he say to you?"

"That it was over between us. At first, I didn't believe he meant it. We were so good together. He always told me how much I pleased him, that I was better in bed than all the others. I was better than all those beautiful women because I wanted to please him. I didn't think only of myself the way they do. But then he went and treated me so badly. I told him I'd leave Martin any time he wanted and go away with him. I would have had his child if he wanted that. He said I meant nothing to him. I can't tell you how he hurt me. When I was young, my father used to tell me how ugly I was, and I hated him for it. He'd say, 'study your books, Joanie, and do well in school. You'll need a good job to support yourself because you'll never get a man.' Martin wasn't much of a man, but he was all I could get until Rick came along. Rick meant everything to me.

"I arranged to meet him for a little while in the utility room, thinking we would have a few moments of pleasure together. But Rick told me that he was going back to California, that his work here was finished." Joan's hand twitched slightly as her finger edged the trigger.

Gardner didn't stir, and Bert was a study in still-life; they watched and listened, waiting for just the right moment to move in on her.

"Bradshaw told you about Martin's connection to the drug thefts?"

"Yes, you're right. At first, I wouldn't believe it, but Rick insisted it was true. He said he was going to report Martin's dishonesty. I begged him not to do it. I told him it would destroy me as well as Martin. He'd be leaving me with nothing. Rick turned his back on me and said he was sick of us both, Martin and me. We were boring, petty people. Then he started to leave. The blood was throbbing so badly in my head I could barely stand the pain. I suddenly hated him so much. He was such a bastard! I saw a baseball bat lying on the floor beside some other pieces of sports equipment. I picked up the bat and smashed it as hard as I could against the back of his head. When I saw him stagger and fall, I hit him again. He didn't move or speak after that. I looked at him and was certain he was dead. I touched him. There was blood trickling from the side of his head. I was glad he was dead. The keys to the utility room were on the floor where Rick had dropped them when he fell. I took them and left the room, locking the door from outside so no one would suspect. I guess I dropped them into my bag when I sat down again. If I'd just remembered to get rid of them, everything would have been all right."

"You found them at April's apartment?"

"Yes, I happened to sit on them one day and showed them to April. She absentmindedly remarked that Sonny must have left his pool keys behind. I decided to borrow them because the utility room seemed like a good place for Rick and me to meet. We only used it that one time. I gave them to Rick just a few days before." Joan licked her lips. "I'm not sorry I killed him." She spoke rapidly, one word stumbling over the next. It was a catharsis for her, Gardner realized, a chance to confess, to express her anger and frustration.

"Why the phone call to Bill?"

"Rick kept pursuing Lou, even when he was seeing me. Maybe I was jealous. They all want the pretty ones like her. I've always been cheated."

"Why don't you let April go? We can't really talk with her around."

"I know what you're trying to do. You think you're so clever. April's another pretty one. I'm going to die anyway. What difference if she joins me?"

"There's no reason for anyone to die. Why throw your life away for nothing? There's a lot more for us to talk about."

"I won't go to prison. I won't! Why should I allow myself to be publicly ridiculed and humiliated?"

"It won't be like that. Give me the gun."

"No!" She still held April tightly, but repositioned the weapon at her own head. For a moment, her hand shook. Bert took advantage of the split second that Joan's resolve wavered. Her movements were fast and sure. Pushing April out of the way, she pounced on Joan Walling. Taking hold of Joan's arm, Bert wrenched the gun away.

Joan Walling cried out. "I have a right to kill myself if I want to! Give my gun back!"

Gardner helped Bert restrain her. They had Joan Walling between them. She began to rant and curse, struggling with them as Gardner cuffed her. He motioned to the other two detectives to join them. Then he read Mrs. Walling her rights on the spot and arranged for Mitchell and Morgan to bring her in for booking.

"Christ, I'm glad that's over with," Bert said as the two detectives drove away with Mrs. Walling.

"Not as much as I am," April Nevins said. She was trembling uncontrollably.

"We'll take you home," Bert told her.

"Will you stay for a while?" she asked, her eyes fixed on Bert.

"I'm not feeling so great."

"A little while," Bert replied.

"You take the car," he told Bert. "Just drop me back at the swim club."

Gardner needed to get back to the pool to let the others know what had happened. As he expected, the announcement of Joan Walling's arrest upset everyone into a shocked silence. After that, the club quickly emptied out.

"I'm glad no one got hurt," Kim said, relief evident in her voice. "I had a fear it was going to end badly."

"You and me both," he admitted.

"Are you satisfied with the resolution?"

He didn't answer her. Something was bothering him about the confession Joan Walling had volunteered, and he kept turning it over in his mind. She'd probably retract it or change it anyway, once she'd calmed down. Instinct told him his work on the case was far from finished. He badly wanted it to be over but knew there was still more to this case. Damn, until that moment, he hadn't realized just how tired he felt. Oh well, as Scarlett O'Hara had said, tomorrow was another day.

"Would you like to come back to my place?" Kim asked. Her gaze caressed him.

"There's nothing I'd like better. But I don't have my car."

"Good. I can drive you for a change."

"Did I ever tell you how sexy you are when you take charge?"

"No, but I don't mind hearing it."

He leaned over and nuzzled her neck. "I don't plan on doing a lot of talking," he whispered into her ear.

She smiled at him. Then for just a moment they joined hands, holding to each other tightly, as they looked out at the setting sun reflected on the undulating water which concealed so much.

SIXTEEN

"THE NEWSPAPER sure gave the Bradshaw case a lot of coverage," Gary Sargent remarked, placing *The Star-Ledger* on the picnic table.

"Big deal," Evie said. "They don't even mention my dad." She picked up a bowl of potato salad and passed it around. "He's the one working the case."

Evie had invited Gary for dinner. Gardner still hadn't warmed to the boy, although the kid was making a definite effort to be pleasant to everyone. Kim was going to join them, and that would make everything a lot more enjoyable for him. Bert had also accepted his invitation.

"Mrs. Walling got a lot of notoriety," Evie said, passing along the coleslaw which was practically untouched. "What's she like, Dad?"

"A very complex person."

Evie groaned. "You hardly tell us anything about your work."

"I don't like bringing it home with me."

"What gave Mrs. Walling away?" Gary asked. His eyes opened wide in blatant curiosity.

"There was something peculiar about her behavior."

"You mean she was real nervous?" Jean took a large helping of the potato salad as she spoke.

"The reverse. She had too much self-control."

"And that made her seem suspicious?" Gary raised his brows in confusion.

"Most people questioned in connection with a murder investigation show signs of tension whether they're innocent or not."

"I just figured she had nothing to hide," Bert said.

"The majority of violent people don't behave like icebergs." Gardner got up and checked the grill. "But icebergs can be pretty deceptive since only a fraction of slippery surface ever shows. Evie, bring the big plate over. The burgers are done and the chicken's about ready."

Gary Sargent persisted on the topic. The young man seemed fascinated by the case. Evie explained that he was planning to be an attorney and, if possible, specialize in criminal law.

"So how do you figure a person like Mrs. Walling?" Gary continued. "I mean, if she's outwardly quiet, passive, withdrawn, how would you ever guess she could explode and go berserk?"

"There are some people who repress their anger and hostility much more than they should. Normal people express their rage—like Evie does when I come home late from work."

She scowled at him. "Dad, when were you ever on time? But I hardly ever get angry. I'm even-tempered and understanding."

He and Jean exchanged knowing glances and Gary smiled.

"Well, anyway," Gardner continued, "there is a type of person that can't let things out, can't communicate his or her feelings, and as a result, tends to feel isolated. Often this kind of person is hypersensitive and is disturbed by real or imagined injustices and rejections. So when the pressures get to be too much, the individual erupts like a volcano. And the blast can be deadly. Mrs. Walling's job as a systems analyst was comfortable and well-ordered. She was happy and secure in it. But her marriage to Martin Walling brought her unexpected frustration that she couldn't manage."

"Why would any woman marry a man who made her that unhappy?" Evie's gray eyes opened wide in bewilderment.

"Where men are concerned, she's always had problems. She believed by not getting married, she was missing out on something. When Martin Walling came along, she saw him as her only hope and desperately set out to snare him. Unfortunately, her success brought her face to face with another problem. She had to live with Martin, and she couldn't stomach him."

"He's really gross?" Jean asked.

"A total slob," Bert said. "Locate porcine in the dictionary and you'll find his picture under it."

"The affair with Bradshaw was Joan's release, her escape. It made living with Walling tolerable for a while. When Bradshaw dumped her, she couldn't cope."

"You think they'll go for a temporary insanity plea?" Gary inquired.

Gardner looked the boy over, relieved to see that he had recently condescended to get a haircut.

"Hard to tell, but I doubt it. For one thing, it's difficult to prove, though with a good lawyer, you never can tell. Still, that woman is far from crazy."

"Dr. Freud has spoken," Evie said. "Let's serve the chicken, Dad."

"At your service." Gardner saluted with a spatula.

"There've been a number of women who got off because their husbands abused them. I mean, who'd ever think a lady could go free after burning her husband to death while he was sleeping in bed or cutting off his…"

Gardner interrupted Gary. "There are children present."

"Sorry. What will happen to Mr. Walling?" Gary was a bulldog, no doubt about it.

"We've got a good case there. We brought him in this morning, and he confessed to being the inside man on all three robberies."

"Did Mrs. Walling kill the lifeguard, too?"

"She hasn't confessed to it. We'll be lucky to get her for the one murder. There are problems with what she told us. And her initial confession doesn't count because she hadn't as yet been Mirandized."

"They're always throwing evidence out of court on technicalities," Gary observed. "I think I'd like to be a prosecutor."

"Dad, if this Mrs. Walling hit the victim on the head with a baseball bat the way the newspaper article says, then how did she manage to put his body in the pool?" Evie tilted her head, her expression puzzled.

"She didn't. Sonny told us he put Bradshaw's body in the pool. He was drunk at the time he told us and slightly incoherent, but we understood him. Sonny thought that April Nevins killed Bradshaw. He wanted to help her by removing any suspicion that a woman might have been the killer."

"I wonder what made him think April killed Bradshaw? The missing keys I guess. But how did he know about the murder in the first place, and why would he think of throwing the body into the pool?" Bert frowned in perplexity, playing with her woven braids absentedmindedly.

"I agree. It doesn't seem like something he would think of on his own."

"Damn, we haven't really finished with the case, have we?" Bert put down her fork in disgust.

"Let's just say we haven't seen the last of the pool club," Gardner said.

"I have a feeling no matter what Martha Rhoades does to it, that pool will never be really clean again." Bert observed.

"The worst part is that your names aren't mentioned once in the newspaper article. I don't understand it." Evie's face wore a glum expression.

"Don't let it bother you, honey. We're not mentioned because neither of us had anything to do with releasing the story."

"Because the case isn't solved?" Gary ventured.

Gardner chewed thoughtfully on a barbecued drumstick and enjoyed the charcoal flavor in spite of the fact it would probably give him cancer one day. Captain Nash had decided that the Bradshaw case was closed with the arrest of Joan Walling. But as far as he was concerned, there were too many loose ends and too many unanswered questions. He was far from satisfied. Gardner pushed his plate away.

"Joan Walling believes she killed Bradshaw, but I'm not fully convinced. Neither is Bert. We really need to get more of the facts straight."

He glanced at the newspaper lying on the table and found himself caught by an article that had received a less prominent location.

"According to this, Mayor Ryan has officially accused the chief of corruption, taking payoffs and bribes. It says the chief countered by stating the accusations were all political in nature because they're in different parties. He says that Ryan is trying to get rid of him and put his own man in office."

"Who's telling the truth?" Bert asked.

"Both and neither," Gardner said with a shrug. "This town has a history of corruption, and I don't think anyone will ever change it no matter how hard they try. It's really a statewide problem. Every politico has deep pockets. That's why things remain second-rate."

"It seems to me, we should all be trying to make things better," Bert said with a deep frown.

"Spoken like an idealist."

She was studying him. "I never figured you for a cynic."

"Just a realist."

Bert shook her head. "Eventually, you'll be forced to take sides."

"I hope not. I live and work in this town and my kids go to school here."

"All the more reason for you to want it clean. You ought to run for public office or something."

"I'm no politician."

"You speak with an air of authority."

"Are you suggesting I'm too full of myself?"

"Maybe just full of potato salad," Bert said with a grin.

Kim joined them at that moment. Gardner welcomed her with a warm smile. The conversation had become too intense. He needed a change in direction. He hadn't meant to discuss the murder investigation with his family. He was going against his own firm principles.

KIM STUDIED THE GROUP of people before her and smiled. She realized how much she wanted to be with them, especially Mike.

"We started without you," Mike said. "Hope you don't mind."

"Of course not. Rush hour traffic was terrible tonight." Just the sight of him helped Kim's nerves relax.

"Well, I'm glad you made it."

She slipped off her suit jacket, folded it neatly and placed it on an empty chair, then joined the others on the redwood benches that faced the large rectangular table. There was a red-checkered cloth and the table practically groaned with plenty of picnic style food.

"Please help yourself," Evie said. "The cooler has a good selection. So choose whatever drink you'd like, as well."

"You're a perfect hostess," Kim said with a friendly smile.

Evie looked pleased. Was the girl finally warming to her?

"We were talking about the newspaper article on Dad's case," Jean told her as Kim opened a diet ice tea.

"I saw it at work today."

"Did you see how they didn't mention Dad?" Evie asked.

"I did notice it." She turned a questioning look on Mike, who merely shrugged.

"I told them no comment. I wasn't ready to share any details. Captain Nash thought otherwise."

The dinner was a pleasant one; a real change for her, feeling like a member of a family. She knew Mike had invited her for that very reason. He wanted her to see what she was missing. All part of his less-than-subtle campaign of courting her. She smiled to herself, not minding the least little bit.

Bert St. Croix also seemed to be enjoying herself. She'd relaxed, kicked back, was drinking a beer. Kim sensed that the outwardly tough police detective was a sensitive woman, one who'd suffered a great deal in her life.

Gary asked a question to the group in general. "Do you think all murderers are crazy?"

Kim bit her lower lip thoughtfully. "I think anyone who consciously plans the murder of another human being has to be mad."

Bert looked stricken. Why should her comment upset Bert that way? Kim was puzzled.

"Sometimes, the taking of a life is necessary," Bert said with emphasis.

WHEN DINNER WAS OVER, Gary asked if he could take Evie out for a drive.

"How late?"

Gary swallowed hard. "Just an hour or so, sir."

Mike looked at his watch. "All right. But first you'll have to drop Jean off at her friend's house. She has a sleepover tonight."

Bert said goodnight and left when the kids did.

"I'll clean up," Kim said.

Mike grabbed her hand. "I don't think so. I have other plans for you."

"You do?"

"I definitely do."

Mike pulled her into his arms and kissed her lips with a smacking sound. He tasted of beer and burgers and something else, an indefinable masculine essence that she found irresistible. Mike led her into the living room, sat down on the couch, pulling her on to his lap. She settled against him, her head pressed against his chest, enjoying the feel of his body, the solid beating of his heart. The strong lines of his face were softened in the glow of lamp light.

"I'm sorry I wasn't more of a help to you the other day dealing with your suspects. I didn't contribute much."

He stroked her cheek. "Having you there was great support as far as I'm concerned."

"You're very good at interrogating people."

"Think so?"

"See, there you go, answering with a question."

He ran his hands down her arms, then along the sides of her breasts and Kim shivered. "For my next question I'll ask how you like being touched by me."

"I'm willing to work with you on your technique."

He kissed her throat. "Good to know." He unbuttoned the front of her blouse and kissed the valley between her breasts. The next thing she knew, her bra was unfastened and she was naked to the waist. "God, you're beautiful," he said.

His mouth found her right nipple and sucked hard as his thumb and forefinger traced an erotic outline around her left nipple. The lower portion of her body was beginning to weep for him. She felt him growing aroused and hard beneath her.

"Mad, bad, and dangerous to know."

"Is that what you think of me?" His hands continued their sweet torture.

"It's how Lady Caroline Lamb described Lord Byron, another seducer of women."

He smiled at her, a wicked, sexy smile that made her heart beat wildly. "In all fairness, I only intend to seduce one woman, that being you. That Byron description might better fit Richard Bradshaw."

He pushed her down on the cushions and removed her shoes. Her skirt and panties seemed to disappear as if by magic. "Lay, lady, lay," he insinuated into her ear. His own clothes came next. She watched through half-closed lids as he ever so slowly removed his shirt, shorts and boxers, kicking off sneakers and socks.

"You have a great body," she said, admiring his well-muscled arms and lean, hard abs. His erection looked enormous. He was more than ready for her.

"You have a strong effect on me," he said, noting where her gaze was focused. "You could say I find conversation with you uplifting."

She found herself blushing but had little chance to feel embarrassed. He joined her again on the couch, his mouth fastening once more on her breast. His right leg moved between her own legs, parting them. His fingers found and touched the spot between her legs where she was most sensitive, most needy for his touch.

"I want you so badly," he said.

Kim couldn't manage a coherent thought after that. And she didn't want to: Everything was passion and pleasure between them.

GARDNER LET BERT do the driving because he was preoccupied. Joan Walling's confession, dramatic as it was, had offered only a partial explanation of what happened the night Bradshaw died.

"I like your kids," Bert was saying.

"You'd make a decent mother," he said. "You've got a way with children."

"Yeah, well, I don't think I'll ever get the chance to find out."

He caught the look of pain Bert couldn't manage to hide.

"You never know in life. Do you have much family? You never mention anyone." She'd been a closed book on the subject, which made him wonder.

"My father took off right after I was born. Guess he didn't want to be burdened with responsibility. My mother never got involved with another man after that. She worked two jobs to support us as best she could. She passed away several years ago."

"You're a New Yorker?"

"Brooklyn, born and raised. Graduated Prospect Heights High School where you were either West Indian or African-American. I didn't fit in with either group since my mother came from the Islands and my father was an American black, product of a biracial marriage. I was a mutt, a hybrid. I didn't belong." Bert's face changed expression as if she feared becoming too close, too personally involved. "So what makes you think there's something wrong with Joan Walling's confession?"

If Bert wanted to change the subject, he'd let her. "Joan didn't cover all the bases. But maybe we can get it straight when we talk to her again."

When Captain Nash saw them, his look of surprise was quickly replaced by one of annoyance.

"What the hell are you guys doing here? You're off-duty today."

"Something we have to check out," Gardner said. With Nash, a terse reply was best.

"If it has anything to do with the Bradshaw case, forget it."

"As a matter of fact, it does."

Nash turned red; the nose that looked as if a steamroller might have gone over it a few times flailed at the nostrils.

"What's going on here? We're finished with that. Everybody's happy with the way you handled things."

"Who's everybody?" Gardner studied the captain's face.

Nash looked away. "Hey, you know."

"No, I don't think I do," Gardner said evenly.

"Look, do you need to have diagrams drawn for you? Important people in this town don't want you making waves. They're satisfied, so leave it alone. Case closed."

Gardner didn't like the threatening undercurrent. It was like a whirlpool ready to suck him under. "There are still questions that need answers."

"Mike, you're no rookie. You know goddamn well small town politics can get ugly. A fella sticks his hand in the john, it might come out covered in crap."

"The way it is now, the case will be thrown out. We don't have enough hard evidence." Gardner walked past Nash and went to his desk where Bert joined him.

"What next?" she asked.

"We've got to get hold of Fitzpatrick and double check Bradshaw's autopsy report."

Gardner had the report itself spread out in front of him. What he sought was confirmation. Luckily, he got through to Herb without much trouble.

"What's up, Mike?"

"I'm not clear on the Bradshaw autopsy report. If you recall the pathology findings, the head wound was not listed as the cause of death."

"Can't this wait? I've got other work."

"It's important, Herb."

"All right then. The head injury was serious but it didn't kill him."

"The knife wound?"

"Fatal."

"You can be sure?"

"The blow to the head would have rendered the victim unconscious for an indefinite period of time. Certainly he had a concussion. There might even have been some degree of neurological impairment from inter-cranial pressure, but

the blow wasn't massive enough to kill him, at least not immediately. I don't recall all the details though."

"The head wound was definitely inflicted first?"

"That's what I've been telling you, Mike." Fitzpatrick
sounded exasperated.

"And about the time …"

"What is this?" the lab man interrupted. "For Christ sake,
we've been all through this before."

"Just bear with me for a couple of minutes. You gave us
the time of death as being anywhere between six and nine
p.m. Was it ever narrowed down further? Could it have been
any later?"

Fitzpatrick sighed impatiently at the other end. "Look,
Mike, you know damn well that Lester Jarvis isn't all that
competent at his job. If his brother-in-law wasn't such a wheel
in the county, that prick would never have become forensic
pathologist in charge of performing all the autopsies for the
M.E.'s office."

"So what you're saying is we can't rely on time of death
as being accurate."

"That's about the size of it."

"I was hoping for something more, something that was
over looked."

"We were as thorough as we could be."

"How could you be sure, for example, that he wasn't
drowned?"

"No water in the lungs. That was the first thing Jarvis
established. Although his lungs were in such bad shape that
was the only thing not wrong with them."

"How's that?" Gardner asked with interest, his initial disappointment diminishing.

"The guy was unquestionably on his way to lung cancer,
but I guess that doesn't help you very much, does it?"

"You can never tell." He thanked Fitzpatrick and ended the

conversation, then turned to Bert. "Things don't feel right. Remember what Mrs. Walling said she used as a weapon?"

"Sure, a baseball bat," Bert said.

"Al Capone used a bat to good effect for murder but apparently Mrs. Walling isn't in his league, if you'll pardon my bad pun."

"So she stabbed him afterwards."

"But she already thought he was dead. We never made public the actual details regarding Bradshaw's death. She just kept on thinking that she killed him and acted accordingly."

"By going on to kill Sonny who'd know her alibi was a lie."

"I'm not certain she did kill Sonny. Remember, she acted in a fit of passionate rage. Killing Sonny would have taken an act of premeditation. Besides, I'm not sure she had the opportunity even if she did have the motive."

"So I guess we'll have to see the lady again and talk to her," Bert concluded.

"Yeah, that's about right."

MRS. WALLING'S LAWYER was less than thrilled about being bothered on short notice, but Gardner had suggested him to represent both Mr. and Mrs. Walling, and he was appreciative of the business thrown his way. Not that Mat Simmons really needed the work; he was the shrewdest and best-connected criminal lawyer in the county. However, Gardner felt he ought to suggest the best since he promised to be fair to Mrs. Walling.

The jail itself was a depressing place. Like other county facilities, it was usually the first place a person was sent after he or she was arraigned. Although far from the worst in the state, it was not a place pictured in travel brochures.

The ominous brick building, set off in a field without fence or sign to identify it, had been built in 1934 as a Depression era WPA project. It was a massive, solid, gloomy facility. The woman's section was in need of paint, Gardner noted. The barred windows were bare, and the sooty brick unadorned. The long line of steel cages left no doubt that this was indeed a place of incarceration.

Joan Walling appeared before them looking more gray than tan. There was a weary expression on her face and when she saw who was visiting her, she became agitated.

"I have nothing more to say to either one of you. You can talk to him from now on." She pointed at her attorney.

"It's all right, Mrs. Walling. Lieutenant Gardner thinks it may help your case if you cooperate." Simmons spoke in smooth tones.

"How are you going to help me?" She let out a sullen, bitter laugh.

"You said that you hit Mr. Bradshaw on the back of the head with a baseball bat and then left, believing he was dead. Had you ever seen a corpse before?"

She shook her head.

"Did you go back later to use the knife on him or did you stab him right after using the bat?" He waited tensely for her response.

She looked up at him in surprise. "What knife?"

"Didn't you stab Mr. Bradshaw with a knife?"

"No, never. I don't know what you're talking about." She looked at him as if waiting for an explanation, but he wasn't about to give her one.

"We'll be talking to you again very soon."

Simmons walked with them and smiled when Gardner thanked him for his help, his mouth a display of dazzling, capped teeth. Handsome bastard. Good courtroom image. These days, it didn't hurt a trial lawyer to look like a movie actor.

"So you think we'll be able to do business with the prosecutor on this?"

"I think so. How'd it go with her husband?"

"We'll make a deal. He has something to offer: the names of the others involved in those robberies. He's not looking at much time. In fact, I can probably get him probation."

"The guy's a creep," Bert said with disgust.

"Justice is blind," Simmons said with a cynical smile.

"You said it!"

Simmons left them in the parking lot and Gardner took a breath of the warm, summer breeze.

"So you don't think Joan killed Bradshaw after all?" Bert sounded let down.

"How does it look to you?"

"Same way," she conceded. "But damn, that means we have to start all over again."

"Not exactly."

As they got into the car, Gardner couldn't help thinking that the landscape in this area was bleak, even in summer. There was nothing much on either side of the highway except for some small, scrawny fir trees closely massed together. Somehow, the term Garden State did not seem quite applicable to this part of New Jersey.

"We know that everyone left the pool by eight o'clock that evening. Sonny told us he locked up then. We have to work on the assumption that when Sonny closed the club for the night, everyone else had gone home and Bradshaw was lying unconscious in the equipment room."

Bert looked annoyed; the whites of her eyes glistened. "Do you know the implication of what you're saying? According to that, none of those people could have killed Bradshaw. You're saying he was locked in there and no one could get to him except Sonny, the Walling woman, Martha Rhoades or the other two lifeguards."

"I suppose that is the implication."

"Okay. We don't think Joan had any reason to return. And except for Sonny, no one else might have a motive for touching Bradshaw. You think the kid killed him after all?"

"Then who killed Sonny?"

"We never asked Joan about him," Bert said.

"I don't think we have to."

"But you can't be sure. I just wish we were done with this case. It's beginning to piss me off."

BACK AT HEADQUARTERS, Gardner went to his desk and put in a phone call to the pool club. There were five or six rings before anyone picked up the receiver. It was the girl called Beth who finally answered, and she got Martha Rhoades for him.

"I'm surprised to hear from you," she said with irritation, "I thought everything was settled."

"There are still some more questions."

"We're awfully busy today," she said in a voice that would have made a walrus look for an overcoat. "I can't tell you how many gum and candy wrappers we've picked up already. Little children have no manners, and these young mothers pay no attention to what their children do. It's a disgrace."

"Yes, I understand. This will just take a moment of your time."

"What do you want to know?" She would never be accused of graciousness.

"Are the spotlights left on at the pool after closing?"

"No, never," Miss Rhoades said. "A total waste of electricity. We have the pool lights on Tuesday night only. That's our movie night. We call it Family Night because we only show films suitable for the entire family. I personally make the selections."

He ignored her unnecessary, self-serving comments. "Mr. Bradshaw wasn't killed on a Tuesday night and the lights were on. You told us that was why you checked on the pool that night."

There was a significant pause at the other end of the wire. "I can't explain it. The lights should not have been on. Sonny had strict instructions from me. To the best of my knowledge, he always did what he was told."

"Is there anyone else who has keys to the club?"

"No, I've already told you that."

"What about the owner, Mr. Page?"

There was another hesitation. "I suppose he might. He was the builder."

"Does he come around much?"

"He is very fastidious where the complex is concerned. He pops in for brief visits now and then. Sometimes he plays golf at the course and then drops by for a swim. He always checks on the flowers. He likes to make certain they're being watered properly. He was favorably impressed by the red and white petunias this year."

"Are his visits always in the daytime?"

"I don't know. Sonny did mention that Mr. Page occasionally dropped by for a swim in the evening."

"And left around closing time?"

She did not seem eager to answer the question, as if she thought there might be something improper about it.

"I couldn't say," she said finally in a guarded tone of voice. "Only Sonny would have known that."

Bert, who was listening in on the extension, shot Gardner a sharp look. Gardner nodded his head at her. His mind flashed with a clear understanding of what had been left unsaid.

"Why didn't you tell us before that Mr. Page had his own keys to the pool?"

"I didn't think of it."

He thought she was lying but supposed the reason behind it was loyalty to her employer. He decided to let the matter drop, satisfied to have found out that his hunch about the builder was correct.

"Maybe we should have a word with Cheryl McNeill," Gardner remarked after getting off the phone with Miss

Rhoades. "We ought to find out if Page and Bradshaw knew each other."

"You think she'd know?"

"Can't say, but it's worth a try."

Before they could leave, Drew Mitchell came over to them. He looked Bert up and down with an insulting stare.

"I really like big women," he said. "Especially big, black women. I hear they're hot in bed." He gave her what only could be described as a leer.

"Get lost, before I report you for sexual harassment." She folded her arms over her breasts and stood tall and straight.

"Saving yourself for Gardner?"

Her eyes glittered like shards of steel as she turned and stalked away.

Mitchell turned to Gardner. "I was just kidding around with her. She's got no sense of humor."

"Leave her alone, Mitch. Call it a friendly warning."

"Sure, Mike." His smile was crooked. "I wouldn't try to claim your territory. Hey, you see the article in the newspaper today about the mayor asking for an investigation of the chief?"

Gardner indicated that he had.

"The Chief's really pissed. Nash told me the old man's worried about the department getting a black eye in the public image. If nothing else, it's bad for morale."

"So what's he going to do about it?"

"He personally phoned the mayor and asked him to come over later to talk."

"Did Ryan agree?"

"Looks that way. The captain just asked me to make sure that a special parking spot be marked for the mayor in our lot as a welcome. It's supposed to separate him from the patrol cars as a sign of respect."

"Sounds promising," Gardner said.

Yet it puzzled him; this sudden courtesy on the chief's part seemed out of character. The truth was, neither man had any regard for the other. But he had other things to worry about and decided to put the matter out of his mind.

He'd told Bert they were close to solving the Bradshaw case, yet he wasn't certain. Things weren't going smoothly; he was afraid they were chasing down false leads. Still, he had to make the effort. He'd felt ever since he met George Page that the builder had a part in this. He was definitely hiding something. Maybe Cheryl McNeill could confirm it. It wouldn't surprise him to find out she'd held back on some piece of important information.

SEVENTEEN

As Cheryl McNeill opened her apartment door, Gardner was again reminded of Bradshaw's excellent taste in furnishings as well as women. He and Bert St. Croix were ushered into the elegant green velvet living room and seated on chairs too good to actually sit on.

"I thought it was all over with. Why do you want to see me again?" She tapped long, vermilion fingernails on a rosewood end table and gave him a suspicious look. "When can I leave for California?"

"Ms. McNeill, we do have a few more questions for you. I hope it won't be necessary to delay your departure. However, you are the one person who knew Mr. Bradshaw best. You also knew his friends."

"Not all of them." Her expression was guarded.

"You knew George Page, didn't you?" His voice was polite but firm.

He watched the tall, slender brunette carefully. Her expression barely changed, yet he could tell the mention of Page's name somehow upset her.

"I don't know who you're talking about," she replied, sitting in a stiff manner.

"I was given to understand Mr. Bradshaw introduced you to Mr. Page." He was playing a hunch. But his unique intuition was rarely wrong.

"I never heard of the man. Look, Joan confessed to killing Rick. Doesn't that end it? I want you both out of here. I'm not going to say another word. I didn't kill Rick. I don't know anything. Leave me alone! I've suffered enough." She pushed her long dark brown hair back from her face, eyes blazing.

He rose abruptly, realizing it was pointless to try and interrogate her any further at this time. "The question of who killed your friend is far from settled. You'll have to postpone your plans and remain in New Jersey somewhat longer. If you do happen to recall anything about Mr. Page or anyone else, give us a call."

She received his final comments less than enthusiastically and slammed the door behind them as they left the apartment. Gardner remembered having once thought that Cheryl McNeill had qualities similar to his daughter Evie; he decided the analogy had been faulty.

THE PAGE RESIDENCE was large and impressive, and about as easy to get into as Fort Knox. They first had to state their business to a man at the front gate. The grounds were surrounded by a high stone wall that extended around the front of the house, and as far as he could tell ended somewhere deep in the woods. Gardner thought of the implications of the poem by Robert Frost: were fences meant to keep people out or to keep people in? Why did Page need a veritable fortress?

They'd done their homework. Bert had phoned Page's office earlier, and after a runaround of being put on hold countless times, finally discovered Page was working from home that day, not from his office.

A male servant opened the door to the Page residence. The face was bearded and there was a sharp, aquiline beak overshadowing the rest of his features. The most impressive thing about him was his build. He looked more like a linebacker than a butler.

"You want somethin'?" The sandpaper voice had a thick New York City accent.

"The fellow at the gate cleared us. We're police officers

here to see Mr. Page." Gardner would have to be blind not to notice the look of cold contempt on the other man's face or the bulge under his jacket.

"It'll be a while. Mr. Page is busy."

"We're willing to wait," he responded without any trace of emotion.

"Let me see some I.D." When the butler was satisfied, he left them standing in the large vestibule on the best pink Italian marble that money could buy. A window of Madonna and Child in stained glass faced him. An ornate chandelier of fine crystal loomed over them. For a moment, Gardner wasn't certain whether he was in a private home or a Renaissance cathedral.

They had to wait at least fifteen minutes before Page appeared. Bert paced restlessly while Gardner studied his surroundings with detachment. When the builder finally appeared, his expression was one of animosity. He looked dapper in a white knit golf shirt and slate gray slacks. As before, his black hair was slicked back. Small creases formed at the corner of his mouth as he frowned at them.

"Why are you here?" he was standing above them on a wide, formal staircase.

"We have a little problem we think you could help us with. In fact you're the only one who can."

Page narrowed his intense, dark eyes. "I don't know anything that could help you and I'm a very busy man." He spoke with the authority of a person accustomed to giving orders and having them obeyed.

"So I understand, but you're wrong about not being able to help us."

Page descended the staircase with a springy movement. "What do you want?"

"For how long did you know Mr. Bradshaw?"

Page licked his lips. "Never met the guy."

"Didn't you occasionally meet Bradshaw in the evening when you went swimming at the club?"

Page made a point of rising slightly on the balls of his feet. He was obviously sensitive about being several inches shorter than Gardner. "If I wanted to swim, I'd put a pool out back. I've got plenty of land for it."

"The pool you built at La Reine Gardens is beautiful. I doubt many resort hotels have anything nicer. And you do consider it yours. It's not unreasonable for you to swim there in the evening when few other people are around. You might even prefer to enjoy the pool after hours, have it all to yourself or share it with a few select guests."

Gardner could see that Page was uneasy. "Look, I didn't know Bradshaw. I never met the guy. Never went near the pool at night. And you can't prove otherwise."

"Suppose I told you I have a witness who puts you at the pool?"

"The night Bradshaw died? I wanna know who that person is!"

"Just like there are things you won't tell me, Mr. Page, there are things I'm not obliged to tell you."

"Get the hell out of my house! Cops or no cops, you're trespassing. I can get you fired if I want."

Gardner was not particularly disturbed by the builder's outburst. It meant that the questions had struck a nerve, proof he was hiding something.

"Thank you for your time and civility, Mr. Page. We can show ourselves out." His mild sarcasm was comprehended by Page, whose face reddened.

Once they left the house, Gardner spoke to Bert. "What did you think?"

"Same as you, the guy knows more than he's saying. Wish we could get him to talk straight."

"I think we'll have to find out more about Page," Gardner said. "But we better tread lightly."

"He's a rich guy with an attitude."

"Absolute power corrupts absolutely."

Bert shook her head. "It doesn't seem right the way the system works. Back in Bed-Stuy, you'd see the big, fancy cars line up and you'd know the pushers and pimps were doing business. Little kids follow them around like they're gods. And why not? They're the ones making all the big bucks. Flaunt it and you get respect, even if you're a piece of garbage. Ask any streetwise kid what he thinks of cops. He'll tell you we're a bunch of assholes because we put our life on the line for a few dollars while the slime lives like kings."

"Yet you didn't give yourself over to it."

"I've got my mother to blame for that. She took me to church with her regular. To her, money wasn't the most important thing in life."

"You wouldn't want to change what you are any more than I would."

"I'd like to change the justice system." Her eyes glowed with bitterness.

"Whoever said life had to be fair?"

"Come on, Mike, doesn't it ever get to you?"

"Of course. That's why I work on maintaining a sense of perspective. According to the philosopher, life is absurd, so I do my best to laugh at it when I can."

"What would your philosopher think of Page? Would he find amusement in the fact that Page, with his connections and money, can turn our justice system into a revolving door?"

"If Page is guilty of murder, we'll get him," Gardner said.

"Now who's being the idealist?"

"Optimist," he corrected. "But why not? It doesn't cost anything extra." He couldn't help wondering what was eating at Bert. Would she ever decide to trust him?

Gardner indicated to Bert with a jerk of his head that he wanted her to follow him around to the back of the house.

"What are we doing?" she asked.

"I'm curious about something. Humor me, okay?"

There was a lot of property to the rear of the house. Where the grass ended, a large area looked as if it had been excavated and then refilled with earth. Although the land had been leveled by heavy equipment, there was a distinct difference in elevation. Nothing grew there. It reminded him of a giant grave.

"What do you make of it?"

"I'd guess from the look of it Page once had a swimming pool back here, a good-size in-ground one," Gardner said.

Bert raised an eyebrow questioningly. Gardner could only shake his head. The answer to the mystery of why the builder destroyed the pool lay buried with it. Gardner heard the growling of dogs and looked up. There were two large Dobermans held on a leash by a burly man.

"What are you doing back here? Did Mr. Page say you could walk around the grounds?"

The dogs barked with savage intent.

"We were just leaving," Gardner said, thinking that the larger of the two animals seemed to be salivating.

"That's good, because these are trained attack dogs and I don't want to have to let them loose unless I have to."

"We agree about that," Gardner said, moving away fast.

THEY DROVE BACK to headquarters and spent the better part of two hours checking on Page and finding out whatever they could about his background. In that respect, the computer was a great help. Since Page haled from New York, Gardner went online and had information downloaded from the mainframe in the city.

They learned that Page's given name had been Georgio Pagenelli and he had a murky background. If he wasn't a wise guy himself, he was well connected. That had to be the source of his money. The fact he wasn't possessed of a major criminal record didn't absolve him. Gardner was well aware that just getting building permits in Webster Township was contingent on greasing the right palms. There were infractions of the building codes all over the township that conveniently went unnoticed by the authorities, all because the right people were paid off.

To build the kind of quality complex that Page had, a large financial investment was required. Page was likely one of the people who took dirty money and invested it in clean enterprises for the families. Webster was the kind of place where no one would ask too many questions. All they cared about was the money itself. Now Page was looking to build a large shopping center. Of course, he wouldn't want unfavorable publicity; his investors would be spooked.

They could always take the easy route and forget about Page; shady connections didn't automatically make a man a murderer. Still, Gardner felt an obligation to learn the truth, no matter how sticky things might get for him personally.

He finally logged off, rubbing his eyes. It seemed as if no other detectives were around, but then, it was dinner hour. Only a few detectives would be there regardless.

"Time to quit for today. I'm ready to chow down," Gardner said to Bert.

"Good idea. I've had it, too."

They were headed toward the parking lot when Drew Mitchell saw them and stepped in their way. "Where you going?"

"Out—why?"

"I wouldn't leave just yet." The sharp lines of Drew's face formed a dark expression.

"What's wrong?"

"Just walk back and stay inside for a few more minutes. It's for your own good. And don't ask questions." He turned to Bert. "If I spoke out of line before, we're even now. This is my apology."

All of a sudden, a rumble went through the building and the walls and windows vibrated.

"Lord, what was that?" Bert said.

They ran out into the parking lot from where the sounds seemed to emanate. A sign saying "Mayor" lay on the ground. Beside it, a car had burst into flames. Gardner flipped open his cell and phoned the fire department.

"Is that why you didn't want us out in the lot?" Bert said to Mitchell.

He wouldn't meet her eyes. "Guess I better let the chief know what happened. He and the mayor are in conference in his office."

"Yeah, do that," she said.

When Mitchell was gone, Bert turned to Gardner. "Why?"

Gardner shrugged. "A warning to the mayor, I guess. Notice they made certain that no one would be injured."

"Nice of them. Real considerate dudes. What kind of town is this? What kind of cops?"

"You'll have to answer that for yourself. The fire department is on its way. Let's get out of here. There's nothing more we can do right now."

GARDNER PHONED KIM using his hands-free device as he drove home.

"If you play your cards right, sweetheart, I'll take you to a movie tonight."

"Is that your best Bogart imitation?"

"Everybody's a critic."

"Jimmy Durante," she said with a laugh.

"You're not old enough to know that."

"Neither are you."

"Just goes to show how much we have in common," he said.

"Wooing me again?"

"You bet."

"What about the girls?"

"Okay, we'll take the kids with us."

"They'll be up past their bedtime."

"What's the good of summer vacation if you can't stay up late once in a while? Can you find a movie that's okay for all of us?"

"I'd have to be Houdini!"

"You're great at that kind of stuff. Just make up your mind that we're going to have a good time regardless." He hadn't meant to sound stern, but that whole business about the mayor's car blowing up had set him on edge.

"All right," she said. "I'll check on what's playing."

It seemed to him that Kim found it difficult to relax and have fun, almost as if it made her feel guilty. She wanted to be happy but mistrusted the emotion.

"Want me to pick you up?"

"No, I'll come by your place."

Evie and Jean were fixing supper when he arrived home. He followed them out to the kitchen, pulled a chilled bottle of Michelob from the refrigerator, fixed some crackers and cheese to go with the beer, went out to the living room, and fooled around with the remote for the TV set. Then he put his feet up on the recliner, feeling drained and fatigued. Just as he got comfortable, his cell phone rang.

"Mike, this is Nash. I'm going to have to take you off the Bradshaw case permanently."

"Mrs. Walling didn't kill him."

"Makes no difference. You've been harassing George Page. Where's your brains? Are you sitting on them? I thought you of all people knew how to handle someone like him with tact. I'm reassigning you."

"I want to finish this," he said in a quiet but firm voice.

"Look, Mike, you've got an excellent record, but you can be replaced."

"So?"

"You got a family to support. It wouldn't be easy starting over somewhere else. You'd be forced to take a cut in pay if nothing else."

"What's your point?"

"I think you know. Just don't step on any more toes. I'm warning you for your own sake."

"What you're saying is that it's okay to arrest a murderer as long as it's someone without any influence like Joan Walling. Just suppose our killer is George Page or someone who works for him? What then? Do we let him get away with it because he's got juice?"

"I wasn't saying that."

"Of course you were."

"You really think Page could have killed Bradshaw?"

"Right now, I don't know, but it's possible. What I do know is that he's hiding something and it could be important to the case. You want it on your conscience that you might let a murderer get away?"

"You're still off the case," Nash said. "That's an order."

"Maybe I should lead the investigation into who blew up Mayor Ryan's car. He might be interested in finding out who's responsible. I bet he's awfully angry right about now. I wonder who he thinks did it. Myself, I just might have a pretty good idea."

"That's blackmail!"

"I don't look at it that way."

"You gonna try a deep throat routine? It won't work."

"Just playing the game by your rules. We'll need a few more days on this case. If we don't get anywhere by then, you can reassign us."

"Damned nice of you!"

"Of course, it is. I stand for truth, justice and the American way, just like our fellow police officers in Webster Township."

On that note of irony, Nash hung up on him. Some good

had come out of evil after all, Gardner decided. At least, they would be able to finish their investigation of the Bradshaw case without further interference. As to finding out who had actually blown up the mayor's car, that would remain an unsolved crime with Chief Morgan promising to make every effort to find the perpetrator—which was like having the fox oversee the hen house.

BERT ST. CROIX ARRIVED back at her small furnished apartment that evening tired and hungry. She'd stopped to pick up a few groceries. The refrigerator was embarrassingly lacking in basic dietary essentials. Living alone, she ate most of her meals out with the exception of breakfast, which generally consisted of cold cereal and a cup of instant coffee. This morning, she'd discovered herself to be out of milk and had poured orange juice over the corn flakes, an experiment she did not care to repeat.

The tiny flat wasn't much to speak of, but she was rarely there except to sleep. She didn't feel comfortable here the way she had in New York where you could walk outside at any hour and see people and life going on around you. It seemed like people just sat mesmerized in front of their television sets at night in the suburbs. She had to ask herself for the hundredth time if she wasn't making a mistake working and living in New Jersey. Maybe when the hurt was less she'd return to the city. Right now, she couldn't stop missing Alva or thinking about her. She put the eggs into the refrigerator and thought how careful Alva always was with them. In her whole life, Bert doubted Alva had ever broken a single egg, but then her life hadn't been very long, had it?

Bert went to bed early, wishing she weren't alone. She knew Gardner would listen if she wanted to talk about it, yet somehow she couldn't. Gardner was okay and so was his family, but seeing their warmth and closeness made Bert feel her loss all the more deeply.

Even Gardner wouldn't understand what she'd done, what she'd had to do. But the nightmares wouldn't go away. There was a knock at the door and she got up to answer it. What happened next was violent and unexpected. Two men were pushing her back into the apartment. For just a moment, she was caught off-balance and someone grabbed her arms with painful force. She was enervated by the pain rather than frightened. The shooting sensation in her arms made the adrenaline start to flow. Her heart pumped fast and hard. Her body tensed, she came back at one of her attackers with a sharp karate-style kick to the groin which sent the man sprawling to the floor. The second attacker grabbed her from behind and Bert brought back her elbow, jabbing him in the gut. There was a deep groan as he fell to his knees. She got to her gun before either of them could recover.

She trained the weapon with an air of menace. "Okay, talk to me," she said to the first punk who seemed to be recovering.

Both men stared at her, transfixed by fear. She decided they were semiprofessional muscle who knew enough to stay still when a gun was fixed on them. Neither man spoke.

"I want to know what the hell you're doing here. Do I have to shoot off pieces of you to get that information? Maybe make you permanent members of the sopranos?"

The older and heavier of the two men spoke. "We're just here to deliver a message."

"Which is?"

"Some people resent you harassing honest citizens."

"And just who are these honest citizens?"

"You gonna run us in?" Small eyes like those of a rodent moved around nervously under bushy brows.

"Depends on what you tell me."

The younger punk gave the older one a questioning look. The older man raised his beetle brows in uncertainty. Bert noticed that the simian appearance belied a certain cunning, animal intelligence as he began speaking for both of them.

"We don't know who sent us here. We got this phone call and the man says our pay will arrive in the mail. Just deliver the message so it'll be remembered."

"No idea who called you?"

"That's right, lady. I just listened, is all. The man never left a name. You might say we're naive, trusting souls. People hear about our service by word of mouth. We depend on referral and our good reputation. We don't advertise in *Ladies Home Journal* or *Good Housekeeping*. We weren't gonna hurt you much. No hard feelings, right?"

She gave the ape man and his friend each a hard shove in the direction of the door. "If I ever catch you around here again, you'll wish I had brought you in. Now get out."

The two men scrambled. Bert locked the door and holstered her weapon. She turned the air-conditioning up high. It had all of a sudden become very warm in the apartment, and the younger punk had worn a cloying aftershave lotion that lingered.

She'd just managed to calm down when there was another knock at the door. This time she pulled her revolver before opening up. April Nevins stood before her, stared at the drawn weapon and blinked.

"Do you greet all your callers this way?"

"Let's just say I try to discourage unwelcome visitors."

"Well, I can see where you'd scare the hell out of the Avon lady. May I come in?" she asked. "You planning to go on an elephant hunt? That gun sure looks like it could handle one." Bert holstered her weapon. "What are you doing here?"

"I'm off tonight," April said, as if that explained everything.

"So?" Bert realized she sounded as irritated as she felt.

"Hot night. Got something cold to drink?"

"All right, you can have a drink and then be on your way.

Juice okay?"

"Sure, whatever you've got."

April was dressed in a raincoat, one of those lightweight beige affairs styled like a trench coat. Her mane of high-lighted honey hair hung in loose and casual curls, undulating as she followed Bert into the kitchen area. "Can't say much for your decorator even if you are a damn sight neater than I am."

"The place came furnished." Why did she feel she had to explain anything to April Nevins? "How did you find out where I live?"

"From the information operator." April smiled as though she were very pleased with herself.

"They don't give out addresses."

"I know, but I have a method for getting them. I don't ask for the address. I give the name of the person, then I give a made-up address and ask if I gave the right one. They usually say no and mention the correct address. It doesn't always work, but it did this time."

"Pretty slick. Maybe I should arrest you for lying to the phone company."

"Is it a crime?" April asked, all innocence.

"What do you want here?"

"I feel we could be friends."

Bert poured April a glass of orange juice. "Drink up. Then haul your ass out of here. We're not finished with the Brad-shaw investigation."

"I thought it was all settled." April frowned uneasily.

"Wouldn't matter. You and I have nothing in common."

After April Nevins was gone, the scent of her lingered. Distractedly, Bert sat down on a kitchen chair and drank orange juice from the glass April had used.

EIGHTEEN

MIKE GARDNER WOKE UP early the next morning. Dawn was breaking outside his bedroom window. He lay very still and listened to the birds sing out their welcome to the new day. A gray light filtered through the slightly crooked curtains. The inside of the house was silent. For a moment, he had the sensation of being completely alone. Then he recalled how he'd managed to convince Kim to stay over last night. He reached over, found the small of Kim's back and began to gently massage her. As she stirred, she moved from her stomach to her back and then went back into what appeared to be a deep sleep. More than anything, he wanted to make love to her again, but now was not the right time. There were promises to keep.

He slipped out of bed and headed toward the bathroom. It was going to be a busy day. Even though he'd bought an extra day or two from Captain Nash, the Bradshaw case would have to be solved with alacrity. Otherwise, Page and the chief would find a way to stop him. He was impatient to get started and went through his morning routine with unusual haste. He wasn't kidding himself; his job was on the line, as well as the comfortable life he'd built for himself and his family. It could all be destroyed like the crushing of an eggshell. Nevertheless, if George Page was a murderer, he was going to find the hard evidence to prove it, and he wasn't going to back down.

He kissed Kim goodbye on the forehead and her eyelids fluttered open.

"You going now?" Her voice was slurred with sleep.

"Yeah, I have to leave."

"I wish you didn't." She placed her arms around his neck. "You smell so good, so manly."

"Funny what a shave and shower can do for a guy."

"It sure is." She gave him a kiss he wouldn't forget the rest of the day.

"You're making it hard for me."

He looked downward suggestively. "Don't I wish," Kim said with a sigh and a smile.

It was some hours later when he presented Cheryl McNeill with a search warrant. She let them into her apartment less than eagerly.

"I'm through answering your questions. I'm going to get a lawyer so you'll have to stop bothering me." She hugged her arms around her body as if searching for security.

"That's your right. We're not here to arrest you. We had this warrant issued to search the premises because we feel there's probable cause. You've been holding out on us."

They walked past her. Only with the greatest persistence, and the fact that he'd once helped Judge Barnett with his son when the boy was rebelling against parental authority and wrecked the Judge's Mercedes, had Gardner managed to get a warrant issued for probable cause so quickly.

Bert began in the bedrooms where she'd been before. Gardner searched the living room. A large, delicately carved secretary sat in one corner of the room. That seemed to be the perfect place to begin, although he wasn't certain what he was looking for, just anything that might connect Bradshaw to Page. He was careful not to upset the papers he found. When he got to the middle drawer, he found it locked.

"Please give me the key," he said to Cheryl McNeill.

She'd been watching his progress with an intent gaze. "I don't have it."

"Why not?"

"Because it belonged to Rick." She spoke in a nervous, halting voice, and he was certain that she was lying.

"Shame to break open the lock. That's a beautiful piece of furniture. Expensive antique, isn't it? Probably wouldn't be worth much after I splinter the wood."

She bit down on her lower lip as if trying to make a painful decision.

"All right," she said grudgingly. The slim brunette walked to a large bookcase and reached into a Lenox vase. "Here," she thrust the key at him.

He took it, opened the drawer, found some financial statements, bank books and stock certificates, and discovered Bradshaw had been very comfortable financially. No surprise there. One bank book was solely in the name of Cheryl McNeill. There were a few small deposits made on a regular basis, then one very recently in the sum of $20,000. The deposit was made two days after Bradshaw's death. Gardner's hand tightened around the bank book.

"Where did you get the sum of money you last deposited?"

Her eyes hardened. "I earned it."

"Doing what?"

"I don't have to tell you that."

"An accomplice to murder is as guilty as the murderer."

The blood drained from her face. "I had nothing whatever to do with Rick's death."

"Shall I tell you what I think? Someone is paying you to keep your mouth shut. That person has serious cash. Did George Page pay you to keep quiet about his connection with Bradshaw? If so, you better tell me now because I'm going to find out anyway."

Her hands tugged at her hair as if reaching for a security blanket. For a moment, he was sure he had her.

"I don't think the bank account proves anything," she

said in a shaky voice. "I'm not discussing it, not without a lawyer."

"We'll leave. But for now, we're holding on to this. It could be evidence." He ignored her protests and signaled Bert.

Standing outside the apartment beside their car, he conferred with St. Croix.

"I doubt any personal checks are involved in that little transaction, and the McNeill girl is scared shitless, so she's not gonna talk."

He knew Bert was right. It had been a small victory at best.

"I bet she's on the phone right now tipping Page off to what happened."

"Good, I hope so. Maybe he'll be upset enough to make a mistake."

Bert scowled at him. "What kind of mistake? Like arranging a permanent accident for both of us?"

"He might just settle for getting us fired."

"That's a relief."

"You really think it's a lost cause, don't you?"

"People like Page with money and influence do whatever they want. I think you're dreaming if you think you can catch him." Bert scowled at him.

"I told you I'm a realist. I don't tilt at windmills."

"I think the sonofabitch might be planning something nasty."

"Don't worry," Gardner said. "I have to stay alive, otherwise my daughters would kill me."

Bert smiled and some of the tension that had crept into her face eased. "We know Page had opportunity since he had a key to the club and sometimes came during the evening hours. But why would he kill Bradshaw? There doesn't seem to be any motive."

"If I could answer that, I'd stop being a policeman, make a few million in the stock market and retire. We've got to look for more information. I can make a supposition though. If Bradshaw came around to consciousness, you have to figure he was in a pretty foul mood. He'd sustained a serious head injury and had to be in pain. If Page found him, they could have quarreled."

"About what?"

"I'm not certain, but that's what we still need to find out."

"Neither Cheryl nor Page will tell us anything."

"Someone else must know. In fact, I've got an intuition about who that might be. The man is vulnerable. It's just a matter of finding his Achilles heel."

"Well, he does have a bad temper," Bert said. "If he loses it, he might lose control of his judgment, as well."

"All we have to do is set up the right situation, and we can count on him making a mistake."

She studied him out of the corner of her eye. "You're not planning to set yourself up as a target?"

"Not if I can help it."

Bert told him about her experience with the two hoods on the previous night. "They were nothing but cheap labor. Still, I don't like it. You better keep your eyes open, too."

"We'll wind this case up within the next few days," Gardner said in a determined voice. "I don't fancy walking around wearing a bulletproof vest for the rest of my life. It would ruin the debonair image I've cultivated." He gave her a wide grin.

"If you say so."

As Gardner surveyed the architecture of the municipal building, he thought the dark brown oblong resembled nothing so much as a dismal prison—or a school. He'd always connected the two in his own mind. It was only when he took college courses that he began to enjoy school. But then, the municipal building did house the court and police headquarters and was not meant to stimulate aesthetic appreciation.

Captain Nash scrupulously avoided them. But no new assignments were thrust at them, either.

"I've thought of a way of connecting Bradshaw and Page. Though probably it's a long-shot not likely to pay off."

"I'm into long-shots," Bert said.

"I'd like to find out if anyone saw Page and Bradshaw together. We can get pictures of both men from the newspaper morgue. My guess is if they did have more than a passing acquaintance, they must have spent some time socializing together. Maybe a drink or a meal was shared, probably somewhere not far from the club."

Frown lines creased Bert's forehead. "We might as well check it out. There aren't that many places around here."

The pictures were obtained; a list was made up, and then divided between the two of them. Four places for each of them to visit. By the time Gardner had finished his half that evening without any success, he was feeling discouraged and thinking that his hunch hadn't been so terrific after all. If the two men had met socially, they could just as easily have gone to a different town.

He wanted to hear Kim's voice, just to let her know that he was thinking about her. He waited patiently while the telephone rang five times before it was picked up. Kim's 'hello' didn't sound right, as though she were nervous or upset about something. He immediately asked what was wrong. When she hesitated, he pressed her about it.

"Mike, I had this peculiar call earlier. I really don't want to bother you about it." She seemed reluctant to continue.

"Go on, what kind of call?" he urged.

"A stranger's voice. He talked crazy. Said to tell my boyfriend that he better drop the Bradshaw case quick or he was going to end up a very lonely man. I didn't like the sound of it."

"It's just some nut. Don't worry about it." He tried to make his voice sound reassuring.

"But how would anyone know about us, and Mike, my phone number isn't even listed. It scares me!"

"I'm winding up the investigation soon. I'm sorry about the phone call. Try not to let it get to you."

She let out a deep sigh at the end of the line.

"Really, sweetheart, it's going to be fine."

"It better be. Otherwise, I plan on haunting you for the rest of your unnatural life."

"Is that a promise?"

"You bet."

He laughed and then quietly told her that he loved her. "Why don't you pack a bag and plan on staying over for a few days?

The girls will be pleased."

"You are worried."

"Did I say that? I'm just looking for any excuse to get you to spend more time with me. In my bed."

"Are you feeling sorry you couldn't stay with me this morning? I know I do."

He thought of the thrill of feeling her body against his. "I get hard just thinking about you. So come to the house as soon as you can."

KIM DIDN'T PUT her phone down immediately. She was still feeling shaken by the strange phone call, more than she'd let on to Mike. Someone must have been watching her. It was a creepy sensation.

She began packing a few things and also slipped a sharp kitchen knife in her handbag, just in case. Then she locked up her apartment and hurried to her Toyota Corolla. Once on the road, Kim checked her rearview mirror repeatedly. She had a sense of being followed and didn't like it one bit.

BERT ST. CROIX HAD checked out three of the local watering holes on her list, and now she was down to the last one. She'd had no success but wasn't at all surprised. She'd saved the Galaxy Lounge for last because she wasn't sure she wanted to see April Nevins. But now there wasn't any choice. She probably should have asked Gardner to go there; why hadn't she?

As soon as Bert walked into the place, she saw April, even before the other woman saw her. Bert went over to the bartender, identified herself and flashed the pictures of Bradshaw and Page. The bartender shook his head and told her to ask the waitresses. By then, April was there.

"Come to visit on my turf?" she said with a smile.

"I'm here on business." She showed April the picture of Page and asked if April had ever seen him before.

April licked her lips thoughtfully. "Looks familiar, but I can't exactly place him."

"Did Bradshaw ever come in here?"

"Rick? Sure, he liked the Galaxy, not just 'cause of me, either.

He came in even after I stopped seeing him."

"Was this guy ever with him?"

"That's it! This other guy was in here with Rick, but only one time. I did notice him though."

Bert felt a sense of excitement, a quickening in her blood. "Try to remember. Did they talk about anything in particular?"

"I should tell you that I wasn't the one waiting on them so I didn't overhear any of the conversation."

"Damn! Do you remember who was waiting on them?"

"Sally, but she quit last week and I don't think anyone knows where she went. Anyway, she was so spaced out she probably wouldn't remember who she served five minutes after they left."

"Hey, April, your customers are getting antsy! Are you working or what?" The bartender pointed to the order of drinks he'd made up for her.

"Sorry." She turned to Bert. "Soon as I serve these people, I'll go on break and we can talk."

Bert agreed to wait. But the time really dragged. When they were alone at a table in the back, April smiled again. "I've been thinking about you."

"Why?"

"I need a friend. Someone I can trust. I'm lonely. You're lonely, too. Right? So what's the big deal?"

"The big deal is you're still a suspect in a homicide investigation."

April lowered her heavily made-up eyes. "I didn't kill anyone, and I'm not trying to influence you."

"Aren't you?"

April met her gaze directly. "No, I just feel there's an understanding between us, a kind of bond."

Bert looked away from her. "Tell me more about Bradshaw and the other dude."

"The one in the picture?"

"Yeah, that guy. Try to think, was anyone else with them?"

"Cheryl was with Rick, which was why I made sure not to serve them."

"Anyone else?"

"Yeah, there was another woman, a blonde. She was older then Cheryl but not bad looking, kind of classy, good bleach job."

"Talk to me about Bradshaw," Bert said. "Tell me everything you remember about that night."

April sighed. "You still consider me a suspect, don't you? I didn't kill him."

"Then help me find out who did."

BERT PHONED GARDNER at home, sounding excited. "Got some thing."

His own spirits lifted. "Go on."

"I'm at the Galaxy Lounge. You won't believe this, but

April Nevins identified Page's photo. She saw him here one evening with Bradshaw and guess what? They weren't alone. Want to know who was with them?"

"Cheryl McNeill," Gardner said without hesitation.

"How did you know?"

"Lucky guess." Gardner was thoughtful for a moment. "Was there another woman with them?"

"Yeah, but April had no idea who she was. I tried to get a description, not much use though. She was too busy watching Cheryl and Bradshaw when she had a free moment. She wasn't serving their table so she didn't overhear any of the conversation. She vaguely remembers that the other woman was blonde and older than Cheryl. Also, she came with Page, not Bradshaw, but that would make sense, wouldn't it?"

"Stay with April if you can. Keep asking her questions. Maybe she'll remember more."

"Right, I'll get back to you."

After he hung up the phone, Gardner tried to watch TV with the girls, but he couldn't concentrate. He was worried about Kim. He knew the threatening phone call had troubled her more than she would say. He felt a deep sense of relief when she walked through the door.

"I brought some of my stuff," she said. "I'll stay with you tonight."

Every night would have been better, but he knew better than to push it.

Evie and Jean surrounded her. "Kim, want to sit with us?" Jean asked. "We're watching a terrific show."

"Certainly. I rarely watch television. It'll be fun."

KIM ENJOYED SPENDING TIME with Mike and his daughters. She was again feeling a sense of family, of connection. It was a good feeling. Not so great was a gnawing fear, an awareness that she could be in real danger. It took her back to the fall when she'd almost been killed. She would have to be vigilant. Stalkers were scary people.

After the girls were in bed for the night, she and Mike sat together wrapped up in each other's arms on the sofa.

"You really are a dangerous man to love," she said.

"Not too dangerous. I promise."

Kim touched his dark, wavy hair, studying the rugged features. "Don't make promises you might not be able to keep," she said.

"I'll try not to. Just do me one favor."

"What's that?"

He caressed her cheek with the back of his hand, sending sensual ripples through her body. "Take tomorrow off from work."

"Mike, I just got back from vacation."

"Call it a sick day or a personal day then. Just do it." His eyes were intense.

"I'm probably no safer here than at work."

"I'll have a car watch the house." He slowly kissed the palm of her hand.

"You don't need to do that."

"I think I do."

He kissed the nape of her neck and she found that, too, was a sensitive area and shivered.

"You can be awfully stubborn."

"But sexy?" There was that wicked smile of his again.

"Don't think I'm not on to how you operate. You use sexual attraction as a weapon of persuasion."

"Is it working?"

She put her lips to his and kissed him deeply. He let out a low groan. Without another word, he lifted her into his arms and carried her upstairs to his bedroom.

"Mike, put me down, I'm too heavy to carry. You'll hurt yourself."

"You hardly weigh anything. Now quiet down. You don't want to wake the girls."

Maybe it was the heightened tension and anxiety, but they made love as they never had before.

She matched his hunger and need with her own. And when her own urgent climax came upon her, he joined her in a sublime, passionate union.

AS HE DROVE DOWN the single lane county highway, Gardner's thoughts wandered. He'd lived and worked in this town for too many years to just write it off. Evie wasn't even born when he started building their house. What he'd liked best was the rural aspect of the land. Coming from a city background, it meant something to live near farms and forests. The township was forty-two square miles in size, a good part of it still undeveloped. There were dense woodlands and even a few lakes. Best of all, they weren't far from the Pine Barrens with their stark, eerie beauty. Gardner couldn't help but wonder what the township would be like in the future. He felt somehow that what he did now would make a difference; but maybe that was just self-delusion.

What worried him most was the indifference of the residents. They had so little regard for others. Very few of the people who moved into the housing developments, townhouses or garden apartments stayed for any length of time. Webster was a bedroom community, a place where New Yorkers lived because they couldn't afford New York City or were afraid of the dangers. Too many residents thought of the town as just a place to sleep as they commuted back and forth from the city each day. Public apathy in civic matters was a tradition in Webster. The only thing that the voters seemed to unite in was defeating the school budget year after year. But who could really blame them? The taxes were strangling them.

Although he might outwardly shrug and say that the graft

and corruption were just part of the system—the inherent
nature of how the game was played—Gardner cared about
upgrading the community. He felt that he had a stake in Webster's future. If nothing else, he could make a contribution
by seeing to it that Webster was a safe place to live.

He'd decided to come home for lunch to check on Kim.
As he drove up to the house, Gardner noticed that the lawn
needed mowing again. There were things he tended to neglect, but he tried not to feel guilty. A question of priorities,
he told himself.

Kim looked very happy to see him, almost relieved. She
actually threw her arms around him.

"Was there another phone call?"

Kim pulled away from him. "I don't want to bother you
about it." She looked pale; small worry lines in the form of
creases appeared at the corners of her warm brown eyes.

"I think you better tell me about it right away."

She began anxiously smoothing her summer dress across
her hips. Without warning, Kim burst into tears. This was so
totally unlike her. He knew from personal experience that
Kim was a very brave woman.

He took her into his arms and hugged her. "Honey, whatever was said, it won't seem so bad if you share it with me.
I might even be able to do something about it." He smiled
at her, touching her tears with his index finger as if to take
away her anguish.

"All right," she agreed.

"Let's sit down in the kitchen and talk. I'd love a cold
drink."

"I'll fix lunch for you."

He followed her out to the kitchen where the family ate
most of their meals. It was a sunny, spacious room wallpa-
pered with bright yellow flowers. He watched as Kim sliced
some tomatoes fresh from the garden and put a substantial
serving on his plate along with some chicken salad.

"There's lemonade and iced tea," she offered.

"Before anything else, sit down and talk to me. Everything else can wait." He gripped her hand.

She nodded, sitting down opposite him. "He said terrible things. I'm fairly certain it was the same man who called before." She stopped then, bit her lower lip, and he had to prod her on.

"What exactly did he say to you?"

She ran her hand through her hair. She was wearing it down today, the way he liked it. But he couldn't think about that now, couldn't let the chemistry that sizzled between them distract him.

"First, he said to tell you that he knows where you live. Then he asked how you'd like it if something bad happened to one of your kids, like maybe not coming home one day. He said you're being watched and so am I. He claimed that I must not have given you his message yesterday and I better do it this time or I'd be really sorry. He said, and I quote, 'If your boyfriend doesn't stop nosing around in matters that don't concern him, we'll give him something to really worry about.' He told me to have a talk with you. It wasn't much of a conversation. He did all the talking."

Gardner was furious; in his entire life, he'd never been so angry. He tried not to show his feelings to Kim and gnashed down on his back molars to hold on to his self-control, but she must have suspected because her look was questioning.

"I'll take care of it," he told her in a tight voice. He took her hand and caressed it, then kissed each fingertip in turn. "Will you trust me to handle the situation? There's nothing I care about in this world more than you and the kids. I won't let anything happen to any of you. Do you believe me?"

She nodded her head vigorously.

"Good. I want you to forget this for now."

"Not so easy. You're the one in the most danger, aren't you, Mike?" Her eyes were like searchlights.

"No more than usual. It's just a lot of cheap macho talk. One of the suspects is a self-important blowhard who over-reacts."

"You think this man's the killer?"

"Honestly? I just don't know, but I'm going to find out quick. That's a promise."

BERT WAS WAITING for him back at headquarters. He hadn't seen her yet today. She'd been assigned elsewhere in the morning.

"Anything else from April?"

"Couldn't talk to her much more. She took a short break, but then had to go back to work. She did remember that Page was flirting with Cheryl, or at least he tried to take her hand a few times."

"Right in front of Bradshaw?"

"She thought that Bradshaw was encouraging it. He, in turn, was paying attention to the other woman at the table who, incidentally, did not look like a bimbo according to April. This lady was class, expensive clothes and jewelry."

"We have to go after Page, hit him hard and get him talking." He saw that Nash was in his office. "I'll let the captain know."

Bert gave him look of disapproval. "Why tell him anything? It might just get back to Page."

"In spite of everything, I think he's a straight cop."

She rolled her eyes.

Gardner walked directly into the captain's office, which was unusual since he always knocked first, but he was in a strange mood. Nash viewed him with a cold expression.

"We've established a definite connection between Bradshaw and George Page. A witness saw them together."

"Just how reliable is your witness?"

"Reliable enough."

"Damn you!" Nash exploded, his face reddening.

"Couldn't you just leave it alone? You're supposed to be a professional, for Christ sakes."

"And just how professional am I supposed to feel when Page threatens my family? What if it were yours?"

"Mike, why this super cop routine? That's not your style. Just lay off Page."

"If we really are professionals, as you claim, then his money and influence shouldn't buy him any special treatment or favors from us. I'm not out to get the guy, only to find out the truth. He's hiding something, and I need to know what it is."

"So damn determined to make me choose up sides, aren't you? Well, if Page killed Bradshaw, nail his ass—but make sure you get evidence that'll hold up in court. I know you've been busting your balls on this case. Just do it right."

Gardner didn't say anything more to Nash; he extended his hand. Nash pushed it away. "No, just get the hell out of here! I'm jeopardizing my pension, and I'm not happy about it."

Bert was waiting for him. He explained the gist of the conversation.

"I've got no use for people like him."

"In three years, Nash can retire on a comfortable pension. He could even work at something else if he chooses. He's not ready for a rocking chair. Plus, he's got three daughters to support, two of them still in college."

Bert shook her head, braids turning. "All the more reason not to trust him."

Soon, they were trying to plan a strategy. Whatever Page was hiding, the lady who had dinner with him, Bradshaw and Cheryl McNeill might be the key. He was pretty certain that woman was Page's wife. There was only one thing to do: he had to find a way to get into the house and talk with her.

Feverishly, his mind began devising a plan that would get him inside the gates of Page's self-styled fortress. He and

Bert went down to the police garage, looking for the right sort of vehicle. He found one finally in a white panel truck used for surveillance. Gardner checked it out; there were even several pairs of white coveralls inside as well as caps. Perfect. "I'm going to get into Page's place, but it'll be undercover. And I don't want you involved."

"How come?" Bert was challenging him again. That figured.

"For one thing, they're likely to recognize you. And the two of us together, for certain they'll make the connection. Besides, I don't want you in danger of being thrown off the force. Not when you just started getting used to working here."

"I'll make my own decisions," Bert said.

GENERAL EXTERMINATORS WAS a company run by an old friend. Gardner had worked with Jim Blodgett in a disadvantaged youth program several years ago, and the two of them came to respect each other. Jim, a large man in his early fifties, had a way with troubled kids, just as Gardner did.

They shook hands, made a little small talk, and then Gardner got down to business.

"I need a favor." He pointed to the white panel truck he'd signed out of the police garage. "I'm working undercover and need some equipment to make me look like an exterminator."

"Not a problem."

Gardner felt both gratitude and relief. Maybe he could pull this off after all.

NINETEEN

KIM SAW MIKE drive up to the house in a white van. He walked up the driveway carrying coveralls. There was a certain look about him, a faraway expression, as if he were lost in thought.

"What's going on?"

"I'm making plans."

"What sort of plans?"

"Hey, who's the interrogator here?"

She studied him, her eyebrow cocked. "Answering questions with questions again. Very shifty. Come on, Mike, give. I'm part of this. Tell me what's going on."

His expression softened. He followed her into the living room. They sat down together, holding hands, and he told her his plan.

She listened thoughtfully. "Even if you disguise yourself as an exterminator, won't Page recognize you?"

"I did some checking. Page won't be working from home tomorrow morning. He'll be at a construction site and then his office."

"I guess I shouldn't ask how you found that out?"

"Hey, it's not just you reference librarians who know how to get information. I got my sources." He gave her a smug smile.

"Okay, but even if you manage to get in, how do you know that Mrs. Page will be there?"

"It seems she's reclusive, rarely goes out. So the odds are in my favor."

Kim was worried. Mike was planning to take a terrible risk. She knew it was all about protecting her and his daughters. She wanted to help make it work.

"You realize you're endangering your job?"

"Hey, being a cop is a risky business regardless," he said with a shrug.

"But you'll be going undercover without authorization. I don't like it at all."

He looked at her intently. "Got a better idea?"

"Well, maybe."

She told him what she was thinking. As she expected, he argued with her.

"You're nuts. You know that? Practically certifiable."

"I don't disagree, but it's the only thing that might work, because, frankly, I don't see Mrs. Page just opening up to you. You're a man and a police officer who'll be invading her privacy. Anyway, they'll be watching you work. You'll never be able to get near her. You need an accomplice. By the way, can you fake it, really look like an exterminator?"

"Sure thing. Blodgett gave me spraying equipment, gloves and goggles. I can make it look real."

"I'll call in sick for work again."

"I'm really sorry about this," he said.

She could see that he meant it. He needed her help. She was convinced there was no way he could do this alone.

"The girls should be here soon. After I call in, I'll fix dinner."

"I'll help you. But it's just you and me for supper," he said.

"The camp took the kids on a trip today so they'll be getting home late."

"Really?" she said. "Well, then, I guess food can wait."

"Not hungry?" Mike asked.

"Not so much." Her voice was husky and she gave him

that special look she had when she was aroused. They were definitely in close communication.

He took her into his arms. "Turns out I am starving, but not for food."

THE FOLLOWING DAY, Bert was outside of Page's gates as they'd arranged. She would stand by as unobtrusively as possible in their unmarked car. Gardner would signal if she were needed.

Gardner found his palms sweating against the steering wheel. He drove up to the main gate, put on a pair of dark-rimmed eyeglasses and pulled the cap low on his head before honking the horn. The guard he remembered from the last visit came forward.

"Yeah, buddy?"

"Exterminator come to do some work."

"Nobody told me nothing about an exterminator coming today." The man eyed him with suspicion and then glanced at the panel truck. He had a dark beard that, although shaved recently, left a coarse blue-black texture along his cheeks and jawline; it made him look sinister.

"They must have forgotten. I got my work order right here." He held up the paper without actually showing it to the man, hoping that his lie sounded believable. Even with all the trouble he'd gone to setting this up, there was no assurance he would be able to get inside. Maybe his plan, born of desperation, had been stupid after all.

"Mr. Page ain't here right now, buddy." The man seemed uncertain.

Gardner thought he was buying the story. Gardner felt a sense of relief suffuse his body. "Mr. Page won't be happy if you send me away. It'll be some time before I can come back again. This is our busy season."

"Yeah, well, all right, I guess it's okay. I mean, they'll have to clear you at the house anyway. I'll call ahead and let them know you're coming."

Gardner drove through as the guard opened the gate. He called back to Kim, who was concealed from view.

"So far so good. Just stay down back there until I call for you."

KIM NODDED her head without saying a word. Her posture was stiff and tense. In her white coveralls with her hair tightly pulled under a cap, she looked like an ordinary worker. Hopefully, she would draw little attention to herself. She took several deep breaths, trying to calm herself.

So far their luck was holding. The huge, white colonial dwelling loomed against the bright, cobalt summer sky. She noticed the large brick fireplaces built on either side of the house and impressive white pillars at the front. The Pages lived well. She wondered what sort of person Mrs. Page was. Well, she would find out soon enough.

GARDNER LEFT THE white van at the front entrance and placed the keys in his side pocket. The spraying equipment and goggles were clutched in either hand for the sake of believability. Then he rang the doorbell and took a long, deep breath. He knew very well that what he had in mind wasn't going to be easy to accomplish, but he didn't know anything else that he could do.

The same hulking manservant answered the door, the voice more gruff than before. Gardner pulled the cap well down on his forehead, feeling sweat drip down his armpits.

"We aren't expecting any exterminator," the man said with a hard look. "Get lost!"

"Mr. Page knows all about it. He wants the company in to look over the house. It's overdue for inspection."

"He ain't said nothin' to me."

"Probably didn't think it was important enough. 'Course, I could always come back some other time, but by then those little critters could have eaten away your foundation. I see many a house sustain structural damage for want of care. I could probably come back again in a few months though. We're awfully busy these days because we're the best in town."

"Yeah, well you sure talk a lot. Okay, come in. We'll see." He eyed Gardner narrowly.

Gardner walked briskly past him into the entry foyer. He looked around for the door that led down to the basement.

"Be right back," he said. "Have to get some stuff."

Back at the truck, he signaled Kim. She took some equipment and followed him inside.

"My assistant will be checking things out upstairs while I work in the basement," he told the big man with an air of authority.

The man followed him down the stairs with a heavy step. Gardner noted the casual shirt and slacks and the jacket that only partly hid his holstered weapon. Gardner decided even if the big man looked like he'd served time at Attica, he was little more than a butler.

Gardner played his part well, inspecting the basement with thoroughness. His every move was watched by the retainer with the aquiline nose resembling an eagle's beak.

"Hey, I just remembered something. This house was termite-proofed when it was built. What are you up to?"

Gardner's heart began to palpitate. "Haven't you ever heard of carpenter ants?" he said. "They'll chew your foundation through good as any termite. And they can be anywhere in the house." He hoped the white coveralls he wore lent him an air of authenticity.

"Don't termite-proofing take care of the ants, too?"

"Nope, they're a hardy breed. Entirely different species of insect. You've heard of the killer ants down in South America? Well, these are related. They can eat through anything if they're not stopped."

"No kidding?"

"Well, I got to look around, fella. These ants breed awful fast. No telling where they are."

The sandpaper voice sounded anxious. "Okay, just do what you have to quick."

"My intention exactly." He walked around with Lurch following close behind.

KIM DIDN'T WASTE a second. She hurried up the stairs to the second landing and quickly looked around. Her heart was beating violently. It crossed her mind that she was now guilty of criminal trespass. It wasn't only Mike who could lose his job. And they might both be thrown in jail. She recalled horror stories of what happened to people in prisons and shuddered involuntarily. What was she doing? She prided herself on being a sensible person. This was totally insane! And yet she kept on going.

The house was large with plush carpeting, expensive furnishings. It looked as if there were at least five bedrooms up here, each with a private bath, but they seemed deserted at first. Then she noticed a small room set off from the others. Kim walked in, aware that someone else was there. A blonde woman was sitting on a velvet sofa with her feet on a hassock watching television. She didn't seem to hear Kim come in at first, which gave her an opportunity to study the woman. Kim thought she was around forty. Although her clothes were well-tailored, there was an aura of neglect about her.

"Mrs. Page?" she asked in a soft voice, trying not to startle the woman.

The woman looked up, puzzled; hazy blue-gray eyes found her own. "I'm sorry, who are you? Was I supposed to expect you?"

She removed her cap. "I'm Kim Reynolds, an academic librarian who works at the humanities library at the university. I came here today to talk to you on behalf of Lieutenant Gardner of the Webster Township Police. He brought me because he found it difficult to get in to talk with you."

For some reason, the woman didn't register surprise. "Georgio doesn't like me to talk to strangers," she said dully. Kim thought Mrs. Page might be on some form of meds.

"I can understand that, since he has such a lovely wife." Kim hoped that wasn't pouring it on too thick, but Mrs. Page actually seemed pleased, offering a wide if somewhat vacant smile.

"Why do you want to talk to me?" she asked, a confused expression on her face.

Why indeed? Kim knew she didn't have the experience and expertise at interrogation Mike had achieved. He knew just what to ask. Mike spoke with authority. They didn't call him *the psychologist* for nothing.

Kim took a deep, shaky breath and let it out slowly. She needed to have more confidence in her own abilities. After all, she might not be a law enforcement officer, but she had plenty of experience framing reference questions. That was an art in itself, asking questions of people to determine what they really needed and wanted to know. And she was very good at it. Being a good reference librarian wasn't all that different from being a perceptive detective, she reasoned. In both occupations, you had to put the pieces together to solve a puzzle. You needed to ask the right questions if you were ever to find the right answers. With that mental pep talk, Kim was able to relax a bit.

"The man your husband introduced to you, Richard Bradshaw? He's dead. Was he a friend of your husband?"

"Friend? I don't know."

"He died under strange circumstances, and we need help finding out what happened. I thought you might know something that could help."

Mrs. Page looked upset; Kim's instincts told her that the

woman did know something. Short lashes fluttered over her distracted eyes. "I can't talk to you. Georgio wouldn't like it."

"It's for his sake. People are thinking bad things about him. You don't want that, do you?"

"I want to watch television," she said.

"Our talk won't take very long."

Kim glanced around the room, trying to get a handle on the woman. Nothing extraordinary: bookshelves mostly filled with romance paperbacks, a sewing machine and some gilt-framed photos. Prominently displayed were pictures of a young boy.

"Your son?" she asked pointing. "A handsome child. You must be proud of him."

Mrs. Page looked away, a pained expression on her face.

"I'm sorry. Did I say something to upset you?"

Mrs. Page turned back and Kim saw the well of sorrow that lay deep inside her. "You couldn't know. The little boy in that photo was my son. He died shortly after that picture was taken."

Kim hated to use personal grief as a device for pumping information, but she knew it couldn't be helped. "Was he an only child?"

Mrs. Page lowered her eyes, nodding miserably.

"I'm not a parent myself, but I can understand how painful it was for you to lose him. My mother lost her younger sister when she was a girl. She had leukemia. It was terrible for the entire family especially my grandmother."

"At least with illness, it's something that can't be helped not some stupid, pointless accident." There was undisguised bitterness in her voice.

So her son had died in an accident. Kim walked to the window and looked out, trying to decide what to ask next. How was she to reach this woman who isolated herself from life, wallowing in a world of grief and pain? Kim looked out at the backyard. Something about it didn't look right.

There was a concave area of dirt where nothing grew. All around, there were plants and shrubs beautifully landscaped and maintained. Why would nothing grow in that large center area? And then she had a vivid flash of insight. She saw the past. She had a clear image of what happened. There had been a drowning pool.

Kim turned seeking confirmation. "Mrs. Page, what used to be in that empty area out behind your house?"

"What?" She seemed startled. "We don't talk about it."

Kim knew without being told. Her special awareness was putting visions into her brain, horrible visions she wished would stop. Kim put her hands to her head and swayed slightly.

"You had a pool back there, a beautiful pool. Did he drown in your swimming pool?"

Mrs. Page's mouth dropped in surprise. "How did you know?"

"I saw it. His spirit is still here. He's suffering. You must go back there and place your hands deep into the earth. I know it won't be easy, but he needs you. Otherwise, he can't go into the light. His spirit won't cross over to the other side where he's meant to go. Only you can help him."

Mrs. Page's head tilted to one side in a look of appraisal.

"You're not pretending, are you?"

"No. I try not to see, believe me. It's too painful."

"You say he's still there?"

Kim nodded. "His ghost or spirit. He's confused. He doesn't understand. Doesn't know that he's dead. He needs you to tell him, to sooth him, to let him go. You must do it for his sake."

Mrs. Page grasped Kim's hand sobbing. "You know, don't you? You have a sensitive look. Not many people understand, and even fewer care. My little boy drowned in our swimming pool—my husband's pool, I should say. My baby sneaked away that morning long before anyone else in the house was awake. He always wanted to do whatever his father did. He knew that he was forbidden in the deep end of the pool, but his daddy always swam there, so he wanted to, as well. It's been a few years now, but the nightmare remains." Her mouth quivered.

In her mind's eye, Kim had a vision of Richard Bradshaw's body floating face down in the La Reine Gardens pool. She tried to shake it.

"I don't know why I told you about it. I never talk to anyone about it except my doctor." Mrs. Page dabbed at her eyes with a tissue.

"It's all right. I understand," Kim said sympathetically.

"Yes, I believe you really do." Mrs. Page was staring at the boy's picture again. "I made Georgio fill in the pool. I couldn't look at it anymore. He thought that I was trying to punish him. Swimming is his favorite recreation. I suppose I was blaming him for what happened."

So that was why Page had built such a magnificent pool in his apartment complex. He'd been trying to compensate for the one he was deprived of at home. Kim wondered if the special pride he took in the swim club had perhaps served as a release from guilt feelings.

"Mrs. Page, you were aware that your husband enjoyed swimming at La Reine Gardens?"

She nodded, her eyes still fixed on the child's picture.

"Did you ever accompany him for an evening swim?"

"I hate swimming pools!"

"Do you know any of the people your husband met at La Reine Gardens? Did you ever meet Richard Bradshaw for instance?"

Her face began to color and she again seemed agitated. "That awful man? I'm sure Georgio didn't know him very well."

"But you had dinner with him once, didn't you? What did he talk about with you and your husband?"

"I think you better go now. I shouldn't have talked to you. My husband wouldn't like it."

How could she get the woman to open up? "Mrs. Page, before I leave, I just want to tell you I believe your husband had some involvement with Bradshaw. You know the man was murdered, don't you? Since Lieutenant Gardner questioned your husband about it, he's been warned that his job is in jeopardy. His family was threatened. Someone warned me on the telephone that if he didn't stop investigating your husband, I too might be killed. What happened to your son was a tragic accident, but if any harm should come to Lieutenant Gardner's children, you can be sure it won't be the result of any accident."

Kim saw that she had reached Mrs. Page; a small tic pulsated in her left eye. Kim viewed her with keen anticipation, hopeful that Mrs. Page would provide the information they desperately needed.

BERT WAS GROWING impatient. It seemed like the waiting had gone on forever. Maybe Gardner and Kim Reynolds were in trouble. She should get in there and see what was happening. The wall had a smooth stone surface, which made it difficult to firmly grasp. It was also higher than she'd first estimated. Good that she worked out whenever she had the chance. Karate and jogging kept her in top condition. Besides, physical activity was the best antidote for depression. She knew she could climb over it.

Bert wasn't even breathing hard when she reached the other side of the wall. There were plenty of trees and shrubs to serve as cover. She kept low, well hidden, and glanced around. The white panel truck was at the front of the house, but there was no sign of Gardner. He had to be in the house. She was wondering which way to approach the house when a sudden rustling in the underbrush caught her attention. She heard the unmistakable growl of a dog ready to attack. Au-

tomatically, she reached for her service revolver as the dog
lunged and ripped at her sleeve. Then another animal came
at her, steel sharp jaws and teeth clamping down on her gun
hand, the agonizing pain forcing her to release her hold on
the weapon. Damn! She should have remembered about the
dogs and tried something like bringing raw meat doctored
with tranquilizers. She'd seen it work in a movie once. But
this was no Hollywood jive, although at the moment, she
wished it were.

"Okay, boys, that's enough. Down, back to the garage!"

Sunlight arabesqued crazily off the gun barrel that was
pointed at her chest. Still, she was relieved to see the two
large Dobermans retreat. She was also aware of the throbbing pain in her hand.

"What are you doing here?" the guard demanded.

She brought up her leg and kicked the automatic from
the man's hand. When the weapon landed on the grass, she
lunged for it with her left hand and almost had it when a
second man kicked it away. Bert looked up and saw this new
turkey also had a gun in his hand, a Magnum from the look
of it. It was the bastard from the house, the big dude with the
beak nose. She brought herself up only part of the way using
her head as a battering ram, butting into the big man's gut.

"Bitch!" he cried with a breathless sound.

Bert felt steel against her back. The sonofabitch had re-
covered much too fast. Should've kicked him harder.

TWENTY

GARDNER WAS ABOUT to claim Kim. He figured she'd used as much time as was wise. The butler had left him a while ago, and that made him uneasy. It was time to get out. As he approached the stairs that led up from the basement, Gardner heard a commotion in the hall above. He hurried upstairs and was surprised to see Bert. Lurch shoved her, a Colt .357 Magnum in his hand. Gardner saw the man who controlled the guard dogs also carried a weapon. Bert's hand was bleeding. It was a nasty, gaping wound. Mrs. Page came hurrying down from upstairs. Kim was behind her.

"Victor, what's going on here?"

"Please don't get upset. Sam found this black broad watching the house, Mrs. Page. She was on the grounds and the dogs attacked her. Sam put in a call to your husband. He'll be here in a few minutes. He's only over at the golf course."

"Who is she?"

"A cop, but don't worry, Mr. Page'll know what to do." Victor focused on Gardner as if seeing him for the first time. "I forgot about this guy. The exterminator's assistant giving you any trouble?"

She cast a guilty glance at Gardner. "I think he's a policeman, too."

The man's countenance darkened; the eagle was ready to peck his eyes out. "Cops!" He spat out the word like a profanity. "You got no right sneaking around here without warrants. You're screwed."

"Please, just get them out of the house. Make them go

away," Mrs. Page said, and dismissed them with a nervous but queenly wave of her hand. She hurried back up the stairs.

Kim came to stand beside him. She looked very pale. Gardner wished he could reassure her. He took her hand and squeezed it gently.

"Well, you heard the lady," Gardner said, and eased toward the front door, signaling Kim and Bert to follow his lead.

"Where the fuck do you think you're going, asshole?"

"Mrs. Page told you to let us go."

Victor shoved the barrel of his big gun against Gardner's temple. "Mr. Page pays us, and he says you stay until he comes. So don't move or I'll have to off a few intruders."

They were obliged to stand in the main hall like delinquents caught writing graffiti on the schoolyard wall, waiting for the principal to haul them into his office for punishment. An indeterminate amount of time passed, in which the silence became nerve shattering. Gardner balled his hands into fists. He barely felt the fingernails dig into his palms. He was angry with himself, furious that he'd put both Kim and Bert in danger. He'd acted stupidly. His plan had been foolish. He could see that now. He knew he'd have to keep calm and in control. He loved Kim and he had an obligation to protect her from harm.

Finally, the front door opened and George Page stalked into the house. Page stood in the foyer staring at them with blood in his eye.

"You ruined a damned good game of golf," Page said.

"Then it wasn't a total loss," Gardner replied.

"Wiseass!" Victor glowered. "We caught these cops snooping around."

"I told you to keep away from here. I guess I didn't tell you strong enough." Page gave them hard looks.

"What do you want us to do with them, Mr. Page? They're intruders, so if you like, I could take them out."

"We don't have to do anything. They've already done it to

themselves. They're going to be thrown off the force. Breaking and entering is a felony. They'll go to prison. Guess how long they'll last there?"

Gardner felt a calm descend over him, as if he were standing in the eye of a hurricane and realized there was really nothing to lose by confronting the storm. "I have a witness who places you and your wife at the Galaxy Lounge in the company of Bradshaw and Cheryl McNeill. She saw the hand-holding and the cutesy stuff that went on there. We also know about the twenty thousand dollars you gave Cheryl to keep her quiet."

"You can't trace that money to me."

"I can prove that you've been lying right along. You knew Bradshaw. And you were at the pool the night he died. What are you so afraid of? Us finding out that you tried frightening us off by making threats?" He paused for less than a moment. "You don't want to tell us anything? Fine, let me try a little scenario. Bradshaw offered to hook you up with Cheryl. I don't know what was in it for him, but I'm sure he would have thought of something. Maybe he just liked the idea of doing an important man a favor so you'd owe him. Did he want your wife in exchange for lending you Cheryl?"

"Shut your filthy mouth!"

Victor moved toward him as if he were about to pistol whip Gardner. Bert quickly stuck her foot out, tripping him, and the big man fell forward.

Gardner continued talking as if he'd never been interrupted. "You met Cheryl at the pool for a swim that night. You found Bradshaw unconscious in the storage shed, or maybe he'd already come around. What happened after that? Did he insult you? He was in a nasty mood, wasn't he? Did he threaten to tell your wife about your fling with Cheryl?"

Page looked furious. "I never spoke to him."

"But you were there that evening." He faced Page. "If you didn't kill him, then why are you so afraid?"

"My people will escort you to the gate."

Gardner didn't budge. "I don't like the way you threatened my family. If anything should happen to my girls, I'll hound you to hell. And If I'm unable to do that for some reason, I'll make sure someone else takes care of it. Even your high, thick walls won't be enough protection, and neither will your bodyguards or your mob connections." Gardner never raised his voice but spoke with intensity.

"I, too, believe in retribution," Page responded in a grave manner, as if Gardner had finally reached him on some level.

"I'm not leaving here until I know what you're covering up. Whatever it is, you can't keep hiding it. The truth is bound to come out."

Page sneered at him. "A lot you know. Money creates its own truth—and it's a silent gravedigger."

Gardner saw that Bert was hurting, although she hadn't said a word. The wound looked like it needed medical treatment. He respected her stoicism and courage. Kim also had true grit. She'd kept silent, a brave woman, but then, he already knew that. It was one of the things he loved about her. Now she exchanged a look with him, a speaking look, informing him she'd found out something that might help them. He nodded to her and she stepped forward.

"Your wife and I had a long talk before you came. She told me about Bradshaw. She wasn't afraid."

Victor came toward Kim. Gardner was ready to take him down if he so much as looked at her the wrong way, but Page signaled his flunky away.

"I don't know what she told you, but my wife is in delicate health. Some years ago, she suffered a terrible loss and hasn't been the same since. She has chronic bouts of depression."

"Is that why you keep her isolated most of the time?" Kim's voice was gentle but firm.

"I do no such thing. She prefers to be alone. How dare you bother that woman with your suspicions? You're nothing but scum."

KIM KNEW IT WAS dangerous to possibly make a man like Page lose control, yet she saw no other alternative. "It's only natural that your wife is depressed. The loss of a child, particularly your only child, is a traumatic experience."

"She told you about that?"

Kim forced herself to stay cool. "I also know why you particularly enjoyed the pool at La Reine Gardens. But you can understand why your wife insisted on filling in yours."

That was too much for Page. His temper was getting the better of him. The color of his face was a mottled purple, as if his rage were beginning to strangle him. Kim wondered if she'd made a mistake.

"I changed my mind, Victor. We'll get rid of these cops permanently. And you can bury them in the old swimming pool. That seems like justice."

Kim felt sick to her stomach. Dear God, she'd only succeeded in making matters worse!

TWO MEN WITH GUNS and Page, who wasn't armed—they could probably take the lot if Bert's hand weren't mangled. Gardner could tell Kim felt she'd pushed too hard. He would have liked to reassure her, but he couldn't. The worst part was that they still didn't know any more than before talking to Page.

"What's going on?" Mrs. Page was poised at the top of the staircase.

"Your husband's decided to have us killed," Gardner told her. "I hope it won't weigh too heavily on your conscience."

"I asked Victor to send them away," she said to her husband, descending the stairs with an awkward gait. Gardner knew he'd succeeded in rattling her.

"Why did you tell the cop anything? Marie, you're a stupid woman. Now I have to kill them."

Her mouth dropped open. "What do you think I told her? Anyway, that woman said she's a librarian, not a cop. They can't prove a thing. I never told her about you."

"What the hell are you talking about? I've been protecting you!" Page blurted out. The land developer realized almost immediately he'd made a mistake by saying too much in front of his employees. He turned to them now with his head high in a gesture of command. "What are you waiting for? Get rid of the cops!"

"Sure, boss. You want us to whack them. No problem."

Sam gave Bert a shove with his automatic. Her leg came up and kicked the guard a hard blow to the groin as her good hand went for the gun, knocking it out of the man's hand and across the room. Gardner had no time to admire her agility in the martial arts, because it was his turn to act. Although Victor was a good four or five inches taller than him and much broader, Gardner brought his elbow up and smashed a hard blow into his adversary's midsection, followed by a fist to the windpipe. Gardner finished with a strong chop downward that disarmed Victor. The eagle had definitely landed.

Gardner quickly unzipped his coveralls under which he had his holstered service revolver. With a gun in each hand, Gardner figured he looked a lot more formidable. Bert, who held Sam's automatic, quickly slipped on the safety and placed it into her jacket pocket. She seemed to prefer holding her own weapon now that she could get it back. The room was suddenly silent.

"I'd like for us all to sit down in the living room and talk like reasonable, civilized people. You don't have to offer us tea and crumpets, but we definitely require some conversation." Gardner motioned to Victor and Sam; they followed Mr. and Mrs. Page wordlessly.

He looked down at Victor's Magnum. It was tiring his hand, but he had no intention of returning the weapon to its owner.

"Mrs. Page, why does your husband think you need protection? Were you at the pool club on the night Bradshaw died?"

Mrs. Page wasn't willing to answer him directly. Instead, she turned to her husband. "You thought that I had something to do with that man's death?" She shook her head incredulously. "Why would I kill him? I barely knew him. He was your acquaintance. I didn't tell that woman anything because I was protecting you."

"Don't start twisting things around, Marie." Page viewed her darkly.

"Fine. Then if you have nothing to hide, and I'm telling you I don't, we should tell them what they want to know." Mrs. Page crossed her legs and folded her arms over her breasts.

"Okay, tell him what you want. I don't suppose I can stop you anyway. You never did have any sense." He turned his face away from her as if disassociating himself.

His wife made eye contact with Gardner, ignoring her husband's insult. "I did go to the swim club the night that man died. At dinner that evening, Georgio and I had an argument, a bitter one. He said we never have fun anymore, that our house was like a tomb, a mausoleum, because I was permanently in mourning. He told me his new friend, Rick Bradshaw, liked me. I knew what was really going on." She threw an accusing glance at her husband. "This Bradshaw was nothing more than a pimp. He offered to let my husband sleep with his girlfriend and in return I was to do the same with him." Her eyes burned with indignation.

"I never said that," Page protested.

"That's what you meant, what you wanted."

"California people are different, much more relaxed and

modern. Rick only suggested it as a way to revitalize our marriage."

She turned away from Page. "Georgio said if I didn't meet this man at the pool, he was going to divorce me. He said he planned to be there with Cheryl, and we'd all enjoy the place together. He put the keys to the club in my hand and then he left. I thought it over for a while. I didn't want to go. Those people were superficial. But nobody in my family has ever gotten a divorce. It isn't done. It would shame me.

"When I got to the pool, everything was locked up and it was dark. I thought maybe there was some mistake. I opened the gate, went in and located the lights. Then I began looking around. The cabanas were empty and so was the pool. I went to the storage room thinking I heard someone moving around in there, found it locked and tried the keys again. When the door opened, I couldn't see anything until I found a light switch. I remember looking up at a small naked lightbulb, then down at the ground. That was when I saw him lying there. He moaned, tried to move and then fell back. He looked as if he were dead. He was so still, and there was blood on his face and hair. I heard Georgio's voice behind me. I remember turning around and staring at him. The girl was there, too. He asked me something, but I didn't hear him. I threw down the keys and ran out of that horrible place, hurrying to my car. When Georgio came home later that night, he tried to talk to me, but I wouldn't speak to him. I just wanted to wipe the whole ugly thing from my mind."

Gardner turned to Page. "Was that how you remember it?"

Page didn't speak at first; a lifetime habit of avoiding and mistrusting police showed in his face. "Marie was there when we arrived. I'd picked up Cheryl at her apartment. We expected to meet Rick at the club. The gates were open and we walked in. Since we didn't see anyone, we walked around. I found my wife standing over Rick. She was just staring at him like she was in shock. I tried to talk to her, but she didn't seem to hear me. Cheryl saw everything that I did."

"So you formed the opinion that your wife had killed him?"

Page's jaw was working but he didn't answer. Gardner turned back to Mrs. Page, the more cooperative of the two. "Did your husband have reason to believe that you might have killed Bradshaw?"

"Georgio was interested in having an open marriage. I did blame Mr. Bradshaw for putting the idea in his head. I felt he was little more than a procurer. I have strong religious beliefs. No matter how I may feel about my husband at times, I strive to make our marriage work. Georgio started talking about how we had to loosen up sexually. That was Bradshaw's doing. The man disgusted me, and I communicated my feelings to my husband."

"Did you assume your husband killed Bradshaw?"

She hesitated, casting her eyes downward. "I didn't know. Georgio has a bad temper. Sometimes, it gets the better of him."

Gardner was well aware that Page considered himself above the law. Mrs. Page probably had very good reason to consider her husband capable of violent acts.

"I didn't kill Bradshaw," Page burst out. "Marie, you need to be locked up in a nuthouse."

"Georgio, you're capable of anything. And I'm not taking your abuse anymore. No more Bradshaws and no more bimbos. I want a real husband or I'm leaving you."

Gardner smiled. Mrs. Page was finally showing some guts.

She gave Gardner an oblique look and shook her head, as if she knew what he was thinking. "It's taken me too long to summon my courage."

"You thought your husband killed Bradshaw, and he thought you did it." Gardner felt discouraged. This wasn't what he'd expected. It seemed unlikely that either of them was the killer. He turned back to Page. "You went to a lot of trouble for nothing. It would've been a lot easier if you'd just talked it out with your wife in the first place."

"Don't lecture me. You're nothing. I buy and sell guys like you anytime I want."

Bert responded to Page's arrogance. "Don't count on it." She waved the gun she held in the builder's face.

"Are you done with your questions?"

"Not quite. We still have a murderer to find. Let's go back to when you left the pool that night. Did you shut off the lights and lock up?"

Page was thoughtful. "I guess I did," he responded with a shrug.

"That's not good enough. Did you lock up? This is important. You must have been in a hurry to leave after discovering Bradshaw in the storeroom. What exactly did you do?"

"I did lock up, but I forgot to shut off the flood lights around the pool."

"When you saw Bradshaw, did you examine him? Did you feel for a pulse?"

"No, he looked dead."

"You didn't think to call for assistance? That the man might still be alive?"

"I had my wife and myself to think about, my reputation and hers."

Gardner didn't comment on Page's selfish disregard for human life; he didn't think it would do much good. "What time were you at the pool?"

"Probably around nine o'clock, not much later."

"Did Cheryl try to blackmail you?"

"Her? No, she's a nice kid. I just wanted to give her a gift. Look, that business before about having you guys killed, I lost my temper is all. I wouldn't really off you. I don't do things like that. I'm a respectable businessman. Let's forget it, okay? My wife and I have cooperated. Now you know we had nothing to do with the murder."

Gardner decided it was nice to see Page sweat a little.

"It's been beautiful," Bert said sarcastically. "Let's do lunch sometime."

Outside the large, colonial structure, Gardner turned to Kim and Bert.

"You were both terrific. We won't have any more trouble with Page."

"Yeah, but we've arrived at another dead end. And I screwed up. If I'd stayed outside, they wouldn't have gotten wise to you." Bert sounded dejected.

"We don't know that for sure. Right now, we've got to get you over to the emergency room and have that hand taken care of. It must hurt like hell."

"I'll take Bert's car back to the house," Kim said.

"Are you okay?" Gardner asked, placing his arm around her.

"Now that my legs stopped quaking like gelatin, I'm terrific."

"That's my girl. You're tough."

"I ain't so tough," Kim said.

"Humphrey Bogart?"

She smiled at him, displaying her even white teeth. "No. Jimmy Cagney's last line in *Public Enemy*."

"You're just full of little tidbits of information, aren't you?"

"It goes with the job."

She gave him a deep kiss and he felt an unexpected surge of desire.

"Catch you later," he said, wondering if she'd feel as frisky once the adrenaline rush wore off. He sure hoped so.

TWENTY-ONE

GARDNER DROVE OFF in the van with Bert after watching Kim leave in the unmarked police car, relieved that they'd managed to survive their ordeal. They were only twenty minutes from the hospital, but the wait in the emergency room seemed unending. While Bert's hand was being attended to, Gardner closed his eyes and concentrated on the Bradshaw case again. They were very close now; he could feel it. Something gnawed at the edge of his consciousness. Why had Sonny thought April Nevins killed Bradshaw? Why had he put Bradshaw's body in the pool? How had he known Bradshaw was dead in the first place? They couldn't ask Sonny those questions. The next best thing was to question April Nevins again. Although she gave the impression of being forthright, you could never tell with a murder suspect. He was anxious to get going but managed to wait patiently for Bert, who finally reappeared with a neatly bandaged hand.

"Does it hurt much?"

"They gave me something for the pain so I wouldn't feel it when the Doc stitched me up."

"I'm going to drop you at your apartment. You've had enough for one day."

"Not a chance. We're finishing this case together. Besides, I'm pretty good with my left hand, too."

"So I noticed. I was planning to visit April Nevins before she goes to work."

"You'll get more from her if I'm around," Bert said. "She seems to trust me."

APRIL PROBABLY HAD been asleep, because she took her time
answering the door and was dressed in her silk kimono, her
hair unkempt. Still, the place looked a little neater than usual,
as if she'd made some effort to deal with the clutter.

"I'm sorry we have to trouble you again," Gardner said
politely. "There are just a few additional questions that need
to be asked."

"Such as?" She eyed him warily.

"Well, let's go over your movements after seven-thirty on
the night Bradshaw died."

She looked at him in surprise. "Lieutenant, I told you all
that before. I don't understand. Didn't I help you enough
when I identified the picture?"

"It was a great help, but we need more."

She shook her head and a tawny lock of hair fell across
her face like a curtain dropping.

"Satisfy the man," Bert urged. "He's a perfectionist."

"Okay, I took a swim and left the club before eight. I
changed there because I didn't have time to waste. I started
work a few minutes past eight. You can check with my boss.
He keeps track."

"For some reason, Sonny thought you killed Bradshaw.
He told you and his mother that. Why?"

"Hell, I don't know. Sonny was dumb."

"What exactly did he say to you?"

She cast her eyes downward. "He said stuff about putting
Rick in the pool for me."

"That's what we need to know about," Gardner said.

She gazed at him, fear in her expression. "I told you all I
know. Please leave me alone."

Gardner saw that she was closing up. He turned to Bert
with a silent appeal.

"April, Lieutenant Gardner doesn't think you killed Bradshaw. Neither do I. It's just that you might know more than

you think. You do want to help us break this case, don't you?"
There was actual warmth in Bert's voice.

"I just don't want to get in trouble," April said.

"It'll be okay."

April's eyes looked into those of Bert. "Sonny claimed he
put Rick's body in the pool as a favor to me. I got angry and
called him some names I'd rather not repeat. Then he got real
sore and said I shouldn't play games with him, that he'd done
just what I asked him to do. I exploded at him. He was drunk
and ranting. That's when I called you guys. I never told him
to do any such thing. Are you satisfied?"

"You did fine, girl."

April studied Bert. "What happened to your hand?"

"A dog confused it with his dinner."

April looked sympathetic. "Let me get you a cup of coffee.
It'll only take a minute." She was in the small kitchenette
before either of them could say anything.

Bert gave Gardner an embarrassed shrug. April returned
minutes later holding a large ripe nectarine, took a bite out
of it, licked her lips, and then handed it to Bert who shook
her head at the offering.

"Take it! Better than a cigarette, right? I seem to be all out
of coffee."

Bert accepted the fruit and took a bite.

"See? No more cigs. I'm reforming like you wanted."

"Don't do it for me," Bert said. "Do it for yourself."

"It's not so easy to stop. I'm an addict. That was the one
thing Rick and I really had in common. We were both chain
smokers."

Something clicked in Gardner's mind. "He smoked at the
pool?"

"Lieutenant, he smoked anywhere he could get away with
it."

As they started to leave, April put her hand on Bert's arm.

"I just want you to know that I didn't kill Rick or Sonny. I hope you believe me."

Bert looked at her long and hard. "I believe you. You're doing good, sister. Keep off the nicotine. Doing things that make you feel good about yourself is the key. You develop self-respect, and others will treat you the same way."

"YOU SURE YOU DON'T want to go home and rest?" Gardner asked Bert after they'd left April's apartment.

Bert shook her head. "I'm okay."

Gardner thought she looked a little gray around the gills. "You might not want to make our next visit."

"Why's that?"

"I have to see Mrs. Blake again."

Bert didn't say anything, but the expression on her face told him the encounter with the Blakes had not been forgotten. "You might need back up today."

"Not with Mrs. Blake. I'm sure the sons are working at this hour. You could rest in the car while I talk with her. I've only got a few questions anyway."

Bert agreed with a look of relief.

GARDNER TOOK MRS. BLAKE by surprise. She placed her hands to her chest when she answered the door and saw him standing there, then led him into the house with something less than enthusiasm. He followed her into the living room. The strains of violins accompanied a tender moment in a soap opera. Mrs. Blake didn't bother to shut off her television.

"What are you coming back here for? Did you arrest the woman who killed my boy?"

"I wonder if we might have a brief talk. Just to clarify something."

"Will it help you get my son's murderer?"

"That's the whole idea."

She seemed to relax a little after that.

"You remember telling me that Sonny was certain April Nevins killed Bradshaw. Why was he so sure?"

Her bony shoulders rose in a shrug. "He was certain is all."

"But something or someone made him certain. Think back. What was it?"

"He got a phone call. Didn't I tell you that before?"

"Go on. Who was the phone call from?"

"Who do you think? That whore! She told him what she wanted him to do and he done it."

"So someone called and told Sonny to put Bradshaw's body in the pool?"

"That's right. He told me it was that slut."

"So a woman called and identified herself as April Nevins—but was it really her?" He was thinking out loud.

"Well, it had to be her." Mrs. Blake spoke in an exasperated tone of voice. She gave him a look that suggested she thought him terribly dense to be raking over the same facts. He didn't care; he wanted to make certain of every point so there would be no mistakes later with the case. Attention to detail was crucial. It could make the difference between conviction and dismissal.

"What time did Sonny get that call?"

"It had to be somewhere between nine-thirty and ten in the evening. I can be pretty sure because one of my favorite shows was on and I remember being annoyed to have to get up and answer the phone. It was a woman's voice, and she asked for Sonny. After he talked to her, his face was like chalk and he went out without saying a word to me."

"Then how do you know it was April Nevins who phoned?"

"'Cause we talked about it after that nasty colored detective of yours come pushin' in here."

He decided to ignore her prejudice and stick with the main

topic. "Do you remember anything at all about the phone call? Background noises for example. Was there music or people talking as if the call were made from a bar?"

"No, nothin' like that," Mrs. Blake said. "But come to think of it, I did hear a dog bark."

He thanked the woman for her cooperation and quickly left the rundown house. He could hear her turn the television set up as he closed the door behind him. Bert was napping as Gardner got back into the car, but she was obviously a light sleeper because the sound of the door closing woke her.

She sat up and yawned. "I think that pill they gave me at the hospital wiped me out. Get anywhere with Sonny's mama?"

"Maybe," Gardner said.

Bert studied his face. "Not giving much away, are you? But you think you know who killed both vics. Come on, give."

"Just a suspicion right now. A woman phoned Sonny and claimed to be April Nevins. She asked Sonny to drop Bradshaw's corpse in the pool."

"Whoever made that phone call was the murderer?"

"I'm sure of it."

Bert's dark, fathomless eyes were alert, and there was concern in them, as well. "You don't think it was April after all?"

"That's the obvious conclusion—maybe a little too obvious."

"I'd hate like hell for it to be her."

"Sonny thought she called him. The question is, if someone else claimed to be April, would Sonny be able to recognize an impersonation?" Gardner rubbed his chin thoughtfully.

"We know he wasn't sharp. Still, he should have been able to pick out her voice."

"Of course, the voice could have been deliberately muffled, or in some respects similar. I'd say it was possible to fool him."

"That person had to know that Sonny and April were getting it on." Bert's eyes became more focused.

"That would include everyone on our list of suspects. It's also possible Joan Walling made that phone call hoping to protect herself. There are several things we have to go over with her."

On the drive back to headquarters, neither of them did much talking, but there was no tension between them. They were both absorbed in figuring out how they were going to solve the case. At the office, they began going over the reports on the Bradshaw case one final time. Captain Nash came by the desk where the two of them sat working. He looked from Gardner to St. Croix, a flicker of a smile lightening the rough, lined face.

"Thought you'd like to know the heat is off. I got word unofficially. It seems George Page called up to say that he was pleased at how thoroughly the police department was investigating the Bradshaw killing."

It was then that the unbelievable happened. Bert St. Croix began to laugh. Gardner stared at her, incredulous. She almost never smiled, yet she was laughing, so hard that tears formed in her eyes.

"What's with her?" Nash said looking annoyed.

"Private joke."

"There was a phone call for you from Jerome McKenna. You remember him? He asked especially for you."

"Sure, he's the representative spokesman for that senior citizens' group, the Gray Panthers I think they call themselves. What's his problem?"

"It seems the senior citizens need a meeting place. They're planning a health festival. The recreation office set them up at Rourke's Funeral Parlor. Mr. Rourke is a big benefactor in this town, as you know. He donated the space as a courtesy. But McKenna says the old folks balked when they heard about it. They think it's bad for the morale of their group to hold a senior citizen health festival in a funeral parlor. Picky old farts."

"Well, I can see their point," Gardner said, suppressing a smile.

"I know it's not the kind of thing we handle ordinarily, but McKenna seems to have high regard for your tact."

"I investigated a robbery for him last year. I guess he remembered me from that."

"Must be. Anyhow, he's worried about offending Rourke. They do a lot of business with him."

"You can always depend on people dying. A real solid business," Gardner observed. "Sure, I'll talk to both of them tomorrow. The library's got meeting rooms. I'll see if they can't book the event there."

Nash left them, his face almost cheerful.

"You thinking of joining the group?" Bert chided. "I'm seeing gray hairs."

"Hey, gray hair isn't so bad. Just ask any bald guy."

"I guess a cop has to consider himself lucky if he lives long enough to get gray hair," Bert said, looking serious again.

"I don't think much about dying—there's no future in it." It pleased him to see her smile again.

GARDNER PHONED Matt Simmons, Joan Walling's lawyer, and discovered she was out on bail; charges had been dropped to two counts of assault with a deadly weapon. Gardner was surprised to learn she'd returned to the apartment. Bert shared his amazement.

"You don't think she's back with that shit, do you?"

"I can't believe Walling'd be willing to live with her,

either," Gardner said. "Not after she admitted to having an affair with Bradshaw and hating his guts."

"Not to mention clobbering Bradshaw with a baseball bat."

JOAN WALLING WASN'T eager to see them at first, but Gardner convinced her they were only going to ask one or two questions that had nothing personally to do with her. She let them into the apartment.

"I'm staying for a few days," she said defensively, answering their unasked question. "I'm packing my things together and going back to my parents' house, although Martin and I have talked." There was a hesitation in her voice. "We might be able to forgive each other and work things out in time."

Gardner checked himself; it was not his place to give marital advice. He hadn't done well in that department himself. "Mrs. Walling, apparently Bradshaw was a chain smoker. You said that he was waiting for you in the utility room. Among his effects at the time of his death were a half-smoked pack of cigarettes and a lighter. They were found in his pants pocket. Did you see him smoke while you were with him?"

"Rick always had a cigarette in his mouth. He was orally compulsive."

She was paler and thinner than the last time he'd seen her, her cheekbones more pronounced, features gaunt.

"Can you recall if there were cigarette butts on the floor?"

"I wouldn't remember that."

"Please try."

"Well, I suppose so. The room was darkly lit and I wasn't really looking, but it was very smoky, and there weren't any ashtrays. I don't understand why it matters." She looked bewildered.

He thanked Joan Walling for her help without answering her question.

He looked carefully at Bert as they walked out to their car. "You're spent. You need to lie down and ingest some of those painkillers the doc prescribed."

"What I need is to finish this case. That will help me rest a whole lot better."

"Okay, but I need to stop by my house and check on Kim and the girls before anything else."

Bert didn't argue. She closed her eyes and rested as he drove. For his part, Gardner was preoccupied with thoughts of how to proceed with the Bradshaw case. He was certain now who the killer was. Proving it was going to be another matter entirely.

KIM, EVIE AND JEAN were in the kitchen when he and Bert arrived.

"We're fixing salad," Jean told him.

"Kim went shopping and bought groceries," Evie said.

He watched Kim chopping carrots and red bell peppers as if nothing out of the ordinary had happened earlier in the day. "You're amazing," he said.

"What? You were low on groceries. Since I decided to stay here for the rest of the day, I might as well make myself useful. Hope you like fresh salmon. I bought the wild salmon fillets. They're the best kind."

"Dad's not much of a fish eater," Evie confided.

"If Kim cooks it, I'll eat it," Gardner said.

Jean giggled. "That means Dad really likes you," she said in a stage whisper.

"Bert, how about you?" Kim asked. "Fish okay?"

"Fine," Bert said.

"How's the hand?" Kim's expression was one of concern.

"Could be better," Bert admitted.

"We hope to finish up the Bradshaw case this evening. Want to come with us?"

"Sure," Kim agreed. "I was there with you at the beginning. It seems only fitting that I should be with you at the end."

TWENTY-TWO

"ARE WE GOING OVER to the swim club now?" Bert asked as they left the house.

"I think it's time, don't you?" Gardner responded.

It was past seven in the evening when they walked through the main gate of the club. The place was almost empty. Gardner looked around for Martha Rhoades, and as he did, he had a sense of having gone full circle like a precise Swiss clock.

Martha Rhoades was supervising clean-up activities. The serious heat of the day was over and long shadows formed along the walkways. Outside the gates, several children played in a sandbox as well as on the swings and slide adjoining the club. Large shade trees bordered the high green vinyl fence. It didn't seem possible that a violent murder could have occurred in such a place.

Martha Rhoades was too absorbed in her work to notice them right away. Gardner observed the curly, close-cropped dark hair that crowned her stern, well-tanned face.

"Why are you back here again?" she demanded when she saw them.

"I think you know why we've come."

"I thought the matter of the Bradshaw investigation was finished." She began folding up a chaise uneasily.

"Mrs. Walling didn't kill Mr. Bradshaw. Someone else did."

"I've already told you all I know. I'm really tired of being bothered. I have work to do. You'll have to excuse me." She called to the young, male lifeguard with the dark-colored hair. "Clean out the kiddie pool. You forgot yesterday." She turned back to them. "That used to be Sonny's job. I haven't been able to replace him this late in the season. It means extra work for the rest of us."

"We need a moment to talk privately," Gardner said in a quiet but strong tone of voice.

"Don't you see how busy I am?"

He ignored her angry response. "We'll talk right here then. Getting back to the night Bradshaw was killed, when you arrived at the swim club, you said you found the lights on."

She cleared her throat noisily. "That's right. They were on."

"Mr. Page visited the pool the night Bradshaw died. He apparently left around nine, and Bradshaw did not appear to have sustained a knife wound at that point. Mr. Page forgot to shut the lights off when he left. Sonny probably arrived around ten o'clock or possibly a little later, and carried Bradshaw's body to the pool, placing it in the water. The murder had to occur sometime between the time Page left and Sonny arrived. We can give a rough estimate of somewhere between nine and nine-thirty p.m."

"Maybe Sonny killed Mr. Bradshaw," Martha Rhoades said.

"Then who killed Sonny?"

Her eyes burned with unnatural brightness; she was finding it hard to control her hostility. "There are other possibilities."

"Such as?"

"One of my lifeguards could have been careless with the keys.

An intruder might have walked in."

"Should I question them about it?"

"Do what you like." She folded up another chair.

"Sonny received a phone call from a woman claiming to be April Nevins. The woman told him Bradshaw was dead.

That was confirmed by Mrs. Blake. The woman asked Sonny to go to the club and place the body in the pool."

"There, you see? You have your real murderer! April Nevins killed Mr. Bradshaw."

"Only one problem with that: she's got a good alibi. She was working at the time of the murder. There are witnesses."

"What about Mrs. Walling? She could have made that phone call. She's already confessed to killing Mr. Bradshaw. It seems logical that she might have coaxed Sonny into finishing the job for her and then killed him to protect herself. There. I do believe I've solved the murder for you." She seemed pleased with herself.

"Except that Mrs. Walling thought Bradshaw was already dead. Then there's still the matter of the lights. You said they were on when you passed the club around midnight. That's what drew you to come inside. You did say that?"

"Of course I did, and they were on." Her lips narrowed into a long, sharp line.

"And so you went into the club to shut off the lights. You told us that you found the gates locked."

"That's correct."

"Then you saw Bradshaw's body in the pool."

"You know all of that."

"You told me yourself Sonny always shut off the lights. It was an automatic part of the routine. Yet you say you found the lights on. Let me tell you what I think, Miss Rhoades. I believe that you did find the lights on, but not at midnight like you claim. I think you came by a lot earlier, saw the lights on and went inside to check. You found Bradshaw, quarreled with him and killed him. Then you phoned Sonny pretending to be April and had him dispose of the body for you. Later you returned, put on the lights again and phoned us."

"That's absurd!"

"Is it?"

"Why would I do such a thing? I hardly knew the man."

"When you checked the utility room, Bradshaw must have been stirring and in a mean mood. What happened then?"

She raised her chin and set her jaw firmly. "I don't intend to say anything. You can't prove your suppositions are factual. I had no motive for killing Mr. Bradshaw or Sonny. Unless you plan to arrest me, please leave these premises." Although her look was fierce, her hands and voice trembled. She diverted her gaze from them back to the beckoning aqua waters of the Olympic-size swimming pool.

"You'd be better off confessing," Bert said in an emotionless voice. "We'll nail you anyway."

"I am going to call an attorney if you persist in harassing me. All you can possibly have is circumstantial evidence. It will never hold up in a courtroom if I choose to deny it, which I do."

"Mrs. Blake heard your dog barking when you phoned pretending to be April. Then there's the matter of how neat and clean the floor of the utility room was. You're the only one who would pick up Bradshaw's cigarette butts and wash the blood from the floor. Also, Sonny's paycheck was in his pocket when we found his body. You lied when you told us he didn't come here for it. You had to be the last person he saw before he died." Gardner was at his best, but Martha Rhoades wasn't yielding.

"All circumstantial. Not real proof."

She began to walk away from them and Gardner had to wonder if Martha wasn't right. Sure, they had evidence, but would it be strong enough to convince a jury? Were they going to be able to prove their case beyond a reasonable doubt?

KIM WALKED INTO the utility shed. Something drew her to the crime scene. The door stood wide open. Some of the chaises were stored inside. But no one else was there. She walked around, feeling surrounded by a sense of *otherness*. She felt dizzy. It was as if the room was spinning. She was out of the present moment. And then the vision came to her. She knew now exactly what had happened here, and the knowledge made her shudder. She felt sick.

It occurred to Kim that there was a way to force a confession out of Martha Rhoades. Mike couldn't do it, wouldn't understand how. But it could be done, although it wouldn't be easy. She returned to his side.

"Mike, I need to have a word with Bert." He nodded his head, a questioning expression on his intelligent, handsome face. Still, he asked nothing. She appreciated the fact that he trusted her.

"Bert, I believe I know what Martha Rhoades is trying to hide. I think you are more likely to get a confession than Mike." She explained her theory as Bert and Mike listened.

"You're sure of this?" Bert asked.

"Fairly certain," Kim said with conviction.

Bert turned to Mike with a questioning look.

"Kim has insight," he said. "She senses things other people miss."

"Okay, I'll give it a try," Bert said.

Moments later, Bert walked in front of Martha Rhoades, blocking her path, her expression grim with determination. Martha Rhoades tried to move around her, but Bert clamped a strong hand on the other woman's arm.

"What are you doing? How dare you touch me!"

Bert took hold of Martha Rhoades and forced her to turn in the direction of Beth, the female lifeguard. "It'll come out at the trial. Everyone's going to know unless you play it straight with us now."

Ms. Rhoades gasped and gave them a horrified look. "I—I don't know what you're talking about." Martha sagged, her self composure suddenly faltering.

"Let's walk over there, and I'll ask your friend right out

if the two of you are in a lesbian relationship. Newspapers love that kind of juicy story."

"You're threatening me?" Her voice was shrill and loud.

The lifeguards turned to listen. Beth came toward them. Martha Rhoades lowered her voice, her face flushed. "You can't do something like that. It would kill my mother. For God's sake, she's an invalid. That kind of publicity would bring on another stroke. You'd destroy her."

"We could make sure the newspapers never pick up on your relationship with a student. It wouldn't be easy, but with a full confession, we'd see to it. You have our promise we'll protect your reputation and help you work a deal if you co-operate."

Ms. Rhoades nodded her head in a defeated manner. Kim was impressed. Bert had managed to persuade Martha to confess with very little difficulty. She was good at her job. As if to prove the truth of that, Bert immediately began to advise Ms. Rhoades of her rights.

"In keeping with the 1966 Supreme Court decision in Miranda vs. Arizona, we are not permitted to ask you any questions until you are warned of your right to counsel and your privilege against self-incrimination. You have the right to remain silent. Do you understand that?"

Ms. Rhoades nodded her head abjectly.

"You are not obliged to answer any police questions. Is that also understood? If you do answer any questions, the answers may be used as evidence against you. You have the right to consult with an attorney before or during police questioning. Now we're going to drive you down to headquarters, and you can give us a formal statement there."

"Must I?" Martha Rhoades was staring into Bert's eyes. Bert assured her of the necessity.

"There isn't much to tell, not really. I never meant to harm the man. I hardly knew him. I was out walking Caesar, just as I said. As we passed the club, I observed that the lights were on. I entered to investigate. Then I heard the noises coming from the shed, just as you thought. I was a bit frightened, but Caesar was with me, so I went ahead and checked on what was causing the disturbance. I found Mr. Bradshaw groping around and turned on the light. He was behaving peculiarly. He raised himself up and tried to stand but couldn't at first. The manner in which he moved and the way his speech was slurred, I thought at first he was drunk. Then I saw the head wound and assumed he'd fallen in a drunken stupor and injured himself. He asked for my help, but when he started to retch, I became disgusted and told him just what I thought of his behavior.

"He laughed derisively, said that he hadn't been drinking, but that it was just like me to think so. He was nasty and abusive. He said he was sick of smug hypocrites like me." Her voice faltered. "He was an exceedingly vicious man. He told me before he left town, he would see to it I lost my job, that it would serve me right for having such a holier-than-thou attitude, for being a hypocrite. He was going to tell the school board that I corrupted the morals of minors. He intended to point to Beth as proof. Apparently, he'd seen us embracing in my office one day. "

"I panicked. The man would have destroyed my life. He would take my livelihood, my reputation, everything. I would never be able to teach again. And what about Mother? What would it have done to her? To him it was just a form of perverse amusement. When he got up and tried to stagger from the utility room, I picked up the knife and plunged it into his back. It just seemed to happen, as if the weapon had a mind of its own. It was as if it were a reflex action. For a time, I just stared at his body lying there. Later, I wiped all my fingerprints from the knife and then I tidied up the horrible mess he'd left. It made me feel better, in control again.

"Then I phoned Sonny, pretending to be April. I hadn't really meant to implicate her, but I did have to protect myself.

I thought you'd believe he drowned. I never thought you'd discover he died in the utility room. I wasn't thinking clearly. I really didn't mean to kill that despicable man. And I never meant to kill Sonny, either. It was just when Sonny stopped by the club for his paycheck, he told me how he was going to meet you and tell you about the phone call."

"I would think that would have pleased you," Mike observed.

"Not really. When he told me about the call, he happened to say that my voice and that of the Nevins woman sounded a good deal alike and wasn't that strange, considering how different we were?"

"And you thought he might have figured out it was you who called him and not her," Mike surmised.

"I offered to walk along with him to Miss Nevins' apartment, to advise him. We were passing by that ravine and I suggested we walk over by it so that we could stop and discuss his problem."

"And then you pushed him?"

"I couldn't seem to help myself."

Bert refrained from commenting, just as Mike did. Kim listened thoughtfully.

"What's going to happen to Mother? She's totally dependent on me." Ms. Rhoades' normally forceful features were weakened by fear.

"We'll take care of it," Bert said. The authority she exuded seemed to reassure Martha Rhoades.

Beth moved toward them, pushing herself between Martha Rhoades and Bert. "What are you doing to her?" the young girl's voice was accusing and frightened.

"They're arresting me." Martha Rhoades said quietly. "I don't want you to worry, dear. You just see to the club."

Beth burst into tears, and Ms. Rhoades tried to comfort her. It was the only time her features ever softened.

"I won't let them do it to you!" The girl exploded into

action. Without warning, she pushed Mike toward the pool. Knocked off-balance, he fell backward into six feet of water. Kim was alarmed. She'd never asked Mike if he could swim.

BENEATH THE SURFACE, everything looked different; Gardner could see clearly without any distortion. He swam up to the pool's surface, gasping for air. He watched Beth trying to land a punch on Bert, who simply gave her a hard shove.

"Get lost, little girl, before I get really angry."

"Do what the officer says," Martha Rhoades ordered. "You can't help me now."

Beth walked away with a lingering backward glance at Martha Rhoades. They exchanged a somber, meaningful look.

"Are you all right?" Kim asked Gardner in a concerned voice, offering him her hand.

"Just a little soggy," he assured her. "Could be a lot worse."

Bert glanced at Gardner and flashed an amused smile. "Seems like you're all wet, Mike, and a little out of breath besides."

"I'll get by. But when I explain to my daughters how my clothes got messed up, they'll probably claim I was just looking for an excuse to take a swim in the pool."

AT HEADQUARTERS, everything went in a smooth manner. Ms. Rhoades regained her sense of composure and arranged for a lawyer to represent her. She even went so far as to make a few suggestions on how they could improve the appearance of headquarters by adding plants. Both Gardner and Bert were fairly exhausted by the time the booking procedure and preliminaries were handled.

"You did a good job with her," he told Bert. "I never thought we'd get her to confess."

"It was Kim's doing." Bert turned to her. "How did you figure it out?"

"Let's just say I understood the situation."

Bert looked puzzled.

Mike wasn't about to explain about Kim's special perception. Besides, it didn't always work. Anyway, Bert would never have believed it. So he changed the subject. "It seems to me you succeeded by using my methods, applying brains instead of brawn when possible."

"Modest of you to say so," Bert responded.

"Actually, you did me one better." Gardner extended his hand in a gesture of friendship and Bert took it. "I think we can knock off now," he said. "Want me to drop you off at your place?"

"Why not?"

BERT FELL ASLEEP in the backseat as Gardner drove. She woke up in a sweat, the same nightmare all over again, reliving what she'd done: there was no escape.

"You okay?" Kim asked, turning around.

"Yeah, sure. Those damn pills. Wonder what they put in them."

Kim reached back and touched her forehead. "I think you're running a fever."

"It's not that." Bert watched the landscape go by like a surreal painting.

"Something wrong?"

"With me? Yeah, you could say so."

What would Mama have thought if she knew? A church going woman who believed in love-thy-neighbor, a woman who forgave, who didn't even blame her husband for running out on them. Mama and Alva, two wonderful women, both dead now.

"You can talk to us, you know," Gardner said.

It came to her that she could trust Gardner and Kim Reynolds with the truth. Even if they didn't understand what she'd done or why, they still wouldn't pass judgment.

"All right, maybe I will tell you. You've known right from the start something's bothering me. That hasn't changed."

Gardner stopped the car, pulled over by the side of the road and turned around. There wasn't anything left but to get things out in the open.

"Four months ago, my best friend was murdered in the city. She was dragged off the street, forced into an alley near the hospital where she worked. Crackheads robbed her. When she didn't have enough money to satisfy them, the bastards got angry and murdered her."

Gardner shook his head, but didn't speak. Kim placed her hand on Bert's own.

"I hunted them down like the animals they were. I shook every snitch till I got answers. I found the motherfuckers, and I killed them."

She waited for Gardner to react, to say something, but Gardner's face never changed expression.

Tears had formed in Kim's eyes. But she said nothing, either.

"They were carrying, so I didn't need to explain what happened. I took them out after I got them to confess what they'd done. Afterwards, I was sick. I couldn't stop throwing up. That was what my life had come to, executing lowlife druggies. But it was necessary.

"Perps walk away laughing, knowing they can do it again and again. A death for a death, I say. No plea bargaining, no getting off on technicalities. I paid dearly for it and I still am, but it had to be done. And in spite of knowing how rotten I feel about it, I'd kill them all over again if it came to that."

She stared at Gardner, who seemed lost in thought. Then he finally spoke. "Just like you, I see the flaws in the justice system. No cop can help feeling frustrated and demoralized by the revolving door if he has any sensitivity or awareness."

"The justice system sucks, man."

"So we've got to do our best to make it work better. We can't execute every alleged killer ourselves. What can I say to you? I'm really sorry about your friend."

"Let's face it, Mike. You don't know what it's like, how powerless a woman feels when she's attacked. I knew I had to make myself mentally and physically strong so I'd never be vulnerable. I thought I could protect the other innocent women out there, all the ones who needed help. But know what? I couldn't even save my best friend! Nothing is ever going to bring Alva back. I did the right thing, offing those scum. So why does my conscience hurt?"

"Because you're a decent, sensitive human being. Look, you want absolution, confess to a priest. You want analysis, see a shrink."

"No. You'll have to do."

Gardner touched her shoulder gently. "You want my advice? Forgive yourself. Put it behind you as best you can. Let go of the anger. You did what you had to do. Case closed."

"That simple?"

"Who said it's simple? But it's something you've got to do, for your own sanity and well being. We're just people, human beings. None of us is perfect. So where are you going from here? Only you can decide that."

KIM UNDERSTOOD Bert's anguish completely. Hadn't she searched for her own friend's killer? "It's time to let go of your ghosts. Mike is right. It's the only way to get on with living your life. Believe me, I've been through it myself."

Bert smiled at them. "Thanks. You're both good people. I guess I do feel better, talking it out with you."

Kim had a strong feeling that Bert would be all right.

THE GIRLS WERE WAITING up for them.

"Good to be home," Gardner told them and meant it. He gave each of them a hug and a kiss. Then he collapsed onto the worn recliner in the living room, his favorite chair.

"I'll get you some iced tea," Evie said. She put her head to one side, studying him with a thorough sweep of her gaze. "Your suit is totaled."

"I know. Let's not tell anybody. I might lose my reputation as a sharp dresser."

"Maybe you could have it dry cleaned." Evie hadn't even smiled; her expression was solemn. "I expect you'll tell us what happened when you're good and ready. Are you through catching criminals?"

"For today," he responded with a cheerful smile. "Forget about the iced tea. I'll get it myself later if I'm thirsty. Go to bed."

The girls both said goodnight to Kim, and left them alone.

"Well, no more threatening phone calls," he said.

"That's good," Kim said. "They get old fast. You better get out of those wet clothes. Take a shower."

"You staying over tonight?" he asked. He looked at her out of the corner of his eye.

"You bet."

"Good. Maybe we'll take that shower together then."

She smiled and kissed him lightly. "Could happen," she said.

He tugged her on to his lap and began massaging the tension away at the small of her back. Then he turned her around to face him again, gently kissed her, and pressed his face into her breasts.

"You're never afraid the way I am," she said.

"More so," he replied.

"You were afraid for me, not yourself. Don't think I didn't know. I love you, Mike. You're a wonderful man."

"You can say that after I nearly got you killed?"

Kim shook her head. "I nearly got myself killed."

He rubbed her arms. "I don't see it that way. I'd never have forgiven myself if anything happened to you, sweetheart."

"Nice to know. How could I not love you?"

"I love you, too, more than I've ever loved any woman," he told her and meant it.

It was a testament to Kim's sensual appeal that he could feel so aroused just holding her after the day they'd endured. He pulled Kim against him and kissed her deeply until they were both breathless.

"Why Lieutenant, I do believe you are guilty of carrying a concealed weapon." She wriggled in his lap and laughed.

"Could be. Maybe you ought to pat me down. Better still, I think you should conduct a strip search."

"You are very bad," she said with a teasing smile.

"Thank you. I sure hope so." He caressed her cheek. "Let's go upstairs."

"What did you have in mind?"

He gave her posterior a pat. "After that shower? Suppose I leave it to your imagination."

* * * * *

REQUEST YOUR FREE BOOKS!

2 FREE NOVELS
PLUS 2 FREE GIFTS!

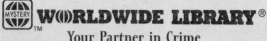

WORLDWIDE LIBRARY®
Your Partner in Crime